DAZZLING PRAISE FOR LESLIE FORBES'S

BOMBAY ICE

"Thrilling."—*Chicago Tribune*

"The elegant musicality of Forbes's writing will . . .
keep readers mesmerized. . . . It can fairly dazzle
you into suspending disbelief."
—*The Orlando Sentinel*

"Enormous fun and truly chilling."
—*Star Tribune*, Minneapolis

"Roz and Smilla would have gotten along just fine.
Top-notch entertainment."
—*Kirkus Reviews* (starred review)

"A literary treat."—*Library Journal*

BOMBAY ICE

a novel

LESLIE FORBES

BANTAM BOOKS / NEW YORK TORONTO LONDON SYDNEY AUCKLAND

This edition contains the complete text of the
original hardcover edition.
NOT ONE WORD HAS BEEN OMITTED.

BOMBAY ICE

A Bantam Book / published by arrangement with
Farrar, Straus and Giroux

PUBLISHING HISTORY
Hardcover edition published by Farrar, Straus and Giroux
in July 1998
Bantam trade paperback edition / June 1999

First published in 1998 by Phoenix House, United Kingdom.

ISBN 0-553-38047-8

Published simultaneously in the United States and Canada

Bantam Books are published by Bantam Books, a division of
Random House, Inc. Its trademark, consisting of the words
"Bantam Books" and the portrayal of a rooster, is Registered in
U.S. Patent and Trademark Office and in other countries.
Marca Registrada. Bantam Books, 1540 Broadway, New York,
New York 10036.

PRINTED IN THE UNITED STATES OF AMERICA
FFG   10 9

ACKNOWLEDGEMENTS

This book is a work of fiction, and while some of the historical characters did exist, the modern characters who form the body of the story are entirely fictitious, as are many of the locations.

Several books were important in the creation of my Bombay: *Monsoons*, edited by Jay S. Fein and Pamela L. Stephens; Alexander Frater, *Chasing the Monsoon*; V. S. Naipaul, *India: A Million Mutinies Now* (the poem by Namdeo that Caleb Mistry quotes on page 229 is from this book) and *India: A Wounded Civilization*; Kishore Valicha, *Indian Cinema*; Satyajit Ray, *Anthology of Statements*; M. P. Singh, *Police Problems and Dilemmas in India*; Benedict Costa, *Bombay Twilight Zone*; J. Seabrook, *Life in the Bombay Slums*; Serena Nanda, *Hijras of India*; S. K. Sharma, *Hijras: Labelled Deviants*; and, especially, Gillian Tindall's wonderful *City of Gold: The Biography of Bombay*. Although I read the last when my own book was near completion, Tindall's work proved to me that the Prospero's Island I thought I had invented did in fact exist.

I would also like to thank Penguin for permission to quote on page 213 from Mary M. Innes's translation of Ovid's *Metamorphoses*; Viking Penguin for the quotation on pages 58 and 318 from James Gleick's book *Chaos: Making a New Science*.

To Professor Nicholas Kurti, Dr. Peter Barham,
and Dr. Tony Blake,
three alchemists who taught me that physics has
more to do with art than with entropy

To Heather Jones, friend and reader, who had faith

And to Andrew Thomas, as always, for his navigation
through all kinds of weather

CONTENTS

CAST LIST

LEADING PLAYERS

Rosalind Benegal (aka Roz Bengal), a freelance radio producer and maker of crime videos for television

Prosper Sharma, a film director, husband of Maya Sharma, a film star (deceased), and now husband of:

Miranda Sharma, Rosalind's sister

Ram Shantra, a computer editor and video producer

Thomas Jacobs, a taxi driver from Kerala

Caleb Mistry, a film director

Ashok Tagore, a maker of archaeological films

Anthony Unmann, an art dealer from an old English family in Bombay

Roberto Acres, a property dealer

SUPPORTING PLAYERS

Shoma Kumar, editor and writer on *Screenbites*, a Bombay movie magazine

Robi, an artist at the Central Props Unit and part-time extra for Caleb Mistry

Satish Isaacs, head of the Central Props Unit

Basil Chopra, a film and theatre actor of the old school

Sunila, a hijra/eunuch, friend of the hijra Sami (deceased)

Gul, a friend of Sami's

EXTRAS/JUNIOR ARTISTES

Dilip, a forensic technician at Bombay's deputy coroner's office

Bunny Thapar, a journalist on *The Times of India*

Bina, guru and matron of the village hijra commune

Salim, Prosper Sharma's lighting cameraman

Vikram Raven, former director of the Central Props Unit

Jigs Sansi, a representative from India's Department of Archaeology

Nonie Mistry, Caleb Mistry's daughter

The biggest single factor in the prevention of cholera in the Third World was the introduction of carbonated drinks, a benefit offset by the introduction of cheap freezers, which preserved bacteria-ridden local water in the form of ice.
Bombay News, *1994*

Ice: vb. to chill or murder

BOMBAY ICE

flashback

BENGAL LIGHT

Bengal light: black sulphide used as a shipwreck signal,
or to illuminate the night.

CAPTAIN HENRY PIDDINGTON,
The Sailor's Hornbook for the Law of Storms

I HAVE SOME KNOWLEDGE OF POISONS. MY MOTHER WAS A GILDER, by inclination as well as profession: she turned base metal into gold with the help of potassium cyanide. At an early age I was taught the precise identification of toxins and their antidotes. Identity is important, if you want to find out which toxin is responsible, and who to blame.

Mum was not the only poisoner in our household. Our old gardener on the Malabar Coast used to collect seeds from a plant the Jesuits called St. Ignatius's bean. The active principle of it and its close relative *Strychnos nux vomica* is the poison strychnine, whose seeds are eaten by many people in Malabar as a prophylactic for snakebite, especially during the monsoon, when cobras are driven from their holes by the rains that revive the earth.

If a history of these monsoon rains could be plotted as a series of fixed points on a map, would they form a pattern, the way planetary orbits do? A whole nest of cobras, perhaps, like the sinuous interplay of radio frequencies when different rhythms come together, or the strobing, flickering patterns of my monsoon summer, a cycle of events that comes back to me as dreams connecting impossible images. I can see the jerky four-frame shots in my head now, the clockwork cartoons of cheap animation.

Let me tell you a movie. Those are the words he used. It had to be a movie because he remained a director, removed from the action. Above it all. So he said. I write this down to try to find some overall pattern to the deaths of that summer, to discover the signal point on that monsoon chart where a flow crossed the boundary from smooth to turbulent. I need to know if the violent weather of our lives could have been reversed.

"This is how it starts," he said, the shot framed using his hands as a viewfinder. "This is the beginning: an opening scene something like Hitchcock's *Strangers on a Train*, with a series of symbolic following shots on feet going first one way and then the other."

The bastardized version, I told him, the Bombay version. Niked, spiked, well-heeled, down-at-heeled, sandalled, sneakered, barefoot, brown. No doubt the Bombay version has a song here and some dancers, dressed to kill. He answered this charge of melodrama by explaining that the map of Bombay is reflected in its movies, and just as the best map is not the one that perfectly represents reality, so the best expression of this city cannot be achieved by celluloid realism.

"You have to picture it," he said. "Train tracks—Hitchcock's camera almost grazing the rails as they speed along their parallels and intersections, a clear glimpse into the nature of the action to be expected. The lens not rising above ground level until the fatal collision, and then just flashes on the screen: old, new, flesh, blood, wet, dry, living, dead."

We will go in much tighter, a telephoto shot (but remember that this lens magnifies images, compresses space; it is an untrustworthy witness):

An open door frames a shadowed figure—two of them; one; we can't quite see.

One shadow pushes the other into the sunlight. Maya, the first Mrs. Sharma—once a shimmering star in the Bombay movie firmament, a sad Indian Marilyn who has outlived her future—stumbles, turns towards us, screams. As her fans used to at the sight of her. As they no longer do. This will be Maya's last starring role.

Quick cut to a close-up: her widened eyes and mouth tightly stretch the skin of her face into a youth that no facelift has achieved. For an instant she *is* the lens—tracking down to the upturned face of the leper seven storeys below. *Then wider again* as she is propelled over the balcony rail. Her heavy scarf catches on the fourth-storey balcony and chokes off her scream, a sudden jerk that pops her upper spinal cord like the beads on a cheap plastic necklace.

That final image—a woman falling—was recorded in newspaper headlines the next day: SNOOPER SCOOPS STAR'S SWOOP! For me it would have been just another statistic chalked on a morgue blackboard, if not for the fact that my sister was destined to become the second Mrs. Sharma. Our stories, my sister's and mine, parallel for a time but set finally on divergent courses, reflect the ambiguous nature of the summer monsoon, a season when the tempo of life and death in India increases.

act 1

FLOTSAM AND JETSAM

flotsam: goods lost by shipwreck found floating on the sea.

*jetsam: goods jettisoned and washed up on shore; goods
from a wreck that remain under water; (fig.) to abandon.*

1

$\mathbf{W}$E WERE SHIPWRECKED ON AN ISLAND AND THE ISLAND WAS Bombay; the monsoon threat held the whole city hostage.

Inside the air-conditioned airport the climate was falsely temperate. Outside, heat hovered impatiently, like an actor waiting for his cue offstage. I shuffled forward and watched a suit survey each line on my landing card with the precision of all men whose souls do not exceed the limits of their uniforms.

"Purpose of visit," he said, stabbing his forefinger down on the offending entry. "TV is occupation, not purpose. What is your motivation?"

What would he say if I broke down and confessed to a murder? If I said that Bombay was not a tourist resort for me, it was the last resort? But it's never a good idea to confuse officials with the facts, so I gave him a version of the truth he could accept. "I'm a journalist. Reporting on the monsoon."

"Anchorwoman?"

"You could say that." If a weighty title got me through the queue faster.

"You are not having such an appearance," said my prosecutor.

The accused stands before him: age thirty-three, five foot ten, swimmer's shoulders, dead straight boot-black hair slicked back in a fifties quiff. On a good day, I like to think the haircut makes me look sort of early Kate Hepburn. On bad days it's closer to late Elvis, as my last lover told me when he left.

"It's not a good day," I said.

With a flash of humour rare in customs men, he waved me

through—"Please to be entering the whirlpool"—and I walked free, into the heat of Bombay.

Here, in the year 1866, my great-great-grandfather was marooned for good, drowned in a bay his engineering skill was helping to drain, and laid to rest in the watery district of coconut groves known as Sonapur, which can be translated as "city of gold"; in this case, a metropolis of gravestones, because to die, the Hindu saying goes, is to be turned into gold. So Great-great-granddad finally found the fortune he had come seeking in this city of celluloid dreams. I picture him on my mental screen, morphing his steely Scottish soul into a softer, more valuable metal, a meltdown process no Glaswegian could regret.

This was my first visit to India in twenty years, a place I've been returning to all my life. I would have liked to begin at the beginning: once upon a time, among the spice forests of Kerala—in old India, where I was born, far down the Malabar Coast. But my sister's letters have brought me instead from London to Bombay, a city with its back to the past. Still, it might suit me better. Built on a shifting humus of decayed coconut palms and rotten fish manure, it has roots that are as shallow as most swamp plants'.

Looking out the window of a taxi headed for the centre, I found myself trying to find some landmark from my last visit. I should have known better. Old maps of Bombay are unreliable, charts of a city which does not exist anymore—or never did. Cartographers here have always disagreed on where land stopped and liquid began. In the seventeenth century, when the future metropolis consisted of no more than seven islands emerging reluctantly from a tidal swamp, every mapmaker altered and reinvented the geography, as if those islands were mere visions based on an insubstantial fabric whose shape could change to suit the audience.

What *was* real has been drained away long since by the urban developers who are dredging up the ocean bottom and using it as landfill to raise Bombay a few more precious feet above sea level. Glossy white hotel towers built with black-market money now stand on land which until a decade ago—last week—yesterday was a cartographer's blue-painted stretch of open water. The city's new identity is not horizontal but vertical, not insular but peninsular, a peninsula shaped like a hand, cupped to call someone back. They call it reclaiming. They say Bombay has been reclaimed from its original twenty miles of mud. The latest road map of Bombay is so out-of-date that even that property supporting the buildings where the map was produced is printed in the deep azure that indicates land still under sea, not yet reclaimed.

But how do you reclaim something that was never yours in the first place?

As the road curved over Mahim Causeway, leaving the vegetal growth of the airport slums behind, I wound down the window and felt the heat move immediately from a supporting role to centre stage, bringing in a gust of wind with the consistency of old lamb gravy. Another, fresher smell overlaid the greasy aroma of drains. Yes, it had rained recently, the driver told me: rain, although not *the* rains, which explained why the temperature hadn't dropped.

I had not forgotten the violence of India's monsoon reversal, nor the scent of soil releasing different chemicals as it turned from dry land into wet. My father, a man whose passion for facts was exceeded only by my mother's for fiction, once analyzed the smell of rain. Its formula, he said, depends upon where it falls—on dry or wet ground. "First there is petrichor, the dry smell of unbaked clay, from the Greek for 'stone-essence.' Later, that muddy, fertile flavour of geosmin." Earth smell: found in the flesh of bottom-feeders like carp and catfish.

Purpose of visit? Transformation from stone into earth.

The driver told me that in the north, near Lucknow, there was a small industry specializing in the smell of Indian rain. They put clay disks outdoors in the premonsoon months of May and June to absorb the water vapour in the air, then steam-distilled the smell from the disks, bottled it, and sold it under the name *matti ka attar*. "Is meaning 'perfume of the earth,'" he said.

Perfume of the earth. I rolled the words around in my mouth, only half listening as my guide ran through a list of this country's other, less volatile attractions. "You are knowing Bombay, madam? You must be knowing then that this is land stolen from the sea."

"So was I." My mother and I left India for the first time to move to Scotland when I was seven, but these broader horizons have scarred my guts in the same way the polio vaccination on my left arm has scarred my skin. A reminder that I've been inoculated.

A sudden gust of wind threw a wave over the seawall, drenching the nearest pedestrians. The taxi driver's eyes met mine in his rearview mirror. "Madam, I think someday soon the sea is stealing back its lost land."

"WHAT IS YOUR GOOD NAME?" ASKED THE HOTEL RECEPTIONIST AT THE HO-
tel Ritzy.

"Roz Bengal. I've already told you twice."

He shook his head. "And twice I am telling you there is not such a
booking."

"There—Benegal, R.," I said, pointing at the entry in his log.
"BBC. Sorry. I forgot I'd given you the Indian spelling."

The man flashed me a smile. "British Broadcasting Corporation!
Why are you not saying? Only I was thinking you would be Indian
lady."

"I am an Indian lady . . . woman. I just happen to have a Scottish skin."

Before I shortened it to Bengal, British colleagues used to have
trouble with my Indian surname. They persisted in pronouncing it
Ben-eagle, like someone the Lone Ranger would've shagged when he
and Tonto had a lovers' spat. The wrong kind of Indian. Bengal is a
more appropriate name for me, the product of Indian weather and
Scottish guilt. And it's easier for the old imperialists: a former British
colony, now divided like Germany into east and west, with religion
down the middle instead of a wall.

In my room, I stretched out on a mattress as hard as Akbar's tomb
and tried to phone my sister, Miranda. The line crackled a few times
before going dead. Desperate for a familiar voice, the best I could do
was the voice mail of a London friend who had moved here years ago:
*"Hello, cyberpunks! You are connected to Ram Shantra Productions.
Fax, phone, or get wired after the tone."*

All my other numbers seemed to be routed through a video arcade
on the floor of the Indian Ocean. The telephone operator told me it
was the start of *Caturmasa*, the four months of India's monsoon, seen
by Hindus as auspicious. "Also as disintegration of the world." I gave
up on contacting anyone and started strafing the networks, nuking
each channel as it failed to satisfy, finally hitting CNN for up-to-the-
minute global catastrophe, my kind of news. Falling asleep to the
sound of machine guns in the Middle East, I corpsed it for sixteen
hours and woke with only the dead and drowned for company.

A face swam up through the snow of static on the television screen:
black-and-white from monsoon interference, flashes of Technicolor
shimmying around the silhouette like St. Elmo's fire. I knew that face.
The face in my dreams. Smeared lipstick. A noose of long seaweed hair
strung round her neck.

The box crackled to life: ". . . *video shot by Bill Thompson, a*

California tourist who found the body on Chowpatty Beach in Bombay just over three hours ago."

The camerawork was amateurish, tracking too quickly from a sea spumy as boiling milk to catch the bare brown feet of a crowd, the cuff of a uniformed leg, a pattern of white eyes in immobile dark faces. The light was murky. Out of the camera's immediate focus you could see only the Christmas lights strung around the street vendors' stalls on Chowpatty.

And then that nightmare face again. My mother's drowned face.

A steadier camera replaced the death mask with a CNN talking head. She turned to the young man seated next to her in the studio. "Mr. Thompson, can you give us details of how you came to take this extraordinary film?"

"I was wading out, taking these shots of the surf. A trip with some old surfing friends . . . headed for Australia . . . when the body . . ." His voice broke, trailed away.

The CNN reporter put her head on one side like a bird listening for a worm, then dug her beak in and gave the worm a tug. "When the body . . . yes?"

"When this streak of yellow wrapped itself round me." He shuddered involuntarily. "Sea snake, that's what I thought."

They used to wash up on our beach in Kerala, helpless as skipping ropes when out of the water, deadly in it. But it wasn't a snake this time. The end of the yellow scarf was tied to a swollen neck, and a gash of blood-red lipstick sliced across a bloated face. Poor Bill. He hauled her in by dragging on the snaking scarf. By the time he got her onto the sand, there was a crowd watching and three policemen to help him lift the body out.

"They told me they'd take her from there," Bill said.

Before they did, Bill had managed to track his camera slowly across the treasure washed up by the waves on Chowpatty. Her hands were a wrinkled fungal white, pocked and pitted from the burrowings of scavengers. "Like one of those wormy mushrooms you find in the woods," said Bill. She had a flat chest and dark, muscular legs, and wore a flamingo-pink embroidered skirt rucked up over a flaccid penis. The camera dipped, lost focus. One policeman sniggered. A second man pulled the skirt down over this sad evidence of misplaced sexuality.

Her arms were heavy with jewellery, not all of it gold. She had played a game of bloody tic-tac-toe on one shoulder. Before that, she had used her upper arms to strop the razor, shredding the skin into brocade, with wide bracelets of exposed sinew wound round both wrists. While her lungs and stomach filled up with water, her blood must have drained out of those fatal armbands into the sea.

Any film director would have killed for that final shot.

It's rare for a real murder to have the drama of fiction. Fictional death has victims with sympathetic haircuts, good lighting, suspense. Movie heroes never wear grey shoes. I should know. Over the past seven years of freelancing I have augmented my radio producer's wages by shooting videos about our daily criminal reality for late-night television. As yet, no serial killings, the twentieth century's ultimate art form, but those are pretty rare, despite cinematic evidence to the contrary.

Instead, the melodrama of real death pays my rent. It's taught me that murder victims die with their pants down, like Elvis, or their skirts up, like Maya Sharma, my brother-in-law's first wife. My job is to make reality more exciting, even when the husband obviously did it. Judicious editing, a little pacey music—and the most banal murder can be given drama.

Few faces touch me now. Only those I recognize: the drowned, the self-mutilators; what my mad mother used to call her "little accidents."

I was remembering, not really listening, when the reporter's commentary filtered through. ". . . *speculation about the presence of an inspector from Crime Branch, Bombay's elite crime-fighting unit, who arrived shortly after the body's discovery. This is the fourth hijra death on Chowpatty in the last eight weeks. Sources claim the hijra may have been connected to the Bombay film world.*"

I put a call through to reception. "What's a *hijra* death? CNN just said there've been four hijra deaths in the last eight weeks."

There was a slight intake of breath before he spoke. "Hijra is man pretending to be woman, madam. Or man who has no . . . equipment that is making man . . ."

"Balls and stick. A eunuch. Thank you."

I haven't seen the eunuch in almost four weeks. The words of my sister's last postcard to me.

2

P*URPOSE OF VISIT, MADAM?*

In the spring of this year all the bonds tying me to London and India were coming unravelled. My mother was dead. My grandparents were dead. My father had died in Bombay before Christmas while I was on a six-month trip through Louisiana, locked into my role as professional vampire, sticking a microphone into other people's lives and sucking out the stories. The notification of his death didn't reach me until five weeks after the cremation.

My sister, Miranda, was the last tie with India—or anywhere else. Both of us orphans by the time she wrote from Bombay:

Thank you for your letter about Dad. None of your old contacts knew how to reach you. I am expecting a son in the second month of Caturmasa, an auspicious time for births, inauspicious for marriages. A friend tells me you are doing a series about the death penalty. My husband is making an Indian version of Shakespeare's Tempest. *People tell me that he murdered his first wife, who was to play Miranda. It is very hot in Bombay. I am being followed by eunuchs and lepers.*

Love, Miranda

Miranda used to write all the time, but her marriage to Prosper Sharma, five years ago, had drawn a veil between us, as though there were a part of her life she wished to conceal. All I heard was that she married a famous film director twenty-five years her senior, an Anglophile educated at Oxford whose parents had named him after the

French novelist Prosper Mérimée. The letters from Miranda in her new role as the second Mrs. Sharma had dried up, become less personal. I put it down to the shedding of her uncomfortable old skin. It hurt, but the hurt could be sealed away, a process I had learned long ago with Mum. My sister was simply one more language I no longer spoke, another country I'd lost.

In reply to Miranda's letter, her first in over a year, I wrote back: "Eunuchs and lepers aren't exactly part of the London experience. Prosper is a well-known film director—there's bound to be gossip." And more along the same lines. Keeping her at arm's length, as she had kept me.

The truth is, I was afraid to let her back into my life. Freed of family ties for good, I could reinvent myself without the history, re-write the past, the way politicians do. It was easier, safer, to cut myself off completely. That subtext in my letter must have been clear, be-cause weeks went by before Miranda wrote again. The day I left for a three-week shift to shoot road-accident footage around Britain, a letter came saying she was going to confront her husband. Intending to write or phone her, I let work get in the way instead, only to be brought up short, weeks later, by that final schizophrenic card:

Remember I used to be frightened of water and you taught me how to float in the bath? Remember the summer you taught me to swim? It's so hot now all I think of is water. Funny that waters break for pregnant women. I haven't seen the eunuch in almost four weeks. Ignore what I wrote you before. No need to come here and rescue me.

Love, Miranda

In a cramped hand, around the edge, my sister had added a postscript, a trace of the old Miranda like a map drawn in dry sand, time running out: "If you come to Bombay we could swim together again—at Breach Candy, a pool built by the British, now used by Indians, shaped like a map of India. Before partition."

That last sentence evoked a picture from the bottom drawer of my memory. Two children holding hands underwater, using touch to com-municate, writing words on each other's hands like sign language: Miranda and I, as we had been during our last summer together, amphibious Siamese twins with pipes of bamboo for snorkels.

One part of me rejected the image as pure sentiment, but when I raised my eyes from the letter there were tears on my cheeks, something that had been happening more and more since my father's death. I would be tracking my lens across the face of a dumpy old lady in a plastic apron, dead for three days before anyone found her, or charting the corporeal geography of a half-charred Pakistani man who lived alone in a damp basement and suffered from bunions—then find myself overwhelmed by a feeling of loss, as if it were someone I knew lying there. "You need a holiday," my boss said recently. "It's bad news when a cupboard full of cat food and stale biscuits makes you cry." Until he spoke, I hadn't noticed the tears. It made me wonder whom I was mourning.

"How will we redeem the lost, drowned lands of Bombay?" asks my copy of an old *Bombay Island Gazetteer*. To reclaim lost land you need to dredge up the past, the drowned. Some of what is turned up by the dredgers is not welcome. Frankly, it stinks. Land must be scarce or precious to justify the effort.

That is how I feel about my sister, this trip to India. The two ideas are inseparable.

It took four weeks to convince the TV station for whom I did my regular crime diary to pay for a story about corruption in Bombay's film world. "Think of the exotic corpses," I said to my producer, a man who wore his cynicism like an impermeable raincoat against emotion. "Machetes, cobra bites, ritual murder."

The ritual murder clinched it, and my remaining costs were covered by a BBC commission for six radio programmes about the history of tropical storms.

But those were just excuses. The real purpose of my visit was there in the postscript of my sister's last postcard. I was here to reassemble that map of a family. Before partition. My own personal monsoon, and nothing to do with the differential heating of land and sea in the tropics.

3

TWO MONTHS AGO MY SISTER HAD GONE TO HER HUSBAND WITH
a story of eunuchs, and within a week a hijra with possible connections to Bombay's film world showed up dead on Chowpatty Beach.
Since then there had been three more hijra deaths on Chowpatty. The
events might be unconnected, but their parallel tracks were enough to
keep me awake. So I had a bath and a cup of tea, and went to take a
look at the scene of the crime.

Walking out through the sweaty, silent streets, I was aware of
searching for something in Bombay's detritus of old empires, some
empirical proof that I belonged here. It was 4 a.m., that brief period
before dawn when the whole of India sleeps, when the hookers in
Falkland Road finally close their doors to everyone except all-night
customers, and people living on the pavement roll themselves up in
their blankets like carpet samples awaiting delivery.

At this hour, the city had the ephemeral quality of a film set. Even
the landscape looked temporary: ugly new office blocks called Il
Palazzo and Acropolis 2000 falling down after only two years of monsoon, half-finished apartments already piebald with mildew while still
being built by companies with the unlikely names of Newhaven or
Goliath Developments. You could almost believe that at the end of its
current economic boom Bombay's façade might be struck and moved
on, just as scenery flats are at the end of a shoot. Then the site could
revert to its original residents—to the Koli people in their dhows fishing for pomfret, the coconut palms, mangoes, and mosquitoes—to its
disparate parts: seven malarial islands once more, separated and connected by a common sea. No family ties. No ancestral memories.

My ancestor was reduced to that—a memory—in the year of my

birth, when his tomb and all the others belonging to the old British dead were cleared away. The burial ground was converted into a playground for children of the well-off Indian families who live along a stretch of reclaimed land extending west of Marine Drive. Turning north along this long avenue, I finally reached Chowpatty Beach at dawn, and waded out from the shore with the Sony mike held low and steady to record the sound of the sea.

I grew up in the sea off the Malabar Coast, where my sister and I used to swim with dolphins and wind up smelling of coconut oil. The Arabian Sea that washed Chowpatty smelled of dead fish, diesel, ozone, hair oil, and shit.

"During the monsoon, debris washes up here from as far away as Saudi," I said into the mike. "Whole villages keep vigil on the shores to collect driftwood for their cooking fires. The sea today is grey and full of rubbish. Full of life, I suppose, or what we've made of it. Six hours ago it was full of death as well." A little over the top, but not bad for a first sound bite, given the jet lag.

There were three policemen on the beach, eyeing me suspiciously: the criminal returning to the scene of her crime, as criminals always do in Bombay movies and seldom do in real life. I showed them the BBC "Temporary Identity" card that is useful for impressing the kind of people who can be impressed by things like that, and asked one of them where the body of the night before had been taken. He told me it was "where they are taking all Chowpatty debris."

"Is that where you do the autopsy as well?" I asked him.

He and his partners laughed. "This is drowning, madam, not case for autopsy."

"It seems a bit extreme to slash your wrists and then drown yourself as well."

"Madam, India is an extreme country," he said.

"But did you see the body? It didn't look like a drowning. Usually you get a foamy mixture of mucus, air, and water around the drowned person's nose and mouth. Sort of like beaten egg white."

Our conversation had attracted an audience of beach vagrants, who muttered and moved closer at my comment. The policeman stopped smiling. "Suddenly you are expert in drowned people?"

"I do know something about it, yes." *She hath no drowning mark upon her.* That's what my father had said at my mother's funeral: Act I, Scene 1, *The Tempest.* But her lungs were wet and heavy. Waterlogged. I logged the evidence in my criminal's diary. "Do you have the address where they took the body?" I said.

"This is not your business," snapped the biggest copper, trying to look threatening, an effect somewhat mitigated by the fact that I could have rested my chin on his haircut. Until he said that, my questions had been not much more than a knee-jerk reflex, part of a pattern established by years of non-stop interviewing that had turned me into a receptacle for other people's opinions. I might have walked away and left the Chowpatty bodies to rot in peace if the policemen hadn't tried to bully me. But I've always hated people who wear their positions of authority like exclusive club ties to bar entrance to the rest of us.

When the coppers gave up acting tough and disappeared down the beach, a man beckoned me over to his food stall. He drew a rough map in the sand, pointed, and said, "Chowpatty bodies," then erased the image with his bare foot. I asked him why he was interested and he just turned away. "No English," he said.

The idea of spending my first morning in India staring at corpses didn't appeal to me. But that's where the day was leading. And it's what I do, what I've been doing for the last seven years. Should the hijra deaths prove to have no connection to Miranda, at least I could clock the time up as research.

THE POLICE STATION WHERE BODIES FROM CHOWPATTY WERE DELIVERED smelled familiar. It shared with corpses and old bureaucracies this odour of organs pickled in formaldehyde, rotting but not yet buried, like the colonial influences in India.

At the reception desk was the kind of man who has learned from his superiors the art of making a little work go a long way. While waiting for him to stop shuffling papers I had plenty of time to read the yellowing clippings pinned on the bulletin board, my back sweating against the plastic chair:

COPS RUN RAGGED IN SEARCH FOR LOST KIDS

Every ten minutes a child is lost or kidnapped in India. 50,000 missing children are rounded up every year but many are never found again. Police and parents are running from pillar to post to stem the losses.

POLICE NAB BIG FISH IN UNDERWORLD

The vigilance branch of the Bombay CID has rescued five girls from a group of fifteen brought for sale to brothels by the villain known as the Sex King, a big fish in the capital's underworld, police reported Tuesday. One girl is believed to have taken her own life.

Eventually, the policeman waved me forward, although he did not look up from his documents for several more minutes. I tried to conceal my impatience, knowing it would only satisfy the man's sense of his own power. An Indian lawyer in London had warned me to beware of Bombay officials. "Lord Macaulay bequeathed us our penal system in the nineteenth century," he told me, "and to the original bureaucracy Britain left behind, India has added thousands of paper incarnations. Now we have as many official documents and forms as we have gods, all in triplicate and quadruplicate."

The man on the desk was a perfect example of the principle made flesh, the carbon-paper copy of an old bureaucratic pattern. He had a face like a pimple that needs squeezing and a stomach that indicated his uniform could only have fit him in some brief period between the time he first joined the force and before he discovered that crime pays. When I told him I was interested in the body of the hijra found on Chowpatty, he handed me a form to be filled out in triplicate. "Name, address, marital status, reason for viewing . . ."

"I've already had a viewing," I said. "It's the autopsy results that interest me."

He continued to wave the papers at me until I handed over my BBC pass with fifty rupees tucked underneath. "We're making a film about India's police," I said. "It's an opportunity to see how you deal with such things."

"So, madam, you are wanting to view our procedurals?" He pocketed the note and smoothed the tie over his belly. "I do not think we can release autopsy details without written permission, but please be seated while I am finding out."

He came back a few minutes later with some files. "On which hijra are you requesting information, madam?" He raised his eyes from the files. "Eight weeks, four hijra suicides. First one is Sami. Other three still unidentified. We are having very little information. Coroner's office have claimed bodies."

"May I see the report on the first hijra—Sami?"

He shook his head. "Top secret. Deputy coroner of Bombay is also having this now, although he is not normally interfering in Chowpatty police business."

"So they'll do the post-mortem examination there?"

The man shook his head. "Drowned, people are saying. Suicides. No need for post-mortem. And deputy coroner of Bombay is for VIPs. Not flotsam and jetsam suicides like these. No-account people get sent straight to crematorium."

"Four hijra deaths in eight weeks seems like too many to be suicides."

"What it is seeming, madam, is not our business. Coroner is satisfied. Hijra community of first hijra also is satisfied. Only you are not satisfied."

"The first hijra—how did you know her name?"

"This Sami is a person of dubious reputation. Man who is working in this office is knowing this person very well."

"What was Sami's connection to the movie business?"

My casual question had a surprising result, hardening the man's soft face into a scowl. "How are you knowing this? I have not discussed such things with you."

So there was a connection. "Never mind. But can you at least tell me how to get in touch with Sami's community?"

"No use." He looked smug. "Hijra people are not telling outsiders about deaths in their community. Not even relations of the dead can come to funerals. Not even venerable BBC. Only I am able to tell you that this hijra community is near Khajra and Barla shrines on the railway line from Bombay to Poona."

OUTSIDE THE STATION THE DAY WAS ALREADY MILKY WITH POLLUTION, A PALE yolk of sun barely visible against the sky's bleached shell, the whole city enclosed in a gigantic egg that was being slowly hard-boiled.

The taxi I flagged down smelled pungently of *bidi*, the working class's cigarettes, although the driver's shirt was as white as his teeth and hair, and he had the round face common to the Kerala people with whom I grew up: small-boned, dark, and ready to smile, as if a fine craftsman had carved him out of polished teak, paying careful attention that every plane curved upwards.

"You would like tour of Chowpatty Beach as well?" he asked, when I had given him the address of my friend Ram's office.

"Not right now," I said, and watched the hope of a big tip fade in his eyes. "But tell me, why do Bombay people go to Chowpatty?"

"People are going for so many reasons," he said, delighted to display his knowledge. "Promenading for beautiful view of Malabar Hill. Or for massage. *Badmash* peoples also are going late at night—men liking men, men liking children, men who are not men. But most especially people are going for regular political meetings being held there. Not hundreds but *thousands* are going to Chowpatty and standing next to statue of Bal Gangadhar Tilak, man at heart of Marathi resistance to British Raj. Himself Marathi—a man from this province of Maharashtra—who is one of Edwardian India's greatest leaders. He is arguing that no good would come of treating British Raj with moderation. They should not be cajoled out of India, he is saying. They should be choked out."

Tilak, imprisoned for six years for inciting his countrymen to violence. The orthodox Hindu who came out of Mandalay jail and electrified India by making a pact with the Muslims. "You know your Bombay history," I said.

"I am taking keen interest, madam, that is so. Part-time driving only."

He reached into his pocket with one hand and passed a printed business card over his shoulder: *Thomas Jacobs, Qualified Driver, Poet, Historic Tourist Guide.* "Should you be requiring tourism services, madam."

"Or a few rhymes." Jacobs: a Christian, as so many were in Kerala.

"Mostly blank verse is my speciality. Like Mr. William Shakespeare: *A plague upon this howling! they are louder than the weather. . . . Shall we give o'er and drown? Have you a mind to sink?* Boatswain's speech, *The Tempest*, madam."

"Very appropriate."

"Yes, madam," he said. "I am immigrant from Kerala, where poetry is our natural medium."

With more than five hundred new immigrants a day coming into Bombay, it followed that lots of people must die here as well. You couldn't blame the police for not being interested in the fate of a few drowned eunuchs. But how did those bodies wind up dead on Chowpatty in the first place? Nobody who earned more than ten rupees a day would ever dream of swimming in those polluted waters: Bombay's only safe beach was Juhu. And if the dead hijra were vagrants, why would the deputy coroner of Bombay have been interested in their deaths?

I tried to summon up more facts about Chowpatty, the images coming back to me as colours from the visit we had made here when I was thirteen. Silver and gold and raw terra-cotta of the figures of Ganesh—Ganpati, as they call him here—the greedy elephant-headed god carried by millions of worshippers into the sea for his birthday in September. Sherbet-wallahs' ices in the improbable limes and violent pinks of Indian saris. The matte green of whole coconuts whose cloudy juice my sister and I sucked up with straws on our last days together.

As a child I would dream of India and wake up in Edinburgh with the cinnamon taste of cassia leaves still in my mouth, an image of light impressed on my retina in reverse, as the sun is after you look away. That's how I remember Chowpatty: a bright light, the contrast with Britain so strong that twenty years later it is still vivid.

4

"HELLO, PETAL," RAM SAID. "ABOUT TIME YOU SHOWED UP."

I smiled to see that my old friend hadn't changed his personal style to fit his new home. "Glad to see you're still out there at the cutting edge of fashion, Ram." He wore a Harvard shirt ripped off at the shoulders and hanging over long jersey shorts, a baseball cap stamped with the logo of some obscure rock band, turned back to front on his cropped hedge of black hair, and red high-top sneakers, presumably a more recent generation than the pair I'd last seen him in.

From the exterior, the building Ram worked in had appeared no more prepossessing than most modern architecture in Bombay, one more vertical imposing itself on this horizontal landscape. His sound studio, on the other hand, looked as if it could take off at any minute and land in the next century. In India, a country dedicated to low tech, it was like trading a sinking lifeboat for the starship *Enterprise*. Panels of buttons covered every surface, the latest in CD/DAT recording machines were stacked on a Milanese shelving unit, computer screens hummed with inscrutable graphs and outpourings from the Internet.

"What did you do, Captain Kirk," I said, "loot the BBC before leaving?"

"You know I've always been good at salvage."

I raised my eyebrows at this, and his thin, impish face broke into a grin. "Okay, Roz, spit it out. I know you're not here to admire the size of my high technology."

"Have you heard any stories about Prosper Sharma murdering his first wife?"

He burst out laughing. "That's my Rosalind—straight into murder and mayhem. But sure, I've heard about Sharma. Bombay makes its living selling those kinds of stories, and he's our very own Claus von Bülow."

"Which means?"

"Depends on whether you think Claus was innocent or guilty."

"Either way, you wouldn't like your sister to be the next Frau von Bülow."

"Hey, the man's a millionaire, right? I could do with someone investing in my business. Still, I might tell her to stay away from insulin."

"My sister is Prosper Sharma's second wife."

That checked him for a minute. "Does she have any money?" he asked, and when I nodded: "Then I'd tell her to stay away from balconies."

It didn't take long to bring him up-to-date on the story. Ram shook his head at the suggestion that there was a connection between the hijra deaths and Miranda's eunuchs, but when he heard about my morning at the police station he said he was surprised that the hijras' bodies had been transferred to the main coroner's. "It's unlikely the deputy coroner of Bombay would take over such an investigation. He's a heavy dude. My cousin in the police says if you haven't got family to stand up for you here, no one bothers with a post-mortem. They just issue a death certificate and then bury it conveniently in the depths of the police filing system, never to see the light of day again."

"Is that what happens with prostitute deaths as well?" I said. "The hijras work as hookers, don't they?"

"Most do. Not all. But if they get killed by a VIP john, he just spreads a little baksheesh—or the brothel-keeper does—and the bureaucratic curtain is drawn."

"Would you be willing to work with me on this, Ram? I need someone on the inside whom I trust, someone who isn't connected to Prosper Sharma."

"Your long-lost sister hears her husband may have iced wifee number one, and in your twisted little brain you have cooked up a conspiracy theory that would do justice to a Bollywood scriptwriter."

"You're probably right. But until I can get more details from Miranda, I have to make do with you."

"You want a hustler," he said. "Is there money in it?"

"If there's a story." I shrugged. "You know the deal. In the meantime, I could pay you to edit my radio stuff. And the company I do the crime diary for should stump up some more."

"My four years in Bombay, movie capital of the world, have not been wasted. Where do we start?"

"I'd like to get hold of the hijras' autopsy reports."

"Autopsy reports are no problem. My cousin the copper is in the same building as the coroner's office. Can we offer him any rewards for extracurricular activities? He may have to pay to get to the stuff."

I nodded.

"Then hold on while I send some friendly E-mail," he said. "Absolute discretion guaranteed: we have our own encryption programme."

He stood up a few minutes later. "Let's leave him mulling that over."

SITTING UNDER AN OVERWORKED CEILING FAN IN A BOMBAY CAFÉ ON THE ground floor of Ram's building, I felt as though it were old times in London. Except that instead of hamburgers we had a vegetarian answer to McDonald's, something Ram called a *pau-baji*—a bun filled with potato chutney, dipped in egg, and deep-fried.

"Quick service," I said.

"Nothing in this city is on time except lunch." Ram laughed. "Bombay is a city of overlunch success—and it's always on the move. You've got your travelling spice merchants who now own supermarket chains and your itinerant storytellers turned movie moguls." He wiped his mouth. "Considering that the film industry used to be itinerant too, I guess the place hasn't strayed far from its roots."

When we'd finished, the proprietor appeared and laid down another plate of what appeared to be a green Swiss roll. He leaned over Ram, talking to him in a rapid-fire language I didn't understand. Asked to translate, Ram shook his head at first, then under pressure admitted he had loaned the man money to buy this little café. He said the proprietor had lost his teaching job when a drought wiped out his village a few years back. Arriving in Bombay on one of the endless waves of people seeking work, he'd soon been reduced to selling his wife's cooking at a street stall under Ram's window.

"They do great food," Ram said. "The family's from an itinerant group of teachers whose caste stopped them from owning land in the past, so they developed this cooking style based on leftovers, stems, roots." He grinned. "Roots again—all the roots other people didn't use." He pointed at the Swiss roll. "This is a speciality. They smear a leaf with masalas, roll it up, steam it, and slice it."

The owner gestured proudly at my friend, *"Goondas! Goondas!"* he said.

"Ram?"

He shrugged, clearly embarrassed by the attention. *"Goondas* are gangsters who have certain *ralka*—certain territories. The small shop-keepers have to pay them protection, and most of the police turn a blind eye, even if they're not actually in on it. My cousin stopped the practice around here, which is another reason I'm always given special treatment."

AT THE STUDIO THERE WAS A LONG E-MAIL FROM RAM'S COUSIN, WHICH IN-cluded some photographs of the hijra victims.

Only two of the four victims had penises. One had old scarring where male genitalia had been surgically removed and cauterized, a puckered hole left to simulate the vagina. In the fourth body the geni-tal amputation was fresher and no surgeon had been involved. A butcher would have been ashamed of the work. The penis had been sawed away, not sliced off neatly. The edges of the wound were rag-ged, with strands of what once had been testicles hanging loosely be-tween the legs. Judging by the look of the cuts, the mutilation had probably been done with a small blade.

"No way these are suicides," Ram said, his voice creased with strain.

"They could be. People who hate themselves have an amazing capacity to bear pain." Most of my mother's cuts were on her upper thighs and abdomen, knotted and white like underground worms. She called them her battle scars.

Turning to the close-ups of the other cuts made me breathless.

Ram stood up. "I can't believe you stare at stuff like this for a living. I'm going to have a cigarette. Press that button when you want to see more."

I looked back at the screen.

Skin on faces and arms was gouged and slashed and peeled. In places, it had been sliced in half-inch strips, then rolled off to reveal the raw flesh underneath, as neatly as my mother used to cut her gold leaves. And herself. Cut to ribbons, I thought. For once the metaphor was appropriate. Whoever had done this had taken his time, enjoyed himself. It must have been a slow, careful process, like gilding, not the work of a frenzied maniac. On one body the strips of skin were still hanging. The others looked as if the action of water and scavengers had eaten the skin away. Thinking that my sister or her husband could be connected to these images, even remotely, made my own skin crawl.

The pictures were followed by a couple of handwritten pages, then some straightforward typed autopsy reports. They all looked pretty much the same:

MALE, ASIAN. AGE APP. 25–35. BODY SHOWS NO SIGN OF DECOMPOSITION ALTHOUGH THERE ARE EXTENSIVE LACERATIONS TO SOFT FACIAL AND BODILY TISSUE. THIS IS PARTIALLY ATTRIBUTABLE TO DAMAGE BY SCAVENGERS AND PARTIALLY TO SEVERE EXTERNAL TRAUMA DUE TO MUTILATION, PROBABLY BY A SMALL, SHARP INSTRUMENT. MUTILATION MAY BE SELF-INFLICTED. CAUSE OF DEATH: DROWNING.

"External trauma. Is that what they call it when they saw your dick off?" said Ram. He was standing behind me. "If they did that to me there'd be fucking internal trauma too." He pointed at the screen. "Tell me, Roz, why do you want to get yourself involved in this kind of thing?"

"I told you. My sister—"

He cut me off. "No, not this particular case. You do this for a living."

His question took me by surprise. "I guess . . . because I want to know why."

"Because the killer is a sick fucker, that's why."

"Not the killer. Why these people died. Why them? Why like this? Did they deserve it?" Seeing my mother's face under the water. "I suppose I want to know if it's just random, what happens to us."

He shook his head. "You should be a Hindu, Roz. Reincarnation would answer all your questions—and then you could move into a better line of work."

We turned back to the pictures of the hijra called Sami, the first murder victim. In life his face must have had a feminine prettiness that death had subdued, enhancing the masculine in his fine classical features, freezing them into a waxy marble beauty, a brown David for Michelangelo. "Can you read these?" I asked Ram, pointing to the handwritten notes attached to the photos.

"Don't you read Hindi?" He seemed surprised. "These must be the originals made by the coroner on site. The pages following should just be neater copies for the files." He frowned. "Wait a minute." He flipped forward again to the typed pages and carefully read through each one. "That's weird."

"What is? The fact that drowning in the sea preceded by self-mutilation is an unlikely suicide method for *one* of India's hijra population, let alone four?"

"Three," Ram said.

"There are four corpses here. All drowned and mutilated."

"That's what it says in the typed manuscript. The original handwritten notes are much more specific about the genital mutilation—one of the lads apparently had the genuine hijra operation. It also says that while three of the bodies were found washed up at the water's edge, the first one, this Sami person, was found on Chowpatty, drowned, but well away from the water. Sami was propped up against the statue of Tilak. And that's not the weirdest bit. Apparently she had the joints of her hips and knees broken as well as the elbow and fingers of her right arm—after rigor mortis had set in. She was holding a cardboard sign in her lap. The guy who wrote these notes has scribbled down the words written on the sign. Roughly translated: *'The great freedom leader Sami looks back nostalgically to the days of Marathi and Hindu glory.'*"

"So it *is* murder. And the murderer is literate and political. Or wants it to look that way."

"Unless it was some kind of political suicide as protest."

"She kills herself—and then her cohorts sit around waiting for rigor before they stick this sign in her hands? Interesting theory."

"I'm not the expert in violent death," Ram said. "So when does rigor set in?"

"Depends on the ambient heat, the weather—it's very unreliable. Some waggish prof said once that if there's no perceptible rigor it means the person has been dead for less than six hours or more than forty-eight. But the interesting part is the broken joints. It suggests she was killed elsewhere, then moved here and arranged. But why display her out in the open like that?"

"Maybe a kind of warning? That would fit in with the sign."

I haven't seen the eunuch in almost four weeks.

Ram was flipping through to the end of the document. "My cousin has added a little personal note to me." He pointed to the screen.

Most common causes of death by misadventure in India: stabbings, hangings, burnings, beatings. Pimps and vice lords seldom bother killing an unwilling hooker. They simply throw acid in her face, disfiguring her for good, then toss her out on the street with her market value considerably, if not completely, decreased. When arrested for such crimes, the criminals often get off (quantities of rupees having made the journey from one pocket into many) or mysteriously escape from jail.

"He's pretty bitter," Ram said. "When he graduated from university he refused to join in the bidding for a good position and that is essential if you want to succeed in the Indian police. So he was stuck much lower down the ladder than he deserved. He was working in Delhi at the time of Indira Gandhi's assassination, and a lot of his fellow police participated in the looting and rape that went on. My cousin filed a report that made him so unpopular he had to move to Bombay. That's why he doesn't mind upsetting the system."

I looked back at the screen.

As to other points: Indians seldom drown themselves. Most people—even fishermen—are afraid of the water and can't swim. Most common suicides are dowry deaths—young wives who burn themselves or stick their heads in ovens because they can't cope with maltreatment meted out by husbands' families. Usual causes of hijra deaths: bleeding to death, trauma or infection from badly handled, non-professional castration, or murder by an unsatisfied sexual client.

If a boy is forcibly castrated to enlist as a hijra prostitute, the hijra mafia or whoever is running the prostitution ring may compel his silence with death threats. Police interfere with reluctance, given that under the penal code the most they could charge the perpetrators with is "abduction and grievous injury with a sharp weapon." INDIAN LAW DOES NOT RECOGNIZE CASTRATION AS AN OFFENCE.

"With a political slant as well?" Ram said. "No wonder the coroner's office is trying to bury it. They must be creaming their gussets. Must be rupees flying about like fuckin' sand in the desert."

I stood up, stretched, and walked to the window. Six storeys below was a small subdivision of houses made out of iron bed frames and plastic shopping bags. A naked baby sat on a piece of newspaper in what passed for a door, oblivious to the pedestrians who stepped over him without a downward glance.

In London I live in a big white room on the top of a rotting tower not unlike this one. The second tallest residential block in Europe, its rent is almost as low as the residents' taste in graffiti, although cheap rent is not my reason for living there. Any money saved is spent on old Indian miniatures of the monsoon, paintings like stage sets for imaginary exits and entrances into a larger world. Infinite riches in a little room—that's what the artist Howard Hodgkin called his own collection. Within a small frame they enclose vast spaces and epic tales.

So it's not the cheap rent that holds me in the tower but the thought that someday—when the smog over London clears, when the clouds lift, when the Number 19 bus runs on time—there might be a wider horizon. The last tenants told me the flat had a view of the sea. My escape route. There are days when their lie is all that keeps me from jumping.

I turned away from Ram's window to watch him flipping through the pages on the screen and scanning for clues, his sensitive features crumpled into an anxious mask. Ram had been a sound editor in London, a genius with the timing of a standup comic and the instincts of a tabloid journalist. I wondered what had drawn him back here to his grandparents' birthplace.

We had met first at the BBC. Passing his tiny office one day, I'd asked about the different lengths of recording tape he kept pinned to his wall. His "museum of pauses," he called it, every variation on the concept of silence, from a double agent's split-second hesitation to a Remembrance Day's two minutes. "That's the *live* two-minute silence," he'd said.

When he swapped his reel-to-reel machine for a digital editing computer, Ram began to turn those pregnant pauses into multicoloured sound graphs on his screen. "Like an artist painting with sound and trading his housepainter's brush for a triple-zero sable," he'd told me at the time. I heard a tape he'd made once as a joke for a couple of mates, splicing together a TV soap commercial and a Conservative politician's party broadcast: "Our policies . . . are the softest soap of all. Vote Conservative: we wash away the dirty facts, leaving no telltale ring of truth." Seamless. By this point in his career Ram could probably inject Hitchcock nuances into a conversation about train schedules.

"Why did you move here, Ram?"

He looked up at me and his face relaxed. "My *dharma*," he recited in a mocking version of a guru's disciple. "Fulfilling obligation to accept duties appropriate to my condition. Upholding moral order of the universe."

"Bollocks! You're the son of a Cambridge physicist, and your brother's a microchip in Bangalore, India's answer to Silicon Valley."

"We Indians are masters of fuzzy logic—what else is Hinduism? Anyway, India is booming, especially in the computer field."

"Don't you miss anything about Britain?"

"Like what? The weather? The climate here may be too hot, too cold, too wet, too dry—but at least it's never boring. Excessive: that's how I'd sum it up. Which may account for the Indians' fatalistic attitude to life."

"What about the British sense of humour?"

"That irony you pride yourself on? Since Vietnam, even middle Americans have developed a sense of irony. It's the humour of all dying empires."

I waved down at the street scene. "And all this?"

Ram hunched his shoulders almost imperceptibly. "It would be going on even if I wasn't here to see it."

I turned away, suddenly tired. "Look, Ram, I'm ready to crash. If you hear any more from your cousin, give me a call at the hotel."

I RECOGNIZED THE DRIVER OF THE TAXI THAT PULLED UP OUTSIDE RAM'S building. "Well, if it isn't my old friend the poet."

"I am returning several times on off chance madam is needing a lift."

"You could've made more money elsewhere."

"Oh no—you have been tipping most graciously."

"So I overpaid you this morning." An illuminated plastic Madonna hung from his mirror now, and a new edging of Christmas tinsel shaded the windscreen. Behind me, a 3-D photo of Shiva kept company with a Buddhist or Jain saintly type and a bad reproduction of some nineteenth-century portrait of Prospero and Miranda. Still, it was nice to have a driver who covered all his bets, considering the nature of Bombay's traffic.

"*Tempest* is a most excellent play for Bombay," said Thomas, pointing at the dog-eared Prospero. "You are knowing it, madam?"

"A little. But I hope you don't mind me taking some liberties with the text. As a qualified poet, that is."

"That would be to make tempest in a teapot, isn't it?" He grinned into the mirror.

Through the window came the musky semen whiff of toddy, the

oily sweetness of fresh coconut from a man with a grater made out of an old ghee can, a nutty blast of frying chickpea batter in a street vendor's *karahi*. Drains and jasmine, bidis and kerosene. All it needed was a taxi driver who quoted Shakespeare. I could read the travel hack's copy in my head: *Come to India, land of contrasts.*

5

MY SUITCASE WAS LYING OPEN, STILL UNPACKED. ON TOP lay the books from Dad's library that my sister had sent me after he died: Piddington's *Sailor's Hornbook for the Law of Storms* and Blandford's *Indian Meteorological Vade-Mecum of 1877*, the most widely used textbook on tropical meteorology at the end of the nineteenth century. In the flyleaf of the Blandford, Miranda had written: "Dad told me he wanted you to have these. I thought you might need them if you came to Bombay. Everyone should have a compass in uncharted territory."

Ringing Miranda's number now, all I got was a watery echo.

The summer my sister learned how to float was for me the window onto a different kind of life, like those family images we used to get in Edinburgh at the hour when people started to turn the lights on in their living rooms, before the curtains were drawn. I was glad I could still remember. Since my mother died seven years ago, since she was killed, my memory has been giving me trouble, although I haven't forgotten that there was a time when Miranda and I were so close we could read each other's mind.

It was the summer we spent together in Kerala. Dad had moved away from the coast and was living by a lagoon in an old teak house on a coconut plantation. A landscape out of Kipling, with tigers to keep us inside at night and elephants instead of tractors to clear the forest. But our father had more elemental concerns. Kerala was the most densely populated region of India, and every bowel emptied its contents into the backwaters that had always been the state highways. The sewage was fertilizing a weed that would soon choke the channels, Dad predicted. A man obsessed with the control of anything fluid, his mission was to find some fluvial engineer of the past who had an answer to Kerala's problem.

Dad had forbidden us to swim in the lagoons, but Miranda and I ignored him, exploring an underwater world where we couldn't hear voices raised or words spat like poisoned darts. Only touch and sight were valid. The water of our lagoon was clear, but where the canals narrowed, there you would run into the snake-green, choking weed—and other things. Once, my sister and I found a tiny skeleton shrouded in sediment, smaller even than the dwarf who worked in the circus school. The size of the newborn baby in our village.

That last summer, I was thirteen, my sister was ten. We had six months together while our parents tried unsuccessfully to—what is the expression?—patch things up? As if life were a quilt that could be stitched to fit. In fact, it was more like a corpse the pathologist had torn apart and sewn roughly back together, minus its organs.

Just six months. Perhaps if there had been other children to play with, the bond between Miranda and me would not have been so strong. Three years is a big age difference for a child, but the isolation cocooned us like a double chrysalis.

After the cocoon broke, we didn't meet again for eight years.

It was in the monsoon summer when I turned thirteen that I first became interested in storms. We were always leaving places I loved in storms.

6

PHOSPHORESCENT EYES, THAT IS WHAT I DREAM. DROWNED Phoenician sailors who rise from their predecessors' ashes, and Belladonna, the lady of the rocks, whose poison is atropine, from Atropos, one of the three Greek Fates.

I woke with the feeling of other eyes watching me: deep-lidded, long-lashed, set in a face the colour of the kippers my maternal grandmother used to buy from the Aberdeen fishmonger on our road in Edinburgh, before my mother moved us to London.

"Yallafish," my gran would say, in a perfect imitation of the northeast accent, although in her voice there were still traces of her own family's Indian roots. She liked kippers, she claimed, because they reminded her of Bombay duck, and she ate them with a strange treacly chutney made of soaked and sieved tamarind pods, a practice her Scottish neighbours found very peculiar. Of course, kippers are nothing like Bombay duck. The *bombil*, that sun-dried, transparent wafer found in Indian grocers, is not a waterfowl but a fish out of water. Like me.

The eyes filled my hotel window. I pulled a shirt over my head and went to examine their owner, who spread over most of the two-storey poster opposite my room. "Goliath!" the text exclaimed, followed by some inscrutable Hindi. His face was unshaven, proof of a Hindu movie hero's machismo and skill in kickboxing. On a villain a five o'clock shadow is just one more example of his lack of moral fibre.

My peeping Tom had welded his jowls so firmly to the cheek of a doe-eyed starlet (the friction caused by contact with his stubble turning her face a lurid salmon pink) that his allegiance to good guys or bad was hard to assess. Looking in the mirror, I could see that my own face was less rosy.

Before I could push that thought any further, reception rang to ask if a Mr. Ram Shantra and friend could come to my room. "Send them up," I said, grabbing a pair of creased white jeans from my suitcase.

RAM ARRIVED WITH A MAN SO SLIGHT AND FRAIL-BONED AS TO BE ALMOST childlike, an impression reinforced by his baggy shirt and wire-rimmed glasses.

"This is Dilip, a lab technician at the coroner's," Ram said. "Friend of my cousin. His brother is a hijra."

Dilip nodded. "Should you not be adverse to departing immediately, I may be able to smuggle you into my office, Miss Bengal. To view most recent corpse."

Everything was happening too fast. If the hijra deaths *were* related to Miranda's husband in some way, I wasn't sure I wanted to get this involved before discussing the situation with her. "Can it wait until I talk to my sister?"

"A press conference has been called," Ram said, "because of all the flak caused by CNN. Dilip figures most people will be out of the office."

"If not taking part in the conference, then at least partaking of lunch. But you will have to be very fast," Dilip added. "What I am doing is most irregular."

DILIP NODDED AT THE GUARD IN THE CORONER'S BUILDING. "MORE PRESS," HE said, and I waved my temporary BBC identity card. The guard took the pass to examine it. "Rosalind Benegal," he said, running his finger down the list of invited press.

"Sister-in-law of Prosper Sharma," Dilip said. Casually reaching for my pass, I managed to slip fifty rupees to the guard, who frowned, then waved us past.

"Fourth floor with others," he called as we got into the lift.

Dilip pressed a button marked SB. "Let's hope the guard isn't watching," he said, when the doors had closed. "SB is the sub-basement, where the post-mortem rooms are."

A Stockholm SOCO, a scene of crime officer, once described what he hated most about forensics. No hesitation. "The smell," he said. To avoid being sick he would take three deep lungfuls of fresh air before starting work. "And even then sometimes you have to breathe through your mouth."

Forensic labs affect me like that. I inhale deeply before entering them. I breathe through my mouth. But it's not just the smell. I have been in morgues all over the world—stainless-steel American morgues, as scrubbed and sterile as industrial kitchens; Danish morgues that look like ads for a Scandinavian furniture chain; Swedish morgues, where they hide the gore behind pale peach curtains. One thing they all share: this is where the final indignities are performed on people we loved, their body fluids drained into the sewer, orifices raped and mutilated by metal instruments. When I die, let it be in the sea.

Bombay's post-mortem lab was older than any I had been in previously, its tiled surfaces more worn and yellowed with years of bleach and chemicals and blood. But basically, it was the same. The jigsaw of what had once been the muscle and tissue of a person lay in unconnected pieces on a porcelain slab in the centre of the room. You could see the rusty stains where excretions had been hosed off the slab onto the tiles. Someone had sawed neatly through the skull to get to the brain.

"What's that for?" Ram pointed to a plastic bucket on the floor next to the slab, his voice shaky.

"Intestines," Dilip replied. He walked over to the corpse and pointed to the penis. "This one was dressed as a woman but still had male genitalia. Second body had no genitalia. It was cut away."

"But it must be obvious when it's a man. . . ." said Ram.

Dilip looked at him. "Not if considerable putrefaction has taken place—if scavengers have eaten away soft external flesh, for instance. In such a case it is useful to know that the uterus is the last internal organ to decompose."

Ram reached for the cigarettes in the pocket of his T-shirt. "I'll wait outside."

Dilip picked up one of the corpse's limp arms and pointed to hatching etched into the flesh. "Coroner was most interested in the cuts on these bodies. Their clean definition seems to indicate a very fine knife was used."

The first time it happened, in Kerala, I thought it was an accident. All that blood . . . The doctor came. Then Dad. One of our neighbours had taken the news to his house.

"Like what?" I said.

"What it is *not* is easier. Not like the more usual machete or flick knife of our Indian gangsters." He smiled warmly. "Perhaps closer to a coroner's scalpel. And whoever did these cuts also did the others. Do you see this cross-hatch pattern across the nipple region? It is identical to the pattern found on the other bodies."

I pulled out the Polaroid camera I always carried. "Do you mind?"

Dilip made a graceful gesture with one hand towards the corpse, like a maître d' welcoming a guest to his restaurant. "But please be quick. I have more to show you and we must be out of here before conference or lunch ends."

I took four or five close-ups of the cuts on the hijra's arms, then Dilip waved me through into another room. "You have read the official typed notes?"

I nodded.

"Those notes are supposedly transcribed directly by a secretary from tapes made by the coroner at time of autopsy."

"Supposedly?"

"I was out of the office testing while the autopsy was going on. When I read the official typed document later, I was interested to know that what I had done had apparently not occurred. Normally I take very little further interest in a case once I have done the tests." He hesitated. "Please to understand, Miss Benegal. It is not because I am not thorough about my job. Only that I do not like to become personally involved with bodies whose elements I examine. Certainly I do not bother to read official documentation. But because my brother too is hijra . . . Anyway, the tape recorder is still set up as it was for the typist. I have wound it to the relevant portion. Please listen."

He pressed the Play button and a colourless, educated voice spoke to us from within the echoing butcher's shop of post-mortem:

"*. . . found to contain very low concentration of chloride when specific-gravity tests were made of the heart blood. A sample of heart tissue when tested for diatoms was found to contain—*"

"Stop it there," I said. "You're telling me you were asked to do specific-gravity tests and also to test for *diatoms*?"

Dilip obediently stopped the tape and favoured me with a small smile. "You are familiar with the reasons for these tests in an autopsy, Miss Benegal?"

"It means they suspected the hijra didn't drown in that particular bit of sea, or was dead before entering the water. A person drowned in a river, say, or other fresh water, has diluted blood. Water saturates the heart and other major organs—even sometimes the bone marrow—which reduces the blood's chloride concentration. That's why you do specific-gravity tests. Both the sea and unpolluted fresh water contain these microscopic organisms called diatoms. You find them by dissolving samples of the organs with mineral acid. If a person is dead before going into the water, you find diatoms in the air passages but not in the blood."

He knew all this already, of course; I was just being put through my paces to check for signs of limp credentials. "And if they drown in the sea?" he said.

"Salt water does the reverse of fresh. It doesn't dilute the blood, it draws water out of it, which is why they use it to preserve meat." You drown more slowly in impure water. In some cases, impurity can save your life. "So it's not only very likely that the other three hijra were drowned elsewhere and then dumped on Chowpatty, it looks as if the deputy coroner suspected it as well."

"So it would seem," Dilip said. "The bodies, at any rate, were drowned in fresh impure water, not in the sea."

"Can I take this tape?"

"Absolutely not—it would certainly be missed. But I will see if somehow I can make a copy." He paused. "Otherwise, I fear the facts about these deaths may be pushed under the carpet.

"You should talk to somebody more senior—the chief coroner, maybe." Dilip gestured to the damp cubicle that passed for his laboratory. Windowless, reeking of phenol and other, less clinical odours, not much bigger than a cupboard. Although the room was chilly, there was no fan; it was cooled by its proximity to the fridge where the corpses were stored. "The coroner knows," he said. "Anyway, I am just a chemist in the basement. Coroner's office is on the top floor. He has air conditioning, framed certificates from famous universities on the wall, and windows facing the sea. Perhaps his windows allow him a broader view of the situation than mine."

My mother had given me a less concise but just as damaging description of Indian society after her initial romantic view of the subcontinent had worn off. Before that, Dad had dealt in histories, Mum in stories. The *Mahabharata*. The *Ramayana*. Other tales of gods who marry dairymaids and produce celestial children. She read too much Kipling, without absorbing his basic message: in India, people know their place. Without this adherence to caste, class, and social considerations, the delicate balance that keeps Indian society stable would be upset. "The dharma/karma nest of barbed wire keeps the poor poor and gives the rich an excuse for holding on to their money," Mum would say bitterly.

"A broader view," I said to Dilip. "You think this is political? The coroner is trying to avoid some political storm by covering up details of these deaths?"

"In India, a country of three hundred and thirty thousand gods, more or less, and two hundred fifty-seven political parties, not counting aspirational Independents, that which is not political must be religious."

Ram put his head through the door. "Someone with flat feet walks this way."

Dilip nervously pushed the glasses up on his nose. "Follow me," he said, opening a door that led into a concrete passageway. "We'll take the back stairs."

Outside the building, Dilip gave me one last piercing look. "You may find it hard to believe, Miss Benegal, but I loved my brother, though he was hijra."

"Is he dead?"

"Not dead. Disappeared. My parents banished him from our home years ago when they discovered his proclivities. It was too much shame for them. But he was not a degenerate and a mutilator of children, as the newspapers are suggesting all hijra are. He was a gentle person, only born in the wrong skin."

"Thank you very much, Dilip, for your help." I didn't like to mention money, although his clothes suggested a few rupees could be put to good use. "Can I buy you lunch on your day off?"

He wobbled his head from side to side in the graceful but ambiguous movement so typical of Indians born on the subcontinent. "Only discover who is doing this," he said.

7

Ram took me to a place around the corner that did fresh mango *kulfi*, an antidote to monsoon fever, he claimed.

"No ice cream for me," I said. "Rules for all foreigners in Third World countries: no water except bottled, no ice in drinks, no fruit or salad stuff that may be washed in water and can't be peeled." Instead, I drank two cups of watery Nescafé while Ram concentrated on the hard little cone of creamy fruit ice on his plate, as if its fragrance could wipe out the less savoury perfumes he had just inhaled.

"I didn't have time to ask Dilip before you came bursting in, Ram, but I presume Sami drowned or bled to death like the others."

"Possibly not. He told me about it on the way to your hotel. He said he found traces of cyanide on her mouth and clothes—"

"Cyanide!"

Ram nodded. "But he can't be sure. Says the forensic analysis was done very late on Sami's body. You'd know more about that than I would."

"The body's metabolism converts cyanide into sulphocyanides very rapidly, and sulphocyanides are present in our bodies anyway. So if an autopsy is left for too long, there may be very little trace of the poison. . . . Still, *cyanide*? How? In a deadly pill? It's the preferred suicide method for Nazi war criminals, but not likely here. So who uses cyanide in India and where do you get it?"

"From a chemist," Ram said, "and even that's difficult. I don't know what you use it for apart from poisoning people—"

"Not to mention exotic butterflies of indeterminate sex. But how ignorant you are, oh navigator. Cyanide is useful stuff. A solution of potassium ferricyanide and iron ammonio-citrate will produce cyanotypes—or blueprints, as we usually call them. A bit out-of-date in cyberspace, maybe, but still a possibility here in the land that time forgot. Potassium cyanide is also used in electroplating one metal onto another. And a solution of cyanide can be used to dissolve gold."

"Why would you want to dissolve gold?"

"To extract the good ore from the waste. Alchemy—or as close as we get to it."

"Apparently the deputy coroner refused to believe Dilip when he said he found traces of cyanide," Ram said. "Claimed the likelihood of hijra suicide by cyanide is about ten thousand to one."

"That could be why they didn't mention cyanide in the official report."

"There's plenty they didn't mention. Dilip said he did—what did he call it?—chromatography on Sami's clothing, and he found traces of sulphides. And even without the chroma-thingy he could see there was a lot of blue wax. As if she'd melted a candle over herself."

"Maybe she worked by candlelight. The factories here are primitive enough."

"Dilip figured that, so he tested this wax against a common Indian brand of candle. The wax on Sami's clothing was much much harder. So hard, at first he thought it was plastic—except that it melted at a lower temperature than plastic."

"Did any of the other hijra have wax or sulphides on them?"

"Negative. Maybe the water washed it away while they were drowning, or maybe— Hey, Roz, you've gone corpse white on me. I told you to have the kulfi, not the coffee. I diagnose a terminal case of low blood sugar—" Ram stopped abruptly and closed his mouth. He spent a few moments rearranging his sticky plate and napkin on the Formica surface of the table. "I forgot. All this drowning business must be hard for you. After your mother . . ."

"I'm just a bit jet-lagged."

"Your mother—did it happen in the sea?"

"No," I said. "In the bath. With Colonel Mustard. Nothing like a mustard bath to relax the muscles."

8

I KEPT TRYING MIRANDA'S NUMBER, FINALLY GOT HER HUSBAND
on the answerphone: Prosper Sharma, a cool, evenly modulated voice,
no hint of an Indian accent. It felt strange to leave the first message for
my sister with him.

Ram had given me the name of the journalist—Bunny Thapar—
who covered the hijra deaths for *The Times of India*. I rang her, bran-
dishing my BBC credentials, and said I was interested in her personal
impressions of the Chowpatty hijra deaths, not the official "suicide"
line she was having to toe.

"Off the record?" she said.

"If you like."

"Murders, definitely. Possibly a warning from their pimp."

"Not political, then?"

"Are you looking for a political connection?" Her voice took
on the disinterested tones of all journalists on the scent of a new
story.

"Actually, I'm looking for a connection between these hijras'
deaths and Maya Sharma's."

"Because of the hijra who was there when Maya fell?"

"What hijra?"

"I worked on that story as a junior reporter. I remember the
photos. There was a shot of a hijra pulling her skirt aside after Maya
fell. One of the witnesses. That's the shot we used. Taken by the second Mrs. Sharma, oddly enough."

I felt my scalp contract as if from a blow. "You mean the *present*
Mrs. Sharma."

"Yes, Miranda Sharma. Her auntie lived nearby. Miranda was opposite the building when it happened, taking photos of the street with one of those motordrive cameras. She gave the film to the police and we got it from them. I always presumed that was how she met Prosper, over the photos of his first wife's death. A bit ghoulish, but Miranda must've seemed like a breath of fresh air to poor Prosper."

"I take it you don't think he murdered his wife?"

"Well, there was gossip at the time, but then there was also gossip that Maya's death might have been political. She and her father were very involved with one of the more extreme political movements—only the fashionable side, of course, like those American socialites with the Black Panthers in the sixties. In fact, I'm pretty sure Maya's death was straightforward: ageing star's depression due to failing career, failing marriage. Infertility in all aspects of life."

"What has infertility got to do with it?"

Something in my voice must have triggered her memory, because there was a pause before she answered. Then: "Benegal—that was Miranda's maiden name. No relation, I suppose?"

I hesitated, reluctant. "My sister."

"Ah. Well. Maya couldn't give Prosper children. No sons: major sin for an Indian woman. But the question of murder was just ugly gossip. Unless you count Shoma Kumar, the editor of *Screenbites*, who was rumoured to be having an affair with Prosper at the time, the only person who would've benefited from Maya's death was Prosper, and he was on set, filming. In your sister's photos you could clearly see Maya coming onto the balcony, then falling and finally dead."

"How did you know the woman in the picture was a hijra?"

"You could tell by her Adam's apple. The police tried halfheartedly to find her afterwards, but she just disappeared. It's easy to disappear in Bombay."

Bunny said she would try to dig out the pictures and fax me a list of people close to Prosper at the time of Maya's death. "But, Miss Benegal, if I were you, I'd start with Caleb Mistry or Basil Chopra. Caleb was Prosper's right-hand man and Basil has been working on a film with Prosper for years."

Miranda had never told me how she met Prosper, never mentioned the photos. They were part of her Bombay life, the years she kept hidden from me. Still, we're a strange family. She is not my real sister—or rather, she is my half sister, although it felt as if I had lost more than half when I left India. I still see her face in strangers sometimes, or in the expression of a young Indian actress in the movies. Half see her, imagining what Miranda looks like now.

Half a sister: her mother was married to my father, my mother wasn't.

9

Mʏ PARENTS MET OVER GOLD AND WATER, EACH PURSUING separate fluvial and gilded myths in the British Library. Dad was on sabbatical from his job as a historian for Kerala's Meteorological Department, in London studying the works of the great hydraulic artists, men who had sought to control the elements either by magic or by mathematics. Like Salomon de Caus, the "Prospero of Heidelberg," author of an illustrated manual explaining how the liquid mechanic might make water perform unnatural feats: rivers flow uphill, golden balls remain in perpetual suspension on illuminated jets.

Dad bumped into Mum over the *R*s. She was about to begin the gilding of a new edition of Sir Walter Raleigh's book: *The Discoverie of the large, rich and beautifull Empire of Guianna, with a relation of the great and golden citie of Manoa (which the Spaniards call El Dorado)*.

She told me in one of her more prescient moments that it was an omen. "Raleigh's expedition to offer European civilization to the tribes up the Orinoco in exchange for their gold was doomed to lose its way and end in death," she said.

Dad tried to explain himself in a letter to me when I was twenty-one. I still have it. He said that the concept of love and sex as an end in itself outside his arranged marriage had never really entered his head until he literally bumped into this tall girl with the wide-set green eyes.

"It was 1959," he wrote. "I had rarely seen my own wife's legs. Your mother was wearing a short tight skirt and a V-neck man's sweater that showed a lot of bosom. All in black, like Cyd Charisse and the Paris beatniks I had read about. She had this long rope of hair twisted up and held with a paintbrush. When I tried to pick up her books, her hair fell down over me. Wave after wave. My wife used to plait her hair so tightly it stretched the skin of her eyes."

"It was a gilder's tip," my mother said, reading his letter later, "not a paintbrush."

In my mind I can open one of her old books, *The Gilders' Handbook of Applications*, mentally turning the pages to find the right one:

> Gold leaf can be picked up only with a brush called a gilder's tip. It should be brushed lightly over the gilder's cheek before each use. A leaf of gold is so thin that static electricity and faint traces of grease from the gilder's skin on the tip are enough to move the gold around.

It has always seemed an apt description of my mother's effect on people. Once she had brushed against them, they were bound to her— however delicately—until she chose to let go.

The first eleven years of my life Mum spent describing how badly my father had treated her. When I was twelve, she began reversing the process, preparing me for the possibility of her reconciliation with Dad, I guess. First she wanted me to be British; then she wanted me to be Indian, like my father. She said that he had seduced her on their first meeting with stories of a waterland where spice forests were guarded by winged cobras. At the time it seemed to her a link to another, lost part of her roots.

People in Edinburgh always used to comment on my rosy cheeks and green eyes. "That's the Scot in you coming out!" they'd tell me, a reward for being a flower with only half its roots showing. I would nod and smile agreeably.

Actually it's the Chitrali. I get the black hair from my mother's grandfather, a pasty-faced, sooty-eyed Glaswegian army clerk who met, seduced, and then married my auburn-haired great-grandmother in the remote valley of Chitral, under the shadow of Tirich Mir, the highest mountain in the Hindu Kush, a place where they make no distinction between legend and history. These were Gran's wilder relatives, from the deep Kalash valleys south of Chitral. They were Kafirs, so-called Children of Nature, and their gods looked like Greek beach boys.

"My people are descendants of Alexander the Great's troops," Gran used to say. "That's why many Chitrali girls have dark red hair and pale eyes. Look at your profile. That's a legacy of Alexander."

So far as I know, Alexander's main column, after leaving the Indus Valley, marched home through the province of Baluchistan, a long way south of Chitral, although I suppose a few independent stragglers might have made it north to impregnate Gran's ancestors. Not that I have met many redheaded Greeks.

To fill the days on the voyage back from Kerala to her widowed mother's house in Edinburgh, Mum introduced me to a new set of stories, of Britons, not Indians, ruling the waves, and palaces of stone instead of teak. We would fit in again, she said, after seven long years of being outsiders.

But she was wrong. We remained outsiders, this time in a cold country instead of a hot one. Reincarnation in a lower form, punishment for our behaviour in a previous life. Gran had shed her half-Chitrali skin like a snake in spring and emerged as a respectable, working-class Scotswoman. The lamia who devoured children, Gran swallowed her own daughter. She never forgot how Mum had disgraced the family. I was the living proof: Dad didn't recognize me "officially" until I was thirteen, after Miranda's mother died. By the time he gave me his name, a new identity was impossible. The gesso I was made of was too liquid a blend. Mum had succeeded in producing a kind of kedgeree instead, neither one thing nor the other, provenance doubtful, just a little bit fishy.

The latest neuroscientists believe that identity, moral choice, guilt are just a question of genetics. A human brain is like an exposed negative, they say, waiting to be dipped in the developer fluid of social conditioning. Your life is down to what's printed on the film—over- or underexposed by upbringing, perhaps, but that print is the genetic map passed on to you, and there's not much you can do except follow the roads on it.

My family passed on a legacy of guilt as other families pass on weak hearts or poor eyesight. Guilt like a slow poison, drip drip drip.

NO MORE THAN TEN MINUTES AFTER I PUT THE PHONE DOWN FROM ARRANGING to meet Caleb Mistry, it rang again: Dilip, calling from the morgue.

"Please, Miss Benegal, I am so sorry to disturb you. But I am wondering if you did—by mistake, I am sure—pick up the deputy coroner's tape?" I heard voices behind him while he tried to be polite. "It . . . seems to have gone missing, and there has been a terrible furore, accusations flying left, right, and so forth. Guard has informed the DC of what he claims was illicit visit of press to post-mortem—"

"I was holding the tape when Ram came in and I may have forgotten to give it back." I fumbled through my daypack and finally found the tape in a side pocket. "Look, Dilip, I'm really sorry if I got you into trouble."

"No problem, Miss Benegal," he said, his voice barely audible over the shouting behind him. "If you would be so kind as to drop the tape off at your earliest con"—the other voices rose an octave—"right away if possible."

THERE WAS A SULKY HEAVINESS IN THE AIR THAT FELT LIKE rain. But I was a tourist in the country of my birth, what did I know? The weather gurus on the taxi radio had changed their tune from yesterday, swearing now that it would be another six days before the monsoon struck. The tenth of June, they said, a mark fixed like a bank holiday in the calendar. And no one doubted them. You've got to admire the faith meteorologists inspire in their religious followers. Weathermen, like most gods, are seldom correct in their prophesies, but unlike anyone else who fucks up a public broadcast, they get to keep their jobs.

"Roz Benegal," I said to the guard at Caleb Mistry's studio gate, admiring his faded uniform, a relic of some spurious cinematic regiment.

"Oh yes, madam." He clicked his bare heels together and saluted smartly before getting into the car just ahead of a crowd of children who had caught up with us. They pressed their faces against the windows, shouting the urgent mantra of street kids all over the subcontinent: *"What iss your nem? What iss your nem?"*

What is my name? The definitive answer always eludes me.

"Only they are hoping you may be some famous movie star," said the guard, before the studio gates shut the children out. We drove across the lot towards a circular, windowless building that looked like a decaying mausoleum for Victorian values. "This is ice house," he went on, "where action takes place. In 1870s, British are storing ice here which they are bringing in huge blocks by sailing ship from North America's Great Lakes, packed in felt and sawdust."

"The last time you could trust the ice in Bombay not to kill you."

"But, madam, this ice too is killing you. When ice house was being converted into a mill, ground was thawing back into mud. Dead ice-man was found buried here." He gave me a sly glance. "Souvenir of your East India Company."

"A frozen stiff."

"Sorry, madam?"

"Who was it?"

"Head and hands have been chopped off, so he has no identity. But Mr. Mistry is keeping a few of the ice-man's *mohars* as souvenirs."

"Molars? He kept this dead bloke's *teeth*?"

"Mohars, mohars, madam—gold coins used in Mogul times and also struck by your East India Company on becoming new Moguls of India. These mohars were crusted with old blood, so perhaps there was foul play."

That was something I knew about. "Gilding once meant to smear with blood."

"Sorry, madam?"

"Just thinking aloud. Is this Mistry's main studio?"

"Actually it was once a textile mill, but since an industrial dispute several years ago Dadasahib is renting it."

It was the first time I had heard the affectionate nickname "Daddy-sir" used to describe anyone other than India's first great director, Dhundiraj Phalke, the man who established the film industry here in 1912. A nickname was about all Caleb Mistry had in common with Phalke, except that the two directors had both produced box-office bonanzas whose profits had to be hauled away in bullock carts— or convoys of Mercedes, in Mistry's case. In the two hours since handing the deputy coroner's tape over to its outraged owner, I had done some homework on Caleb Mistry, and his credentials read like a Hindi script synopsis: street kid made good, bad poet, benefactor to his people. A life in keeping with his art. Like most commercial Hindi directors, he produced schlock musicals, the kind Busby Berkeley would have made if he'd had the Indo-Pakistan war as a plot. In the magazine *Tinsel Town* I read a synopsis of the standard Mistry movie:

Mr. Underdog has been exposed to death, failure, and brothels. Loves pretty Miss and fighting the system. Finally, Underdog, the lone barker, goes on a biting spree. Rewarded with pretty Miss in the last reel.

Inside the ice house, four different seasons coexisted within fifty yards of each other. Doors were kicked down in a monsoon downpour, women were raped and beaten under a spring moon, men spilled stage blood into salt snow, and, to this muted drumbeat of head jabs and knee thrusts, a man had his eyes gouged out under the cobalt brilliance of a 10,000-watt summer.

Ten feet into the studio an almighty crack of thunder made me jump.

"No problem," said my guide. "Is metal sheet they are using for thunderclap."

But the jerry-built set was genuinely lethal, G-clamp hell, an electrocutioner's wet dream. The Code of Safety for Bombay films must be not so much lax as laxative: this set would have loosened the bowels of any European inspector. I stumbled through the offstage twilight over electric cables whose safety coating had worn away in places to reveal venomous live wires jammed into floor-mounted sockets inches from leaking taps. This did not disturb the barefoot stage crew, who tripped blithely over the wires, unaware of the danger, or used to it. Karmic immune. It was Hollywood in the 1920s: stuntmen here not only looked as if they were defying death; they actually were. A bloody prop crowbar for the next scene was in fact a real crowbar. Perhaps it was real blood as well: one actor who had crashed through a window was being treated for cuts.

"Does Mr. Mistry have real gangsters playing the gangsters?" I asked the guard.

"Oh no, madam, Mr. Caleb is employing many street people, for he too was having to haul himself out of the gutter, but not villains."

Someone must have set off a dry-ice machine nearby, because the studio ahead of us had disappeared under a billowing mist. The guide turned and shouted, "Lady from BBC, Dadasahib!" We moved forward a few feet until a group of figures began to emerge from the white clouds, heads first, like Cheshire cats.

Caleb Mistry sat in a pool of light, surrounded by acolytes and actors. He wore faded jeans and flip-flops and had rolled the sleeves of a baggy Hawaiian-print shirt up over his powerful arms. He was broad and muscular as a bull, with a handsome, fleshy face and eyes of a strange pale grey, the colour of ashes. For one moment when he grinned at me I thought his teeth were stained with blood: Central Casting had gone terribly wrong, and this guy should be playing the cannibal, not the saint. Then I saw the auburn splashes of betel juice around his chair and realized he was chewing the mildly narcotic *paan*. Mr. Kurtz meets Cecil B. DeMille in the Heart of Darkness.

"How do you do, Mr. Mistry." I stumbled over the double mister.

"You want tea?" he asked abruptly. "Of course: all English girls want tea—*Chair!*"

He crossed one leg over the other and waved his hand in dismissal at the boy who was fanning him with a big piece of cardboard. "For some reason you make me think of a T. S. Eliot poem," Mistry said. "What are the words? *Something something come and go, talking of Michelangelo.*" Poetry that fit him like the wedding ring on a hooker.

"I'm not much for poems," I said.

"Pity." His full mouth turned down in what might have been mock or genuine disappointment. "I suppose you'll want to sit. *Chair!* And give me some light!"

A spot switched on from high up in the gods. The chair and the tea arrived.

"You look hot. *Fan!*"

An electric fan the size of a Volvo started up and blew a small typhoon our way, dissolving the last of the dry ice. "Is that better?" Mistry said. "We use it for giving our heroines' hair that windswept look. Most appropriate for a representative of the great British Broadcasting Corporation."

"I'm only freelance." I put my cup down and got out my tape recorder. "And I'm not English. I'm half Indian, part Scottish, and an eighth Chitrali."

"And a little pedantic." He paused. "So what are you wanting of me?" There was some wariness in his question. He was a man with the outward face of power, whose accent and language kept slipping from one continent to another. He had the manner of a supporting player forced into the star's ill-fitting costume at the last minute, and I got the feeling that both of us were inadequately rehearsed for the roles we were playing, as I have always felt in Britain. It gave Mistry an attractive vulnerability, a bond with me: two outsiders.

"I'm here to make a series about Bombay directors," I said, altering my story to fit the circumstances, while trying to look like a woman who posed no threat. "Judging by what I've seen on your set today, this is no romance." I pressed the Record button on my DAT machine and smiled sweetly.

Mistry raised his eyebrows and smiled too, not at all sweetly. "Why? Are all love stories bloodless? But in this case, it's the Good

Guy beating up the Bad Guy. In Bombay movies we have a simple masala: eight songs, four fights, one rape, and a mother-in-law/ daughter-in-law confrontation." He paused. "Then they all make up and live happily ever after," he said, but the skin of irony was very thin. "The poor people's twenty-five paise supports our movies, and they like happy endings. So when the Good Guy has finished, he goes home to his family and makes love to his wife. Not on screen, of course, our censors wouldn't allow it." His mouth twitched as if he wanted to smile. "And the bad guys screw."

"What about their families?"

"Bad guys don't have families."

"You're divorced, aren't you, Mr. Mistry?"

"Oh, I'm the bad guy, definitely. If that's what you're asking. Or maybe I'm still looking for True Love. . . ." He eyed me up and down as if I were stretched out on an invisible casting couch.

Dickhead, I thought, but smiled winningly, flirting a little to soften him up for the tougher questions. "Your films have definitely changed since the days with Prosper Sharma," I said, glancing across to where a chorus of chubby hoofers with plastic Kalashnikovs were practising a dance step.

"And read Plato and Shakespeare—especially Shakespeare, thanks to my guru." He trapped the word "guru" in mocking quotation marks, the shrine for a false god. "Oh yes, thanks to my guru I know an Elizabethan fag's sonnets better than I know the Vedas and can rip off a Hitchcock film better than Truffaut could."

"You sound like an unwilling pupil. Who was the guru?"

"Prosper Sharma. I thought everybody knew."

"But you made him sound English."

Caleb shrugged. "He might as well be. Prosper's family were like coconuts—brown on the surface and white underneath. They came here from Lahore when the Hindus were kicked out of Pakistan after Partition. But like so many well-connected families, they managed to have enough forewarning from their political friends to smuggle out their loot."

"It hasn't all been smooth sailing for Mr. Sharma. His first wife—"

He didn't let me finish. "A marriage of convenience, like his present one."

Like his present one? I tried not to show my surprise. "Why did you work with Sharma for so long if you disliked him?"

"Not *with* him—*for* him. He pretends to run a democratic studio, but when it comes to taking the applause, it's always Sharma up on the podium."

"So how did you manage to start your own studio," I began dryly, leaving a two-beat pause before finishing the sentence, "if not with help from Sharma?"

"Here's a tip for playing Happy Families: tell the audience what she wants to hear. That's how you strike gold." He had a remarkable voice, deep and melodious; a storyteller's voice that made you want to keep him talking.

"Well, you've certainly struck gold in this ice house," I said. "Is that why you kept the mohars? As a souvenir of independence?"

"Who told you the mohar *story*—the guard?" He turned away, and for a moment his profile, dark and clearly outlined against the light, appeared more Roman or Greek than Indian. After a slight pause, he said that the ice house was a reminder to him that the British didn't belong in Bombay.

"The Moguls introduced the idea of artificial ice to India, not the British," I said, a bit more crisply than I'd intended, and went on quickly, before he could change the subject. "By the way, you worked on Prosper's Mogul version of *The Tempest*, didn't you—the last picture Maya made before she—"

"The Moguls didn't belong here either," Caleb cut in, his odd greyish-green eyes locked directly into mine again, so that I knew he meant me to take the comment personally. "Like Prosper, their interests lay elsewhere."

This time I wasn't going to be deflected. "Didn't you set up your own studio the year she died?" Watching his eyes changing like water, shifting as I spoke. How odd, I thought: we have the same eyes.

"What are you implying? That the two events are connected? Or are you just being provocative?" A minute pause while we rested, verbal fencers sizing each other up. I was trying to work out what the real dialogue was here—both of us attracted and repelled by something we recognized in the other? Then he spoke again, his voice teasing: "Roz . . . may I call you Roz? You strike me as one of those Western women with a big chip on their shoulders. Not at all like your sister, Miranda."

"How do you know I'm Miranda's sister?"

He smiled even more broadly. "A long shot. Her maiden name was Benegal. And she told me once she had a sister who worked for the BBC. I know her well enough to see you could be the vanilla version of her. Except for your eyes. But your face is less expressive. More like a statue's. Impassive—that's the word. Like impasse, a dead end." Winding me up. A man who knew my weak points—but how? "Miranda is rounder, sweeter."

I wanted to ask him who the fuck he thought he was. But how could I argue with his image of a sister I hadn't seen in years? Impasse, a place from which there is no way out. "I'm not surprised she's rounder," I said, standing up to leave. "She's eight months pregnant with her first child. A son. You don't have any sons, do you, Mr. Mistry? Just one daughter, I believe—in America?"

"When you see Miranda," Caleb called out as I walked stiffly towards the studio door, "ask her if she thinks her son will take after Daddy. Do you think it's inherited, that gene, like a feeling for music?"

I spoke more sharply than I meant to: "What gene is that?"

"Like a feeling for music," he repeated, enjoying my reaction, "a feeling for murder. You should have a look at Mr. Sharma's films. And remember that he's named after a writer whose speciality was the hoax." With that, he swivelled his chair around to face Stage One. *"LIGHTS!"* he shouted. The cold, revealing tungsten flared on another part of the set. *"SNOW!"* An invisible hand attached to some production assistant on a ladder out of camera range released a muslin trough full of multicoloured confetti onto the stage.

"Who used the coloured paper?" Mistry's furious voice rang out of the darkness. "I told you: white white *WHITE!*"

All I could see of Caleb Mistry as I left was a faint glow of fluorescent lettering on the back of his chair: *DIRECTOR*. So everyone would know who was boss when the lights went out.

Y EXIT FROM THE FILM LOT WAS LESS DIGNIFIED THAN MY
arrival, as exits so often are. There was no sign of my car, nor of my
friendly guard, and beyond the narrow span of movie dawn filtering
out of the ice house, darkness had arrived suddenly. *Lights!* I could
almost hear Mistry's voice, with the muffled sound of a velvet safety
curtain hitting the stage. The stage manager had laid on big raindrops
as well, warm as tears, which managed to reach me under the shelter
of the doorway. I stood there for two minutes hoping my taxi would
reappear, and using the time to record the individual raindrops as they
built into a single liquid chord.

"Monsoon effects, Bombay, fourth of June," I muttered into the
mike. Then added, "Or maybe just rain." When did one begin and the
other end? Even Nehru had complained that no one could tell him.
Bombay's monsoon rains could come with pomp and circumstance
and overwhelm the city with their lavish gift, he said, or they could
sneak in like a thief in the night.

When it was clear that no white knight was going to appear with
an umbrella, I held my backpack over my head and started off across
the quarter-mile lot towards the light of the studio gate.

The drive had turned into a river of slurry, rapidly melting back
into its origins as a tidal mudflat. It was so dark I had to feel my way
through the ankle-deep mud, sliding one foot slowly forward and then
the other, thinking of how cobras used to love swimming across our
garden in the first monsoon burst.

Halfway between the ice house and the gate, the roar of rain eased.
I heard footsteps behind me and turned to see a man whose hair was
plastered to his head with bright blood, rivering down his face to join a

bloody dam on his cheek. A shirt like a butcher's apron. I cried out, and he put a hand to his head.

"Only it is stage blood," he said, wiping his hand on grimy jeans. In the other hand he held an umbrella. "Mr. Caleb has sent me." He opened the umbrella over my head, using the proximity to examine me carefully. "You are concerned about Sami at Chowpatty, isn't it? I am a friend—Robi. I am seeing you at the beach."

"And you are . . . the star of this work of art?" Under the stage blood and bruises he had the finely chiselled classical features of a hero.

"Oh no!" He looked shocked. "Hero is always big fellow. I am only part-time villain. Not hale and hearty enough for hero. Mostly I am working in props. Before Mr. Caleb gave me this job, I am Chowpatty beachboy. And Sami is many times coming for *bhelpuri* with me. We were friends."

"I'm very sorry about your friend." We were almost at the gate.

"Please, miss," he said softly, "take care. Don't walk alone on Chowpatty too late at night. And don't be talking to wrong people about Sami."

"Is this Mistry's idea of a joke?" I said. The scene stank of his kind of script, all the prose in shades of purple. "Tell him to stuff it. Tell him Gothic melodrama has never been one of my favourite art forms. It's too much like real life." I left the umbrella's protection and ran the last fifty yards into the road through the rain, with Robi just behind calling, "Miss! Miss!" Jumping into a passing three-wheeler, I said, "Hotel Ritzy, please."

The driver turned around. "Gateway of India," he said, "with Towers of Silence where Parsee people are leaving their dead for vultures to eat? No extra charge."

"In *this*?" I roared. "Are you mad?"

"Only I am doing my job, madam. No call for yelling."

The driver hurled us out of the quiet back streets into the heaving pulse of traffic. When we reached Hutatma Chowk, the Piccadilly Circus of Bombay, he shouted back to me, "Formerly Flora, formerly Frere Fountain," and skirted the main clot of vehicles, past a statue at whose feet sat a man surrounded by signs offering Ayurvedic cures "for rumatism, hair falling, piles, fistula, and sex weakness." Then we were swept in, our dangerously unstable vehicle like a contagious virus entering the city's bloodstream. Horns blared, a painted Afghan lorry missed us by inches, a man on a scooter with his family of three crouched in the space between his legs swerved into the path of a bus packed with people.

I didn't open my eyes again until we emerged into one of the city's less choked arteries, where the rain stopped as suddenly as it had started. Steam rose off the asphalt like dry ice on the film set I'd just come from. A bird cried out twice. Caleb Mistry would've loved it.

"Listen!" said the driver.

The bird cried again, a strange four-beat call: *"Paos ala! Paos ala!"*

"Is brain-fever bird," said the driver. *"Paos ala*—in my language, Marathi language, means 'Rains are coming! Rains are coming!'"

Hindus would call it dharma and leave it at that, a feeling of destiny, of belonging; a barely discernible pattern that could not be reduced to an equation and plotted on a graph, as mathematicians and meteorologists have attempted to do with the Indian monsoon. Not yet, at least.

I used to believe God was a mathematician. You get to the Pearly Gates and before they let you in a guy with a halo of white hair and a tooth-tickler asks you three questions on the theory of relativity. You think, Damn! I knew I should have listened harder to the number-crunchers, clocked up more owl time over the calculus. Then I figured, What did Einstein ever do for the Jews? and switched to meteorology. For a while I listened to the weather report religiously. Having faith in it the way some people have faith in the Pope's broadcasts, I began to assemble a library devoted to the great storm prophets.

Their story begins in 1686 with Halley, the man who notes the differential heating of land and sea as a driving force for the trade winds. Then, in 1838, Colonel William Reid publishes his *Treatise on the Law of Storms* and presses the East India Company to initiate an investigation into typhoons. There is a renaissance in storm analysis. In 1852 comes Captain Henry Piddington, who coins the word "cyclone" to describe an Indian typhoon and collects monsoon data with the enthusiasm of a pubescent stamp collector, filling his hornbook with thousands of brightly coloured miniatures: descriptions of famous cyclones, extracts from ships' logs, the minutiae of daily sailing. Later, he adds philosophy to his storm memorabilia: "It is upon the track of a storm (as upon that of a pirate) that the seaman's manoeuvres must depend."

Unfortunately for nineteenth-century seamen, Reid's and Piddington's diagrams of tropical storms have a crucial error. They show the wind's circular disturbances but fail to indicate their inward spiral. Like the coils of a snake, the winds tighten around innocent ships, sucking them into a common centre.

A grave error: it sends sailors to their graves.

Fortunes are lost, yet meteorologists prosper; they are Prospero's men. Psychiatrists charting the turbulence of troubled minds, these weather shrinks believe that identification of the problem will lead to its solution.

Each generation adds a new system for tropical weather prediction. Theory upon theory. Weather pattern upon weather pattern. Taking into account the swirl introduced to the winds by the earth's rotation, the sensitivity of the monsoon to solar radiation and early snow over the Himalayas, the effect of clouds and aerosols and the Nile's rising.

I have amassed a two-hundred-year catalogue of scientists' valiant attempts—and ultimate failures—to corral the phenomenon known as the Indian summer monsoon, to reduce its striking fluctuations to a predictable formula on which accurate long-term forecasts may be made with absolute conviction.

To pretend that there is order in the universe. An orderly God. Meteoreligion.

The recent books are pure mathematics, incomprehensible to me. I keep them for the tragedy implied in the latest weather wizard's manifesto. "Recent developments involving chaos theory include applications to meteorology," he says, and you can almost hear his tears, this man who has devoted his life to the idea of a fixed chart. "Weather patterns exist within the Earth's atmosphere, but it has been discovered that these change constantly and have never exactly repeated themselves." He has read his fortune in the clouds and it looks as bleak as a Yorkshire coal mine. If there is no pattern, no logic, then meteorologists and climatologists will be reduced to the level of village soothsayers. "This lack of regular behaviour indicates that the atmosphere is in a chaotic state." Mourning the inevitable conclusion: that weather is unpredictable.

A friend of my father's explained it to me years ago, although at the time I wasn't ready to listen. "A very small cause which escapes our notice determines a considerable effect that we cannot fail to see," he said, "and then people say that this effect is due to chance." He waved an imaginary wand. "They prefer to believe in magic. Art, weather, the oscillations of our hearts and brains, all these seem unpredictable and erratic to them. In fact, it is only that we have not yet discovered the right magic ball in which to peer."

I thought about my ridiculous scene with Caleb Mistry, trying to fix the point where he'd shifted the balance of the interview away from himself. My clumsy questions about Maya and his studio had annoyed him, that was obvious. But the shift had come earlier, I thought, perhaps with the mention of Prosper's *Tempest*. I was sure Mistry had known exactly how to divert my attention, which argued that his knowledge of me was greater than he had pretended.

"When do you expect the monsoon?" I asked the driver.

"Bombay or Delhi, madam?"

I laughed. "You can predict both?"

"Must be watching for monsoon bird, madam." He smiled, pleased that he had a happy customer once more. His tip secured. "*Megha papeeha*—songbird of the clouds, most accurate monsoon herald. He is arriving in Bombay three days before monsoon, flying on to Delhi at more leisurely pace, arriving in capital fifteen days after monsoon has broken over our Western Ghats."

1 2

THERE WAS A FAX FROM BUNNY THAPAR AT *THE TIMES OF INDIA* waiting for me in the hotel: names on one page; addresses, numbers on the next.

People who stood to gain from Maya's death:

- Prosper Sharma (inherited her family cinema chain)
- Nonie Mistry, Caleb Mistry's daughter, who starred in Maya's last film (but dropped out after Maya's death and subsequently married an American real-estate developer)
- Caleb Mistry—indirectly, if you consider a brief movie career for his daughter to be a gain
- Shoma Kumar, editor/writer for the film mag *Screenbites*, if Prosper had married her (but he didn't)

People closest to Prosper at time of Maya's death:

- Basil Chopra, fading (in fame, not weight) film star
- Salim (no one knows his last name), Prosper's lighting cameraman and inspiration, a genius
- Anthony Unmann, an English dealer in Asian arts, an old university chum of Prosper's

Who wanted Maya dead?

- Almost everyone (she was a bitchy prima donna on the skids, her nails dug in like a cat going down a tree)

Yet, in her day, I thought, Maya had lit up the screen. Not one of the current crop of pneumatic Bollywood beauties whose collagen implants turned their mouths into vaginas, she was slim, almost boyish, yet unquestionably a star. What had changed her? The years married to Prosper? And what did that say for my sister's chances?

Into my head came a folk song recorded by Maya in one of her last films:

> *Who is the winner, who is the loser,*
> *and what is the price?*
> *Father is the loser, father-in-law the winner,*
> *and I, the bride, am the price.*

It seemed an appropriate epitaph. She was mourned by no one, least of all her husband, who had remarried within a year of her death.

Marriage is one of the *samskaras*, my mother had told me, the Hindus' sacraments, their signs of spiritual grace. "The only samskara open to women," she said, "and other low-caste people. That is how your father treated us, Roz, like low-caste citizens. Because he couldn't leave his wife for fear of losing her little nest egg, he wouldn't grace us with legitimacy." Marriage: when Mum finished, every version of it sounded like a visit to the dentist: strapped into the chair without an anaesthetic. Hold still and it might not hurt.

I started typing into my laptop:

Bombay Ice: Premeditated murder (all 4 iced elsewhere?)

Motive: Note genital mutilation—possible connection prostitution ring/pimp/customer/brothel. Religious? (Look into hijra traditional role Hindu society.) Political? (Sami's location by statue of Tilak, implications of sign cover-up police and coroner's.) Note: traces of sulphides (type?) on Sami's clothing, also blue wax.

Questions: How did bodies get to Chowpatty without anyone seeing killers? Miranda said, "People tell me my husband killed his first wife"—who is "people"? Did she ever confront Prosper, as she told me in her letter she intended to? Caleb Mistry also hinted Prosper was murderer (mischief-making? resentful gossip?).

Link to Maya Sharma death: Who was hijra at scene?

That was as far as I'd got when Ram called to say he was in the bar downstairs.

"IT'S EIGHT O'CLOCK—WHY AREN'T YOU HOME FEEDING YOUR INSATIABLE appetites?" I said to Ram, peering at him through cigarette smoke so thick that the Ritzy's management should have invested in gas masks instead of peanuts.

"I found some info on your brother-in-law that made me think the connection between him and the hijras may not be so farfetched." He pushed a stack of pages towards me. "Thought you might like a printout."

"You're happy drinking beer for the next week or two while I read?"

"Save the bio film stuff. Skip through to the last two pages."

I didn't feel any wiser at the end. "This is a geography lesson?"

"You didn't read it carefully. Look again at why Prosper didn't use Salsette."

On the old maps of this lost archipelago, Salsette was the last stepping-stone to and from the mainland. Its identity had vanished under landfill in the last twenty years, and creeping vines had strangled the gravestones and churches in the original Portuguese walled city by the sea, yet Salsette still embodied the idea of departure and arrival. As the site of Bombay's international airport and many of its film studios, it was now a stepping-stone to the less firm ground of fame and fortune. At Bombay's Salsette studios, VIPs were always turning up on the set expecting to meet the most famous stars, just as both rising and falling stars expected to meet the VIPs. The sliding scale of power was delicately balanced, and confirmation of success was valid only when reflected in the mirror of another pair of starry eyes. To add to the sensation of perpetual motion, actors in Bombay often worked on thirty projects at once, zapping from one studio to the next like Super Mario in a manic computer game. Prosper had side-stepped these potential hazards by building a studio two hours away from the allure of Salsette. And he didn't install telephones, a precaution which had since become outdated because of the rise in mobiles.

"I know most of this, Ram. What's the connection?"

"Sometimes the whole cast sleeps at Island Studios. Prosper and your sister may be there now." He paused. "You get there on the railway line to Poona."

"So? It says in this article you've found that Prosper chose the location because—let me find the quote. Here: 'Poona is the former capital of the Marathi people, who in the seventeenth and eighteenth centuries shared a sense of nationalism almost unique in India, and whose warriors beat both British and Mogul armies.' Unquote. And he's making an epic Indian version of *The Tempest* set in that period."

"The only things of interest near Prosper's studio are some Buddhist shrines." Ram tapped the table. "Are you hearing me, Roz? The Khajra and Barla shrines."

If I hadn't been so jet-lagged it would have hit me earlier. "Near the town of Sonavla," I said, "where a hijra called Sami lived."

"Now listen to this. It's cheaper these days to use real locations rather than rent studio space, and Prosper has been reduced to doing commercial stuff to finance his *Tempest*. So he only uses Island—the Poona studio—when he has funds. He may shoot for weeks and then not get back to shooting for a year, like Orson Welles with *Don Quixote*. Often there's no one but a caretaker there."

"No witnesses," I said. "We have to check if the dates when this Island studio was empty match up with the hijra deaths in any way."

Picking up Ram's Cobra beer, I placed it next to a dish of chilli-fried peanuts and spread out a line of blue cocktail napkins beside the empty Kingfishers left by the booth's previous occupants.

"These napkins are the sea," I said. "And these peanuts are the statue of Tilak. The Cobra is murdered—with cyanide, let's say—and brought to Chowpatty with a cryptic message in her hands."

"A warning: 'The great freedom leader Sami looks back nostalgically to the days of Marathi Hindu glory.' That's what Prosper's doing with this *Tempest*, Roz. Looking back to the time of Shivaji, the Marathi leader who harassed the Moguls."

I pointed to the remaining bottles. "And these three Kingfishers are brought to Chowpatty as well, having been drowned first in fresh water."

"A river, a lake—"

"Or a bathtub. Let's look at where and when the three bodies are *found*."

"Chowpatty Beach, all of them around midnight, except Sami—the Cobra—she was found much later."

"If these killings are a warning, I figure it's for someone on the beach at midnight—and what's it like on the beach around midnight?"

"Crowded, but not the family audience."

"Hookers of all persuasions, pimps, perverts . . ."

"Anybody who sleeps rough," Ram said. "Except when they have all-night performances of the *Ramayana*, when there'd be even more people."

"So how did the bodies get there? You can't dump a dead body without being seen, certainly not three of them. And if you throw them in the sea, how do you guarantee the bodies wash up there? Come on, Ram, you know this city better than I do—who else is around Chowpatty Beach at midnight?"

"No one, apart from hippie tourists."

"Poor Bill."

"And fishermen, I guess—believe it or not, there's still an old fishing village on the beach, right in the shadow of modern Bombay."

"A fishing boat. Or something got up to look like one. That's how they got the last three bodies here." I finished off the last of my beer.

"It's only your opinion, Roz, and you know what they say about opinions. Like assholes, everyone's got one." Ram picked up the Cobra. "What about Sami?"

"Sami we investigate on her home ground." I dropped a peanut into the bottle top. "The village of Sonavla, near my brother-in-law's own little island."

"Why not take a break? Life's a marathon, man. No sense in wearing yourself out in the first two-hundred-metre sprint."

I shook my head in amazement. "Do you get your philosophy from fortune cookies? Or have you been reading *Reader's Digest* again?"

He laughed. "Okay, but I'm serious. You've been here thirty-six hours and spent most of the time looking at corpses."

"I'm having lunch with Shoma Kumar at the Taj Mahal Hotel tomorrow. I won't be heading for Prosper's studio until the next day. Is that enough of a break? Or would you suggest I try some more beachcombing?"

RAM HAD TITLED THE NOTES HE'D MADE "WHO IS PROSPER SHARMA?" AMONG the many clippings was a copy of an interview Prosper had done in Shoma Kumar's magazine, *Screenbites*, written in the simple question-and-answer format her readers favoured. Shoma had watched several scenes of his *Tempest* being filmed, then accused Prosper of misinterpreting Shakespeare's original.

Shoma: What about all the corny tricks you've used—the snake charmers and nail-walkers and hijra dancers? Haven't you lost Shakespeare's original intention in your efforts to transpose the story to India? One scene is no better than the daily show at Chowpatty Beach.

Prosper: What you see as a distortion of the text is in keeping with Shakespeare's time, when there was not such a distinction between magic and religion. Much closer to an Indian villager's view—and to current trends in the West, where, having lost religion, they are moving towards astrology, UFOs, and the like. Elizabeth I and her court were great fans of John Dee, an alchemist with as many devotees and sceptics as our infamous guru Sai Baba. There has been some suggestion that Dee was the model for Prospero. So I have included a scene for my Prospero where he mints new mohars. A literal interpretation of alchemy, don't you think?

Shoma: What I think isn't important when Bombay's own Prospero weaves his magic, Sharma! Until the next spell is cast, that's all from Shoma, your roving eye on Bollywood's elite.

Clipped to this interview was a photocopy of John Dee's biographical notes:

DEE, John (1527–1608): English alchemist, geographer, and mathematician, he earned a reputation for sorcery as astrologer to Queen Mary. Imprisoned on charges of arranging her death by magic, later acquitted. A scholar of international repute employed by Queen Elizabeth I as Astrologer Royal and, sources claim, as spy. A member of the Royal Society of London, he observed the weather for seven years, acquiring such skill in prediction that he was known as a witch. For most of his life concerned with the search for a Northwest Passage to the Far East, he later became involved with Edward Kelley, a con man whose ears had been cropped for forging. They parted company not long after Kelley reported that angels had commanded that he and Dee share everything, including their wives. Dee's wife is reported to have burst into a fury of anger at the suggestion. Dee died in poverty, discredited.

By THE TIME I GOT TO MY ROOM, THE FAT MEN OF EXHAUSTION were trampolining off each eyelid. But I knew sleep wouldn't come until I talked to my sister, the prosecution's main witness. This time when I rang her, a man's voice answered.

"I am Tusker, butler and odd-job man here. Miss Miranda was on her way to bed, but she will surely wish to hear from you." He sounded pleased for us. I was all nerves.

"Rosalind! How wonderful!" my sister said a minute later. Three years since our last phone call, yet her voice was still familiar, a version of my own with a faint Indian lilt that gave some music to the huskiness. It had the ridiculous effect of making me feel as if I belonged. That's what families are for, I thought, to provide a mirror in which we can adjust the makeup of our own identities.

"I couldn't believe it when I heard your message," she was saying. "Why didn't you tell me you were coming?"

"I didn't get it together until—" I said. Until what? Until I got that last schizophrenic card from you, Miranda? By the way, how's the wife-killer? I was tongue-tied by what couldn't be said on the phone. So many things I wanted to ask. Do you remember the cinnamon-peeler, Miranda, or the word for cassia? Do you still have the feather I gave you that the Syrian Christian priest at Kottayam swore had come from the wing of the Archangel Gabriel? But instead of risking anything that mattered I chose neutral territory. "Any chance you're free tomorrow? For tea, maybe?" Very British.

"This is terrible, Roz. Not that you're here—I can't wait to see you!" I tried to measure the level of sincerity in her voice and was defeated by the monsoon hum on the line. "But Prosper and I are going back to his country studio tomorrow for a couple of days." She sounded overexcited, almost feverish. "Why don't you come with us?"

"Tomorrow I've got an appointment with a writer called Shoma Kumar. What about the day after?" This fitted my plans exactly. "I could take a look at those Buddhist shrines near you and—"

"That would be lovely." Miranda cut me off, as if she were already having second thoughts. "Roz, why are you seeing Shoma?"

"I read an article about her. Seems she dispenses sexual favours with the same open-handed generosity with which Mother Teresa dispenses charity. Not your typical Indian matron . . ." Blah blah blah. I could hear myself chattering like someone applying for a job after years out of work. See how clever I am, Miranda? See what you've been missing? This wasn't how I'd imagined it. In the film of our reunion there were no uneasy subtexts and misunderstood silences.

"But the message said you were doing a series about the monsoon or . . ." She trailed away, leaving an impression of underlying anxiety. "I hope this has nothing to do with those letters to you. I was . . . tired. It happens when you're pregnant." In the portentous, juddering consonants of that final word Miranda found her own safe ground. She started to tell me about the clothes she'd been buying for the baby, the cot, advice other mothers had given her. I listened as the Miranda I remembered vanished under the disguise of Happily Married Indian Mother-to-Be, a national costume missing from my cultural wardrobe. Her voice got brighter the more she talked, the musical note now as artificial as a canary's—the kind they take down mines to warn of poison gas.

"That reminds me," I said, figuring I'd blown the subtle approach anyway. Or was I trying to stop that relentless, excluding flow of maternity? "Remember the eunuch who kept following you? What was the eunuch's name, Miranda—did you ever get a name?"

I listened to an underwater hum on the line for a while.

"Miranda? You still there?"

"Sami." Exhaling the name like a slow puncture. "Now I must go. Prosper and I will be delighted to give you lunch the day after tomorrow." The bedroom door shut firmly.

This is how a weather pattern builds. First the cool wind lifting the hairs on your skin, then the drops of rain, then the storm.

1 4

T HE NEXT DAY I TOOK A TAXI TO THE TAJ MAHAL HOTEL.

"Our meeting is my dharma, your karma, madam," the driver said, and I saw he was my friend Thomas. "Each life is a judgement and next life is the verdict."

"Don't tell me," I said. "The *Ramayana*, am I right? Or do you want me to believe Shakespeare quoted Hindu philosophy?"

"No, madam." Thomas grinned. "Louis Malle."

"Shakespeare quoted Louis Malle? Are we talking reverse incarnation here?"

"You are joking, madam. Louis Malle is French New Wave director famous for such screen gems as *Pretty Baby*, *Atlantic City*, and *Zazie dans le Métro*, which is featuring Philippe Noiret as a female impersonator and—"

"I know who Louis Malle is, Thomas."

His grin widened. "You may be interested to know that in 1960s, when Mr. Louis Malle is making his famous documentary here on India, I am his driver."

He dipped into his bag and produced a dog-eared photograph. Louis Malle, sure enough, standing next to a much younger Thomas. How could I have doubted it? I read the note on the back: "With best wishes to Thomas, for his poetry, Louis."

Thomas's brown eyes in the mirror were hopeful. "A modest retainer is sufficient. And you may be calling me on my mobile telephone any time."

"You have a mobile, Thomas? I'm impressed."

"Why, madam? Mobile is only way to be avoiding monsoon interference."

We agreed that his hours would be arranged at the end of each day. "But don't push the karma line, Thomas. I'm not a believer."

"I will be correspondent to command," he said.

"You do that. And keep your eyes on the road. I'm not anxious to join the world of elves and fairies just yet."

Shoma Kumar had told me to meet her in the café of the Taj Mahal Hotel, in the Colaba district. Another drowned island, Colaba had been swallowed up to form a base where the first Europeans could build their cotton presses and their military cantonment. Bombay had put on weight since then. It had eaten well, fleshed out its frame. Only in a few places was the original skeleton still evident beneath the fat of reclaimed land: a rib cage of Victorian docks enclosing the city's new business heart; a backbone of the old fort rampart, now Rampart Row, curving up to Flora Fountain. As more and more land was stolen from the mud, the original Koli fishermen who gave Colaba its name had been squeezed out to a small thatched village at the extreme end of Colaba Causeway. Unwanted fingernails on Bombay's claw, eventually they would be snipped off into the sea.

THOMAS DROPPED ME OPPOSITE THE TAJ ENTRANCE, AT THE SEAWALL, ON which a hungry flock of half-naked boys were perched like bony birds. For a few rupees these scrawny waterfowl would dive into the sea looking for treasure, through the oily film left by the tour boats on their six-mile sea journey to Elephanta Island, where the monumental statues of Shiva appear as Ardhanari. "Uniting both sexes in one body, all opposites resolved." That's how the guidebook put it. But for twenty-five rupees you could hardly expect Marcel Proust.

Around the late-Edwardian triumphal arch known as the Gateway of India a few crude signs were painted in a script I didn't recognize. I asked one of the little boys what it meant.

"Mumbai!" he cried delightedly, and all his friends cheered.

A man next to me spoke up. "Pardon my interruption, madam. It is local Devanagari script for Mumbai Devi, benign mother goddess. Shiv Sena's work. They want city returned to its old name of Mumbai, not Buan Bahia, the 'good harbour' of Portuguese. They wish to remove all traces of foreign influences, even foreign languages. Most amusing when you think that Mumbai is a goddess with no mouth. Like Bombay, she has no common language."

"What are Shiv Sena?"

"The Army of Shiva—regional political movement here, most

important among poor people, taking its name from Shivaji, seventeenth-century warrior and leader of Maratha people, who ruled whole west of India in the vacuum between Moguls and British. Shiv Sena is wanting Maharashtra for Maharashtrians."

"Are you Maharashtrian?" I asked.

"Most certainly not, madam. I am of Kashmiri origin, a Muslim, only here three generations. Shiv Sena is pro-Hindu. I am to be got rid of."

What iss my nem? I thought. Four beats of the drum, an echo in my head. Passport: British. Allegiance: unresolved. Where would Shiv Sena place me? Not even a coconut like Prosper, my skin is as white as any other Scot's. Only in hot climates does it take on the faintest glow of gold, a sort of jaundiced yellow.

THE LEPER ON A SKATEBOARD IN THE TAJ'S DRIVEWAY WAVED HIS STUMP AS I walked past, but I ignored him and nodded at the Sikh doorman's salute, entering a lobby where there were no cracks in the weather-proof barriers, no nasty seepages of poverty. Diseases transmitted here only by credit card and mobile phone.

In the ground-floor café the birds were less bony than those on the seawall.

"The fattest women, the ones with the Pirellis of flesh exposed, are the rich Gujarati housewives," Shoma Kumar said to me, no trace of any Indian accent in her husky voice. She was already picking fastidiously at a chicken salad by the time I slipped into the café booth. I wouldn't have recognized her from the Bombay *Who's Who*, which had given her age as forty-eight. In fact, she could have passed for a Milanese aristocrat of ten years younger. She had that same pale olive cashmere skin, and the smooth bobbed hair favoured by regular Armani customers. Even her sari forswore the magentas and emeralds of India for a chic mud palette more often seen in Rome or Turin.

She was not fazed at all as I miked her up for our interview, carrying on unchecked in her description of our neighbours. "It's all the ghee and sugar—Gujaratis eat three kilos more sugar per year than India's national average. Their husbands are the ones in the short-sleeved safari suits tightly buttoned over paunches. Not for nothing are they called the *middle* men of Indian business. The woman in green is a dhokla millionairess." She pointed at a woman who bore a striking resemblance to W. C. Fields. "Made her money producing dhokla, a sort of Indian doughnut. Like her. And the pretty boy with the Elvis hair who can't see his hamburger for his Ray-Bans is one of our current screen idols."

Shoma's sari showed off enough of her fine-boned body to prove that she at least was not addicted to buttery snacks. "If you belong to the family of people worth knowing, darling, the Taj Majal Hotel has always been the place to stay," she said, "ever since it was built in 1903, just before the Gateway of India out there. Tourists and travel writers *adore* all that pastiche palace architecture. The Raj symbols of arrival. Nothing like a cheap metaphor to please the masses."

She was chain-smoking, stubbing one cigarette out long before it was finished and lighting the next. "Our more recent arrivistes, the oil sheiks from Dubai—or *Do*-Buy, as we call it here—prefer to forsake heritage and install their harems in the Taj tower block." She stopped, her expense-account eyes, pale green and calculating, assessing the effect her words were having on me. I gave her my impressed look. "But you told me you wanted to talk about less recent arrivistes, darling—Bombay film directors. Did you pick me for my artistic opinions or because you hoped I'd dish the dirt?"

"Would you?"

"Depends on the director."

"Caleb Mistry?"

"Ah, the devil with the Midas touch; the ex with the gold Amex: ex-beachboy, ex–ticket tout, ex-draughtsman turned director, ex-junkie, ex-husband: widowed once, divorced once, one daughter who can't stand him. Self-made man—with a little help from Prosper Sharma. Currently living out of a suitcase at his studio. Hung like a Coke can, so I've heard. What else?"

"What kind of help did he get from Sharma?"

"It's well before my time, darling, but the story goes that Prosper was making a movie about Bombay street life years ago, and he happened to film Caleb, who was a pretty little hustler sleeping in the *chawls*—that's the slums to you. Caleb later had some minor criminal trouble and Prosper got him off and gave him a job. Next thing you know, Caleb is helping Prosper make very intense films about freaky subjects—druggies, hookers—all with great camera angles, all commercial flops and critical successes. Caleb was still on drugs, but seeing a series of gurus to try to get off. Finally went to this one guy who told him to get rid of his other gurus—including Prosper, I guess—because when Caleb got off drugs, he started up his own studio."

"What was Caleb's relationship with Maya Sharma?"

"Couldn't stand her. She thought he wasn't good enough to wipe her bottom. Maybe she resented his friendship with Prosper. But dislike for Maya wasn't unique to Caleb. I hated the old bitch too."

"Enough to kill her?"

Shoma stubbed out her cigarette and stared into the ashes, considering my credentials. "Switch off the tape."

I did as I was told, or made it look that way. Removing her mike, I clipped it—head up and running—inside my bag.

"This has nothing to do with a programme about directors, has it?" she said.

"In a way. It has to do with my sister, Miranda, the second Mrs. Sharma."

She narrowed her eyes and looked me over, from my Elvis quiff, across my great-grandmother's tribal earrings, down to the scuffed sneakers on my feet. "So you're Miranda's sister. Last I heard she was selling Gujarati sun-dried tomatoes and Tibetan goat's cheese to fat Bombay housewives who wanted to make California pizza. You don't have quite the same naïve girlish charm, do you?"

"It takes up too much room."

"I can see the resemblance now," she said. "It was your grunge style that fooled me. Your sister has all her *shalwar kamiz* designed by Prosper's chum Neruda, the fag son of an ex-maharajah who spends his time writing bad copies of Auden on the cocktail napkins of a luxury hotel that used to be his granddaddy's country cottage. The family has to slum it on the top floor, but even so it's still the tenth largest private residence in the world."

I tried to absorb this new addition to the portrait of my sister.

"To give you the scale," Shoma went on, "its mod cons include a pool shaped like a 1935 Rolls and ruby glass chandeliers that had to be lowered from the roof by a team of nine elephants. Eight of them, stuffed, line the main entrance."

"What happened to the ninth?"

"The ninth elephant fell through the roof and killed an old family retainer. The elephant was killed too, though not disfigured. Unlike the retainer. But it was felt to be in bad taste to have either one of them stuffed."

"People say you had an affair with Prosper Sharma," I said.

That stopped her. "Where did you learn your interviewing technique—in a police cell?" She lit another cigarette, shrugging off my question in the process. "Caleb Mistry's daughter also had an affair with him. So? Prosper has always liked a variety of dishes. People

were surprised when he married Miranda instead of—" Shoma closed
her eyes and blew smoke in the air.

I used the opportunity to check the sound level on the tape machine. The red light on the machine was speaking nicely between –3
and 0, just as it should. "Instead of you?" I said innocently.

"No, darling." She laughed, a sound like coins rattling. "Instead
of Caleb's brat. After Prosper iced wifee number one, your sister appeared out of nowhere."

"You think Prosper killed Maya? He was a long way off when she
died."

"Had someone do it, then. A subtle shade of grey. Either way it's
not a problem. Our own Prospero is in with all the right people. If he
can't charm them into doing what he wants, he has the clout to give
them a push."

"The right people?"

"Goondas, gangsters, hit men. Darling, where are you from? Half
the films here are funded by gangsters, stylish guys who love having
their pictures on TV. Like all celebrities, they believe media fame
equals eternal life: reincarnation on the airwaves. We have gangsters
to stop politicians defecting, gangsters to speed up construction, gangsters to make movies. What's new? Look at Frank Sinatra and George
Raft. Movies were always married to the mob."

"But why would Prosper have his wife killed, assuming he did? If
he wanted to marry you, why not just divorce her?"

"Look, I just fucked the guy a couple of times. He never intended
to marry me. He's got expensive habits, like moviemaking. Talk to
some of his buddies if you want the inside story—Basil Chopra, or
someone from the old days. All I know is there were nasty rumours
about Maya."

"Did the rumours have anything to do with Sami?"

"Sami?" Shoma frowned and shook her head.

"The hijra found at Chowpatty two months ago. An extra at Caleb
Mistry's studio threatened me about it. Very melodramatic. Like a
scene in a movie."

"The melodrama doesn't make it any less a threat. Gangsters here
model themselves on film stars—blame the criminals' plots on Bollywood. Only here could you get such a multilayered mixture of crimes
and criminals: insider dealing on the stock market, cattle rustlers,
insurance frauds, witchcraft—"

"I'm worried about my sister." The statement came out almost against my will and had an immediate effect on Shoma's brittle plastic armour of charm.

"Let me give you some advice," she said, her voice softer than it had been since I arrived. "Miranda's going to give Prosper the son he's always wanted, and Indian men respect the mothers of sons. But you could get yourself in trouble if you start poking around. This isn't your country. We don't just make fun of Don Quixote and blackball him from the club; we kill him. It keeps our windmills intact. Now I hate to eat and run, but I must get back to work. We're doing a big feature on kissing and I've made the mistake of leaving a little virgin in charge."

We walked out of the Taj into air so humid you could wade in it— heavy, thick air that had been chewed, digested, and excreted by too many people. It felt as if someone had wrapped a wet dog around my head.

"God, I wish it would rain," Shoma said. I offered her a lift, a perfect opportunity to winkle more criminal insights out of her, I thought. But until we hit the commercial district she kept up a shield of commentary on Bombay restaurants, as if to ward off any more appeals to her better nature. She had just started on Delhi's lack of gastronomic prowess when the traffic ground to a halt.

"I thought the lunchtime traffic jam would be over by now," I said, feeling feathers of sweat tickle the skin between my shoulder blades.

"It is. This is the two o'clock traffic jam."

Beggars appeared from the alleyway opposite, threading their way nimbly through the traffic to tap on my window. Shoma was un-moved. "They know you're a tourist," she said. "If you feel guilty, donate something to charity."

Suddenly she wound her window down and gave a twenty-rupee note to one of the crowd. "I'm sorry," she said, "it's all I have today." The woman who took the money had a five o'clock shadow and lips painted the colour of hybrid dahlias.

I was surprised by Shoma's about-face. "What was special about that one?"

"She's a hijra. If you are rude to them, they curse you and threaten to show their deformed genitals. It's very bad luck." She gazed out the window and cast the next words over her shoulder reluc-tantly, unwanted baggage inherited from a distant relative. "They might turn your sons into hijra. And I'm pregnant."

"SUCH A REGRESSIVE ATTITUDE TO HIJRA IS NOT UNUSUAL," THOMAS SAID, ON the slow taxi ride back to my hotel. "People here who are not being Christian, as I am, are still being bound by mysticism and magic."

"You think Christians are not bound by mysticism and magic?"

He shrugged. "At least India is emerging from fog of snake charmers, maharajas, and rope tricks. No more hocus-pocus."

"What, no snake charmers? I'm disappointed."

"Very few, madam, according to recent survey, whose aim is to create a map of human surface of India. Snake charming is risky business, not for every Tom, Dick, or Harry. First catching snake, then removing poisonous fangs, then training of serpent, lastly feeding of same and suffering taunts of hoi polloi."

Thomas said he wanted me to appreciate the elasticity of Indian identity, a characteristic that Shoma's abrupt compass swing from Western cynic to Eastern mystic had already pointed up. Like the India rubber it resembled, identity here could be condensed from the latex of various tropical plants, as Shoma's was, or used to rub out the pencil marks of previous generations. I needed someone to shake the bones of superstition and fact together and put their random configurations into context. Thomas, for all his insider's viewpoint, could help only up to a point. And Ram's grasp of the political and religious ramifications of this case was almost as tenuous as my own. The guru I had in mind was a friend of my father's called Ashok Tagore.

1 5

HE WAS BORN INTO A FAMILY OF WANDERING HOLY MEN AND philosophers in the foothills of the Himalayas. An ancestor of his was a Tuscan mosaicist, expert at the inlay of delicate floral designs into marble, who came to India from Italy three hundred years ago as one of the twenty thousand labourers and craftsmen working on the Taj Mahal. Traces of those intricate Florentine arabesques survived in Ashok. He had a talent for mosaic.

I had kept in touch with his career through my father, when Dad was alive, and later, through mutual friends. The last time I'd heard, Ashok was living in Bombay making archaeological films, although for a scholar of the antique, his life seemed curiously bound up with the more colourful fragments decorating India's modern history—in Bangladesh when it went up in flames, in Kashmir for the 1990 Quit India movement. Dad had said of Ashok that unlike many people in India who suffered from the altitude sickness of corruption when they climbed, Ashok had a head for political heights. "He will have no problem in rising."

I was five when Ashok first came to spend a monsoon with us in Kerala; he was twenty, already with a D. Phil. from Oxford. He had what Dad described as "the mind of a boy from the roof of the world, a clear view." If I was looking for an interpreter of patterns on the ground, Ashok Tagore was a good place to start. I had tried his number the first day without success. At the hotel, I tried again. After five rings, the phone was picked up and a deep, calm voice answered.

I MET ASHOK AT THE GATE OF THE HOUSE HE HAD INHERITED FROM HIS UNCLE. The single-storey white bungalow had been the garden villa for a grand colonial mansion long since torn down to build Malabar Hill's first high-rises. Walking back through the tamarind trees and banana palms, we stepped over the remains of the old house, half-buried stone corpses in a cemetery for Bombay's architectural past: fluted columns, gods' faces freckled with mould, the broken bones of a dancing faun.

Ashok stopped to pick a mango, then sketched a salaam and passed the fruit to me. "Niculao Alfonso, aristocrat of mangoes. An Afghan ambassador to Akbar's court once arranged for a shipment to be sent to Isfahan to await his arrival."

His face was as I remembered: lean and brown as a leaf, with smile lines deeply etched by years of Himalayan sun, the bones so close to the surface that they whitened his skin when he was under strain, as tent poles do with canvas in a high wind. "Do you remember telling me about Akbar and his miraculous ice cream?" I said.

Ashok smiled. "And are you still, like salt, a converting substance?"

The day that Ashok tells me about salt and ice, I am seven. My parents' union is splitting apart at the seams, rotten as old sari fabric in the heat and humidity. It is about 36 degrees centigrade. Ashok and I are eating coconut water ice after a monsoon storm. "They are fighting about me," I tell him, looking out over our canal, a stripe of black between the steaming green plush of the paddies.

"That's not true," Ashok says.

But I know it is. "Tell me a story about Kerala," I say.

"I will tell you a story about ice." He licks the sticky coconut juice off his hand. "Water is a great leveller. You cannot carve it, only give it channels along which to flow. It seeks the low point. But ice is different. Ice forms peaks. It has form."

In the last quarter of the sixteenth century, he says, more than a hundred years before a certain Signor Procopio will make his fortune by introducing ice cream to the city of Paris, twenty-five years before a brash plan conceived by a few intrepid sailors and visionary London merchants will crystallize into the East India Company (whose massive imports of New England ice will lead to the appointment of the first American consul general in Bombay three hundred years later, "a sign of how influence can spread like water"), Akbar the great Mogul constructs the *Ibadat Khana* as a meeting place for the coolest brains of his empire—scholars and freethinkers and theologians of all persuasions—and teaches his new people the Oriental magic of saltpetre, a miraculous oxygen salt that can transform pandanus-leaf syrup into *sharbat*, the Persian water ice.

Offering me my heritage in the guise of a fairy story.

"Salt is above all a converting substance," Ashok says. "Stolen from the sea, yet prized for its ability to dry, it preserves as well as it corrodes. It is salt we use to seed pregnant monsoon clouds in July. Salt makes ice and also melts it."

Behind us, a ripe fruit hit the ground with the amphibious sound of a frog flopping into a tank, and the past slipped back into the present. A serpentine trail of notes carried across to us through the trees. I heard something slither away into the shadows. "What's that?"

"Come with me," said Ashok, "but stick to the path."

We pushed through huge leaves to a clearing where a man stood playing a flute. His eyes closed, he swayed as if in a trance. Next to him was a lidded basket. "An old rogue," said Ashok. "Every year he charges more, and if you don't pay . . ."

"What are you paying for?"

"You don't remember—from Kerala?" He was surprised. "The snake catcher. At the first rains, he comes to lure the cobras out, then sells them to the hospitals to be milked of their venom." Ash walked over and lifted the basket lid. Inside were three large, cross cobras. "If you don't pay him enough, he lets them go again nearer the house." The snake catcher was oblivious to Ashok's comments.

"My tape should be running," I said. "I'd forgotten your talent for turning life into history."

He frowned. "I've tried to bring history to life. But you may be right." He led me onto a deep verandah where green rattan chairs had been drawn up under a mahogany fan that whirred in sporadic waves, like the sea. The impression was of a cool, underwater cave. Surveying the number of Indian sweetmeats his cook had laid out, he suddenly looked anxious. "You wouldn't prefer . . . crumpets?"

"What? No diet Coke?" I plunged a spoon into some spongy little dumplings in cream. "*Rasmalai*, my favourite."

Ashok relaxed. "People change, Rosalind." He stopped. "You have changed. You used to work in theatre, with musicians. Your father told me you have become more interested in . . . observation, documentary."

"I got tired of the drama. You don't have to be tactful. Dad hated my work."

"Perhaps he worried you might lose your way?" As your mother did: the unspoken text. But he left it at that, no more than a question mark.

One murder at a time, I thought, deferring further questions from Ashok by launching into a description of the hijra deaths and their possible connection to my brother-in-law.

As the story progressed, Ashok's body became increasingly still. "It is a tale requiring certain leaps of imagination," he said at the end.

"I know. And the more I talk about it, Ash, the more it sounds like one of those Bollywood melodramas with the song-and-dance sequence after every big scene."

"An interesting analogy. Bombay cinema interpreted as Greek *melos* drama: plays with songs interspersed, strict attention paid to poetic justice."

"And how would you interpret my interview at the ice house with Mistry?"

He said nothing at first. Then: "The waters of my beloved Walden will blend with the sacred waters of the Ganges."

"What?"

"Thoreau: it is what he is said to have remarked on hearing that a hundred and eighty tons of ice from the frozen lakes of Massachusetts had been shipped to Calcutta and arrived with two-thirds of the cargo intact."

"Is this relevant?"

"The clear waters of Western philosophy cooling our naïve and overheated Eastern minds," he said, his voice very dry. "Did you know that the Indian coolies who hauled in the first ice complained that it 'burned' their backs?"

"At the moment I'm more interested in these hijra deaths."

"Perhaps the subjects are not mutually exclusive. I could lend you a book on the hijra. Did you know, for instance, that Arjun, a great hero of the *Mahabharata*, was required to live one year as a eunuch?"

I broke in before Ash could lapse into the kind of Timeless Wisdom that can overtake the most prosaic Indian when asked for a straight answer: "Most people seem to think it's unusual that this case has been taken out of the hands of the Chowpatty police. Both Ram Shantra's cousin and the forensic chemist at the coroner's office said that the inspector who turned up at Chowpatty was from the Criminal Investigation Department—Bombay's subversion of Scotland Yard, Ram calls it. He claims the CID here is mainly used for crimes with interstate ramifications. Is that right?"

"I see your sources of information are broadly spread." Ashok made it sound as if I'd been selling my story to the *News of the World*. "Of course, crime is not my field. But I wouldn't think it strange for a crime-branch inspector to take an interest. Local police are more concerned with keeping the peace. The CID crime branch has resource to a unique scientific team often brought in when there has been some suggestion of . . . partiality."

"Corruption in the local coppers, you mean," I said. "Ram told me about that. But why did you say CID *crime* branch? Is there another branch?"

He studied me closely. "Do not be so quick to use the word 'corruption,' Rosalind, or to trust completely the judgement of—Ram Shantra, you said his name was? But yes, there is also a CID Special Branch. During colonial days it was seen as the eyes and ears of the British administration."

"And now? What's so special about it?"

He poured us some more tea. "If I remember correctly, its officers do not wear uniforms and for the most part are unknown to the local police."

"So if they're involved, no one at a low level would know."

"Special Branch also cover public demonstrations where there is suspicion of political unrest." Ashok rinsed his hands in the bowl of lemon water next to his plate. When his eyes met mine again, they were cool and critical, as if I were a candidate in the process of failing an important exam. "Have you considered the admittedly remote possibility that the Bombay CID, while not actually of the Himalayan standard set by Scotland Yard, are nonetheless quite capable of doing their work without your assistance?"

The cold disapproval in his voice stunned me. "I considered the possibility, Ash. But the facts prove there's been a cover-up at a high level. And it looks as if there's a connection between my brother-in-law and these hijra deaths."

"Does it?" He raised his eyebrows.

"A hijra witnesses Maya Sharma's death, a hijra named Sami trails my sister around town with warnings that Prosper murdered his first wife, a hijra named Sami turns up dead on Chowpatty Beach? I would say these were firm grounds for making a connection, yes."

"These facts, as you call them, may turn out to have a purely coincidental pattern. Coincidences are dangerously attractive, but their form tends towards the random rather than the conclusive. Some patterns are too large to observe." He folded his hands in his lap: the guru has spoken; the acolyte may withdraw.

Not enough is made of the fact that it was Indians who created mathematical zero—the Big 0, half of all computer language. The Sanskrit word for zero implies "a wide emptiness," perfect for a country largely made up of distant horizons. Conversations with Indian intellectuals can feel like that at times. Combined with Ashok's natural gift for mosaic, it was making my head pound. "You're wasted at the university, Ash. With your gift for preaching, you should be in politics or religion."

"Religion is what we would like to believe," he said. "Politics is the result of trying to put those beliefs into practice."

"Come on, Ash! I ask for a few facts and you come over all Indian on me, like some Mahatma dispensing pearls to the masses. You used to be more direct."

"I'm sorry to disappoint you, Rosalind. Perhaps I no longer have the knack of being British." His face had lost its handsome planes. The skin, deflated, hung off his bones loosely, making him appear older than his forty-eight years. He stood up and gestured for me to follow him to his library. "Allow me to make a small peace offering."

Treading a careful path between piles of magazines, I read their titles in passing: *The Indian Sceptic, Journal of the Indian Rationalists' Society*. There was very little room for anything other than the written word in Ashok's house. Recent English paperbacks overflowed from boxes onto the hardwood floor, and the only chair was imprisoned behind turrets of yellowing manuscripts tied with ribbons.

On his desk lay a narrow piece of wood the length of my forearm, heavily scrolled with gilt.

"A Florentine barometer," Ashok said. "Fairly unique. Look: the artist who made it included Sinclair's storm markings of 1664." He ran his finger down the words *tempest, stormy, much rain, rain, changeable, fair,* and *long fair*. "An ancestor brought it to India, about sixty years after Torricelli's first experiments in the 1640s. I gave it to your father the day you were born. When he was dying, he sent it back, with the instruction that it was for you, should you return to India. He said you had a certain interest in predicting the approach of storms."

"And if I hadn't come back?"

Ashok smiled. "But you did." He handed me a document stamped with the insignia of the Archaeological Survey of India. "You may need this. Without such permission it is illegal to export art objects more than a hundred years old." He glanced at his watch. "I feel I have been of little help, Rosalind. But I promise to find that book on the hijra and bring it to your hotel in the next few days."

"Not tomorrow. I'm going to see if I can talk to the hijra community near Prosper's studios."

Ashok frowned. "You will not leave it to the authorities? I hoped—"

"What can I say? Murder—it's not much, but it's a living."

He shook his head at my flippancy. "Then please try to avoid jumping to conclusions. Remember that clouds are not spheres."

"Another inscrutable gem of Timeless Hindu Wisdom?"

"Not at all." He smiled. "Mandelbrot. An American mathematician. Clouds are not spheres: it's what he said to explain the need for fractals, the complex fractions he introduced to calculate the dimensions of real objects like clouds. And of infinity, of course."

"Of course," I said.

"The principle is that natural objects contain within them the geometrical proportions of the smaller organisms of which they are constructed. You should know about them, with your interest in film. Special-effects departments in Hollywood use fractals to create extraordinarily realistic computer landscapes—although Hollywood came to the idea much later than our own Satyajit Ray. Ray said that the presence of the essential in a minute detail, which you must catch in order to express the larger thing, is a very Indian tradition. From Rajput miniatures to the caves at Ajanta, the *essence* is a combination of the cosmic and the microscopic."

THE ESSENCE: A LEG LAY STIFFLY ON THE WORKBENCH.

"Observe that where the bone is close to the surface at the knee and ankle, the soft tissue has split and ruptured," said the small, neat man next to me. He had the overly scrubbed and manicured hands I always associate with forensic pathologists, his cuticles almost raw where they had been pushed back by some instrument better suited for dissection. And his eyes were slightly too big for his face, as if he were peering at me through the glass in an aquarium, an impression reinforced by the dim blue strip lights that illuminated the large L-shaped room.

"Except for the lack of bruising around the wound," he went on, "it is almost as if it has been slashed with a knife. This is caused by the burning. As is the extreme flexion of foot and knee, an effect we find when high heat first contracts and then coagulates the muscles."

The man's hands were neater than his work space. Everywhere I looked there were bodies and limbs in different stages of dismemberment. Next to the leg in question was a cone of newspaper filled with something yellow and greasy. I felt my stomach contract. The man saw me staring.

"Sorry," he said, "the remains of my tea. *Poha*, typical Bombay snack: flat rice flavoured with lime juice, chillies, and peanuts, a late-afternoon pick-me-up for those of us who are working late. Most tasty. A street vendor brings it in at five-thirty, so my staff call this 'collective poisoning time.' Street food, you know . . ." He was apologetic, looking in vain for somewhere suitable to hide the rice, finally stuffing it into the pocket of his stained work apron.

Then he went back to the leg. "This is some of my best work," he said, proudly pulling back a flap of skin on the thigh to reveal the intact nerves and blood vessels underneath. "Sure sign that the burn was suffered while the victim was still living. Basically, veins and nerves are intact because the blood has cooked." He cast around for a comparison. "Like your famous fry-up of liver and bacon!"

The liver itself was not that challenging an organ, Satish Isaacs explained, being so well-defined. Easily sliced, as he put it. Unlike the vascular system, which was an elusive network of solid and liquid. "Bodies are models of infinite complexity, Miss Benegal, each one a separate country with its own history; every organ a state having its own microstructure. Some invisible, even, like the immune system, as complex as any spy network for decoding data about threatening invaders. And then there is this." He put his hand in the general direction of his heart, launching a soulful look at me across his butcher's table. "Brain is our government, heart is our legal system, precisely meting out life and death. A living record of our own and our parents' abuses of its country's laws."

I owed my interview with Satish Isaacs, head of the Central Props Unit, to Ram. He'd been trying to get in touch with Robi, the boy who'd approached me at Caleb Mistry's studio. "He wasn't there, Roz, and no one knows where he lives," Ram had said on the phone at my hotel, a note of suppressed excitement in his voice. "I got the number for Central Props, though, where Robi works. That was more encouraging."

"Why—did you reach him there?"

"No, it seems he's rarely called in. 'For what kind of jobs?' I ask the guy who answers the phone. 'Jobs which Robi is specialist at,' he says. 'What's his speciality?' I ask, thinking we might figure out his schedule. 'Very specialist work,' the guy says. At that point I give up and ask for the unit's address and Robi's next date of employment. They didn't know when he'd be in again."

"This is what you call encouraging?"

"Wait for it, Roz. Guess where the Central Props Unit is?" He had been excited, a small boy who'd caught a big fish. "In the basement of Prosper Sharma's city offices, although it seems Sharma shares the prop service with whoever can pay. I took a taxi there to be sure. Late-sixties building, big windows onto the street, Prosper's office clearly marked: seventh floor. Maya must have made her fatal nose dive right past those props workers six years ago."

BUT SATISH HAD BECOME HEAD OF THE PROPS UNIT ONLY THREE YEARS EAR-lier. He had no knowledge of anything to do with Maya's death, or Sami's, and neither did any of the artisans I questioned in the studios. They knew Robi, who was an excellent sculptor, they said, "in the Indian fashion." Sami's name drew a blank, although Satish admitted that she might have been in the unit under the previous director, Vikram Raven, who was in semi-retirement and came in now only to supervise the finer museum and gallery work.

Satish waved at the head of a woman whose face had melted into a red pulp. "We call this our Museum of Wounds and Diseases," he said. "Bombay's greatest directors have used my wounds." I could tell he liked his work. He paused, then went on shyly: "I don't suppose you took in *Streets of Fire*?"

I shook my head.

"Ah well, it is perhaps not your kind of thing," he said, a little wistfully, "although it had one of my best decapitations, and also a very fine bludgeoning—a close-up shot, so we had to show splinters of skull bone embedded in the brain, with strands of impacted skin as well. Absolutely true-to-life, I promise you."

"Sorry I missed it," I said, "but how do you know what it should look like?"

"We are obtaining frequent permission to do—shall I call it life drawing?" His eyes creased up, as if he wanted to laugh. "At central morgue."

"Why go into such detail for a movie prop?"

"One might be saying the same thing of a costumier who spends hours on a shoe that is to be hidden by a long skirt. A question of job satisfaction. No pain, no gain. But in fact, my finer pieces are mostly being used as teaching props for universities, and apprentices often come down here to draw."

"Medical students, you mean?"

"Also artists and students of forensic pathology and other such people who are making a living out of death." He laughed at his own joke.

"Are your wounds modelled in wax?"

"Oh no! We use synthetic latex. Wax is most out-of-date. Although I can show you a few old pieces." He led me to a strange figure in one corner of the room and blew dust off where it had settled in the crevices of the grotesque features. The creature was so lifelike it seemed familiar, ready to stick out a hand to beg.

"Not much call for lepers these days," said Satish. "So few left, thanks to modern medicine. Still, the work is very fine, don't you think? But from before my time. I believe this one was modelled from life, although the artist has had the bad taste to dress him in a maharaja's jacket. The artist has even named it—there, at the base: *Gulkand*. Meaning rose preserve. Possibly a play on the poor chap's name—Gulab is 'the rose,' you know. Here preserved in wax."

"Is this all you do?"

He smiled. "Are we limited to reproducing the weaknesses of men's flesh, you mean? No. I can show that also we provide testaments to the durability of his soul."

We walked through several large, well-lighted studios, their floors white with plaster dust. Long trestle tables crowded with plaster casts were arranged closely together against walls papered with charcoal drawings of Hindu gods and goddesses. It was like stepping back into the era when artists still learned their craft by copying from classical sculpture. Another time warp, I thought. More graffiti from the past.

Satish unlocked a heavy steel door and asked me to leave my backpack outside. "What you see here may be fakes, Miss Benegal, but still they are gilded fakes."

Even in the dark, the room glowed with a metallic light of its own: bronze Krishnas, plump silver Ganeshas, and golden Shivas danced along worktables lining each side of the room, some of the figures shining like liquid, others still leaden, waiting for a final polish to come to life.

"What processes do you use?" I asked.

"All sorts: some are gilded, some sand-cast, some moulded in plaster."

"How about gold paint?"

"Oh please, Miss Benegal—that is for other prop houses, without our heritage."

Satish explained that if a director had an actual piece in mind, a sculpture he'd seen at a museum or historical site, the Props Unit often took photos and worked from those, as well as from drawings made on site. They had their own photo studio and darkrooms and a huge reference library.

"Your brother-in-law has asked us to make Prospero's cell for his film of *The Tempest*. Such a stickler for historical accuracy. Look at what he has given us." He passed me sketches of Renaissance-style grottoes, with a handwritten note:

> For the 1611 production of *The Tempest*, Prospero's cell might have been a grotto in the style of the French garden designer Salomon De Caus, who in this period planned English gardens with fantastic caves and grottoes at Somerset House and Richmond Palace. This corresponds with Jahangir's reign, so it is possible that Mogul gardens were influenced as well. Or vice versa.

"It is to blend in with Elephanta caves, where Mr. Sharma is shooting final scenes," said Isaacs. "Of course, few directors pay for such precision. But over the years our fame is spreading far and wide. Even museums abroad are asking us to produce copies for temporary replacements during exhibitions and so forth."

My initial exhilaration was gradually draining away, sucked out by Satish's precise descriptions of latex moulding, plaster casts, and surface films of sulphur. There seemed to be no hidden secrets here, but on the way out I took one last look, noticing some boxes by the door. "Gold ingots?" I said, half-joking.

Satish smiled. "Hardly, Miss Benegal. These are today's delivery of wax."

"You said you didn't use wax." I tried not to make the statement sound important, but Satish's clever marine eyes bulged slightly more at my tone.

"Not beeswax, and not in the way you implied: voodoo figures or Madame Tussaud's. This is carver's wax for precision work."

He pulled one of the boxes open, revealing hundreds of little disks, each about the size of a large coin. They were bright blue and shiny, more like plastic than wax. I picked one up and ran my nail across it. The disk was so hard I left only a fine white scratch in the surface.

"For jewellery, medallions, coins, small statues," Satish said. "We use a process called *cire perdue*, or lost wax technique. It's—"

"I know what it is," I said. "My great-grandmother was a Chitrali goldsmith."

Gran always claimed that her mother had inherited the jeweller's skill from long-lost followers of Alexander, and it is true that lost wax has more than a passing connection to my family, if not in the way Gran meant. Cire perdue is a technique of hollow casting dating from classical antiquity that was used by the Greeks to reduce the weight of their monumental statues. The first step is to carve a model in wax, or to take an artist's work and make a replica of it in clay, enveloping that copy in wax. In either method, the wax model is then surrounded with a heatproof mould, the wax melted out—"lost"—and molten metal poured in to replace it. When the mould and core are removed, a hollow metal sculpture remains, only its inner surface preserving scars of the artist's original modelling. Hidden, as the scars of abused children may be. In this way an artist transforms a solid lump of rough local clay into a hollow work of art, its gold or bronze walls as thin as the wax skin they replaced.

When an artist models his original copy in clay, a new mould may be made from it. But wax models are destroyed in the casting, and no replica is possible unless there is recourse to an earlier model. If this is another portrait of identity, then for me it may be too late to recover the original model.

Satish unlocked a steel door at the end of the room, returning with a figure in the palm of his hand: the gilded bronze statue of a goddess, no more than five centimetres high. Where the gilt had worn away, the bronze was sea-green with age.

"Greek?" I said.

"With her toga, one might think so, but look." He pointed to a lotus leaf on the base. "Sign of Indian origins. In fact, she is the mother goddess. A recent copy."

"I would never have guessed it was a copy. How did you get the bronze patina?"

"But, my dear young lady, that is what I have been telling you earlier! We Indians are masters of the instant antique. One monsoon, one summer of sandy winds, and—Bob's your uncle—a new piece acquires ancient Indian heritage. This bronze patina so greatly admired by collectors?" He winked. "This we can do in a day with solutions of oxides or sulphides such as liver of sulphur."

I wondered if Dilip the chemist had identified exactly what sulphide formula was present on Sami's skirt.

THOMAS GAVE ME A SMILE THAT WAS A PALE IMITATION OF HIS USUAL EAR-TO-ear special.

"Sorry, Thomas. You've waited far beyond the call of duty." I fumbled in my bag and handed over a fifty-rupee note.

He waved it away. "Daily fare is no problem, madam. First I am thinking this is only my poetic imagination," he said. "At end of the day I am not so sure."

"Of what, Thomas?"

"Of car which is following us all day, from start in morning at hotel."

"What car, Thomas?"

"Beige Hindustan."

"That's a big help." Thomas was driving a beige Hindustan. The cars on either side of us were beige Hindustans. The cars in front of us were yellow-and-black Hindustans. With few exceptions, *all* India's cars are Hindustan Ambassadors, based on the British Morris Oxford design of 1952, the momentous year in which someone had given crayons and the concept "car" to a few preschool children who came up with an engine of the most rudimentary form encased in a solid, square body, with the corners rounded, like a vehicle invented before the law of aerodynamics had been discovered.

"Driver is small, dark-brown man in black T-shirt," said Thomas.

"I'll keep that in mind, Thomas, in the unlikely event I come across any small, dark-brown men driving Hindustans in the next few days. Now could you take me to the Ritzy so I can pick up my bag? I'm going on a train ride."

act 2

AMPHIBIA

*amphibious: leading two lives; living or adapted to life on
land and in or on water; (of military operations) in
which troops are conveyed across the sea or other water
in landing barges, and land on enemy territory; of
double, doubtful, or ambiguous nature.*

1

VICTORIA TERMINUS, A VAULTED GOTHIC ALLIANCE BETWEEN the Industrial Revolution and some vague Indo-Saracenic past, was built when railways were part of New Bombay, which sets it firmly in what is now known as Old Bombay, an era that always ends about thirty years ago and extends back indefinitely.

Like all railway stations, VT represents the Indians' vision of their history as an endlessly repeating cycle of arrival and departure. Looking around at the platform full of squatting families with their entire lives rolled up into clothbound bundles, I guessed that many of them were waiting for trains that had been delayed by as much as eight hours. Yet everywhere I saw expressions of infinite patience, as if the function of this or any other train station were only to provide a temporary platform where these people could fulfil their own function, which was to wait without complaint or expectation. Unlike me, they genuinely believed that their train would come, if only to take them on one of those interminable rail journeys, the backbone of Indian daily life, whose end would mean arrival at yet another platform where the wait might be a little shorter, a little less uncomfortable.

AT 5:10 P.M. PRECISELY, THE *DECCAN QUEEN*, FILLED WITH ITS USUAL QUOTA of commuters, slipped out of Victoria Terminus headed for Poona, the old British capital during the monsoon, where many workers now chose to live to escape Bombay's daily escalating rents. They made the 192-kilometre journey twice daily, and at three and a half hours this was the fastest—therefore most desirable—train. I was lucky to get a seat, as the ticket superintendent reminded me, asking slyly if I was going to the Shree Rajneesh Ashram to seek Enlightenment with the Sex Gurus. I told him that in fact I was a follower of the Mystic Rose, a regime that involved laughing for three hours a day for seven days, then crying for three hours a day for seven days, and I was going to Poona to see the armour of fish scales in the Raja Kelkar Museum.

In fact, I planned to get off long before Poona, at a station not far from Sonavla, where the hijra Sami had lived, less than a hundred kilometres from Bombay. Thomas would have driven me—glad of the money—but trains were a part of my Indian history I was looking forward to reclaiming.

My friendly Ritzy porter had warned me to be prepared for "sharp rains." He gave me a black umbrella the size of a small tent, a relic of many years on this monsoon coast, if its rusted fabric was anything to go by. "Built to last," he said, "by oldest umbrella manufacturer in Bombay, who is gearing up for boom season. But arrival of monsoon is in dispute. Every day she sends to Trivandrum weather station for latest report. Lack of rains could mean ruination."

In Bombay it is easy to forget that Asia is essentially an agricultural world, only gradually releasing herself from the vagaries of the monsoon, despite all the strides forward India has made since Independence. Starvation was only a missed monsoon away, Indira Gandhi said. One missed periodic wind, as explorers used to call the monsoons. A female thing: natural but bloody messy.

WITHOUT THE HUGE BLACK UMBRELLA I WOULD HAVE BEEN AN OUTCAST ON the train, although like so many other badges of belonging it inhibited freedom of movement as much as it reassured.

Next to me sat a man with his wrist manacled to an attaché case on which he beat time and sang along to the music being piped through the compartment.

"*Choleee kay peachayayay . . . choleee kay peachayayay . . .* This is having the irritating tenacity of all pop music," the man said. Then he continued to mouth the chorus of a Hindi movie song that was vaguely familiar to me.

I tried not to look encouraging, but he insisted on telling me the history of his life anyway. I have that kind of face, a lens, a receptacle for other people's images. The man claimed to be developing a wristwatch that would warn the wearer when he was threatened by exposure to nuclear radiation.

"How useful," I said, in what was meant to be a quelling voice. It had no effect. The man went on to confirm my suspicions that the human race is blowing all its redundancy fuses. This century is going out in a global fireworks of watches that buzz the hour on the wrist of the unemployed, camcorders that recycle the daily life of the terminally dull, forests denuded to produce the newspaper record of ecological apocalypse.

When I could get a word in between the microchips, I asked the man about the song he was singing. "The vendors of pirate tapes in Bombay play it constantly."

He was delighted by my interest. "All our movies are dubbed," he said, "often with older singers whose voices add allure to young, no-talent actresses. This is Rajasthani folk tune sung by our most famous movie playback singer. *Choli* is brassiere-like contraption worn by tribal women. *Choli ke peeche.* Means"—he smiled apologetically— "means: 'What is beneath my blouse?' Some people say it is a heart, some say a bosom. This song has scandalized Indians even up to parliament in Delhi, where there have been questions about the moral decay implied by its popularity. We are a country, after all, where the first cinematic kiss was introduced only a few years ago."

To prevent any further sexual revelations, I raised my newspaper, searching for a mention of the dead hijra. The main news was all about a member of the Congress Party who had shot his wife, then stuffed her into a restaurant's tandoor oven. Her smouldering remains had been raked out by the chef when he was baking his first naan in the morning. Police had tracked the politician to Varanasi, where he was reported to have been found having his head shaved prior to taking an annual bath in the holy waters of the Ganges. The headlines read: GETAWAY DIP FOILED BY COPS.

On the same page I read of a man questioned by police regarding counterfeit antique coins. His name was given as Roberto Acres and he had been released for lack of evidence. Other than that, there were two more stories about profit and loss: current fashions on Paris supermodels (rich women got up as Holocaust victims, Latino whores, Eurodykes), and a fast observed by retired Indian circus artistes whose pensions had not been sanctioned by the government in six years.

Nothing about the hijra on Chowpatty Beach. It was as if she had been washed away by the next day's tide.

The train picked up speed outside Bombay. We passed whole cities of scrap-iron shacks that clung to the landscape like rusty lichen, the last of the film posters, a scattering of tea stalls. Then, the country: a goatherd as black as licorice standing motionless under a thorn tree, with only his goats and a small stone goddess splashed with carmine for company, an elemental scene like the geography of my childhood, reminding me of the clay rain god that had been wedged into the elbow of a tree branch in Dad's garden.

Into my head walk the rainmakers from our village in Malabar. One is a scientist, with a master's degree in climatology from Madras University, who fertilizes plump clouds with sprays of electronic messages in a code that only he understands. One is a master of the monsoon raga, a song to invoke Indra, god of rain and thunder, and to milk liquid from the cumulous udders of uncertain skies. His songs the whole village knows. Both men are magicians, living at opposite ends of our village in old carved teak houses whose roofs must be rethatched every year after the monsoon. Continuity, that is what the village is about.

I remember the feeling on my skin of the warm, sleek rain dispensed like medicine by those cloud doctors. It arrived in a wide deluge, too heavy to distinguish individual drops, bringing a sense of unity with the earth.

The Malabar Coast breeds men who understand water. It was once as famous for sea pirates as the interior is for train robbers. India's current crop of upwardly mobile gangsters peddle drugs instead, all the usual ones: alcohol, videos, package tours, holiday homes, heroin. Bombay has always prided itself on keeping up with the West. Step right up, madam. Get your smack here, only fifty rupees a gram, just over a quid, a buck fifty, the cost of a beer.

Halfway to Poona, the train slid to an unmarked halt and the air conditioning switched off. The dust-curtained window revealed no clues to the cause of our sudden stop, only a vast pink bubble slipping below the horizon, draining the anonymous plain of light. I got up and walked to the back of the train to join a very suntanned girl in a Disneyland shirt who was taking pictures of the sunset.

"Have you ever seen anything like it?" she said, her accent American.

"Just like it, in fact. I was born here."

At that moment, five men clad in dhotis took the opportunity to leap off the train and squat companionably together to have a shit beside the tracks. The girl screwed her face up with an expression of disgust, then looked at me and blushed. "Sorry—it's my first visit. You're more used to it than I am."

"Sure," I said, smiling at the turd-brown Maginot Line that will forever divide East and West. "Shitting in the open is the thing I miss most about India."

The girl turned away and walked back to her compartment.

Forget the starving millions. Sometimes I think it is India's lack of toilet training more than anything else that upsets Western visitors, who live in the smug belief that any turd washed up on their own beaches has been purified with a chemical that guarantees immunity. You can't take it personally, as you can Indian turds. It is no longer your turd or my turd. It has lost its identity. In the West we don't like to confront our own waste. We are too used to flushing it away and letting others look after the dirty work.

As the train shuddered to life again I held my microphone out the window and taped the dry grinding of the brakes' release. In the near distance, a woman by a well—her narrow, spare frame elongated into a totem by the brass waterpots on her head—watched us pull away as if she had never seen a train before, as if it had not passed by her well every day for decades, as if it had chugged out of some unknown future.

2

THE NEXT MORNING, I SHARED A TAXI WITH SOME STUDENTS
from my guesthouse. They dropped me at Sonavla, where the hijras
who had claimed Sami's body lived above the public baths, about
three kilometres from the Khajra and Barla shrines and ten kilometres
from Prosper's studio. The houses were single-storey, brightly painted
in glossy cerulean or magenta acrylic when the owners could afford it,
and limewashed in subtle earth pigments when they could not. At the
junction of the four main lanes, four rocket-nosed Hindu temples in
white marble anchored each corner of the town square like Art Deco
salt and pepper shakers on a tablecloth. More temples rose above the
rooftops, and old remnants of what appeared to be temple carvings
stippled the walls of newer residential houses. Where an American
town would have had a strip of joints dedicated to the worship of
McFood, this one sprouted wayside shrines to Ganesh and Shiva, for
grazers of the quick spiritual uplift, the fast food of religion.

The women tending the bathhouse were as slim and lightly muscled as marathon runners. They waved me through an inner courtyard
and upstairs into one of the shadowed, immaculate rooms of my village childhood. Windows no bigger than hand towels were set into
thick walls that had been washed in ice blue to enhance the feeling of
coolness, then painted with an exuberant frieze of white curling flowers and leaves. A rope-strung charpoy bed stood in one corner, piled
with folded quilts; above it a small shrine to the Mother Goddess.

But there were more incongruous things here: plastic vases sprout-
ing lavish bouquets of silk flowers, a television set, still in its box, an
acrylic wallhanging of Shiva embroidered in the electric blues and
pinks of cheap foreign liqueurs.

Four women welcomed me with a soft chorus of "*Namaste.*" One had her sari pulled well forward to cover her face, but what I could see revealed features so finely etched it was impossible to believe she had once been a man. By contrast, the hijra's guru and leader, Bina, was taller than me by several inches, with a Mount Rushmore jawline and the nose and eyebrows of a boxer who has taken one too many punches. I had been told downstairs that she spoke good English.

"Does that surprise you?" she asked. "Most of us speak several languages, because we travel all over the country. And we are not all low caste. I myself am from a middle-class merchant family and have studied English up to college level." She poured some tea. "You know you cannot see Sami's body or even discuss the burial? That is a secret part of our rituals."

"I just want to ask some questions about why you think Sami was in Bombay."

"She preferred Bombay since five or six years, coming here to rest and then—no warning: here today, gone tomorrow, mixing with wrong kinds of people."

"What was wrong with them, Bina? Who were they?"

"Lowlifes from shady outskirts of movieland, hoodlums, *zenana*—boys who dress like hijra but only for making money from sex. I am a decent woman, trying to bring my daughters up properly. Many times I have had to fine Sami: fifty-one rupees here for riding a bicycle, fifty rupees there for using a razor instead of pulling out beard with tweezers so her skin stays smooth."

I winced, remembering the pain I had suffered the single time I had my legs waxed. "Your daughters are not allowed to shave?"

"This is the right of a household's guru to decide," she said with the confidence of an elderly stateswoman. "Hijra may choose to live alone, but to be without a guru is like having no mother. How will you have a position in society? Everyone will say, 'See, she doesn't have a mother. How can she exist?' Mother is identity."

"Did Sami ever resent your punishments?" I said.

"Would you allow your children to criticize your behaviour?"

"I have no children." There are enough unwanted mothers in the world.

"But children represent hope! And you are of an age . . . quite pretty." She looked over my boyish clothing disapprovingly. "Where is your security? In old age, we can always find a place in the hijra family. Who will look after you when you are old?" Bina shook her head. "This is a thing I never understand about Western women. My dream is to have children. Still, guru here is Mother of all, and some hijra when they first come are young children. They do not even know who are their real parents. Slowly slowly they are learning to act modestly like ladies."

"And Sami? Is it because she disobeyed you that she wound up on Chowpatty Beach?"

For the first time Bina's air of command wilted and maternal feelings struggled over her pugilist's features. She told me that Sami was a good Christian girl who had attended convent school up to the ninth standard. "And always reading, reading. But before she found us, she was selling her body because her papa and mama did not want her. They said she brought disgrace on them because she dressed in girl's clothes. But Sami was very artistic." Bina gestured at the wall frieze. "She copied this from a book. She could copy anything." She studied my face a moment before coming to a decision. "This way, please, and I will show you what kind of a girl Sami was."

We walked through the house to a smaller room whose walls were frescoed with a pattern as densely detailed as eighteenth-century needlepoint.

"This is Sami's room," Bina said. "She did all this. What other things she had, we buried with her. Only this we kept." She picked up a book from a small table by the bed. "Because it was not ours to bury."

It was an expensive edition entitled *Fine Arts of India and Pakistan*, published by the National Heritage Trust of India, with a stamped warning inside:

PROPERTY OF CENTRAL PROPS UNIT, BOMBAY
NOT TO BE REMOVED FROM REFERENCE LIBRARY

Flipping through the pages of glossy photos, I saw that a draughtsman of considerable skill had filled the margins with exquisite copies of the book's photos. Not satisfied with this, the same hand had used a separate sheet of paper—from somewhere called the Hotel Rama—to sketch a smiling Shiva from several angles. These drawings were too full of a living sensuality to have been copied from any photograph, as if the artist had caught Shiva before the god turned to stone. "If Sami did these," I said, "she was more than just a copyist."

"She did them. This sketch I think she did at the shrines nearby. You may keep it, if you promise to return the book to its owner. I do not like stolen goods here."

"Bina, what do you think happened to change Sami?"

She shook her head. "I can only tell you *when*." She led me along the balcony. Around the courtyard on the ground floor, a mural of dancing girls had been painted in the virile brushstrokes of Rajasthani desert artists. The last two girls had no faces. Their clothes had been sketched in but not painted. They looked like ghosts.

"Sami came to us from Rajasthan," Bina said. "Yet she spoke Marathi with a Bombay accent. So perhaps her family was from that city, but Rajasthan is where she wound up after she left her family. I think she was always looking for home. I gave her permission to paint this, even though mural painting is man's work. She seemed happy until five years ago. That is when she started to go to Bombay."

Years ago, I interviewed an explorer who prided himself as much on probing the pubic jungle as on penetrating the Amazonian rain forest. He had a theory that heterosexual men are drawn to jungles and caves and men who are uncertain of their sexual inclination prefer deserts.

Is Bombay a desert or a jungle?

The other women had appeared at the doorway, fluttering towards us in their bright butterfly colours. "Do you think the pictures are important?" I said. "Could the pictures and the book have something to do with her death?"

"It is possible that those pictures are a clue to what she was going through, yes. And this year . . ." She stared down at the faceless paintings below. "No matter."

"What about the sign on her chest? Was she involved in any political movement that could have done this? I'm sorry to press you, but I am worried about my sister and I think there may be a connection. Tell me, did Sami ever mention Prosper Sharma?"

I immediately regretted my questions. Tears slid down Bina's face, etching ditches in her thick makeup. "I can tell you only two more things. And these only because I know what it is to worry about a sister. First is that most of us have been operated here."

"Operated?"

She made one swordlike movement of her flattened hand downwards across her genitals. "Only way to have true hijra identity and gain power. Like this we are true servants of the Mother. If you go to perform a dance, people are asking if you are *pukka* hijra. Then you can show them it is so. Otherwise some are mocking you as a fake, just an impotent man, empty vessel, like all men who go with their own sex and are the passive partners in sexual intercourse. Sami wanted more than anything to be operated. That is why she went to Bombay in the first place. Hijra midwives there are better. But the operation is costing a lot, and even when she has money, she is sending instead these things you saw inside."

"Where did she get the money?"

Bina gave me an old look, a look that had been around the block, down the alley, pushed up against the side of dusty cars. "There is a famous Punjabi folk song," she said. " 'Dancers cannot help taking dance steps. One who has to dance for others cannot live away from dancers.' "

3

IF THE DRAWINGS BINA HAD GIVEN ME WERE DONE AT THE Khajra and Barla shrines, then those shrines might be a good place to find clues to Sami. Like so many voyagers, Sami and I were trespassers, violators of boundaries. Through our compromising liaisons with aliens and barbarians (anyone not speaking the right language or sleeping with the right colour people, in other words) we are the means by which chaos is introduced to society's stable centre. In the Bollywood version—all singing, all dancing—it is the voyager who brings the monsoon.

They say here that the monsoon is preceded by a time of working up a thirst, and the thirst hit me about halfway up the path that wound from the endless flat farmland around Sonavla through steep scrubby hills to the shrines. By then I would gladly have traded Sami's heavy book for a single bottle of ice-cold beer.

Gradually, the roaring of broken exhaust pipes from the main road below was drowned by the hot rasp of crickets. An insect hypersensitive to changes in the weather, it creaks louder as the temperature rises. To distract my attention from the thought of beer, I tried to apply to the cricket's noisy metronome an old equation of my father's. "For the temperature in Fahrenheit," he said, "count the number of creaks in fourteen seconds and add forty." But the crickets fell silent at my footsteps, then took up their creaking again as soon as I passed.

I stopped to catch my breath. The plain was spread out like one of those 3-D maps of India we used to make as children in Scotland, little flags stuck on them with Plasticine, proof of my first country's lack of progress: mud village, waterwheel, fields ploughed with oxen. The land below me now, which would acquire a pubescent fuzz of green within three days of the monsoon breaking, was still dun-coloured. Using my black umbrella as a walking stick on the steeper parts of the path, I watched its cotton fabric and my black sneakers dissolve into the same colour as the dust.

The dust made no impression on the black rocks bursting through the skin of the hill like boils. Those stony outcroppings grew as I climbed, giving me the uncanny impression that someone was following me. But it was Thomas who had put the thought in my head, I was sure. My pursuers were only shadows fusing humanoid shapes out of the stones' negroid surfaces. For the last hundred yards I had the company of a platoon of dark mineral figures twice my height.

My guidebook didn't specify how many shrines there were. The first one I came to was as high and airy as a cathedral, a huge scallop of stone carved out of the rock at an angle that allowed the sun to fall on a tall Buddha from the second century. Set into deeper impressions at the base of this were still older Hindu statues, while around the hill away from the marked path the shrines got smaller and more primitive. The smallest, not much more than a giant's thumbprint in the cliff face, held one of the strange stone phalluses called *linga*: Shiva's dick, the one he chopped off and used to fertilize the world. Linga are supposed to have emerged naturally from the rocks here at about the time that Christ emerged from the sand of the Middle East. But like everything in India they were prematurely aged: they felt like the oldest things on earth.

Bina had told me to look for Sami's figures in the last shrine, on the side of the hill farthest from the road. And there he was, carved into the back wall, a Shiva about the size of a tall man, not really big enough to live up to his reputation as the deity who is supposed to destroy the universe when it becomes overrun by evil. Perhaps this was a different incarnation: when I leaned forward to look more closely at the god's face, the image—the god as half-man, half-woman—didn't seem to match Sami's sketches. Disappointed, I stood up and moved out of the sun to try to claim what cool I could in the figure's shadow. It was so quiet, almost too still to breathe, that I wanted to make some noise to fill up the huge, empty silence.

It was about then that I noticed the crickets had stopped, which made the heat even more oppressive. I thought I saw a shadow move behind one of the black rocks. I called out "Hello?" feeling slightly ridiculous, as if I had identified too closely with the heroine of an Edwardian novel. But the two figures who then stepped out of the shadows were not imaginary. Smaller than I, their faces black against the light, they moved towards me without speaking.

My first reaction was not fear but disbelief. This kind of thing doesn't happen on a sunny day. I stepped around them.

They moved to block me.

"Let me pass," I said firmly, and stepped the other way.

This time they were more deliberate, pushing me backwards against the rough wall of the shrine. People ask you afterwards why you didn't knee them in the balls, stamp on their insteps, rip their hearts out with your bare hands. Always the same answer. It happened so fast. I didn't expect . . .

But this happened very slowly. My mind went split-screen, one half wondering how to defuse the situation, still disbelieving, the other saying: *Yes! Hitchcock*, North by Northwest. *The scene in the cornfield. Bright sunshine and a blank, open countryside and Cary Grant being hunted down by a plane.*

I tried to slip away. The men ran their hands over me and pressed so closely I could smell rose hair oil and the fried fat from their moustaches. The smaller one stuck his face up to mine and shouted. Then the other one. The smaller one again. Back and forth, pushing against me and grunting animal sounds. I couldn't understand the words, but I figured it was the usual things.

I was still holding the umbrella. When I got fed up listening, I raised it and plunged it down as hard as I could—one-handed, but with all the force of my anger and my swimmer's shoulders—into the bare foot of the smaller man. The long metal tip must have pierced the flesh between his bones, because for an instant it stuck there like a flagpole in soft ground. I had to pull hard to release it. The man cried out and bent over his foot, and as he did, I kicked out at him and pushed past. The second man grabbed the backpack off my shoulder so quickly that I didn't realize what he'd done until he turned and ran. I followed, down a narrow goat track that twisted steeply around the hill towards the road a kilometre or so below.

He was quick and agile, but his legs were shorter than mine. I was gaining on him, pushing myself hard until the breath tore out of my lungs, when he suddenly ducked past a rock and the sound of running stopped. Giving the rock a wide berth, I circled round to see where he'd gone. Behind the rock was an entrance to one of the smaller shrines I'd looked at earlier. Not much bigger than a cupboard, but the rock blocked my view. I threw a handful of stones. A figure lunged out. I hit him in the head with the umbrella's wooden handle and made a grab for my bag. He swung out with his left fist and caught me at the side of my neck, then kicked me hard in the thigh. My leg trembled and collapsed.

The man ran off.

After a minute, I stood up and followed, limping, hearing a matching set of limping footsteps behind me. The hill was steeper now, the path zigzagging down the hill like a snake. I looked back, catching sight of the second man on a rise above, and as I did, my sneakers slipped on the dust, bringing me sliding down onto my coccyx so hard I thought I was going to be sick. Half falling, saved by the umbrella's point in the ground, I grabbed at thorn bushes with one hand to break my passage down the hill, slid ten metres, and dropped off a vertical bank onto a lower section of the path. One ankle gave out and I sat down in the dust. A crow of laughter from above brought me to my feet again. Sun and dust stopped me from getting a clear view.

Faint traffic noises rose on a hot thermal from the Poona road below, where trucks swept along, safe in a world of petrol fumes and acid rain. Next to the road was a soft-drink kiosk advertising Thums Up, India's favourite cola. On a bend in the path a hundred metres down the hill, a figure was leaning over, his hands in my backpack. Another hundred metres below was a party of tourists.

I ignored the path and threw myself down through the scrub again, digging the heels of my sneakers in to get a grip in the dust. When I hit the next section of path, upright this time, I started running and calling out, "Stop! Thief!" Again that very English fear of seeming ridiculous.

The man looked up at me, then back down the hill at the tourists, who were shouting and pointing at us. He started running, along a side path away from their route, and disappeared into a copse of trees.

When I reached the trees a minute later, the man had vanished. My backpack was sitting on the ground in the middle of the path with my wallet still inside. I limped halfheartedly a few metres along the path and checked up and down the hill. Nothing but crows and crickets. The hill had swallowed up both men.

My leg was throbbing where I'd been hit, and my neck was so sore I could barely swallow. I staggered over to a big rock and sat down. A few minutes later, the party of Indian tourists rounded a bend in the path and rushed forward. They insisted on escorting me all the way down to the main road. At the soft-drink kiosk they bought me a Thums Up and a banana and sat me in the shade of the stall on the vendor's upturned soft-drink crate. They apologized for not having a car or a mobile phone to call for an ambulance; they fretted about my ability to survive the rigours of Indian public transport, explaining the bus schedules to me in detail, although I had long since stopped listening.

Not until they'd gone did I realize what was missing: Sami's book. Only the sheet of sketches remained. The man had missed it in his rush to get away. But why would a common Indian thief be interested in a book of fine art?

I must have fallen asleep, because the next thing I knew, the kindly soft-drink vendor was shaking me, saying, "Taxi! Taxi!" He had managed to flag down a passing cab and the passenger was willing to drop me at my brother-in-law's studio.

4

IT WAS NOT MY LUCKY DAY. MIRANDA HAD RETURNED TO BOMBAY for an emergency check-up, Prosper with her, and shooting had stopped until his return. The only people around were extras too poor to afford the fare back to the city, and the lighting cameraman, Salim. When he saw the state I was in, he apologized for the studio's lack of facilities, then disinfected my cuts and found me some clothes of Miranda's to wear.

"Oh, Miss Rosalind," he said, "you should be in the bosom of your family. What can I do to make up for this misfortune? Lunch? A tour of our set?"

"I'd like both those things."

He was a small, quiet man in his late fifties, with the oversized ears and eyes of a garden gnome and the permanently anxious expression of someone accustomed to stopping the bucks instead of passing them. To quote one of Ram's magazine articles: "Even in Sharma's less illuminating entertainments, there is always Salim's camerawork to make the screen worth watching. His lens could find the poet lurking within our crudest screen villain." Better still, and more useful in terms of critical, if not commercial success, it could find the actor.

It would have taken more time than I had energy to tour all of Prosper's set, a life-size section of the Red Fort that included a formal Mogul garden with mulberry trees and pomegranates and a mock village. The village took up twice the space of a real village, Salim explained, because the huts had to satisfy the demands of India's audience, who expected to see their own lives reinvented, with better drains.

I asked Salim if Prosper was shooting a historical feature as well as

The Tempest, but he said the set was just for the usual Bollywood fare. "Gangs, smugglers, shoot-outs." Searching for other late-twentieth-century pastimes. "Dope fiends, rapes. Nothing special. Hero is unemployed village boy." Salim smiled. "Obviously, the clothes he wears cost more than most of our extras could afford. Not up to Mr. Prosper's artistic standards at all, but it is paying for a few more weeks' work on his *Tempest*, and set is doubling for Prospero's island."

"Your shooting schedule over the last six months must be pretty schizophrenic. Any chance of a look at it?"

"That can be arranged." He led me through the far end of the studio lot, where an army of gods stood, every size from domestic to monumental. Carved or cast by the props department, Salim said, then left outside to acquire the patina of age. "Always useful for lending authenticity."

"It must cost Prosper a fortune." I bent to admire the fretwork on a temple and Salim pulled me back. "I am afraid our reconstruction is so authentic we have even attracted a temple cobra. Very big fellow: at least four feet long. An extra who crawled under those steps to enjoy some illicit hooch was nearly bitten. Snake hit the bottle instead."

"I hope he liked the brand. Was it a king cobra?"

"No, this was *naja naja*—from the Sanskrit *naga*, you know, meaning snake—true Indian cobra, our man said, very dark colour. Although of course there have been pure white ones. But these are rare, like albino Negroes."

"How did the man get away?"

"As your great cobra expert, R. Mell, theorized, anyone with requisite calmness can approach cobra and with a light but firm pressure by the hand push upright forebody of the cobra until it loses balance and topples backwards." Salim smiled. "Our man was not so keen to test Mell's theory. But his father is a snake charmer, so he knew that vision is a cobra's most important sensory mode. Once it is oriented towards such things as a waving hand, it heeds no other stimulus."

"Hail, Sesha," I said, only half mocking, and saluted the temple steps. Sesha, the dark snake on whose thousand heads rests the entire universe. In Hindu mythology, the earth is like old Bombay before the reclamation. There are seven islands and seven seas, and below the earth are seven layers of worlds inhabited by demons and semi-divine beings, and below the seven worlds is Sesha.

Salim smiled. "So you are knowing our stories, then, Miss Rosalind?"

"I grew up on them. My mother used to say that the most sophisticated Indian lives in many centuries all at one time. India is like a wall, she claimed, with the surface chipped away to reveal the graffiti of previous generations."

"Perhaps that is why everything takes so long to change here," said Salim. "We are always reading too many messages at once."

"Like Prosper—he's been working on *The Tempest* for—what, twenty years?"

He looked hurt. "Maximum we are working on it is four weeks per year. In linear terms, Coppola took much longer for his masterpiece, *Apocalypse Now*. And Orson Welles much longer for his *Don Quixote* that was never finished. Still, it is true there have been problems with our production . . . first Mrs. Sharma's death, rising cost of shooting such an epic, script changes."

"Could I see the script?"

"I will get my copy. And shooting schedule, so you can see why it takes so long."

PROSPER'S SCRIPT HAD BEEN CROSSED OUT AND REWRITTEN MANY TIMES, AND the cast list—not surprisingly, considering the time span—had seen more changes than Bombay's telephone book. "Great working title," I said, *"The Sea and the Mirror."*

"A reference to Mr. W. H. Auden's verse commentary on *The Tempest.*"

"Viewers will have to catch up on their reading before taking in Prosper's film," I said dryly, scanning the script synopsis on the first page. "Could I have a copy of these opening notes? And the schedule?"

"Of course." He was delighted. "Mr. Sharma is so clever. See how he has made Prospero the usurping colonizer, as the Moguls were, who lands on the island—that is, India—and by force deprives native inhabitants of their Hindu inheritance, just as Prospero forces his language and morals on Caliban. Based on Caleb Mistry's original idea, of course, but much expanded."

"You worked with Caleb Mistry for a while, didn't you?"

"On only one film, *The Cyclone.*"

"Why only one? Was it so bad?"

"No, not bad." Salim hesitated. "You see, Miss Rosalind, a director must trust his cameraman completely, because cameraman frames the shot, does panning, tilting, tracking. Advised, of course, by the director, but still it is only when the director sees the rushes that he knows if his vision was interpreted correctly."

"I can see that, yes—it's a partnership in which each partner must trust the other, a sort of marriage. And with Prosper?"

"Mr. Prosper is always in charge totally, like Alfred Hitchcock. He likes to use a studio, where he can simulate daylight by using bounced lights, or a set like this one. He likes to control even the weather. Caleb used to build Mr. Prosper's miniature cardboard models of the sets, everything perfect down to the last detail. No room for error. But when Caleb started directing, he wanted to shoot always on location, working very fast with a hand-held Arriflex, even in the rain. Other cameramen also told him you couldn't shoot in the rain and he was too naïve to know that what they said had an element of truth."

"An element of truth?"

He shrugged. "He did it and it worked."

"So what was the problem?"

"Caleb took too many risks. No fixed boundaries, shooting script changing daily. He said Mr. Prosper's method was like the cameraman being a blind man led by a dog. But then Caleb would fly into a rage if we did not get it right. Now he is more controlled. Dadasahib, they are calling him. He has come round to Mr. Prosper's way." He checked the time. "Perhaps you would like some lunch?"

We retraced our steps to some picnic tables under a grass roof. Salim brought me a bowl of pumpkin curry and a battered tin plate of potato croquettes stuffed with pellets of fresh coriander chutney so full of green chillies it cleared every passage in my head. Salim grinned as my eyes watered.

"I think your tastebuds are out of practice with Indian food, yes?"

"I'm out of practice with India, Salim, not just the food."

"So now you must start practising if your sister is to find a husband for you."

I choked on my beer. "If she *what*?"

Salim's eyes twinkled. "Everybody must get married and have children."

"I've just been talking to the hijra community—what about them?"

"Even sometimes hijra are forming a bond almost like marriage, although they are not supposed to. Part of what you might call their brief."

"Do you know any hijra?"

The question seemed to make him uneasy. "All of India's many-faceted society is in *The Tempest*. Mr. Prosper has Caliban played by hijra, and in the end, when Prospero releases him, Caliban is turned into a real woman, reincarnation of Mumtaz, Shah Jahan's great love."

"Did Prosper have any particular hijra in mind for the role?"

"In Shakespeare's time all women's roles were played by men."

"What about a hijra called Sami?" I said.

He shifted about in his chair before answering. "You don't want to know this Sami, or the kind of people she knew."

"Prosper did know her, then?"

I didn't think he would tell me. But I waited. Then: "Sami was a prostitute working the area where we made a movie. She used to turn up and watch us every day. Then it seemed she got some fixation on Mr. Prosper."

"A prostitute. Did he give her money?"

"Mr. Prosper has a very kind heart. Anyway, this was so very long ago."

"When was it, Salim?"

"Oh, maybe five, six years. It can have nothing to do with Sami's death."

So he knew she was dead. Was that why he was so quick to deny the connection?

"Was that before or after the first Mrs. Sharma was bumped off?"

Salim stood up. "You must never never say this again. Mr. Prosper was—he *is* a great artist. Do you know how hard it is to be an artist in India at this time? In the 1970s our government was at least giving film artists development money. Now he is having to make four bad pictures for one good one. You are a journalist, someone who looks in from the outside. Mr. Prosper is an artist."

"We're both telling stories." Thinking: I never suggested Prosper was connected to Maya's death.

"I will get a car to take you back to Bombay. It will save you—the bus and train journey."

5

IN BOMBAY THAT EVENING, I TELEPHONED MY SISTER, AND Tusker informed me that Miss Miranda and Mr. Prosper were back from the hospital, and Miranda was fine, but sleeping. "She was most sorry not to be at the studio to welcome you. She said if you rang I was to invite you for a swim at Breach Candy baths tomorrow morning at eight-thirty."

"Give her my very best wishes when she wakes up. And ask her—" It had been a long time since I'd had family to worry about, and the need to tread carefully made me feel as though I were being forced into favourite shoes I had long since outgrown. "Ask her—only if she is feeling better—if she has those photos she took when she first came to Bombay, of Prosper's city studio."

The hotel receptionist had given me a fax from a friend of mine at Christie's in London, with background on the art dealer Anthony Unmann, the university friend of Prosper's. "The genuine article," she wrote. "Galleries in London, Germany, and the States, where he has regular exhibitions of Asian art, absolutely above reproach." She had sent a list of the exhibitions, as well as some stats of Unmann's catalogues over the last year.

I rang Bunny Thapar to find out the latest news about the hijra deaths and discovered that her editor had told her to drop the story. "What, until you have some more evidence?" I asked.

"Drop it, full stop. His exact words: 'Hijra are not a happening story.' He says the hijra subject always makes our readers uncomfortable."

"What if you told him that I was mugged while trying to find out more about the deaths?" Briefly I explained to Bunny what had happened at the caves. "It seems pretty likely, doesn't it, that someone followed me to the hijra baths to get that book of Sami's?"

"Could be." She didn't sound convinced. "I'll see what he says."

For dinner, I took a couple of Nurofen and a handful of chewable vitamin C. I checked Prosper's shooting schedule against the dates of the hijra deaths. No luck. Was I looking for connections where there were none to be made, as Ashok had suggested? My job was to record, not to convict. But I couldn't let go of Sami's death, perhaps because everyone else wanted her to disappear for good, and because she was an outsider, a trespasser, like me.

The anthropologist Margaret Laurence wrote that the best people in her field sought to send human voices through the thicket of our separateness. The thicket surrounding the hijra seemed impenetrable. Within Indian society they had a traditional role dancing in the temples and at marriages and the birth of sons because it was believed that their blessings could confer fertility. Yet they were impotent; powerless. Neither man nor woman.

How do the powerless gain power? Talent, blackmail, religion, sex.

Politically correct Americans like to say that sex is what you're born with and gender is your identity and social role, what you've made of it. The difference between fate and choice, between life and the movies. Movies rewrite life and give it a neat ending. Art is what we do to prove we have some control.

The last thing I did before falling asleep was to tape Sami's drawing of Shiva to my mirror, with one of the pages of clippings Salim had given me from Prosper's *Tempest* notes:

> Before entering the Alchemic Citadel, one condition required was knowledge of the *Great Work*—preparation of the great alchemic transmutations into gold.
>
> There is a masculine and a feminine principle in the Work. Nicolas Flamel wrote of it: "Thou hast conjoined and married natures, masculine and feminine, and they are fashioned in one sole body, which is the androgyne of the ancients." This phase of the operation is figured in all the treatises by the symbol of the Hermetic Androgyne.
>
> —Grillot de Givry, *Some Concrete Notions about Demons and Alchemy*, 1931

Below this, someone (I presumed Prosper) had added a handwritten note: "*Phoenician*, from the same root as Greek *Phoinix*: anything that arises from its own or its predecessors' ashes. Adopted as a sign by chemists through association of the phoenix with alchemy, the transmutation of base metals into gold. Eliot's Phlebas the Phoenician in *The Waste Land* refers to Phoebus/Apollo, the Greek sun-god. As opposed to Icarus, who was burned by the sun's fire and did not rise."

There was more along those lines, drawing in Hermes and Apollo and a lot of fringe gods I'd never heard of, but the only connection to Sami I could see was the date this page had been written—a week before her death.

I'd had enough literary references for one day. I switched off the light and closed my eyes. From the video stall outside my window a pirate tape whined its question: *Choleee kay peachayayay* . . . until I fell into restless sleep.

IN MY DREAM, I AM SWIMMING AGAINST A CURRENT THAT DRAGS ME DOWN AND under. Looking back through the dark water I see that it is not the current or the weed that holds me. It is a hand, with a wide bracelet of exposed bone and sinew around the wrist. Farther back, beyond the hand, there is something I do not want to see. Not Sami. A face I know, floating up through the weed to claim me.

6

Next morning, the air conditioning was so icy it made my bruised body ache arthritically. I turned the air-con dial from Hi to Lo, but it had no effect on the wind-chill factor. Flipping through the complimentary newspaper that hotels in India push under your door every morning, I spotted an item halfway down page 2: OUR STREETS OF SHAME: DIRECTOR'S SISTER-IN-LAW IN CAVE ATTACK: LINK TO OLD SUICIDE! Thank you, Bunny.

To combat the room's arctic conditions, I filled the bathtub and lay up to my nostrils in scalding water mixed with six packets of the hotel's *Supasoftee Sandalwood Bath Oil. It makes your skin feel like singing!* I waited for the surface of my body to break into a tune. With the exception of a few minor scrapes, most of the damage from yesterday was muscular. True, my left ear, neck, and cheekbone had turned the streaky pale mauve of a baby aubergine, but to counteract that, my bottom lip had the petulant swell of a sulky Brigitte Bardot, an effect some women pay thousands to achieve. Just how a girl wants to look when she's going to meet a heartthrob.

When I'd phoned Basil Chopra the night before to ask for an interview, he'd said, "Why me, dear girl, with so many younger chaps around? I'm an old ruin."

"I like ruins."

"Only tourists come to see ruins."

"And archaeologists." On reflection, that was not the most tactful compliment I could have paid him. "Actually, Mr. Chopra, I've had a crush on you since I was fifteen," I said quickly, "and saw you play the poet in my brother-in-law's film."

"Why didn't you say so first of all, dear girl? Fans are so rare these days. Do come by for a spot of brunch after the swim with your sister tomorrow. Though I fear you'll find me sadly disappointing."

As I left the hotel the receptionist gave me a fax from the independent TV company for which I often worked, telling me that my leads on the Bombay film corruption story sounded strong enough to follow through. I hadn't mentioned that the chief suspect for the moment was my own brother-in-law.

BREACH CANDY BATHS WAS ON BHULABHAI DESAI ROAD, A KILOMETRE NORTH of the Hanging Gardens. "These gardens are being built to cover reservoirs supplying water to whole of Bombay," Thomas informed me. "People are joking that vultures picking up sections of corpses from nearby Parsi burial ground are dropping them into reservoir. Now since 1881 we are having gardens with noted collection of hedges clipped into animal shapes."

"It's seven-thirty in the morning, Thomas. I'm not ready for your topiary tour."

All I could think about was meeting my sister, how to broach the possibility of her husband's guilt. The prospect filled me with an oppressive feeling that couldn't be put down to the weather, whose weight had been cleared in the early morning by a brief, heavy downpour. Above Breach Candy—one of the great "breaches" or creeks through which the tide used to rush, drowning the flatlands and transforming the city's high ground into seven islands—the clouds looked as if a wig dresser from the court of Louis XIV had been up early combing and teasing the vapour into a fanciful creation of ringlets, pouffes, and billowing pompadours.

Breach Candy had been reclaimed; filled in, some cynics claimed, with the city's nightsweepings. Its name belonged now to a peeling twenties building that served as a sort of clubhouse for the pool. The official at the gate informed me that foreign guests could not enter without a passport. Hearing that I'd left mine in the hotel, he shrugged and went back to reading his book, *Jeeves and the Yule-Tide Spirit*, by P. G. Wodehouse.

"Please," he said, when he saw me reading over his shoulder, "what is Nietzsche?" He pointed at a passage: " 'I once got engaged to his daughter, Honoria, a ghastly dynamic exhibit who read Nietzsche . . .' "

"German philosopher. Big with the Nazis. Believed in the Superman, who would rule with no need of traditional morality. Death of

God, that sort of thing. Died of syphilis, I believe. Moral of the story: Keep the God option open."

"Thank you, madam. It is so important to put these comments in context."

"You like Wodehouse?"

"Mr. Wodehouse is *most* popular in India, useful to uplift our English."

"That explains a lot," I said. "Now can I come in?"

"Oh no, madam. We must be keeping up standards."

Fortunately, my sister and her husband were only twenty-five minutes late, practically early by Bombay standards.

Miranda was easily recognizable, despite the years since our last meeting: her face, framed by shoulder-length black hair, was a milk-chocolate version of my own, as if the artist who had created the first sister had simply changed to a softer, darker clay for the second.

"Roz!" she said, moving towards me with the sailor's gait of a pregnant woman. She tried to put her arms around me, giggling as her belly kept us apart. "It's simply scrumptious to see you! And I'm glad to see that the horrid cave incident has not affected you too much."

I felt myself stiffening. Was it affectation or did grown women really use words like scrumptious and horrid? I stood back, judging her, trying to find the original model of my sister inside this elegant matron's skin. I would have liked to meet Miranda alone, to explore common ground without an audience, but behind my sister stood a tall man whose brush-cut hair was the lustrous silver of expensive cutlery: Prosper Sharma, immediately recognizable from scores of old film photos.

At fifty-four Prosper had the skin and build of a man ten years younger. He wore immaculate ice-blue linen *kurta* pyjamas that made me acutely aware of the egg-yolk stains on my shirt, and when he took his sunglasses off I could see that his beautiful, deep-set eyes were hazel, framed by seal-smooth eyebrows, so perfectly curved they looked plucked. Everything about Prosper looked plucked. From his voice to his handshake he was cool and cultivated, the resident of a different climate than the rest of us. He exchanged the kind of warm smiles and introductory chat with me that indicated how civilized he was, a charm I found hard to match, given that his boyish smile never quite reached his upper face. He seemed to be playing a role—brother-in-law eager to please—while his eyes gauged its effect precisely, adding a few more winning words when he saw I was not yet won over, as he might do with an actress who was giving him trouble on the set.

Perhaps I did him an injustice. This was someone I knew only by reputation, a man who had once made great movies—ten, maybe twenty years ago—but was still dressed in the suit of that outdated fame. A man who might have killed his first wife before he married my sister.

"Going swimming in emeralds," I said, touching the large studs in Miranda's ears. "What are they—your second-best?" I wanted to say something warmer, more intimate, but found the sisterly words impossible under Prosper's gaze.

Miranda blushed. "Prosper gave them to me last week. I haven't taken them off since. But I'm just watching today. I'm too big to swim."

"You must be a regular here, Prosper," I said as we passed through the pool entrance with no problem about my passport. "I'm surprised."

Ahead of us stretched a vast map of India, a continent in reverse, where the land was watery and the ocean concrete. Beyond the pool was the sea.

His fine eyebrows flew up. "Why?"

"I would've thought you'd prefer one of the more exclusive clubs."

Over his handsome features passed the faint suggestion of a frown, but not enough to cause any permanent damage. "When I am in town I like to swim before work, and this is convenient from my office."

"The office above the Central Props Unit?" I asked. He nodded.

Miranda leaned over to whisper in my ear. "Actually, we come here because it's cheap, and it amuses Prosper that this pool was built for the Europeans, so they could be sure of swimming with no contamination from brown skin. They used all the remaining money of the Bombay Steamer Fund for that purpose."

Prosper overheard her comments and shook his head slightly. Her smile froze.

"This pool was presented to the Municipal Commission in April 1876 by Major General Harry Barr of the Bombay Army," he said. "My great-grandfather served with the general, but they couldn't swim together. Of course, this is not the original Edwardian building. It was built in 1927, after the old premises fell into disrepair." He waved at a row of cubicles. "You can change in one of those. We'll meet you by Calcutta, near the seawall."

I put on my black Speedo, slathered myself in Factor 15, regretting once again that I had not inherited my father's dark skin, and walked down the east coast of India to where Miranda and Prosper

were already seated. My brother-in-law immediately rose and introduced me to two men who he said had provided great technical expertise for his historical features. Neither one looked as if he came from
the same class as Prosper, not even the same planet. The first man had
a belly that rivalled Miranda's: Jigs Sansi, from the Indian government's Department of Archaeology. The second, with a black moustache poised above wet red lips like a shiny beetle ready to feed on raw
meat, was Vikram Raven.

"Raven by name, graven by nature," he said. "Call me Vic."

"His grandfather was an English stamp designer, and Vikram too
is a very fine engraver, as well as being a director at the Central Props
Unit," Prosper said.

"Delighted to meet you, Mr. Raven," I said. "Ever since finding
out that I can't take real antiques out of India I've been dying to buy
one of your copies from the Central Props Unit. I had a great tour of it
from Satish the other day. Your artists' talent for giving fakes the feel
of legitimacy was very impressive."

"If you want the real thing, you have only to speak to Jigs," said
Raven. He winked. "I'm sure he could arrange some relevant documentation."

"You're not suggesting my sister-in-law break the law, are you?"
said Prosper.

The sickly smell of coconut oil rose off Raven's body, cut by a waft
of sea air. "Only joshing, old boy."

"You have such a broad range of interests, Rosalind," Prosper said
after a few moments. "What exactly are you working on now?"

"A series about corruption in Bombay's cinema."

"Ah yes. That explains why you took such an interest in my shooting schedule. It's odd, but I'm sure Miranda told me you were researching the monsoon."

"If I have time. But I'm more interested in the corruption angle. I
gather smuggling is a real problem in Bombay."

Everyone started to laugh, with the exception of Miranda, who
rushed to defend me. "Don't laugh," she said. "Roz doesn't understand the situation." It was an odd sensation, having family on my
side. I was used to fighting my own battles.

"You've been watching too many Hindi movies, Roz," Prosper
said, "where every film must feature a villainous smuggler. In reality,
India couldn't run without them. We have two economies here: the
white and the black, and even European residents have no colour
prejudice against the black one."

"What is commonly called 'Number Two,'" said Raven. "Not bowel movement but financial movement. As our eminent author Shashi Tharoor puts it, Number One is money you can afford to piss away by cheque."

Prosper's face barely registered the vulgarity, but it was obvious he didn't like it. "Of course," he said, turning his body slightly away from Raven's, "new arrivals immerse themselves in such films as Caleb Mistry's, whose every hero gives a stirring speech against smuggling. In truth, civilized society could not keep its head above water without black-market goods." He squeezed a tube of Clinique sunblock and spread some on his pale brown chest. I was surprised the sun dared to touch him. "Our government, in their wisdom," he continued, "passed punitive laws effectively banning import of quality foreign goods, thus protecting local businessmen who produce their own shoddy copies."

"Indian industrialists are lining politicians' pockets with the ill-gotten gains they earned as a result of protectionist policies," added Raven, going on to point out that Bombay, as the centre of India's gold, diamond, and property markets, was responsible for a third of the income tax paid on the subcontinent. "Cash economy, so-called black money system, is thriving here like nobody's business. Politicians are helpless and hopeless to stop it, even if they want to."

"The highest-earning smugglers simply contribute Number Two to the politicians' campaign fund," Prosper said, smoothing more sun lotion onto his thighs as if he were stroking the fur of a prized Siamese cat.

"Without smugglers," said Miranda, "there would be no drinkable gin or champagne, no edible marmalade or biscuits."

"How do the politicians get support for laws that deny the nation Cooper's Fine Cut and Alessi cappuccino machines?" I said.

"Whole of India is drowning in Number Two, that's how," said Raven.

"Sounds like an effective system," I said. "Anyone for a bath—I mean a swim?"

I dived in around Nepal and swam steadily underwater in the general direction of Madhya Pradesh. There were only three other swimmers in the whole map of India. Everyone else was up to their chests in water, their arms waving gracefully as plankton, while their feet remained suckered firmly on the bottom.

I learned from my mother that water plays a crucial role in the genesis of ores, and from my father that you can wear it like a second skin. It was he who taught me the art of swimming: to let the water make you weightless; if swept out to sea, to swim with the current until you understood it, and then at an oblique angle, not directly against the flow. Unlike my sister, I had never learned to apply the same principle to living.

When I put my head above the surface again I saw Vikram Raven sitting with his feet in the water. "So energetic you are in this heat," he said. "What we in Bombay are calling three-shirts-a-day weather."

I pulled myself out. "It must be fascinating to work at the Central Props Unit," I said to Raven, who smiled happily. "You were there when the first Mrs. Sharma died, weren't you?"

He stopped smiling and shifted his bottom from cheek to cheek. "Not actually in the building. It was Ganpati's birthday, when half the city are parading handmade elephant gods to Chowpatty. My chaps at Central Props are making their own clay statue to immerse, and each year's figure is mother of next, for we are putting a morsel of one year's clay into following year's statue."

"But Prosper was working that day. Why, if it was a holiday?"

"Prosper is such a workaholic. He was filming festival on Chowpatty for a scene in his *Tempest*. But he is reshooting scene again in controlled location next time, as genuine festival was too tempestuous. Whole shoot was a disaster."

"I'm sure Maya would've agreed," I said. "By the way, Mr. Raven, do you know an artist called Robi?"

"He is not with my team, but most appropriate to our discussion. He learned his craft making sand sculptures of Ganpati on Chowpatty, did you know?"

"You don't happen to remember Robi's friend, the artist called Sami?"

Raven slid off into the water. "Sami . . . no, I can't recall any Sami. A Satish we have . . ." He strode purposefully away from me through the map.

Prosper was standing where I'd left my towel, talking to a tall white man, although to call him white was misleading. His skin was pinkish-grey, the colour of canned tuna, and he had an eely look to him, not unhandsome, but with all the features too close together, including his shoulders. If eels had shoulders, those were the kind they'd have. No hard angles to get a grip on.

A boy of twelve or so ran past and dived into the pool, slicing the surface as neatly as a knife. I watched as the tall man's face turned away from my brother-in-law to follow the boy's progress.

When I joined Prosper, he introduced the eely man as an old friend from Oxford days, Anthony Unmann. "Rosalind is here to put a stop to smuggling, Tony. She's an expert on the subject."

"Impressive after just five days in India." Unmann laughed. So they'd already been discussing me.

"And what are you here to do, Mr. Unmann," I said, staring pointedly at his pallid chest, "get a tan?"

"I live here. One of my houses in Bombay isn't far from Prosper's."

One of his houses. "Slumming it?" I said, with a smile as close to pert as a five-foot-ten half-Scot could get.

Unmann laughed and unwrapped the towel from his waist. He threw down a wallet, a handful of keys, and some coins onto the table next to us. Five of the coins were gold.

"Mogul," Unmann said, as I picked one up. "I keep them for luck."

"Anthony has a famous collection of coins," Prosper added.

"Almost as good as your brother-in-law's." They smiled smugly at one another, two insiders, the genuine articles. Absolutely above reproach. "Prosper, you must bring Rosalind along to my monsoon party. You know how I enjoy new people. Make it the thirteenth." He stepped over to the pool edge.

I could see myself reflecting badly in their shiny surfaces. "Would you mind if I brought a friend from Christie's?" I said. "He'll be in town that day from London and I've promised to look after him."

Unmann's smooth stride hesitated for a moment. "Of course. Bring as many friends as you like," he said, and slid into the water.

Prosper followed his friend's slippery progress through the pool. As soon as both their heads were underwater, I used my towel as cover to scoop one of the gold coins off the table. Adding kleptomania to my list of accomplishments before joining Miranda under her umbrella.

"Remember when you used to read these to me in Kerala?" she said, holding up a book of Hindu myths. "You always liked the ones about battles and demons."

"And I remember you used to insist on the ones where the moral order was sustained and everyone lived happily ever after. That should have warned me."

Miranda opened the book at a page she had marked. "Here's one you loved—about Sandhya, the melting, liquid times between sunset and darkness, 'between black night and bright dawn, an hour full of whispers and suggestions.' "

She was trying to re-establish our old bond, but it wasn't going to be easy. Too many unanswered questions between us. She flipped a few pages and pointed at the drawing of a flying monkey: Hanuman the monkey chief. "That's what you called Daddy the last time we met—in London, remember? Hanuman, whose children inherit his capacity for havoc and subversion. I couldn't believe you could be so cheeky."

I couldn't believe she still called him Daddy. But even as a teenager Miranda had given the impression of belonging to an earlier, more innocent generation than mine. A different breed altogether: sheltered, thoroughbred, no bad blood.

"I'm so happy you're here. There's so much we have to talk about," Miranda said, touching my hand almost tentatively, as if she sensed the reluctance in me to let down my guard.

"Yes?" I said, wanting to reach out, but held back a barrier that neither of us could cross unless she answered that question I was afraid to ask: How much did she know about Prosper's involvement with the murdered hijra? Until I found out the answer, we would have to stay on separate sides.

"Do you still blame Daddy for what happened to your mother?" she asked suddenly. "He said you did, when he came back from your mother's funeral in Scotland. He said you accused him then of keeping your mother in our village like his *bibi*"—she searched for a word—"his mistress. Just as the white planters used to keep a *bibi-khana*, a lady-house, in the corner of their estate. He said you claimed your mother would still be alive if he'd left Mummy before I was born and married Jessica."

Jessica, I thought, how ill-suited those soft, pretty syllables were to my angry mother. *I don't want you to blame your father*, she had written, before one of her early suicide attempts, *it's not really his fault*. So I thought it was something I'd done. Perhaps I still do blame myself, for the loss of my mother and my country, for the strange half-loss of this sister I no longer knew. "I've spread the blame around now."

"Your mother wrote to him, you know," Miranda said. "I found the letters after he died. They go back to the 1960s, when you were still in India. Before my mother died. They were postmarked in our village." She tried out a tense little smile. "Do you remember the letters I wrote from the convent after that summer you came out here? I still have the ones you sent me."

Her letters to me were lost somewhere on the road with Mum. We always travelled light, no room for childish things. Still, I remember the details: Miranda sent away to a convent school in Madras only a few weeks after our summer together. She was ten, officially an only child; Dad (a Rhodes scholar himself) claimed he wanted her to have all the benefits of a classical English education. As a teenager, she wrote to say that she thought it was more likely he couldn't bear to have her around as a reminder of his own failures with my mother and with hers. She described her life to me—bad food, bullying, loneliness—in the letters she wrote every week. From Madras, aged twelve, she was sent to board in Bombay, where the girls mocked her dark southern skin and she cried herself to sleep for weeks. Later she went to finishing school in Switzerland, the year I hitched across America meeting a different kind of Indian, the kind Columbus discovered by mistake when he was looking for us.

Miranda and I met only once again after our long summer together, for tea at Claridges with my father, when she graduated from finishing school. Slouching into the hotel half an hour late, I could see even from a distance how proud my father was of her, his legitimate daughter, immaculately turned out in a little silk dress that must've cost twice my monthly salary. Dad frowned at my T-shirt and jeans and asked if I hadn't anything more appropriate to wear. I told him that what I was wearing was perfect for our family reunion: frayed at the seams and grubby under the collar. Miranda, staring at her plate, absolutely still, maintained a silence I took for condemnation of my behaviour, as if her letters had been written by a different sister. I remember feeling the same sense of betrayal after meeting an author I admired and discovering he was a lesser man than the hero of his own novels.

It seemed that as adults Miranda and I could communicate only through the written word. In a letter she wrote a few years ago, she told me that she felt sick at the coldness between us that day in Claridges. She hated her dress, the patronizing manner of the hotel waiters towards my small brown father, the rage and scorn she saw in my eyes whenever I looked at her. In fact, that last meeting was a mirror of today. I had arrived desperate to talk to her, only to be discouraged by the company she kept.

There are so many ways of poisoning people, even more in India. Our gardener had an uncle who killed his family and himself during the monsoon by lacing a fish curry with *neagala* root instead of ginger. To poison unwanted foetuses, both *Croton tiglium*, of the *Euphorbiaceae* family, and *Plumbago rosea* are used, although they can also cure dyspepsia, fever, piles, rheumatism, and paralysis. But *Croton* is so dangerously purgative that the oil from its seeds can be used internally only after extracting the poison. Then it cures convulsions, gout, worms, whooping cough (in an infusion of ginger)—and insanity.

My mother was four months pregnant when she arrived in Kerala. She did not know yet that my father was already married, to the daughter of one of the great landowning families, or that the continuation of his studies depended upon the good graces and substantial cash input of his wife's family. Without them, he was just one more MSc in a nation full of underemployed university degrees.

Three years after I was born (in as much secrecy as is possible in a small Indian town), my sister's arrival was celebrated in her mother's estate on the outskirts. From the beginning we were facing in different directions.

In London, years later, browsing through Mum's books, I came across a mildewed copy of J. F. Menon's dictionary of South Indian medicinal plants, published in 1959, the year before I was born. It still smelled of Kerala. One page was marked with a piece of paper. Almost transparent, like most Indian paper, the writing on it appeared to be a prescription in Malayali, Kerala's language, but with the words *Plumbago rosea* written at the top. I read the lines about plumbago marked in the text:

Uses: The root is acrid, diaphoretic, abortifacient; as an *abortifacient*, chiefly used externally, the root-bark introduced into the womb mouth.

I was fourteen when I read that note. For years I lived with its implications, another form of poison. But it wasn't until the night of Mum's death that I confronted her with it. She denied having asked for that old abortive prescription (*"I always wanted you. Always. Believe me!"*), claimed it had been written by my father's wife and signed— falsely—in his name. *"To make me think he didn't want you—but he did!"* I didn't believe her. Sitting here in the sun next to my sister, I began to wonder, Is this why I have come back to India? I wouldn't recognize Dad's handwriting in Malayali, but I still had the note: would Miranda recognize her mother's? Was she a witness for the prosecution or the defence?

"The letters from your mother," Miranda was saying, "stopped for a few years after I was born. They didn't start again until you moved to London."

I looked away. "The first couple of years back in Scotland were quite hard. Living with Gran. Mum never liked that house. Too many bad memories. It was better when we moved down to London, when she got back into gilding."

"There's something I must say, Roz." She took her sunglasses off. Maybe she thought they were the cause of the distance between us. I didn't help her. "Daddy told me he wrote to you several times offering what he could. But you wouldn't accept anything from him."

I shrugged. "He didn't have much anyway. Mostly books. Everything else—the house, the land—it all belonged to your mother's family. You're the heiress: they left it to you. That was Dad's punishment for being a naughty boy with Mum."

"Can you blame them?" The answer shot back at me. So she wasn't quite the meek Indian matron she seemed. Maybe she was in there somewhere, the Miranda I remembered. "The last letters from her, Roz . . . they were . . . they sounded . . . crazy. The accusations she made about my mother . . . that Mummy had tried to get her to take . . ." She left it there. Waiting for me to deny it, to clear her mother. We each had questions that could not be asked. Easing me into it: the confession; giving me a chance to open up. Girl to girl, heart to heart. Gee, sis, life's a bitch. This is what you wanted, Roz, what you came here for.

I stared down the watery coastline of India before Partition. While Pakistan and Bangladesh were still part of the big happy family.

"There are some things Daddy collected over the years that he always wanted you to have," Miranda was saying. "And I wanted—I want—you to have them too. He said it might take time for you—"

"Do you think the rains will start soon?" I interrupted. At the Tamil Nadu end of Breach Candy children were splashing in Ceylon, a shallow kiddies' pool. "That reminds me—did you manage to find those photos I mentioned?"

Turning back to my sister, I saw that her eyes were raised above my head. "What photos are those, Rosalind?" It was Prosper, back from his swim.

"Rosalind was interested in how I met you, Prosper. I told her it was over those pictures I took of . . . at your building." Miranda turned to face me again. "I had a terrible crush on him, you know. I used to cut out pictures of him from all the screen mags. That's why I was taking pictures, hoping he'd walk out the door."

"And did he?" I said, then laughed to show it was all in fun. Ho ho ho. Is your husband a ladykiller? No one joined in. "I'd love to see some more of your films, Prosper. Can I get them on video?"

Prosper considered my question for a moment, walking stiff-legged around it in his head, searching for hidden teeth, then seemed to relax. He smiled at me, a warm smile this time, that lit up his eyes and exaggerated his good looks, giving his face that combination of strength and almost feminine beauty common to some Indian men. For the first time I could see why my sister had fallen for him. "Only pirate videos." He laughed. "And I know how you disapprove of smugglers. My films aren't the popular kind shown in the big cinemas here."

"Prosper has lost money everywhere, Miss Benegal," said Anthony Unmann, sliding into the frame next to my brother-in-law. He glanced down at the keys and coins in his right hand, then back at me. "Even in Russia, where everyone made money on the black market, Prosper's rubles became rubble."

"If you go to my office this afternoon," Prosper said, "I'll leave a message there that someone should give you a screening of any film you'd like."

"Will you come to lunch with us today?" Miranda said.

I checked my watch. "Sorry, I'm having brunch with Basil Chopra."

She stood up awkwardly and gave me a big hug. "Supper tonight, then?"

Prosper frowned.

"I forgot . . . tonight's a bad night," she said, stumbling slightly over the words. "Tomorrow lunch?"

I smiled noncommittally and waved goodbye. Punishing her—but for what? Loyalty to a husband who clearly made her nervous?

7

If HOLLYWOOD HAD BEEN CASTING THE SET FOR A BOMBAY VER-
sion of *Sunset Boulevard*, Basil Chopra's mansion on Malabar Hill
would have scooped the role. All it lacked was William Holden's
corpse floating in the pool. The house was gangrenous from too many
monsoons, its walls streaked with bird shit. Inside, years of paint and
plaster were peeling off to reveal a century of baroque taste in wallpaper, the red velour on the ebonized rosewood sofas had alopecia,
everything sagged—including the pillow of Basil's stomach, whose excess hung in folds like the heavy ruched curtains of an Edwardian
theatre. He was only fifteen years older than I, but he had the bulk and
decay of two people twice my age. Dressed all in white, a fat Mr.
Havisham, his eyes alone belonged to the poet of Prosper's early films.

"You see what I am reduced to?" Basil said, pointing to the
marching damp. "One of the last of the old Bombay houses, but no
repairs get done because these gangland developers are beating up any
builder who dares come here. They want my house to fall down
around me. Everyone is selling out to hoodlums who give penthouse
suites as bribes to the former house owner. Even the meanest two-
bedroom flat is now costing a million, million and a half dollars."

"It's sad to see history with a price tag on it."

"Even street people have to give five hundred rupees to secure
their piece of pavement from the former owner. And then another
thirty rupees a month in bribes to stop hoodlums tearing down their
shack." He raised his lustrous poet's eyes to the sky. "But I am forgetting my manners. Brunch is laid."

Basil's taste in food was locked in the same decade as his language, somewhere on the road from Rudyard Kipling to Noël Coward.

For brunch I was offered devilled eggs, the yolks whipped with coriander, butter, and shreds of green chillies, crisp samosas filled with
minted lamb, fishcakes with a tamarind dip, a pile of hot buttered
toast wrapped in a starched napkin, several cut-glass jars of Scottish
marmalade, a solid silver platter the size of a table, mounded high
with steaming kedgeree flecked with red lentils, and a matching platter of sausages.

He was the West's idea of a maharaja, although the Chopras' social elevation was pure sleight of hand, all smoke and dry ice. From
his grandfather to his grandson, every member of the star's family had
been in film or theatre.

"We were raised on Olivier and Gielgud," he said, "my gurus."

I expressed surprise at his support of British rather than Indian
actors.

"Where would we poor Indians be without the British, dear girl?
They gave us the language which united India and ultimately turned
us into revolutionaries. Like Prospero with Caliban, the British created
their own enemies in a simple effort to have better clerks." He
coughed. "Sorry. I have been playing Prospero for too long—twenty
years in your brother-in-law's *Tempest*. With his constant money
problems and refusal to compromise, my stomach will be the size of
Orson's by the time we complete the picture." He patted the stomach
fondly. "Or it will kill me first. But Prosper is so brilliant he could get
away with murder."

He picked up a ground-chicken kebab as round and plump as the
breast of a nursing mother and popped it into his mouth.

"I see this *Tempest* as his son," he said, licking each finger delicately. "He can't bear to have it judged by the cruel world. And now
that he has discovered new technology, we will never finish. The bit
Shakespeare lifted from accounts of Sir Thomas Gates's shipwreck on
Bermuda—*that dreadful coast . . . supposed to be enchanted and
inhabited with witches and devils, which grew by reason of monstrous
thunder, storm and tempest*—is to be run on screens above us now.
And since watching the rushes of *Jurassic Park*, Prosper is determined
to use computer animation to accomplish the magical transformations,
all those sorcerers and androgynes in Ovid's *Metamorphoses* that inspired Will."

"Ovid isn't high on my bedside reading list. I'm more into popular
culture."

"How does one define popular culture, dear girl?" He shrugged dramatically. "I myself am a slave to the great British directors, as Prosper is, and most Hindi cinema is influenced by Hollywood's worst excesses."

"But even Hindi copies of Hollywood are remade to fit an Indian frame—that archetypal concern for the value of an extended family. Poor people love them. Their sense of security is reinforced. The rich get richer. Everyone's happy."

"You mean drugs and property gangsters get richer," Basil said, and grimaced. "Their taste brutalizes our films. Where once we had classical musicians, now we have wet saris and that vulgar 'Choli' song. As if everyone couldn't tell what precisely is beneath her blouse."

He rolled his eyes and pursed his mouth. "We are reduced to three plots. One: a young couple has brief idyll of happiness, followed by death of one or both. Two: family breakup because of nefarious doings of a villain. Climax, melodrama, followed by prompt reconciliation. Family reunited and villain forgiven and/or violently blown away. Three: the good and bad siblings—good one devoted to Mum; bad, sexy one, cruel and indifferent, a naughty entertainer if she's a woman, smuggler if a man. After long separation and much gratuitous violence, a reunion. Even better if the siblings are twins, giving audience a childlike pleasure in seeing two images of the same person in a single frame—"

"And integrating the two selves, good and bad," I said. "Just like Shakespeare—all those separated twins. Three plots: love, death, and the middle bit."

"Ah, but the master's hand—who can forget the monsoon from Prosper's *Living and the Dead*, where Maya throws herself from the roof to drown in the tank. Proving, by dying again, that she has not died. And all the while it rains."

"Maya was also in Prosper's *Tempest*, wasn't she?" I said.

"She started out as Miranda, but by the end she was too old to satisfy Prosper's backers—or the audiences, for that matter. Maya must have been—what—at least forty-five?"

"What role was she playing when she died?"

"That last day . . . I think it was the day that Caleb presented his new script—"

"Mistry wrote the script?"

"He did many things for Prosper . . . but he never saw eye to eye with Maya. His idea was that instead of Roman goddesses appearing in Prospero's masque at the end, there would be Indian goddesses. Caleb had given Maya the dual role of the witch, Sycorax, Caliban's mother, and Kali."

"An old witch and a goddess of death. Nice casting."

Basil tried not to smile. "Actually, you know, they were very powerful roles."

"Great costumes too. Did Caleb give Maya that necklace of severed heads that Kali wears? And the tongue dripping with blood from her sacrificial victims?"

Laughter rose out of Basil's belly and rolled across the foothills of his mountainous face, displacing them briefly, as if an earth tremor had passed. "Not to mention Kali's sagging breasts and habit of haunting cremation grounds. Caleb's boards were very precise. One can hardly blame the poor woman for causing a scene."

"Caleb did the storyboards as well, did he? And there was a scene?"

"Another scene, I should have said. Prosper fought very hard for her. But Maya was always causing scenes, delaying shooting, making wild accusations."

"What kinds of accusations?"

"All very vague, dear girl, and even vaguer six years later. She knew something or someone that could change everything. Typical threats of a desperate woman."

"What happened on the day of her death?"

"I remember it cinematically—the shots, not exact dialogue. Let me see . . . Maya did several bad takes with Nonie, who played both Miranda and Annapurna, the goddess of plenty and fertility—Caleb had sketched her in as a peasant girl brimming over with milk and carrying a ladle, as she does in the little Maharashtra shrines. Nonie made some derogatory comment and Maya slapped her so hard she left a handprint as red as those ones you see on old walls, where wives have committed *sati* after their husband's death. She kept looking at Prosper and then back at Nonie, screaming, 'Shall I tell her? Shall I tell her?' Quite hysterical, you see. Finally Prosper ordered her off the set."

"Nonie. That's Caleb Mistry's daughter. Was it to do with Prosper's affair with her?"

"I say, are you taping all of this?" He leaned over to look at my machine. "It seemed at the time to have some wider meaning."

"What about Shoma Kumar—did she have anything to do with it?"

"By then, darling Sho was well on her way to some other woman's husband."

"And then Maya was murdered."

Basil shook his massive head. "Many people think that, but I really do believe the poor woman killed herself. By the next film there would have been no more playback singing, not even providing the voice for a younger woman's face. She had lost virtually everything that made her Maya Sharma, don't you see?"

"I'd love to see that script of Caleb's."

"The early version was aborted years ago, dear girl. The reasons it was written no longer exist—and neither do the actors, apart from me. I'm sure Prosper would let you have a copy, or a look in that book of his, his shooting diary. The one we call his *Atharva-Veda*." He noticed my blank expression. "*Atharva-Veda*: the Brahmins' Secret Book, like those Black Books of early magicians and alchemists . . . Anyway, I know Prosper is very secretive about it—but as family . . . And he keeps all manner of fascinating things in it—ideas for scenes, rough storyboards, photos of the cast, any snippet of information pertaining to the history of storms and *The Tempest* that he might use." His voice trailed away. "Curious, your face keeps reminding me of someone."

"My features are quite similar to my sister's."

"Miranda? No, someone else. Terrible thing, how one's memory goes."

8

"Thomas," I said, "where would I go to buy and sell antique coins?"

"Best place for smuggled goods is Mutton Street in Chor Bazaar—Thieves' Market. There they can sell you spare parts stolen from your own watch, so good are the pickpockets. Whole street is chock-a-block antiques." He was passing a truckload of bananas and for a brief, spellbinding moment we were on the wrong side of the road with all of Bombay hurtling towards us.

"Also, there are Javeri and Dagina Bazaars selling king's ransom in gold and silver," he said, as we pulled back into safety. The car grazed a station porter in a red jacket with a brass licence disk on his armband, Victoria Terminus's distinctive uniform, but I saw him trot off unhurt, swinging a bag full of plantains the size of cigarillos. "But in your case I think we are taking Mohammedali Road, heading for Masjid Bunder, largest spice market in India. Right side of street: spices; left side: diamonds. Only street in Bombay cleaned six times a day." He ruffled through his bag with one hand and passed back a business card with a map printed on one side. "I am knowing just the fellow for you. This fellow is part-time jewels, part-time gold."

"I never doubted it for a minute," I said.

THE MARKET STREETS OFF MOHAMMEDALI WERE JAMMED WITH HANDCARTS, bicycles, housewives armed with brutal black umbrellas, hawkers flogging mechanical Taiwanese dogs, India-wide lottery tickets, raw cashews from Kerala, Kashmiri rose incense. I shrugged off a man with no teeth who was trying to sell a signed photo of Roger Moore in

Octopussy and stumbled over a boy sitting cross-legged on the pavement offering to clean customers' ears with a selection of metal instruments that looked as if they'd come out of a car mechanic's tool box. Next to him, rows of teeth grinned up at me from the flowered table-cloth of an open-air dentist, and the dentist flashed a flawless set of gold molars when I showed him the jeweller's business card.

"Yes yes, madam." He waved towards the densest knot of humanity. And then I could smell it: waves of turmeric and ginger. I had only to follow that smell to its source, trailing the beggars who doubled here as human bloodhounds, scouring the surface of the street with their bare hands for a microchip of glitter. In Bombay, city of leftovers, these leavings of the diamond merchants were the most valuable leftovers of all.

I found the jeweller behind a velvet-covered desk at the back of his shop. Thomas had told me that Shrenik was a Jain from Gujarat, like 50 percent of the diamond and gold merchants in this market.

"How may I be of assistance?" he said, raising his eyes from an old Sotheby's catalogue. "A ring of engagement perhaps?"

"I have a gold coin I'd like appraised."

"Some tea first—just the ticket on such a stinking hot day." He gestured to a small boy crouched at the front of the shop, then screwed a jeweller's glass into his eye and held out his hand. "Coin please."

After turning it over several times under his glass, he weighed it on a tiny set of scales, then got a book down from the shelves above his desk, pushing aside a decade's worth of New York, Frankfurt, and London auction house catalogues. He placed my coin on a double-page spread of coins and grunted.

"So it's a fake," I said.

"No, this is real. See Jahangir's name? One of the coins he had struck in 1602 to confirm sovereignty after seizing Allahabad from his father, shortly before he had his father's historian murdered and all his male relatives assassinated."

"Nice fellow."

"Oh yes. A great supporter of the arts, Jahangir, a man who could spot a fake a mile off. In his memoirs he is writing: 'If there be a picture containing many portraits, and each face be the work of a different master, I can discover which face—even which eye and eyebrow—is the work of each of them.' Like a mother recognizing her baby amongst thousands."

The boy arrived with a tray of tea in small glasses. Sipping the milky spiced drink so typical of Gujaratis everywhere, I had a wave of nostalgia for Kerala, where the Gujarati merchants used to serve my mother their favourite tea masala while she bartered for goods.

"May I see that book?" I asked. The title was *Fine Arts of India and Pakistan*, published by the National Heritage Trust of India.

"Essential book for all serious students of Indian gold and bronze works, as well as stone," the merchant said. "See the quality of photographic reproduction, and exact measurements and weights next to each object? Most useful for checking authenticity."

"Is there a market for fake gold coins?" I said. "Or real ones?"

His wise yellow eyes assessed me. "Old coins, not much, except for disguising black-market money. Gold medals and small bronzes is whole other kettle of fish. Most profitable. Best is to container-load to Europe or U.S."

He told me that despite the regulations Ashok had described to me, even genuine antiques could escape the eagle eyes of the Department of Archaeology. You bought a piece of furniture containing some secret compartment—a tribal wedding chest from Rajasthan, say, or a Goan clothes cupboard, an *almirah*—old, but not so old it needed a letter verifying its lack of antiquity, then filled it with smaller art objects and shipped it out. You paid by volume. With half of India's foreign port traffic to deal with, Bombay officials couldn't check everything. The trick was to present the objects in the secret drawer as a surprise find to a potential buyer in the West.

"Of course, I am no specialist in these things, you understand," said Shrenik. "For that you are wanting this man"— he wrote a name and address on a scrap of unheaded paper—"in old Portuguese quarter. He may be able to help."

THE SKY WAS VERY CLOSE AGAIN, ITS WEIGHT REFLECTED IN PEOPLE'S EYES. A man beat the bandaged stump of his arm against Thomas's window.

"Faster, Thomas."

He put his foot to the floor. "You should not let these people upset you, madam. I am thinking of Caliban's address in Mr. W. H. Auden's prose-poem *The Sea and the Mirror*. Most Hindu in its sentiments. I happen to have learned part of this text out of library book." We stopped at a red light and Thomas began to recite as if to a larger audience: *"We should not be sitting here clean and cosy—"*

"Cosy?" I asked. "You're sure Auden used the word *cosy?"*

"—clean and cosy," he persevered, *"with our bellies full, in best seats house is offering, unless others were not here . . .* I am quoting

from memory only, madam, but see how appropriate is this? . . .
*others failing to navigate the tempest or to whom natives of foreign
shores are not so friendly, others whose highways and byways famine
is turning aside from ours to pass through—*"

"Thomas, the light's green."

One eye on the road, he continued to recite: "*—others not repel-
ling invasion of malaria or who are being crushed by . . . by an
insurrection of the bowels . . .*"

At that moment, Thomas broke wind. "Sorry, madam. I have a
nervous stomach. And now I have destroyed mood of poem."

"That's all right, Thomas. You have the true poet's sense of timing."

9

I T WAS CALLED THE ELEPHANT HOUSE, SHRENIK HAD SAID, BE-
cause of the carvings on its stone gateposts. Typical of the town houses
built by rich merchants here, its delicate fretwork and three tiers of
deep, overhanging roof were reminiscent of a truncated Chinese pa-
goda. Suitable for an Oriental turn of events, I thought. Above the roof
rose a few tall palms, some of the few that remain of the island's
original toddy-producing coconut trees. But there was no longer any
evidence of the fishing village—Machcha-grama—that had given this
old Portuguese quarter of Mazagaon its name, unless my quest could
be considered a form of angling.

Nor did the dealer look as if he should have de Souza engraved on
his letterbox. He sat cross-legged on a string bed opposite mine, bare-
chested and solid, with the rounded edges common to 1950s electrical
appliances. High above us, flies buzzed around a single 40-watt bulb.
From time to time a more adventurous insect would descend and the
dealer's tongue would appear between his thick lips like a frog's, his
flyswat would rise, and—THWACK—another corpse dropped from mid-
air. Each time he did it I jumped.

Shrenik had warned me that there would be a certain ritual before
we got down to the nitty-gritty, but I hadn't expected anything quite
so primordial.

A servant opened an old Portuguese-style wardrobe, the only other
piece of furniture in the room besides the tin trunk between our two
charpoys, and removed a selection of bundles in faded red cloth. I took
a sip of tea from a translucent Chinese cup and unwrapped the first
package. Inside were some erotic miniatures, showing the excessive
attention to detail of so much bad Indian work.

"They shouldn't have used such bright gouache on the penises," I said. "And the women's pubic hair is too carefully painted. Still, not bad." I stared directly into my examiner's eyes. "For copies."

The dealer remained silent, but his eyes narrowed.

The next package was more promising. The first painting, of a gazelle-eyed girl contemplating monsoon clouds from a palace window, crumbled into four pieces as I picked it up. In the second, spotted with mildew and ravaged by white ants, boldly painted figures in vivid saffron and rust red were seated at a low, octagonal table.

"Marwari," I said. "Stunning."

The dealer's eyes gleamed.

"A very fine copy." My hands had started to sweat. "Late-nineteenth, early-twentieth-century, I'd say."

THWACK. Another life extinguished. "From a period when our artists were still allowed to go into museums to copy the masters," said the dealer. "Which is why it is good. Now they copy other copies. Or worse, use their imagination."

He waved to the servant, who packed up the remaining bundles and returned them to the wardrobe. "So. We have established that you are not just tourist in search of dirty pictures. What do you have for me, madam? Or want to buy?"

For the next twenty minutes we danced themes and variations on the Indian trading minuet, establishing that I had a collection of Mogul coins of great value (unspecified), acquired in a manner I could not go into, to sell at some future (unspecified) date, and that I would be pleased to sell through him—provided, that is, that my (unspecified) other interested party did not offer more.

"My dear young lady," said the flycatcher, whose manner had warmed with the exertions of his ancient dance, "I cannot imagine how anyone else could be offering such good returns on your outlay."

"But he has offered much more, in fact. It's just that . . . well, I am a loyal citizen of India, despite my British aspect, and I don't like the idea of this collection of Indian artefacts being sold through an Englishman and leaving our country."

The dealer's eyes closed with satisfaction. "Ah, now you are letting the feline out of the bag. And you have been misinformed by your go-between. Only one English dealer offers such good prices as I on items of . . . questionable provenance. And he is not buying these days, only selling."

"Who are you referring to?" I said. He smiled and shrugged. "Anyway, you must be thinking of someone else." I took Unmann's coin out of my pocket and tossed it a few times in the air so he got a good look. "A few days ago I sold a whole sackful of these to him." Praying to whatever gods were watching that there was such a sackful to be sold.

The dealer uncrossed his legs and leaned forward. "But why would Unmann—" He saw me grin, and his mouth snapped shut as if it had finally caught the fly. Then he summoned up what passed for a gracious smile and told me that if I changed my mind, his own offer would hold until the end of the month.

S ATISH ISAACS HAD TIME TO SPARE FOR ANYONE WHO SHARED
his enthusiasm for the Museum of Wounds. The reincarnations he
performed in this small part of the Central Props Unit were his family,
and he ruled over them like a stern patriarch.

"I'm in a bit of a hurry, Satish—"

"Yes, yes, no problem. First you are seeing my work. Seeing is
believing!"

Leading me through the Museum of Wounds—acid burns on the
right, bludgeoning on the left, Gulkand the leper staring morosely out
of his dusty corner—he brought me to a new figure. "Look! My masterpiece."

It was Sami as I had seen her in the morgue photos, down to the
last strip of peeled flesh. Her bra lay against the flat male chest like an
old woman's useless udders. Satish had even caught the awkward arrangement of her arms. Perfect. Except that Frankenstein's figure
wore the mask of a generic Hindu hero.

"Where did you get the details from—and why the mask?"

Satish rubbed the fingertips of his right hand together. "Before the
coroner's people took body away, one Chowpatty officer there took
Polaroid snaps. I am giving money to several police stations for inside
info on up-to-the-minute deaths."

"Why the mask?"

"Rama, hero of *Ramayana*!" Satish said, surprised at my igno-
rance. "Body was found on day before Ramanavani, when temples all
over India are celebrating birth of Rama."

I could feel my patience fraying. "But how would Rama have
anything to do with the death?"

"Week leading up to birthday, *Ramayana* is widely performed. One reading is happening on Chowpatty Beach. Not long afterwards, body was found like this, covered in sand, only head and sign sticking out. Police say no one spotted the death because people are thinking at time it is only one more sand sculpture."

Not fishermen, then. An all-night performance of the *Ramayana*, as Ram had said. I held out Unmann's coin. "I picked this up by mistake on my last visit."

Satish turned it over to read both sides. "Impossible. We are doing last batch of Mogul coins like this maybe three months ago, for Mr. Sharma. And your coin is genuine article, I would say, not copy."

"What happens to the coins and other work after a director finishes filming?"

"Those they can use again they save. Others are sold or melted down. Right now I am turning a copper medallion into a silver one by simple electroplating. Are you familiar with process?"

"Broadly speaking," I said.

"For small pieces, we are using very amateurish method, I am afraid. Articles to be plated must be perfectly clean. For silver plating we use solution of potassium cyanide and silver nitrate in water. Current is passing through solution with silver anode and silver is deposited on object in thirty minutes. Article is then polished. Gold also can be deposited. Of course, this costs more."

I SPENT THE REST OF THE AFTERNOON UPSTAIRS WATCHING CLIPS FROM PROSper's old films. His assistant gave me a catalogue that listed Island Studio's last twenty years of work, with each film's plot synopsis, the cast and production team, as well as awards won. But what was I looking for? Insight into my brother-in-law's character? Cinematic evidence of homicidal tendencies?

Director, Key Grip, Foley Editor, Best Boy, full-length features, shorts, documentaries—after a while the categories started to blur. Although the catalogue was in English, most of Prosper's films had been made in Hindi, with the odd co-productions, which meant that I would fall asleep in a short Hindi drama set in a Calcutta slum, only to open my eyes in a French co-production about the Dalai Lama in Tibet.

After about three hours, the sound of a loud, wet crack jolted me awake. A woman's body facedown in a gutter. Tentacles of blood filtering out into the water from her head, the camera tracking in until the screen fills with red. Cross-fade through to the red stripes of a fluttering U.S. flag. Hold that image long enough to register. Roll credits. One final frame on the screen, three lines of white type, deliberately shot so they flicker like the subtitles on a silent movie:

> *The iterating of these lines brings gold;*
> *The framing of this circle on the ground*
> *Brings whirlwinds, tempests, thunder and lightning.*
> —MARLOWE, *Dr. Faustus*

I turned around to the projectionist. "Can you wind that back to the death?"

"You want actual fall again, madam?"

"Yes, please."

An open door frames a shadowed figure—two of them; one; we can't quite see.

One shadow moves backwards into the sunlight. A woman stumbles, turns towards us, screams.

And then quick cut to a close-up: the whole frame filled with widened eyes and tightly stretched mouth. Another cut: for an instant she is the camera lens—tracking down to the faces of pedestrians seven storeys below. Then wider again as she is propelled over and her heavy scarf catches on the balcony below, choking off her scream before the final fall, the final frame of red.

"Critics are saying this image is comment on our increasingly violent society," said the assistant, who had appeared beside me halfway through the last shot.

"When was it made?" Seeing my sister on that balcony instead.

He flipped through my catalogue to the page of film details. "There: *Cyclone*—two years after first Mrs. Sharma died. Rest of film is not relevant to her death, only this bit. Story of woman at the time of monsoon who is taking her own life due to cancer. Silver medal, Venice."

"I thought *The Cyclone* was a film by Caleb Mistry."

"One cyclone started by Mr. Mistry, many years ago, but never distributed. This cyclone by Mr. Sharma based on Mr. Mistry's original."

"Why wasn't Mistry's version distributed?"

He shook his head. "Not similar. Mistry's film is about woman who kills herself because of loss of faith in Mrs. Gandhi's Congress

Party and death of her idealist son in police firing squad. No one is distributing it because of politics."

The lights came on. The technician pointed to the clock above the screen. "We are shutting up shop, madam. And it is best if you are home. Sky is having blood-red tinge to the cloud. Sure sign there will be real humdinger of a storm."

WHERE DO I DRAW THE LINE BETWEEN FACT AND FICTION? I FEEL AS IF I AM trying to predict a cyclone that has already happened, charting its course by the broken trees and damaged property it has left in its wake—but it is so long after the storm's passing that the scars are barely visible.

When Piddington, the great storm prophet, was writing his masterpiece, he welcomed every source of information, however humble. Meteorologists and mariners of all nations offered him their celestial and atmospheric signs.

Two captains in the Bay of Bengal report that nets come up covered with all the muck of a muddy sea. Another mentions great waves of turtles floating in the dead calm preceding the cyclone, all apparently in a state of stupor. Many captains' logs remark on "a most awful silence, during which the quicksilver disappeared in the barometer," and then a series of peculiar noises preceding and following the storm. "Plaintive," one of them says, and another describes "an awfully hollow and distant rumbling," a moaning that rises and falls like that heard in old houses on winter nights, known on some parts of the English coast as "the calling of the sea." A Captain Smith, foundering in the South Indian Ocean during a gale preceded by a sound resembling the scream of a steamer's whistle, overhears his Malay crew. "They call it the Devil's Voice," he says.

"Act Four, Scene One," I read in Prosper's stage directions. "Prospero starts suddenly, and speaks; after which, to a strange, hollow, and confused noise, the Reapers vanish."

One sign is considered infallible by all authorities, Piddington included, and that is the colour of the atmosphere before the cyclone strikes. A Mr. Burdett, passenger on the *Exeter* in the May cyclone of 1840, writes in the Calcutta *Englishman* of his distress:

On the morning of the 30th, the day appeared to break full an hour before its time, and all was seen through the medium of bright crimson. Sails, men, sea and even clouds, the whole hemisphere gradually assumed a flame of fire; the sea appeared an ocean of cochineal and the ship and everything aboard looked as if dyed with that colour, as if bathed in blood.

The first of May was one of the loveliest days Mr. Burdett had seen. May 2 was the only fair run the ship had had. On the night of the third and the morning of the fourth there was such a storm that the ship was dismasted and went down. Most passengers were lost, and all the crew. Those who survive remember the colours. A lurid red, they say. Bright crimson. A brick-dust haze on the horizon. The colour of dried blood.

I am starting to believe I can predict the weather.

11

IN THE HOUR BEFORE MEETING RAM FOR A DRINK, I SAT AT THE Ritzy going through my notes, making a list of all the coincidences and near-misses of the past couple of days, putting the commas and the semicolons in the right places. Cross-referencing my data with Ram's original information, and multiplying the result by my desire to change from voyeur into player, it still didn't add up. I didn't trust my charming brother-in-law or his friend Mr. Anthony Unmann. So? I didn't trust the leaders of any of the world's political parties either. That didn't make them murderers. Not all of them, anyway.

I was going round in circles, trying to find a pattern that fit the facts, or facts that pointed in one direction instead of fifty, when the phone rang. "Package here for you, madam," said the receptionist, "from *The Times*."

The package contained three photocopies of photos taken at the time of Maya's death. Bunny had written a note: "Dug up some of the snaps from our morgue. Call if you want better reproductions."

I called her immediately. "I am sorry, madam, but she has left," said her secretary. "May I take a message?"

"Can you tell her that Roz Bengal would like better copies of those photos. She'll know what I mean." I looked with frustration at the blurred and inconclusive vision in my hands, a truth just out of my reach.

"I FOUND OUT THAT YOUR FRIEND ROBI USUALLY WORKS THE EVENING SHIFT at Mistry's," Ram said. "From six p.m. to midnight. The day shift finishes at 5:30 p.m. Most Bombay studios have two shooting shifts.

Mistry is using both shifts now, because he's coming up to the end of a film. He's an old hand at the movie game, and he always works with the same crew, but he probably still gets only about half an hour of usable film from each shift. The guy on the phone said Robi might be there tonight. But he wasn't sure if they were calling in the part-time villains or just the heavyweight thugs."

"What about that performance of the *Ramayana* on the night Sami was killed?"

He reached into his briefcase for his notebook. "After you rang me from Prosper's, I called a few religious groups and found out it was organized by a big arts charity called the Tilak Foundation."

"Tilak, as in the statue where they found Sami?" I said.

Ram nodded. "But don't get too excited. The Tilak Foundation supports religious festivals, pays for repairs to temples and historic buildings, that kind of thing. I looked up this Tilak dude. When the British banned crowd assemblies in 1894, he claimed the Ganesh festival on Chowpatty was religious, and then managed to get across his political message disguised in a dance drama. But I couldn't figure how that connected to Sami."

"Who runs the charity?"

"A mixed bag—some Indian directors, some U.K. I didn't get any names, but here's the number I phoned. Talk to a guy there called Jay."

"And Dilip—any more on the sulphides?"

"Dilip hasn't got anything to report," Ram said. "I think he's been having trouble getting access to the information . . . because of that tape you took."

"Shit. I'll try to think of a way to sort it out. In the meantime . . ." I laid the morgue photos of Sami and Co. on the table next to the ones Bunny had sent, and tapped the close-up of Maya.

Of my sister's three pictures, one was clearly enlarged from the other, perhaps in an attempt to identify the hijra. But the hijra's face was turned away from the camera, and from that angle she could have been anyone. The third photo was a wide shot of the building that Miranda must have taken minutes after the fall: Maya's body surrounded by a crowd, a strip of Prosper's office entrance, people streaming over to gawp. Bunny had marked the fourth picture "police photographer": the audience cleared away, Maya's corpse laid out on a stretcher, the view from her feet back towards her face. She didn't look too bad. Most of her bleeding would have been on the inside. The photocopying had left streaks and obscured precise details, but if you looked closely you could just make out a set of parallel marks extending from above Maya's sari top to her face. On her cheek, the one that wasn't streaked with mud, the tracks overlapped. Impossible to be sure, given the quality of the print, but to me the intersecting tracks looked like a game of tic-tac-toe.

I started doodling on my napkin.

"It could be dirt on the photocopier," Ram said, but I could hear the suppressed excitement in his voice.

"There are better prints at *The Times*." I stopped my doodling. "Bottom line, Ram: do you think Prosper is connected?"

He hesitated for a moment, then nodded. "Absolutely. But I don't think you'll be able to prove it." He tapped the photos. "The Maya ice is too old."

"What about Sami and friends?"

He looked away and hunched his shoulders the way he had the first day, when I'd asked him about the pavement dwellers. "I think most of Bombay doesn't want to know about people they consider to be well beyond the pale, and the ones who do want to know are going to a lot of trouble to hush the whole thing up." He reached over for my napkin. "What's this—some kind of weather map?"

I nodded. "A kiddies' version of the monsoon chart produced by Edmond 'the Comet' Halley, the fellow who first reported on monsoon physics." I pointed to the triangular shape on the right-hand side of the sketch, where the word "Maya" was written. "This is Maya, full of hot air, sitting on top of her mountain of money. And this spiral over here is Prosper and his *Tempest*, at first just a stiff sea breeze, but gaining momentum as the years roll along and there's no son and no great success and the money drains away and the backers put on pressure."

Ram started to grin.

"D'you know how a monsoon works?" I said. "You get heat rising off the land, sucking in cool air from the sea, gradually building into this great spiralling weather system." I held up my hand to forestall any sarcasm. "Prosper's *Tempest* rolls forward like that, carrying him along. He's obsessed. He identifies with the characters; it becomes the most important thing in his life, the film that's going to clear all his financial and artistic debts."

"Until it hits the mountain."

"Even if he's not directly involved with the destruction, Prosper is the eye of the storm. Around him are the most violent winds. Or maybe a series of cyclones, like those families of depressions that whirl into India like giant Catherine wheels." I added the words Mistry, Unmann, Raven, Shiv Sena to my drawing.

Ram smiled down at it. "The Maharashtrian love of poetry must be getting to you. Save me a seat in court when you present this graphic cocktail napkin as evidence. But what makes you think Maya was the mountain? Maybe she was part of the storm blowing towards a different obstacle." He took the pen, crossed out one word, and wrote in another. "So now who is in everyone's way?"

In place of Maya's name on the mountain, Ram had written mine.

12

THE HOTEL RECEPTIONIST GAVE ME A MESSAGE FROM ASHOK, garbled beyond comprehension by the operator. I rang him to clarify it, but the static on the line was so bad I gave up. "Monsoon is coming soon," the operator said when I complained again later. "Are you expecting phones to be working come hell or high water?" The cables were not laid in ducts, he explained, which meant that during heavy rainfall water seeped in to distort or disconnect the lines of communication.

It was too late to try the number Ram had given me for the Tilak Foundation, and my call to Caleb Mistry's studio was cut off as soon as it connected, so I couldn't quiz the director about the cyclone he had shared with Prosper.

The story I was involved in reminded me of a series of letters my father had written when he heard about my developing interest in storms.

"Flow has always been easily measured as long as it remains calm," he wrote. "We map it with a series of points called 'attractors,' which act like magnets to limit behaviour to a fixed orbit. But once disorder sets in—turbulence of any kind: a waterfall, the sea, a cyclone—knowledge collapses. It is one of science's most puzzling problems, turbulence. It makes those fixed points lose their magnetic attraction. Instead, we have the same limited space filled with erratic compass points. Imagine a submarine sailing across the Indian Ocean, manned by an anarchic crew determined never to retrace the same path, never even to intersect it. For if its orbit ever intersected, the sub would be dragged back into an orderly route. To prevent this happening, the course charted is infinitely long, a series of chaotic loops and spirals, which, nevertheless, eventually form a pattern—and this pattern is called a Strange Attractor."

I wrote back: "Doesn't the discovery of these chaotic patterns undermine the root of your Hindu faith in life as a series of cycles endlessly repeating?"

He wrote to me: "Doesn't the discovery undermine your atheism?"

"How can there be an infinite number of paths within a limited space?" I wrote. "And if things never repeat or intersect, where is the pattern?"

"Strange patterns. Physicists also find it difficult to believe in God," he replied. "But remember Emerson, who said that if we meet no gods, it is because we harbour none."

I wrote: "I do not think one should use God to justify one's unjustifiable actions, claiming that they form part of some larger pattern." Between the lines we could both read what I had not written: *You had a choice, my father.*

We did not write again for several years.

THESE HIJRA MURDERS HAD AN ELEMENT OF STRANGE ATTRACTION. EVERY time I got a point fixed on my compass, the needle started to waver and another set of points appeared. True north not yet established.

The weather report on television interrupted my train of thought as if programmed by the pilot on that erratic submarine of my father's, static giving every face the shadowy silhouette of a lost twin:

"*. . . coming to you from India's most famous weather office, the Meteorological Centre in Trivandrum, Kerala's capital, where the Monsoon Officer formally announced today that the monsoon had finally arrived. After the usual gusting, forty-knot winds from the southwest, classic prelude to the burst . . .*"

The monsoon was expected to arrive in Bombay in four days. After another beer, I started to see Prosper and his chums as a massed rank of cumulonimbus, subject to the monsoon clouds' phenomenon known as Conditional Instability of the Second Kind. All I needed was something to shake that instability. I remembered a summer when the monsoon clouds were clearly visible for day after day, refusing to rain. Heat building up, people cracking under the pressure.

"*. . . Two days ago at the village of Vilappilsala, a thirty-two-year-old woman hanged herself by tying her sari to the beam of her verandah,*" said the talking head on my television. "*She was found with her feet only two inches off the ground. Neighbours claim that her* *nagging husband drove her to it, himself driven to distraction by the heat. Monsoon madness is building up in the north as well . . ."*

There was a rainmaker famous for having broken a drought by sending electronic impulses into the atmosphere for ten minutes every three hours. It took him eleven days, but the result was a monsoon storm that demolished roads and power supplies for a week.

". . . Five died today during rioting in the Punjab, and at the town of Amreli, famous for its excellent quality groundnut oil, a clash between rivalling shopkeepers left three dead and six gravely injured . . ."

In Kerala, rainmaking was not unusual. My father knew a pilot called Krishna who was paid to fly his Dakota into the rain clouds and seed them with a fine dust of ground soapstone and salt, a mixture that was ejaculated from the plane's undercarriage into the clouds' bellies in a white burst of spume.

Shortly after Krishna had taken off on his mission one day, I overheard our gardener talking to a friend. This was during the brief period when I understood Malayali. By the time I came back, six years later, I had lost the language as one loses baby teeth: only a few words and phrases remained under my pillow.

"There goes the cloud-fucker again," said our gardener.

"Do you think his sperm will be fertile this time?" asked his friend.

"Oh yes." He tapped the side of his nose. "Old Krishna can smell the plump ones like ripe mangoes. Still, there is always a risk."

The risk lay in not differentiating between the dark rain clouds and the dangerous thunderheads. One error in judgement and your plane could be sucked up by the storm clouds' spiralling ring of low pressure, thousands of feet in seconds, to the top layers, where the air was a heaving maelstrom of ice crystals charged with static electricity.

"That would be like fucking an angry bull," said the gardener.

Henry Piddington advised three ways of managing a ship at the approach of a tropical cyclone. One was to run from it, avoiding any confrontation. The second was to tack around the dangerous centre. The third was a strange and startling solution for sailors of the time: to *profit* by the storm, to use its fury to increase your speed. This advice comprised just a few words: study the storm, read its signals, then, with the transparent storm cards which he provided in his *Sailor's Hornbook*, plot its course, and "If circumstances allow, sail with it." To run on the crest of a storm like a surfer, that was the art. My problem was that I had lost the transparent storm cards Piddington provided.

After my third beer, everything became much clearer. I saw that one could learn about the pattern of another person's life only by following that person into the same maze. Useless to keep a map of the maze in your pocket: when the person you were following retraced his steps for the fiftieth time, the temptation to take the quick way out would be irresistible.

It was like my mother's lack of interest in travel books. They were boring, she said, because you knew from the start that whatever dangerous paths our hero the narrator had to walk, he would always live to write another book.

"And if the narrator is not the hero?" I asked her. "If the narrator is unreliable, what then?"

I switched off the TV, left my sister's phone number with the hotel receptionist in case of breakthroughs from Ram, and went to pay a visit to Prospero's cave.

13

WHEN MIRANDA MARRIED PROSPER, HE'D LIVED IN A HUGE old house on the Malabar Hill. Recently, the house had been torn down and they had moved into the penthouse suite of the apartment block that replaced it.

Prosper did not exactly welcome my visit to his eyrie with unfeigned joy. "Roz. You should have telephoned. Your sister is at the hospital again. A spot of high blood pressure, but she'll be there until morning. No more visitors tonight."

"Aren't you going to invite me in?"

"It's not very convenient at the moment."

"Nonsense, Prosper!" a man's voice called out. "We've finished work."

My brother-in-law stepped back reluctantly, framed against the Mogul court dress of some distant relative, which hung behind glass on plaster walls polished to a dull buff that must have taken hundreds of fingers hundreds of hours to achieve. The lighting was too discreet to let you read the fine print at the bottom of your contract, but bright enough to prove that every detail in the penthouse was conspicuous by its implications of modern taste and antique money, the kind of money so dusty with age and respectability no one remembers it was ever new. Or how it was earned. To reinforce the metaphor, a case of old gold coins was visible through a door into a room off the main hall.

I tried and failed to fit the sister I knew onto this stage. A sister I used to know.

The entrance to the living room was framed by two Gujarati temple columns tall enough to let an elephant pass through with ease. It looked like a place where an elephant might tap-dance in, carrying the drinks tray. You could have fit the Savoy's ballroom into it twice but not three times, and a row of eighteenth-century Rajput noblemen stood like dancers waiting for the ball to begin against one living-room wall, their picture frames finished in a silky gold.

"Nice flat," I said, tapping one of the frames. "Good-quality water gilding. It all depends on the original gesso work, did you know? Has to be perfectly dry if the burnishing is not to damage it." Expert gilders like my mother could tell whether it was ready just by lightly tapping the surface or by running a burnishing stone gently over it. Some of the oldest burnishers were made of wolves' and dogs' teeth. "The largest burnishers used to be made of haematite, a word that means 'bloodlike stone,' " I said. "Blood and gold have a long association." Another tap on the gesso, less gentle this time; I was feeling the effect of the three beers I'd had in the hotel. Prosper blinked his long lashes several times but did not seem visibly distressed by my probing. "I guess this stuff was your family's?"

He looked around. "Some, and some is from Maya's family."

"They must've been loaded too."

He frowned slightly.

His business partner did not look as if he considered gold vulgar. From the gold bracelet around his left wrist to his white silk suit, everything about him was new. Except his skin. It gleamed with expensive face lotion, the kind that promises eternal youth. He was not a good advertisement for the product. He had skin the colour and texture of very old chip fat.

My brother-in-law tossed me his guest's name as if he didn't want it caught. Big in property, I gathered, although Prosper wasn't clear. When the man got up to shake my hand, I expected him to leave an oily mark on the ivory linen sofa. Just when I thought I was going to have to remove my hand forcibly from his, he kissed it. "I truly admire the BBC," he said, staring at my breasts as if he were interviewing them for an outside broadcast.

"I'm only freelance," I said. "And I'm thinking of giving it up. I don't like the quality of the audiences we're pulling these days."

When Prosper offered me a drink, I asked for a Scotch. "A double."

"Ice?" he asked.

Only distantly concerned that the water might not have been boiled, I said "Lots" and sat down well away from the greaseball, slurping the alcohol like mother's milk. It went straight to my head and formed a deadly alliance with the beer, giving me that carefree feeling of unreality that is so unwise in interviews with gangsters or prospective employers. I wondered if it was murderer's Scotch.

"You seem to have recovered from that incident in the caves," Prosper said. "Perhaps the swim did some good."

"I've been thinking about that." I gave him a knowing look. "You didn't happen to tell any of your heavy friends I would be in those caves, did you?"

"I'm sorry, Rosalind?" Prosper knotted his sensitive brow.

Oh, he was good, my brother-in-law. "I've been running back the reel of that incident," I said. "I mean, those guys didn't steal Sami's book of pictures by accident, did they? They knew what they wanted."

"Sami?" said the greaseball, and knotted his brow as well. His knot wasn't such a good rendition of honest perplexity as Prosper's, but then he hadn't had my brother-in-law's years in the theatre.

"You remember Sami, Prosper?" I ignored his friend. "The sand sculpture they found on Chowpatty? The one who was hanging around at the time of your first wife's . . . um, death? Those pictures of Sami must have really made you sweat."

"What are you talking about, Roz? What pictures?"

I got up and helped myself to another generous slug of murderer's Scotch, rattling the ice loudly and fixing Prosper's guest with a canny glare. Roz Bengal, ace reporter and sleuth, hot on the trail and as subtle as a game show.

"What amazes me," I said, "is that everyone in this town knows you had your wife killed and won't do anything about it."

"What was that about pictures?" said the man with the tan, his voice congealing like saturated fat.

Cogs in my head slipped out of sync. "What've you got on this one, Prosper? He looks like someone you buy your nose candy from."

There was a long silence. Then the oily rag stood up. "You stupid bitch."

Prosper grabbed his arm. "She's very drunk. Please, just leave."

For a second the man looked as if he would ignore Prosper. Before he walked out he had one more parting shot: "Journalists are like assholes—full of shit."

"Nice twist," I said. "Great friends you have, Prosper. Good grasp of English vernacular for a raghead."

The door slammed. Prosper ran his long artist's fingers through his silvery hair in a ham actor's theatrical gesture of despair. "Roz, Roz. You don't know who you're dealing with. This isn't a game. It isn't Fleet Street."

"Fleet Street doesn't exist anymore," I said, and sat down abruptly on the sofa.

My brother-in-law the murderer, confidant of gangsters, went into the kitchen and made us a pot of very smooth, very strong espresso from Coorg coffee beans so rare that Indians rarely export them. He poured it into two porcelain cups and we drank it without exchanging a word. I had got around to reading my fortune in the coffee grounds before Prosper spoke again.

"What pictures were you talking about, Rosalind? The ones Miranda took of Maya's death? That you mentioned this morning?"

"Have you got them?"

He shook his head. "She couldn't find them."

"Bollocks. But if you want to play cat and mouse, that's fine with me."

We faced each other on the two sofas, divided by an old Kashmiri rug and a mistrust the size of Spain. After a few minutes of this, Prosper leaned forward, closing the distance between us. The theatrical lighting in this apartment smoothed the lines on his face, giving him the Vaseline beauty of a twenties film star, an Indian Valentino. "Miranda told me about your mother's . . . instability . . ." he said, picking his way through the minefield of my family history. "She wants—we both want—this visit to work for you." He said they had talked about taking a long trip with me after the baby was born, showing me India. His voice as smooth and sticky as warm toffee. He was coming dangerously close to making me believe him. "But you don't make it easy, Rosalind. I know it has been a difficult year for you, losing your partner, your father dying, but—"

I stood up abruptly, to break the spell. "Is there such a mundane thing as a telephone in this abode of the great?"

Prosper waved to a heavy old-fashioned phone behind the sofa.

I dialled the ice house. The man who answered told me that Robi had not been called that night. "May I speak to Mistry?" I said, enunciating carefully. "Tell him it's the BBC." It took a few minutes. "Hi, Caleb. Any chance of talking to you about that film you made, *The Cyclone*, and about the work you did on Prosper's *Tempest*? Tonight? Great. I'll be there in about an hour."

"Don't you think you've done enough interviewing for tonight?" Prosper asked when I hung up. "It's late. You'd be better off in bed sooner rather than later."

"Who says I won't be?"

Prosper was much too well-bred a fish to rise to my bait. He said the rain had started again and I would never get a taxi in this neighbourhood, so he called his chauffeur and told him to drop me at Caleb's.

Murderer's Scotch, murderer's car. Does murder wear off in the rain, I wondered, as water-gilt does?

MOST PEOPLE WHO GET SICK IN BOMBAY ASSUME IT'S THE RESULT OF SOME filthy native cooking. They say, "I never *touched* the water! It's full of bacteria." In fact, the poison often comes from a more familiar source. They forget about Bombay ice.

The Moguls used to ship ice from the Himalayas by boat downriver to Lahore, and then by teams of post carriages to Delhi. Twelve pieces of four kilos daily. Imagine the telly ad: red-coated nineteenth-century toff sips his Scotch and calls for ice. Cut to the snow. "More ice, boy!" echoes off the peaks, and thousands of little brown men start hacking off another Himalayan glacier. Two thousand miles and boats, carriages, bearers later, it reaches our gent. The mountain has melted to a molehill. "Damn it, boy," shouts our military man, "I asked for two cubes!"

Ice in the tropics: ultimate symbol of civilization. In Bombay they used to believe that iced water must by definition be pure, regardless of its origins. It was offered as a medicinal drink to guests at bedtime, a hot-climate answer to a warm milk or Horlicks. It looked so clear and cold and Western, so incompatible with India. But that's just packaging. Buried inside is the germ that makes you sick. It's the thing you trust that kills you.

Scotch, beer, and Bombay ice, with a splash of bile. By the time I arrived at Caleb's studio I felt more than slightly nauseated. Unfortunately, the guard must have been off duty: there was no one there to give me a last chance to turn back.

CALEB WAS SITTING IN HIS DIRECTOR'S CHAIR READING A novel called *The Black Dahlia*, the story of its author's obsession with his murdered and mutilated mother. On the floor next to Caleb was a bare mattress stained with what I presumed was stage blood from some recent cinematic violence.

Not until I was quite close did the director look up. "Good book," he said. "Did you know that in murders of extreme passion, a killer always betrays his pathology? According to Vollmer, who wrote one of the textbooks on criminology, if a detective sorts his evidence objectively—blood splatters versus spurts, splashes, pools, smears; patterns of bruising versus laceration marks typically caused by bludgeoning, with strands of skin, tissue, and blood vessels deeply impacted into the bone—and then *thinks* subjectively from the killer's viewpoint, he can often solve crimes that are baffling in their randomness."

"Clearly, it's better to be dispassionate when performing a murder. Is this relevant? You see some crime in my past that baffles you by its randomness?"

He smiled. "Everyone has a crime in their past. I'm interested in blood. You know—blood ties: genes. What Mummy and Daddy are passing on to the kiddies. Whether good wombs can bear bad sons and bad wombs good ones."

"I wish people would stop quoting Shakespeare at me. What d'you think—we spend all our time in Britain strolling around in bowler hats reciting iambic pentameters? Make do on bad days with a few sonnets about the royal family?"

"My old auntie loved the royal family," Caleb said. "She lived in the chawls. First time I went to London, I told her, 'Anything you want, Auntie, a cashmere shawl, the crown jewels, just tell me.' She asked for a signed picture of the Queen, the one with the corgis, circa 1959. That was as high as Auntie's ambitions went. She's dead now."

"So are the corgis."

"You're kidding me—I've seen them in pictures."

"Stuffed."

He laughed. Put the book down. Glanced at the mattress.

"I had a look at Prosper's films," I said quickly. "What was I supposed to find?"

"You didn't recognize anything?"

I shook my head, and felt the Scotch hit the side of my brain with a splash.

"Not much of a film buff, are you? Here's what you missed: the great Prosper Sharma is a fraud. There's not an original bone in his body. Like the rest of us in Bollywood, all his work was born in the West. Only difference: he picks better source material. Check it out. Antonioni's *Zabriskie Point*, De Sica's *Bicycle Thief*, Hitchcock's *Strangers on a Train*—"

"Mistry's *Cyclone*?"

"So you *were* paying attention."

"Why didn't you get distribution?"

"You should've asked Prosper. His chums were largely responsible." He pointed to the bruise on my face. "I heard you had a run-in with some of the quaint local Eve-baiters who think a woman's place is in the home."

"Not quite. I was in the Khajra shrines and some guys grabbed—" I stopped.

"What?"

"Your eyes. The first time we met, I thought they were grey."

"My mother was a blue-eyed hag seduced by a British gentleman. Seduction by the Brits goes a long way back in my family." He waited for a minute, letting this sink in, drawing up a new set of ground rules. Then he took my hand and ran his thumb over my palm and forefinger.

"You don't have a developed mound here. That's a sign of degrading proclivities." He ran his own forefinger very gently over the bruise on my face. "Such pretty white skin for an Indian," he said, "but then you are only half an Indian, aren't you? Or what was it you told me—some curious fraction?" He curved his finger round the cut on my cheek and along my bottom lip to the scab on my lip. "Nice lips," he said, and pressed lightly on the scab. He pressed again, harder, until I felt the scab split and blood slip out. It was an odd sensation.

"Blood of Rosalind," Caleb said, "pure blue. I wonder what blue blood tastes of?" He licked the blood off his finger.

"Not pure blue," I said.

I want to rewrite the next hour. Shoot it over again, blur the explicit Western camerawork, take out the tits and ass and cunt and dick and the smell of sweat. I want Satyajit Ray's sensibility: a long, slow shot of the couple silhouetted behind mosquito netting. Ray said of his love scenes that if he went in for close-ups and lit the action more clearly, catcalls from the lower stalls would ruin his delicate mood-setting sound track of shrilling crickets and distant howling jackals.

When Caleb had finished licking his finger, he said, "Shall I be your guru? Let's begin at the beginning." He told me what he was going to do first and then he did it. When I asked him not to, he did it anyway. No man has ever talked to me so unrelentingly while he made love. If you can call it that. Sometimes talking can be a kind of sadism, and listening can be purely masochistic. Most of the things we did I never want to do again.

The camera executes mainly pan shots, picking out with almost studied unconcern moments of extreme but controlled pain and pleasure. The rhythm is elaborated further in a study of textures: hardness alternating with a lingering softness, penetration with reception, a rhythmic tension in a harsh grey light that gives a sense of foreboding.

After it was all over, I lay on the mattress in the damp odours and the snail trails, feeling cold and emptied, as you do after vomiting, a sour taste in my mouth. Nothing of me left. It's what I looked for: a rinsing of memory. That sense of someone else choosing the close-ups and the long shots.

Caleb pulled on his jeans and lay back, crossing his arms behind his neck. A mouth like a Rajput's moustache, permanently curled up at the corners.

"You see?" he said. "If it's done well, there's hardly any blood."

The skin on his chest had a gloss of sweat on it. I didn't know whether to lick him or spit on him. I rolled over on my stomach and crossed my arms underneath, pulling in my extremities, presenting a hard carapace. This is the glue, I thought: the fight, the scars; not the gentle interlude. Crime and punishment, they go together like love and marriage.

"I didn't like that," I said. "I think I'll go now."

He laughed. "Not bad for a first audition, but no screen test. You played that line too much like one of those Hindi screen heroines, a curious combination of the modern and the traditional. At first they are very sensual, very uninhibited in front of men. Then, at a crucial moment, they switch over to being a virtuous lover of all the traditional values. I find them tedious."

I sat up with my back to him. "Shall I tell you the real problem? The problem is that in India a woman has no identity separate from her prescribed role as mother/sister/wife/daughter. The only way she can have her own identity is to reject sex. She then becomes an enigma. She's on her way to being deified."

"So now you want me to treat you like a goddess? Very good: in most Hindi films there is a comic turn after the melodrama. But frankly, you don't have the looks for an Indian goddess; you need at least three more pairs of arms and legs. Or a longer tongue." He smiled. "At least that could be useful. Would you like a bit of Krishna's flute music now? Shall we sing a duet? Every crucial turn of Indian love life in the movies has a suitable song. Like Greek melodrama: that's the kind of fact Prosper quotes to arty film magazines. I quote box office."

"Did your box office improve when Maya died?"

Caleb rolled off the bed and walked across the studio to pour a drink. Leaning against the makeshift bar, he said, "If you go round making accusations—"

"Did Prosper phone you after I left him?"

"—you could wind up in a lot of trouble. Everyone here has to do business with people whose methods you might not approve of. It's the way things are in this city. Think of Bombay as Palermo or Atlantic City: the mafia is in charge here and politics is dictated along their lines. You do what you're told or you're dead."

"I'm sure I've read that in the *Lonely Planet Guide*. Or maybe it was an old movie. Now I'm supposed to speak out of the side of my mouth and say something like 'I go where I want to, with anyone I want. I happen to be that kind of girl. It took more than one man to change my name to Bombay Lil.' "

He looked as if he would like to hit me. "You don't understand Bombay."

"So everyone keeps saying. Try a new tune: 'You don't understand Einstein's last theory, or Kierkegaard's concept of irony.' But Bombay, for God's sake."

"I forgot. You're familiar with violence. Your sister said you used to work in pop music. Sex, drugs, and rock-and-roll. All those televisions out of windows."

"You obviously haven't been to London recently," I said. "Things have gone downhill since then. Musicians now are vegans terrified of AIDS. The only people they're violent towards are smokers, journalists, and makers of faulty condoms."

He laughed, and the tension between us eased up. "So let me give you a little advice. I know something about this Sami you're worried about. She was turning tricks for the rough guys around Great Palace Street, the hijra prostitution area. After a while she started shacking up with one of them, playing wifee. These guys can't tell a toilet from a soup bowl, and some of them who look like they've got their heads above the slime are just scumbags in suits. Sami's friend gave her lots of expensive stuff. Then she shafted him."

I thought of the gaudy litter in the hijra bathhouse. "For someone on the periphery of this story, you know an awful lot."

"I used to be connected."

"Weren't your contacts more specific about why Sami was killed?"

"I'm trying to warn you off, not get you more involved." He took a mouthful of rum and rolled it around his tongue. "Your sister's worried about you."

"My sister! What—"

"And she's not the only one who's told me you've been acting as if you know something that could hurt people in high places. What are you doing it for? A woman who killed herself six years ago and who no one mourns? Or for some eunuch whore who was selling her ass for drugs?"

"There were no needle tracks on Sami's arms."

"Whatever. You've got proof she wasn't killed for mouthing off to her pimp?"

"Call it a hunch."

"That's not the impression you've been giving. And Sami's friends wouldn't think twice about slashing you with a razor, then pouring on the acid. It's all in a day's work. Ever seen what acid does to a face?"

"Do you know who did it?"

He shook his head, not so much denial as disbelief. "You think *I'm* involved?"

"Are you?"

"I know the kind of people who do this kind of thing. Listen to me, Roz, and try to take in what I'm saying. For years, India was the only country in the world where a statement made to the police—outside or even inside the police station—was *not* valid in a court of law. There used to be a club near Chowpatty that was opened in 1971 by a scumbag called Bondi. His chums could drop in whenever and for whatever they liked—child sodomy, snuff porn, coke—as long as they first produced a promissory note to prove solvency, signed—wait for this—*by the Governor of the Reserve Bank*. Entrance to this exclusive club required sponsorship, of course: by a half-dozen of their fellow rapists and pimps. This was *known*, Rosalind—it went on for years. Very few policemen tried to stop it. One of the ones who did was returning from his prayers on a motorcycle along Grant Road when he found an iron bed blocking his path. He gets down to move it, someone slits his throat. Middle of a crowded street, no one sees a thing."

"Great story. What happened—the club blackball you for bad behaviour?"

Caleb poured another drink. "You want to start a one-woman campaign to clean up the city, fine. My advice is to stick to lifestyle stories with more style and less risk of sudden death. Or go back home and clean up your own city."

"I was born in India." But not *this* India, I thought.

"So learn to live by the rules. And if you've got hold of something you think is ammunition, get rid of it . . . before it goes off in your face."

"Maybe I'll just load it up and point it." I started to pull on my clothes.

Behind me, the door to the ice house opened and shut: three men, two of them carrying machetes, the tallest wearing a green demon's mask.

"Studio's closed," said Caleb.

"My my my, what have we here—the bitch in her lair?" the tall man said, his voice muffled by the mask. "Do you feel the heat? I think it's getting hotter." He unbuttoned his silk shirt down to the Gucci leather belt at his waist. Elegant brown leather shoes buffed to a liquid shine.

The other two men were small and feral, with the narrow muscular limbs and concave chests of Indians born on the street. The kind of men who will never live to be fat. One of them carried a roll of wide adhesive tape.

"Machetes?" I said. "What is this—the fucking *Jungle Book*?" It's hard to sound tough with your knickers round your ankles, but I did my best.

The tall man nodded at the man with the tape, who stuck the machete in his belt and limped over to bind Caleb's wrists. Then he did the same to me, first pulling my arms viciously behind my back and wrapping my wrists so tightly that the veins in my arms started to pound. He smelled of oily flowers, coconut milk, and garlic. He pulled the machete out and ran it over my pubic hair.

"Nice," he said. Caleb cursed and started forward.

"Easy, easy, Mistry," said the tall man. "Nothing is going to get out of control."

"Give her some clothes," said Caleb.

"She'd only get them messed up, then, wouldn't she?"

"They know where I am at the hotel," I said. "I left a message there."

"We are going to walk out of here," said Caleb. "The guard on the gate will hear and set off the alarm. A million people will be here in minutes."

"Seems your guard got paid some overtime and took the rest of the night off," the tall man said. "And that night watchman finally got enough saved up to buy himself a ticket home to visit his family in Madras."

"This is ridiculous," I said. "You can't hold a BBC journalist and the head of a studio like this. Who do you think you are?" I started walking towards the door. It wasn't courage that made me do it. Stupidity, maybe, or an inability to take the scene seriously. It was too badly staged: the mask, the machetes.

One of the men raised his machete and swung it against the side of my head. I fell with all my weight onto one shoulder. My arm went numb. Blood from my ear ran down into my mouth. The man with the machete stood over me, holding his knife loosely in one hand between his legs, as if he were holding his dick. Miles away I saw Caleb being pushed across the studio to the back room.

"You shits," I said. The man kicked me.

"Who do you think *you* are?" said the tall man. "Running around mouthing off to everyone, like you have a dick between your legs. You're not a fucking cop."

"You're not Indian," I said.

"You think? Personally, I'm not nationalistic. I like to think of myself as an international businessman. A citizen of the world. No fixed abode. Right now I like Bombay. It's a real frontier town, a ripe mango, and everyone wants a bite. Ideal for development. Great beaches."

"You'll have to get rid of all the shit and poor people first."

"That's what I like about this place. Give an Indian half a chance and he'll grab it and haul himself out of the muck. Bombay people know there's no Big Brother waiting to pick them up if they fall. My friends here, they're local boys, they understand shit and poverty. They clawed their way out of it and they don't want to fall back in and drown. They're old-fashioned, though. They like women who do what they're told. Me, I like a bit of a struggle. Like you and Mr. Mistry."

"You watched us."

"To pass the time until we made sure no junior artistes turned up. Now you just tell me where Sunila has gone with Sami's pictures and we'll all be happy."

"Who's Sunila?"

"That's not the right answer, girlie. But I saw the kind of games you like. B? I call these guys B and C because their names are so fucking dumb."

B came out of the back room and locked it. He was carrying a bucket that was too heavy for him. C went to help. "I am having to add water," B said. They dropped the bucket down in front of me and it sloshed red liquid onto the floor.

"Don't you worry, now. Your lover-boy is okay. It's just stage blood," said the tall man.

"I don't believe this. A bucket of blood? Are you *serious*?"

"It's a colourful touch, don't you think? I could've been in movies. You won't know which is your blood and which is fake. It's the thought that counts."

"You've got to work on your dialogue," I said, wondering whom I was fooling with this hard-boiled act. Certainly not myself.

He nodded at B and C, and they grabbed my arms, sending a band of shooting pain across my collarbone. They hauled me onto my knees in front of the bucket. One of them thrust his hand into my hair, wrenched my head backwards, and plunged it into the bucket. I forgot to shut my eyes. Everything went red.

They hauled me out again.

"Not a pretty sight on such a pretty lady," said the tall man. "But maybe I shouldn't call you a lady after what I saw tonight. And you like to act like you've got a dick, don't you? You know, when an Indian boy wants to be an Indian girl, they have to cut off all his goodies. There's a lot of blood then too." He paused to let me think about that. "They don't use doctors. Another hijra called a midwife does the cutting. Funny, isn't it? They even give the patient a forty-day recovery period, just like they do when a woman gives birth. They have to be very careful because of the risk of infection, so they rub sesame oil into the wound." He pulled the lining out of his pockets in a comic gesture. "Sorry! All out of sesame oil!"

"What has this got to do with Sami?" I was trying to stay calm, but my teeth started to chatter as I spoke.

"Oh, Sami's part of it, but that's still not the right answer." He nodded to B.

"But I don't *know* anything!"

They pushed my head into the red bucket again. This time they held me down for longer. I tried to concentrate on holding my breath. Strange ideas floating in my head. Such as: it doesn't take a lot to drown a person. Dennis Nilson killed two of his victims by getting them drunk and drowning them in buckets. Death is much faster in fresh water than in salt, due to the short time "pure" water needs to dilute the circulating blood and reduce its capacity to carry oxygen.

When they hauled my head up I was retching and blowing red bubbles out of both nostrils. The watery stage blood had filled my eyes like red tears.

"Seeing red?" said the man in the mask. Big laugh. "We can keep this up for longer than you can. Next time you'll be under a lot longer and you'll start seeing more than colours. That's when you forget to hold your breath. If that doesn't work, my friends here have got methods you might find more persuasive."

He nodded to the other man. I went under for the third time.

When I was a child swimming off the Malabar Coast, the divers there taught me how to hyperventilate so I could hold my breath like a seal underwater. I would dive down into the sea until it pressed against my lungs and eardrums and forced me back to the surface straining for air. Once I stayed down for three minutes. But I was young then. Even so, if I was down too long, there would be this same feeling that the surface was miles away, that I should just let go and become part of it. Breathe in the fish, the weed, the blue, the red. The tiny skeleton. My mother's open mouth. And then the roaring of a reluctant sea like giant conch shells in my ears as I struggled back up to the light.

"Fuck," said the tall man. "Who set off the siren?"

B crashed into the bucket and knocked me onto my shoulder again as the three men ran out of the studio. Red liquid poured out around me. I lay in the middle, pink and drained as a stuck pig. Footsteps and men's voices in the distance. Too tired to do anything. Bone tired. Blood tired. My thoughts splattered like the rain that was bringing the

168 / LESLIE FORBES

summer smell of wet dust through a leak in the roof, I heard the shrill cry of a bird, then my father's voice: "*Clamator Jacobinus*, the pied crested cuckoo, who every year sails the monsoon winds across the Indian Ocean from Africa a few days ahead of the rain." I remembered the meteorologist Dr. S. K. Bannerji, who proved that a westerly stream of air could not climb over the Western Ghats unless it was fed by some other source of energy.

The footsteps stopped. A familiar voice said, "My God!"

I opened my eyes and blinked to clear them. "Hi, Ashok." The green demon's mask grinned up at me. "It's what you call a real bloodbath." I started to giggle. "Don't worry, most of it's not mine."

Vacation in India, Land of Contrasts. From P. G. Wodehouse to *Titus Andronicus*, no change of scenery.

THE MESSAGE GARBLED BY THE OPERATOR HAD BEEN TO SAY that Ashok was coming by the hotel later to drop off a book. When he didn't hear from me, he rang the hotel again and they gave him Prosper's number. Prosper had sent him here.

Ashok cut the tape on my hands and wrapped a sheet around me. "The driver is ringing the police," he said.

"Caleb Mistry is somewhere back there," I managed to say before drifting off. By the time I was conscious again, two policemen had arrived and I could see Caleb answering their questions and rubbing his wrists. From time to time he glanced over to where I sat with Ashok.

Then it was my turn. The police asked why I had come to the studio so late. Hearing that it was for an interview with Caleb, they exchanged smirks. Did I know the reason for the attack? It was to do with the hijra called Sami, I told them, and pictures I didn't know anything about belonging to a person I'd never heard of called Sunila. They asked if I had recognized my attackers.

"There was a man with a limp. He had a bandage on his foot. The guy in charge called him B or C. I think he may have been one of the men who attacked me at the cave. Three days ago. I stabbed his foot with an umbrella."

"An umbrella." The police stopped taking notes. It seemed ridiculous, even to me. "And the other two men?"

"The tall one wasn't Indian. His voice seemed familiar. I'm good at voices. But I'm really not sure—under the mask . . ." It sounded feeble. "But it must've been someone who understood the studio system—"

One of the policemen laughed, stopping abruptly when Ashok frowned.

"Why is he laughing, Ash? He didn't let me finish."

The second policeman was less intimidated by Ashok. "He laughs because every rickshaw driver in Bombay understands studio system. This is a movie city."

After a few more fairly fruitless questions and answers, they told me I could go.

"I'll take you to my house," Ashok said. "You shouldn't be alone tonight."

"Do you think the police can do anything?"

"Our best chance of catching the men who did this is if they are known criminals, with traceable addresses. Although given your description . . . And, if they *are* known criminals, there may be other difficulties."

"Like what?"

His mouth tightened and it was clear he was reluctant to answer. "I must be honest with you. There are politicians here who use criminals to get work done faster than could be done legally. If your attackers have that kind of backing, they can move from one safe house to another every night and the police will have barriers put up in front of them that are difficult to break down."

I saw him assessing my nakedness under the sheet and trying to frame a question the police hadn't asked. He settled the problem obliquely. "How is your shoulder—are you sure it's not dislocated? You should see a doctor."

"I'm fine, Ashok. They didn't do anything except rough me up." To diagnose death by drowning is one of the hardest tasks in forensic medicine.

ASHOK'S LIVING ROOM HAD ALMOST AS MANY BOOKS AS HIS LIBRARY, BUT AT least he had left space here for a couple of chairs and a table. "I have no air con," he said apologetically. "I usually carry my charpoy onto the verandah on these hot nights before the monsoon. If you wish to do that, I'll close the bamboo blinds, so the peacocks don't disturb you. They mate during this season and the rattle of their tails can be as noisy as a room full of ladies with ivory fans."

"Where will you sleep?"

"I'll make up a bed here on the sofa while you have a bath. Then I'll cook us a snack. You should eat." He gave me a towel and a fresh bar of sandalwood soap and some of his cotton pyjamas, neatly folded and smelling of fresh herbs.

But even after the bath, my clean surface was only a thin shell around something that couldn't be washed off. Seeing Ashok sitting up in his big chair made me feel as if I were entering a courtroom. He would have looked even more like a judge if it hadn't been for the pot of tea and two cups next to him.

"Rosalind," he said, after I had sunk into the sofa, "you didn't tell the police the whole truth. I could see it in your face."

Yeah, Ashok, I was shagging Caleb just before the bad guys turned up and they had a grandstand seat. "I'm sure Prosper was involved," I said. The musky smell of black cardamom floated towards me from my cup. "The man in the mask . . . he might have been a friend of Prosper's I met tonight. I have to warn Miranda, get her out of this situation." That man in the same house as my little sister.

"Why on earth didn't you tell the police?"

"Did you see how they looked at me? As if I were making it all up? And Indian police are not famous for inspiring trust and loyalty." The teacup slipped in my fingers and I watched its contents stain the rug. "I'm sorry," I said.

Ashok came over to sit on the sofa next to me. "No, *I'm* sorry, Rosalind. You know how I feel about . . . your family." The hesitation as light as a gold leaf drawn over my skin. "It's been too rough a night to subject you to another interrogation." He took my hand in both of his, the first time he had touched me since I was a child, Indians not being great hand-shakers and face-peckers. I had forgotten the strength in his hands and arms.

As if aware of my thoughts, Ashok let go of me and stood up. "Perhaps I've lived too much with books," he said. "Since my wife died and the boys were married, I've built walls of words—cities of words." His eyes took in the room, and he sighed, the air so still I felt the weight of his breath on my skin. He brushed past me and walked over to stare into the dark garden.

The rasping fiddle of the frogs almost drowned his next words. "You know I was in Kashmir when the troubles started there in the late eighties? My wife wasn't well, we had taken a houseboat on the lake because the doctor said the air would do her good. Five years earlier, my wife had given twenty-five thousand of her family's books to a school in Srinagar, Kashmir's capital. Some of them had been in her family since the ninth century. Her ancestors were travelling scribes and teachers, and when they had no ink or parchment, they wrote in blood on leaves and carried the manuscripts throughout the Himalayas, reading the old stories to the people of those remote places. I loved her books like old friends. I used to go to the school to look at them. Many were illuminated with paintings—one-offs, irreplaceable.

"When the real fighting started in Srinagar, I knew we would have to get out. The Indian police were shooting at shadows, the Muslims were running in gangs up and down the streets smashing windows, starting fires in Hindu shops. There were rapes of schoolgirls, beatings, all the atrocities that erupt when this usually peaceful country lets go of its control. Partition all over again. Finally, I got us tickets on a flight to Delhi. On the day we were to leave, one of the Muslim boat boys, who was a friend of my family, came running to say that a gang was threatening to burn the library. He took me to the school. There was smoke everywhere. Some of the teachers had been badly beaten. Instead of helping them I ran to the library. Boys were pulling books off the shelves, tearing pages out, urinating on them, lighting them with torches. I tried to make them see that it was their own history as well as my family's they were destroying."

"A gun would've been useful."

"I don't believe in guns. It's just that I was the wrong man for the job." His Adam's apple moved as if he were trying to swallow. "Perhaps I made it worse, standing there and talking while they laughed at me and burned a thousand years of scholarship. I stood there all night, long after our plane to Delhi had gone, watching the fire, doing nothing. The next morning, when I went back to the boat and told my wife, she turned away. She said the boys had burned her family when they burned the books. She died not long after. She was dying anyway. But I shouldn't have told her."

"Who burned the library—Muslims or Hindus?"

"There were injustices on both sides. Those boys are part of a pattern which one cannot alter by eliminating a few threads. It would be like trying to change the weather. You with your interest in storms must have heard of Edward Lorenz?"

I admitted that I had. "He created a machine which reduced meteorological patterns to a series of numbers on a screen," I said.

Ashok nodded. Like a pat on my head. "And realized that while one could change a weather pattern, the act of changing it would prevent discovery of how it would have turned out without such interference."

"I'm sure the people whose lives are wrecked in tropical storms would prefer to forgo the pleasure of knowing what it's like to be hit in the face by a flying sofa."

"Perhaps." Ashok moved his head from side to side in that very Indian gesture, neither acceptance nor denial. "Yet by diverting a cyclone one creates only a local pocket of order, while increasing the risk of disorder elsewhere."

I had spent too many years with my mother not to recognize a gilder's touch. It made me wonder what unpleasant truth Ashok was gilding with his expert storytelling. "Was the moral of your library tale that my sister would be happier not knowing her husband had me beaten up?"

"You have no evidence that Prosper was involved. And there are certain situations we have to walk away from. Why not let others do their job?"

"Like the police?" I laughed. His words beat Dad's old Hindu gong of tolerance that I found so foreign. Mum's family had bequeathed me an earthier identity: an eye for an eye, never turn the other cheek, a good offence is the best defence. Yet half of me had watched and listened and accepted for years and not acted. My mother's act of leaving India had neatly split me in two. "I'm starting to get hungry," I said.

Ashok smiled. "You must be feeling better. Fortunately, I know how to cook. My father insisted that good cooking was the sign of a civilized man."

"Do you have any bad habits, Ashok?"

"Remind me to tell you about them when we're both less tired."

I followed him into the big kitchen, enjoying the coolness of its tiled floors on my bare feet and the faint brown scent of spices that hung in the air.

Ashok selected an ivory-white cauliflower from a basket. He heated some mustard oil in a karahi and separated the florets of the cauliflower as carefully as if he were arranging lilies, adding a teaspoon of shot-grey mustard seeds to the hot oil and slapping the lid down as they started to explode. They smelled of popcorn, the smell of my father's southern kitchen. A clove of garlic and a thumb of peeled fresh ginger were crushed to a paste in a rough stone mortar with some coarse salt, then stirred into the pan with the cauliflower and a little water. He covered the pan again, all his movements sure and unhurried. At the last minute he threw in a handful of grated fresh coconut that had been sitting in a metal bowl with a piece of muslin over the top.

Hands broad across the palm with long, strong fingers and beautiful nails. I wondered what they would feel like on my back.

"The cook is asleep," Ashok said. "I hope you don't mind having rotis left over from my tea. They can heat up in the oven while this cauliflower is cooking."

We sat at a low table in the living room to eat, and Ashok talked about the film festival that was showing one of his documentaries in two days' time.

"They want me to give a speech before the film . . . I'd like it very much if you would come." He paused, then changed the subject abruptly. "Your father was a great inspiration to me. Do you remember the stories he used to tell you?"

I shook my head and concentrated on scooping some cauliflower onto my roti. "My memories of that time are very liquid, hard to pin down. I remember the elephants, and the smell of the sea off the coast, and our wooden house on the plantation. And that we had to travel by boat, boats like gondolas with black-skinned gondoliers in white dhotis." The contrast between black and white.

Ashok nodded. "When I first came to visit your father, it seemed there was water everywhere, and you were always in it. Even in the monsoon, you wanted to swim." He smiled. "I suppose you know why he called you Rosalind?"

"I thought it was Mum's choice."

"Your father was a great lover of old English pastorals. And he'd read that Shakespeare based Rosalind in *As You Like It* on an earlier Rosalynde."

"Another cross-dresser?"

"She was the heroine of a sonnet that Thomas Lodge wrote on a privateering expedition to the Canary Islands: . . . *hatcht in the stormes of the Ocean, and feathered in the surges of many perillous seas.* Like you."

"I remember that what you thought was firm ground in Kerala often turned out to be floating weed. Step on it and you were up to your neck in shit."

Ashok flinched. "You seem angry with me about something, Rosalind."

"I don't like to romanticize history. Dad told me once that I was like the monsoon. I figured it reflected his ambivalence about me, the way Indians feel both joyous and anxious about the monsoon's arrival. He said that the poetic mood of the rains is *viraha*, the torments of estrangement. Like the estrangement of my parents after I came between them."

"I can't believe your father meant such a thing."

"Can't you?" I knew how much Ashok had admired my father. Why did I want to puncture that balloon. "Dad was very fond of pontificating about the evils of capitalism and Western society. 'What is the point of having two houses when a man can only live in one at a time?' he would say. One day he was going on about this as usual, sitting on the verandah with Mum and Miranda and me, and I said, 'But you always had two houses, Dad, and you managed to live in both. The secret is to have two wives as well.' It was during the monsoon, I remember. During the monsoon the land around our house was always threatening to turn back into sea. The garden used to flood, and snakes would often swim up onto the verandah."

"What did your father say to this?"

"You mean when he slipped away from his wife in the big house to be with his mistress?" Mum's words in my mouth. I pushed my plate away and took a sip of water, letting the coolness trickle slowly down my throat. Ashok waited.

"Dad told me not to fear snakes, but to treat them with respect. In fact, I liked them. Not for any religious reason—I liked them because they always went their own way and everyone stepped aside. The gardener found me playing with a cobra one year and killed it with his machete. Dad was furious. I guess he felt my life was no more precious than the snake's."

"I'm sure that's not true, Rosalind."

"What I remember best about Kerala is the leaving of it. Mum taking me back to Scotland." And Dad letting her. "Because it was driving her mad."

"It wasn't easy for her. She was more Scottish than Indian. I suspect you are too. You certainly look it."

I was tired of talking. My hair, still wet from the bath, had flopped forward over my face. Ash leaned over and tucked it behind my ear, brushing the side of my cheek with his fingertips. I waited for his next move. The antivenin.

The great screen lover Raj Kapoor got around these awkward moments by having the two lovers staring into each other's eyes, and experiencing the agony and longing in them, then moving apart at the crucial moment. Immediate cut to two swans or two flowers or two birds to indicate a kiss.

But nothing happened. I was always misreading signals in this damned country. Ashok stood up and stretched his long, narrow body backwards, as if pulling away from an invisible brink. "We're both tired. I hope you'll be all right on the verandah. Good night, Rosalind. Sleep well."

I DIDN'T SLEEP; I PLAYED TIC-TAC-TOE INSTEAD: PROSPER; CALEB; ASHOK. MY sister, the mother. And thought about history, that map of the past we rewrite to suit the roads we wish to follow. Like a map, history protects our sense of who we are while linking us to something bigger than ourselves. History is simply the stories we inherit.

Each mother passes on to her children the sins of her fathers. One of the lessons my mother drummed into me when we moved back to the widow's house in Scotland was that I was never to be caught alone in a small room with Granddad's twin, Alex. Every few months Alex would come from Glasgow to visit Gran, and I would watch the tension in my mother increase. Years later, Mum told me that what she really feared was Alex's face, the mannerisms he shared with Granddad. If they shared those things, what other, less innocent things did they share?

As part of the cure for her affliction (our affliction), my mother was asked by her shrink to do a self-portrait, like one of those naïve body-maps anorexics produce to compare their real and imagined silhouettes. But my mother was an artist, so her paintings were gouache miniatures of her hands, her feet, her head, her genitals—all on separate pieces of paper, the parts never joining up into a whole. No complete portrait exists. After she died, I taped her paintings together into a loose humanoid shape. A graphic violation, a portrait done with a meat cleaver, like something by Francis Bacon.

Let us consider a subject who finds any show of love or kindness suspect, who believes all sensation to be fraudulent—other than pain. Only pain is real: you can *see* the results. The child of an abusive parent becomes an abuser in turn, or a self-mutilator, or at least learns the art of manipulating others, as my mother did. The abuser claims the child has led him on: the child's complicity is proof.

In my mother's youth, incest wasn't a subject discussed in front of the children.

Consider Britain and India: empire as incest. If it is true we wind up nursing our parents through a second childhood, is Britain the mother, or India?

My mother used to tell stories of how influential her father had been. It was years before I learned that he was a butcher, the first to use chill-cabinets to display the results of his butchery. She grew up in one of those cabinets, each part of her neatly sliced and labelled for his future consumption. She simply rewrote her history. But that's what gilders do: cover truth in glitter to increase its value.

My father represented another side of India. Like the Rajput prince Jai Singh, who between 1728 and 1734 designed the largest stone-built astronomical observatory in the world (including a sundial accurate to within two minutes), my father was one of that great tradition of Indians who put their faith in numbers. Some were clerks. Some calculated auspicious days for marriage. He mapped meteorological chaos on a computer. One of the first things he taught me was that it was India who gave the West its numerical system. Numbers had names in Sanskrit, he said, so they could be easily remembered in the form of verse: arithmetic poetry recited like sums under a banyan tree.

What form of abuse, what repetitive sequence of events, turned India into a country of storytellers and computer scientists and clerks?

My mother's story was always the same: a person who started drowning at age ten and was going down for the third time. From her I learned that sickness is a habit that can be acquired like any other. A certain kind of sex can give you the rush and scars of heroin. It establishes a pattern, lets loose the snakes. Nothing is ever the same again without it. No one can ever love you the way Daddy did.

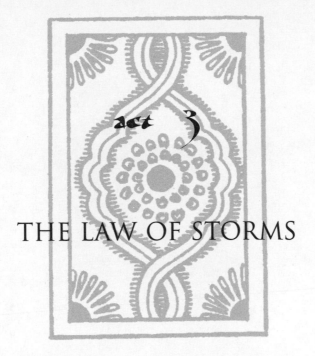

act 3

THE LAW OF STORMS

The wind in a cyclone has two motions. It blows round a
centre in a more or less circular form, and at the same
time has a motion forward, so that, like a whirlwind, it is
both turning round and rolling ahead at the same time.

—CAPTAIN HENRY PIDDINGTON,
The Sailor's Hornbook for the Law of Storms

1

I T WAS THE RATTLING OF A PEACOCK'S TAIL THAT WOKE ME, OR perhaps the stripes of sun through the slatted blinds. From inside the house soft voices floated out, and soon a barefoot woman appeared with a cup of tea and a note from Ashok:

> I am sorry not to be there when you wake but I have an early appointment. I hope you found the tea with black cardamom a good antidote for a hangover. We must discuss other results of yesterday's events.

I cleaned up and walked out towards the road, hearing once again the snake charmer's slippery flute notes, and thinking of the story I had told Ashok the night before, and of what I had not told, of the day our gardener in Kerala found me sitting cross-legged on the verandah watching a cobra that had come up out of our flooded garden to find a new, dry home. Both snake and I weaving rhythmically in a strange dance of mutually hypnotic fascination. He was a long snake, muscular and thick through the body, and I recognized him from the year before. After the gardener had killed him, I asked for a piece of the skeleton. It sits on my mantel at home in London, one long curve of vertebrae, a reminder of that lost garden.

I GOT BACK TO THE HOTEL IN THE EARLY AFTERNOON TO FIND THAT MY SISTER had left several messages. She sounded very strained when I rang.

"Where *are* you, Roz? I've been so worried!"

"You heard what happened at Caleb Mistry's?"

"That's what I was calling about. Prosper told me what you'd said to him last night, and then I rang Caleb—"

I interrupted her. "Miranda, did you and Prosper talk about taking a long trip with me after the baby is born?"

"Yes, this morning," she said, her voice puzzled by the change of topic. "Why?"

"Just this morning? Not before? I only wondered why you hadn't mentioned it at Breach Candy."

"No, it was this morning. He said it would do us all good, after such a bad year. Why?" One of those long pauses into which the listener reads too many things. Then: "Both Prosper and Caleb told me you seemed determined to continue with this hijra story."

"Did Prosper tell you about the charming guest he had last night?"

"I don't know the man who was at the flat," Miranda said quickly, "but Prosper says he's a client who is—who *was*—going to invest in *The Tempest*."

"If that's where Prosper is getting his money, I'm not surprised you've been having nightmares."

"Prosper can't get hold of him anywhere. He seems to have disappeared."

"What a gaping hole that will make in this thriving metropolis."

"Prosper is very worried. It could mean the loss of his studio."

"I grieve for him. But excuse me if I prefer straightforward thugs who don't try to introduce you to their analysts. Give me a nice, honest psychopath any time."

"You can't mean Prosper?"

I found it difficult to adjust to her change of tune. "Is this the same wife-murderer you wrote me about, Miranda?"

"I shouldn't have done that."

"Why did you, then?"

"I don't know. I haven't got many friends, none I could tell that kind of thing to. Most of them are Prosper's . . . Anyway, you didn't write back for weeks. And by the time you arrived, I knew it was all a mistake."

"What if I get you proof?"

"Proof of what?"

"Proof that he killed his first wife, or at least was responsible for her murder."

"I don't want proof. Prosper is my husband. He will be my child's father."

Again we listened to each other's silence, while I puzzled over the strange wording of her last sentence. Was it intentional? Or just another misread signal?

"If you love—if you care for me at all, Roz, you'll stop this."

I had my answer: Keep off. The line was still drawn between us. But I couldn't let go. "There's no such thing as past tense when it comes to murder, Miranda. Once a killer, always a killer. Murder requires some form of retribution." Even if it's self-inflicted. "I know marriage is all about ten percent promise and ninety percent compromise, but murder is quite a compromise. I hope he doesn't snore as well." I wondered if she'd been pushed far enough to give an honest response. "If I get you the proof—"

She stopped me before I could take the next step. "I can't take any more of this." Her voice had the furry sound that told me she was close to tears. "Perhaps we should . . . wait a little while before we see each other again."

"We've only seen each other once since I got here."

"Perhaps we both need time to think."

"About what? Your husband or his ex—"

She cut in: "It's not how I imagined it would be. You coming back. I'm so sorry, Rosalind, I'm really very sorry." And hung up.

MY SCREEN LOVER'S EYES STARED INTO THE ROOM, DARK CARDBOARD POOLS IN the magenta face of a larger-than-life hero, the kind of a guy who would know exactly how to handle this situation. It was easy for him. All he had to do was read his script.

In the script for a good Hindu girl the first lines read "Loyalty to family." Which includes brother-in-laws. I glanced at the phone, that subtle instrument of torture, wondering if I should call Miranda back. Apologize, promise to stick to sisterly subjects in future: shopping, babies, the joys of motherhood. Maybe launch into a monologue on flower arranging and macramé.

Scribbled on the pad next to the phone was the Tilak Foundation's number from Ram. I picked up the phone and rang the man called Jay.

For who can say with absolute conviction what our dharma is, or what it takes to make a family. Six months one summer when you're thirteen? A week? Or the brief glimpse of Sami's shadowy figure, half-finished, like the figures she had painted on Bina's mud wall? I had seen my sister as a sort of causeway into a happier part of my family history. The truth was that the causeway had a tollgate on it, and I wasn't sure that I wanted to pay the price.

JAY COULDN'T TELL ME MUCH ABOUT THE *RAMAYANA* ON THE NIGHT SAMI WAS killed, only that it had been a dance drama with a group of itinerant performers whose numbers swelled and receded like the tide. "Sometimes they work for movies, sometimes for festivals," he said, and most used stage names.

A list of the Tilak Foundation's sponsors was easier; they were printed on the annual report. Thirty or so names, from Anwar and Bhat to Vivekananda. As Bombay's roll call of race and religion marched past, I stared out the window at the place where the horizon should have been. But the sea and sky had merged into one solid grey mat the colour of roofing felt.

"Sorry, could you repeat those last few names again?" I said.

"Santiago, José. Sharma, Prosper."

"What about Anthony Unmann?"

"One of our English sponsors, yes," said Jay. "A most generous man. Even today he is down at the Hindu temple near Haji Ali Quay. He has given money to restore the gold jewellery on the gods there and he is seeing to the work."

2

I T WAS LOW TIDE, BUT THE WATER WAS CHOPPY AND DIRTY WITH hidden turbulence, as littered with floating debris as Brighton beach after a bank holiday weekend. The waves kept breaking hard against the long causeway leading to Haji Ali's tomb, splashing the hundreds of beggars where they squatted patiently waiting for alms and rice from the Muslim pilgrims coming to pay homage to the saint. The money changers at the start of the causeway, who, for a small commission, would change single rupees into paise, so that charity could be measured out in minute proportions, cursed as each wave threatened to turn their miserable profits into papier-mâché.

At one time this area, The Flats, had been part of the drowned lands separating Bombay's islands, although there is a map drawn just ten years after the British arrived—long before major land reclamation had begun—which shows it as firm ground, all the islands joined into one, as if the cartographer had simply raised Bombay's cupped hand out of the sea and poured away what liquid was left.

Walking west past the Japanese Embassy towards Mahalakshmi, a temple on the very edge of what once had been the Great Breach, I spotted Unmann long before I got to the temple entrance. With his expensive clothes and well-fed, glossy finish, he stood out in the sea of small brown men like a great white shark in a school of pomfret. As I got closer, I saw him touch the shoulder of a slim boy in a white dhoti. He kept touching the boy's shoulder in a proprietary way. One more part of India to be consumed.

Unmann looked up at my approach, and his urbane smile slipped a few millimetres before he could drag it back. "Miss Benegal, what a surprise."

"I hurried down here as soon as the Tilak Foundation told me what you were doing. I hadn't realized you were a philanthropist as well as an art dealer."

He had his smile more under control this time. "Come in and have a look." We kicked off our shoes. "Do you know anything about gilding?"

"My mother was a gilder."

"I'd forgotten. Your interests range so widely. Crime, smuggling, the weather—"

"Forgery."

"Forgery as well. What a fascinating life you lead." He put his hand on my arm and propelled me gently through the temple door. The smell of incense and jasmine wreaths inside was overwhelming. "It's dedicated to Lakshmi, the goddess of wealth," he said, "so appropriate for Bombay's grasping soul." He pointed to the three goddesses at the back. "They are said to have been found in the sea. My people are restoring some of their jewellery. Although you may find it a bit vulgar by British standards, it suits the local people's taste very well."

"Do you find Indians vulgar, Mr. Unmann?"

"Some."

Like so many Hindu temples, this one had a lot in common with a Roman Catholic cathedral. That same obsession with smoke and sacrifice, the magpie love of shiny baubles, almost interchangeable gods and goddesses. You can see why Hinduism and Catholicism are so popular. Something for everyone: gold, blood, sex, masochism, violent death, a place for the poor to spend their money.

Unmann told me that the men outside were *sadhus*, holy men, who took a special vow of not travelling during the monsoon so they wouldn't commit the sin of trampling on any life, not even on the insects that spread typhoid during the wet weather. The first rains always brought an influx of them. "A temporary overpopulation of world renouncers—*sannyasis*—at pilgrimage sites is a major cultural feature of the monsoon, Miss Benegal, didn't you know?"

"I didn't realize you could achieve holiness at such a young age." I gestured to the young boy Unmann had been with earlier.

"He's one of the artists," Unmann said smoothly. "Now, I'd love to spend more time with you, Miss Benegal, but I have to retrieve my car—it's at the Mahalakshmi Racecourse down the road."

"If you don't mind, I'll walk with you." And even if you do, Mr. Unmann.

He nodded somewhat curtly and set off, his long, brisk strides making no concession to the heat.

"I'd like to pick your brains about Hindu art," I said, almost running to keep up. "It all looks the same to me—all those girlish men, those women with melon breasts and too many arms. I imagine it's pretty easy to fake, right?"

Unmann blinked rapidly several times, as one does when a photographer's flash goes off. "Not really. There are tests. Of course, India has an advantage in that the arts here have never been interrupted by an industrial revolution. There is a long tradition of craft; it hasn't had to be reinvented as it has in the West. So at a lower level—not museum quality, you understand—authentication can be difficult for the amateur." He gave me a long sideways look. "Until Christie's of London rang yesterday to ask if what you'd said was true—that I was selling my collection of coins—I hadn't realized you were so interested in art."

"Is that what they said?" Bastards. I had told them not to mention me. "Actually . . . it was *you* who interested me . . . after seeing you at the pool." I couldn't blush on cue, but I tried to inject a sort of blushing note into my voice. "I said my brother-in-law was thinking of exhibiting his collection and you were his usual agent."

Unmann frowned. "Prosper? He never exhibits."

"That's what they told me. Under no circumstances. Odd, when he used to be such an exhibitionist. Articles about his home life, TV appearances at the drop of a dhoti, and then—bang! Six years ago, he gets a dose of the Garbos."

Unmann stopped to light a cigarette. He took a deep breath of smoke. "Blame it on your sister. He's got much more private and philanthropic since he met her."

"Like you. Helping Bombay restore its oldest temple. The man at the Tilak Foundation said you were involved in the restoration of a lot of Bombay's most beautiful buildings. Also that you were building a temple or something? With the price of property here doubling every day, that must cost."

"This is the Unmanns' last good deed."

"You're going in for bad deeds now?"

"What I meant was that I'm leaving India." He measured the words out carefully, as if I should recognize their value, his patience with me clearly wearing thin. "My family has been here since Catherine of Braganza brought this piece of mosquito-breeding ground to Britain as part of her dowry. My great-great-grandfather was responsible for dredging the swamp and turning it into a habitable piece of property. One of my relatives built the railroad that connected Bombay to the cotton-growing Deccan plains—"

"Thus transferring the balance of the East India Company's interest from opium to cotton," I said, and opened my eyes very wide to show that I had no grudge against drug dealers, given a decent lapse of history.

"We *were* this city, Miss Benegal. There used to be streets named after my family. Now they've replaced our names with new Indian ones—"

"That's true—the geography of maps in Bombay used to be a sort of pictorial title deed for the British. But you should be reassured by the fact that everyone except the politicians still calls the roads by their old names. You know: Elphinstone College, Flora Fountain—"

"The only record of a lost landscape which overpopulation is destroying," Unmann continued.

"Charles Correa, the Indian architect, said that every day Bombay gets worse and worse as a physical environment and better and better as a city."

He gave me an ironic look. "Correa is welcome to the new Bombay. In public, we are all liberals. In private, many people accept that Sanjay Gandhi had the right idea when he ordered the sterilization of any man with more than three children. By the millennium, India's population will have outstripped China's."

"The largest democracy in the world," I said. "Inspiring, isn't it?"

"Democracy doesn't work in India." He had stopped in front of the racecourse entrance. "Here we must part, sadly. I have an appointment on Marine Drive."

"Oddly enough, I'm heading for Marine Drive as well. Chowpatty, in fact."

"Then you've been walking in the wrong direction."

"Have I? I get so turned around in this city."

"While giving the impression of being fixed directly on course." We both waited, to see who would crack first. "May I offer you a lift, Miss Benegal?"

FOR A MAN WHO HAD BEEN ALMOST COERCED INTO PROVIDING TAXI SERVICE, Unmann was quite gracious, giving me a potted-history tour of each area we drove through and recommending a stall holder called Das if I wanted bhelpuri on the beach. "A sixth-generation immigrant from

Uttar Pradesh, like the rest of them. But he has a subtle touch with spices. When I come to the beach I always eat there."

"So you don't mind the risk of poisoning." I waved at the striped wooden bhelpuri stalls between us and the water, each one lit up with Christmas lights like a miniature Harrods on wheels. "Of course, with all these potential poisoners around, it would be difficult to single out the culprit."

That strange, staccato blink again. "I have a strong stomach. And even stronger nerves. Besides, I like to gamble."

"Phlegm."

"*What* did you say?"

"Phlegm. Isn't that the word?" I practised my innocent look. "The English are famous for it, right? Sounds nasty to me, like something you should spit out."

But nothing seemed to pierce his smooth skin, not even the two hijra who wiggled past us to the statue of Tilak, stopping at the statue to lay flowers.

"Odd," I said, "the way transsexuals exaggerate the worst aspects of femininity."

Unmann wound his watch. "Nothing like our sexuality for mocking us."

"And the men who visit them . . ." I said. "It's hard for me to understand the concept of fucking a man dressed as a woman."

"Our erotic preferences don't always come up to our moral standards." He gave me a smile I didn't like. "Do they, Miss Benegal?"

"I've been investigating the deaths of those hijra on Chowpatty," I went on, "especially the one who died the night the *Ramayana* was performed. A friend of one of the hijra made an odd comment: One who has to dance for others cannot live away from dancers. So when I found out it was you who organized the dancing I thought—" I stopped.

"What did you think?"

"I thought you might know more about the dancers who performed that night. They may have seen the man who killed her— Sami, I mean."

"All I do is donate the money and suggest the talent, Miss Benegal. I don't attend the performances." His voice was bored. "You should have a longer chat with your contact at the Tilak Foundation. What did you say his name was?"

"That's it, you see: I think there might be a connection."

"To what?"

I lowered my voice. A storyteller's voice. "This is how far I've got. There is this great star—call her Maya. Isn't that what Hindus call the illusionary world? She falls from a great height . . . or is pushed. So, a falling star. Someone sees her fall, watches all the events and people involved: Sami, an artist."

"Is this fairy tale heading somewhere?" said Unmann. "I don't like to rush an artist's demise, but—"

"Fast forward: Sami can reproduce anything—from a Mogul coin to a Rajput mural. But like most artists, she's a bit short of cash. She is creative, though; she's the goose that lays the golden coins . . . eggs, I mean." Pure speculation. I kept checking to see if any of it was getting through, but the words ran off his skin like water. "Why would anyone want to kill the goose," I said desperately, "unless maybe one day she decides she wants to keep some of those golden eggs?"

"Fascinating," said Unmann, his voice not even mildly interested.

"The acquisition of property—isn't that what this society's built on?" Thinking of Prosper's guest—something to do with property. But ready to toss in the towel. "You buy a house, flog the original details to an antiques shop, replace them with cheap copies . . ." Unmann switched off the ignition and turned towards me. For the first time I had his complete attention. With the engine off, I could hear the drum note of big waves breaking on the beach, long rollers sweeping in from the open sea. The wind had picked up too, blowing a fine salty spray in through the window.

"What has property got to do with this?" he said.

The tone of his voice made the hairs on my neck and arms prickle, like static building on cheap transistor radios before an electrical storm. Such crude meteorological signs have been neglected by our techno age. What we can't measure on a computer graph now, we reject. But early ham-radio operators knew that radio signal forecasting was up to 90 percent accurate.

"That's where you and the Tilak Foundation come in," I said, trying to pick up that signal again.

"We do?" Unmann turned his face away.

"Tilak was concerned in getting India for the Indians," I said, feeling my way now, "and the sign on Sami tied her to Tilak . . . and then there's your Tilak Foundation, with its restoration of old property. A kind of linked fence around a central idea, don't you see? These deaths are a big sign reading KEEP OUT."

He turned his head back towards me very slowly. "And are you going to tell me what that central idea might be, Miss Benegal?"

No, I wasn't, because I was just twisting the dial, trying to improve transmission. "I thought you might be able to," I said weakly.

"Did you?" Unmann's voice was thick with laughter. I'd lost him. "I'm almost sorry that I have other work which prevents my offering assistance." He started the car and looked pointedly at my door. "But it will be a pleasure to hear more of your entertaining tales when you come to my monsoon party."

"I've been reading about the monsoon." I refused to be dislodged. "Amazing phenomenon. Did you know that dice was the classic monsoon game of the Mogul period? In palace circles they used to play dice wildly during the final months. Art collections, estates, even whole kingdoms—all kinds of property—were lost on a single throw."

Unmann smiled and leaned across to open my door. As I got out, he said, "Be careful on the beach, Miss Benegal. Chowpatty can be dangerous during the monsoon. Even this early in the season. Huge rocks can be scooped up off the seabed and flung at unwary tourists. They have been known to cause fatalities."

He was still smiling as he drove away.

3

I TRANSFERRED MY GAZE FROM UNMANN'S DISAPPEARING CAR TO the sky above it, searching for Mirg, the monsoon star, as I used to in Kerala. My father's friend the monsoon seeder claimed that its ascending was a sure sign of the rains' onset. "If rain does not fall," he said, "then it is necessary to seed the clouds with a mixture of dry ice and sodium chloride." He had talked to me once after he'd ridden through those massive slabs of cloud above Kerala. His Dakota was a tank of a plane, but he said that each time it rammed the side of a monsoon, that big machine would bounce, flex its wings, and slide down it with no more impact than a pigeon hitting a window.

"And then?" I said.

"If I am lucky and my engine is strong enough, it is bringing me through into the monsoon's curdled heart. Then, if my luck is holding, the Dakota is carrying me out again. And the rain will fall."

FOR THE NEXT HOUR AND A HALF I CRISSCROSSED THE BEACH, TRYING TO glean more information about the hijra deaths, Sami's in particular. I asked who had seen the *Ramayana* performance, and if anyone knew the other hijra, or maybe a boy called Robi, a friend of Sami's. There were vague answers, but most people were close-mouthed. Giving up after the twenty-fifth blank stare in a row, I sat down in the sand next to a man on a grass mat under a huge beach umbrella. He was painting copies of Indian miniatures of the monsoon. At his feet was his inspiration: six postcards with bad reproductions of paintings from the Purshottam Mawji collection in Bombay's Prince of Wales Museum. I asked him if he knew any of the other artists on the beach.

"All," he said, and offered me one of his paintings. "Two hundred rupees."

I shook my head.

"Painting of hijra at Mogul court," he said, his expression unchanging.

I passed over the two hundred rupees.

"Artist you seek does not work here anymore," said the painter, pocketing his money. "Although often he comes here at this time of day—to visit statue of *Tilak*." He stressed the name Tilak.

"I am interested in a more detailed work as well. For this, I could pay more."

He looked through his portfolio and passed over a larger work, a group of ladies in the courtyard of a large palace, spraying each other with red dye. "This is allegory." He pointed at the women. "These ladies are not real ladies, and they live all under one roof, in another part of this *great palace*." Stressing the last two words. "Red dye is warning them to get out of palace."

"Who owns the palace?"

He pointed to a prince standing on a terrace watching the lightning. "Who owns palaces? Always the same: rich men." A continuous beeping sound started up from under his waistcoat. He reached into an inside pocket and pulled out a mobile phone. "My agent at Taj Mahal Hotel," he said to me, and held out his hand, palm up. "Five hundred rupees, please."

By the statue of Tilak, a Chowpatty vendor was roasting corn over his portable coal brazier. He squeezed some lime juice on a cob for me and sprinkled it with a potent mixture of dried red chillies and salt: red fires and white neon. Behind him, a string of lights like electric blossoms through the bare-branched trees triggered memories of other Februaries. From the end of February in north India, garden flowers start to wither in the heat and the wild flowering trees replace them; first the silk cotton, then the coral Flame-of-the-Forest, and lastly the golden laburnum with its poisonous seeds. Then the trees lose their flowers as well as their leaves. They are stripped bare. Fires spread.

For an Indian farmer, dryness during the four monsoon months denotes sterility; it is untimely. He longs for rain as he does for a son, using elaborate methods for detecting symptoms of cloud pregnancy. Literary forecasters resort to the monsoon proverbs of Ghagh, a seventeenth-century poet-astrologer. "When clouds appear like partridge feathers and are spread across the sky," wrote his wife, the even more learned Bhaddari, "they will not go without shedding rain."

"Is the monsoon coming soon?" I asked the corn vendor.

"Monsoon is good for business," he said. "Everyone has picnic here. Jasmine is blooming and jasmine sellers making necklaces for people to wear." He scanned the horizon. "But this is time of false hope. Now we have only mirages at noon."

I stood picking corn niblets and chilli seeds out of my teeth and watched the sea change from pewter to bronze. A man set up a stall selling plates of mangoes, guavas, and false noses. In front of me the snake charmers, sand sculptors, fire-eaters, pickpockets, jugglers, naked sadhus, beggars, gymnasts, child prostitutes, tightrope walkers, miracle curers, and performing monkeys worked the crowds on Chowpatty with displays of marvels: the whole minutiae of Indian rupee-shavers lit by kerosene lamps, their feet stirring up dust into a cloud that softened the light like a gauze safety curtain laid over a stage. Everyone breathless with anticipation, waiting for the punters and the rain.

A voice comes back to me from Cochin: "The monsoon's roots lie in *mausam*, a word that defined a whole season of certain risk and potential prosperity for the old Arab navigators." That sounded like my voyage home, although I have not followed the example of the Arab pilots and used epic poetry instead of navigational charts to guide me here. They mapped the sea with stories, as we map our history, unrolling acceptable fictions to find a route from one year to the next without losing our way.

Do you remember the stories your father used to tell?

I remember. He told me that long before Vasco da Gama arrived to claim the Indian Ocean, spice traders from Africa sailed the monsoon across to Malabar using rafts of logs bound with coconut fibre, which could withstand the winds because they were more flexible than fixed-mast boats. "When they untied the ropes, the boats lost their identity and turned back into logs," my father said. "Often, a flexible identity can be useful." I was seven. At seven, a child wants a fixed identity.

This is what I know about the monsoon, things remembered from childhood, meteorological fairy tales told to me one night in a billowing tent of mosquito netting, while the coconut palms bent double on the beach and a watery battering ram of rain hit the house. *Once upon a time*, when he should have been reading me "Sleeping Beauty" or tales from the *Ramayana*, or instilling fear of the dark and the unknown into me; these are the tales my father told:

1. The tropical revolving typhoons common during the monsoon

are known as cyclones in the Arabian Sea and India, from the Greek word *Kuklos*, meaning circle. Or *kukloma*, the coil of a snake.

2. There is a coiling, eely wind called the Eksman Spiral that breeds monsoon clouds, a phenomenon known to drag cold air upwards in a corkscrew into the sky, sucking birds and insects with it, then mirroring this action in the sea, so that fish and sea snakes as well are spiralled up from the deep to the surface.

3. The Nagas, deities who appear on earth in the form of snakes, have always been honoured during the rains, for floods often force them from their usual habitation into gardens, courtyards, and houses.

4. During the monsoon, snake deities are propitiated with special attention by barren women in want of sons.

I kept coming back to the snakes.

The prophylactic powers of strychnine impressed our old gardener in Kerala. He kept a supply for use against serpents in the monsoon. Why my mother should choose to steal strychnine from the gardener to kill herself, when she had her own cyanide, she never said. No one asked. It's not the kind of question that comes easily. She left a note: "Dear Rosalind, Men cannot help themselves. And you are too young to know better." That February, she got the dose wrong and lived. Later, she found a more effective killer.

The last time I saw my mother alive, she told me I had turned into the image of my father.

When something touched my arm, I was prepared for ghosts. And I recognized her at once, my little fish sucked up to the surface from the deep. Although she had painted her face this time with more chalk than you'd find on a school blackboard. It was the shy, beautiful hijra from Bina's community.

The difference in our builds made a nonsense of our sex. Mine had all the outward signs of a liberated, meat-fed swimmer; hers (but for the Adam's apple) was a caricature of feminine beauty: narrow where I was broad, curved where I was muscled. Even her hands were as rounded and dimpled as a young girl's.

"Please, miss," she said, "I need to talk to you. My name is Sunila."

4

"Pretend you don't know me," Sunila said. "We are walking away from here."

"Right. We are walking, you are talking. Tell me about your pictures, Sunila."

She shook her head. "Not here, miss. I am taking you to safe place."

For over an hour I followed Sunila on and off buses so crowded that by the time we escaped into a quiet part of Colaba the air outside smelled positively alpine. I sucked it up like soup as we walked through the streets to a narrow, dead-end alley where pots of jasmine vines screened off a few tables.

Sunila ordered us fish steamed in banana leaves and some coconut rice. "This is enough for you? It is coming with chutneys."

"Fine. But why this place?"

"Chowpatty is watched. Police too are involved, but here are good people in trouble with police. You see man with scars on his face like running water? He was collector of waste paper. But he is not paying bribes. So goondas are burning his go-down with kerosene while he is sleeping inside."

It's important not to listen too carefully when you do this kind of interview. Not to let the image get close and lodge itself in your personal nightmare file. *A house of cards. Faded bales of newspaper. The muscles of the face burning, running.* Keep aloof, check for battery level, concentrate on the technical details. And stick to the facts: homicide by burning is rare outside India because it is so ineffective. Hard to get the fire to burn intensely enough to destroy flesh and bone. Here it is used mainly in the so-called kitchen deaths, where a bride is burned by her husband to get her dowry.

"Cook is scarred when Supreme Court decrees people living on pavements are dangerous," Sunila was saying. "Police smashed her camp to make way for new apartments. First time, cook's people took down their camp themselves to save their things. Second time, police are head-bashing and stealing everything."

"These are people who arrive after one monsoon and are washed away by the next. If they keep building shanties on the open spaces, eventually no one will have room to breathe." It could have been Unmann speaking.

Sunila shook her head. "They were twenty years in that camp. This man walks eighteen kilometres every day to sell postcards outside Taj Mahal Hotel. He sends his son to school. Lady works with stuff you people throw away."

She brought me a yellow watering can made of old coffee tins that had been flattened, shaped, and welded back together, part of Bombay's endless cycle of reclaiming itself. Everything inorganic goes back into the working bloodstream of the city. Everything organic is digested by cows, goats, pigs, dogs.

In front of me the scarred woman laid a banana leaf, the melamine tray of India, and ladled on coconut rice and yellow dal with a daub of lime chutney and the leaf-wrapped fish. A cook's palette. She spoke to Sunila.

"She says that the invisible ones must stick together to be seen," said Sunila, her face taking on the jutting masculine conviction of an advocate arguing his case in court. A butterfly stuck halfway through the process of metamorphosis.

"Let me get this straight," I said. "You're saying the government has been involved in destroying the squatters' homes. But what's it got to do with Sami?"

"Before she moved into the chawls, Sami lived in same camp as these people. It was she who is telling them to save their things by tearing down shacks and then to rebuild after police are gone. Second time, police hit her first and put her in jail. But these people remember her, what she did."

I got the tape recorder out of my bag. "Let me set this up."

Sunila grabbed my hand. "No. If someone recognizes my voice I am dead too."

"I can't help you otherwise."

She shook her head, her lips shut. Not until she could see that all my recording equipment was safely out of sight did she begin, like all the best storytellers. "Once there was a time"—her eyes closed—"before Sami."

I lifted the tiny clip mike just clear of the bag.

In the time before Sami, Sunila lived on the streets and paid the police two rupees a night to sleep in the park, a rupee to the gardener for water. One day people came with a sign: BEAUTIFICATION OF BOMBAY and moved her on. "So I went to Chowpatty."

"How did you survive?"

It was the Bombay story. She survived by begging, at first. Then she sold bottled mineral water to the tourists—labelled bottles that she had collected from hotel dustbins and refilled with pump water in the park. A friend had worked out a way of making the seals look new. But if they were caught, the police beat them and took them to jail with hundreds of other street kids. In jail, Sunila was often made to share a mat with grown men, one after another.

"They would fiddle with me and finger deep into me. If I am resisting . . ."

"What happened?"

Her makeup turned into a map of fine brown lines. "Better not to," she said.

I thought, But this is why people have families? To protect themselves from these things? This is why people make maps, so we won't get lost in such places?

One good thing came out of her jail experience: it was there she met Sami, and Sami told her stories to pass the time.

"What kind of stories?"

Stories of the old times, when the hijras were respected, stories of hijras from the *Kama Sutra* and the *Mahabharata*—the longest and oldest poem in the world. With pictures drawn on the floor—they shared a love of drawing. "She gave me the name of a group, the All India Hijra Kalyan Sabha, who are looking after the rights of hijras and trying to prevent such things as forced castration of boys."

And Sami told Sunila of a policeman who would let young hijras off jail time and pay them good money to suck his cock for him behind the station. But competition was brisk.

"Some friend, this Sami," I said.

"Yes," Sunila said, missing the irony, "it is better than jail. Only one man."

"Tell me more about Sami."

Sami was a special case. Even as a very young boy, she had made up her eyes with *kajal*—eye black—to be more like a girl. She had a delicate beauty that attracted older boys, who took her on their laps to fondle. "Her father is hating this so much he is never at home." As she got older, the shame to the family became too great, until her mother was forced to give her to a hijra family. "Maybe twenty years ago? She is nine, I think. Before her mother leaves, she is saying Sami's father is great man in Bombay movies."

Every orphan's dream. To be different from the other lost boys. A story that could have come straight from Ashok's book of hijra case histories.

"Her mother gives Sami some family pictures, saying someday Sami's father is coming back to claim her." Sunila's voice faltered. "But he never does. So she runs away to Bombay to find him, and there on Chowpatty we meet."

"I thought you met in jail."

"First in jail," Sunila said quickly. "Later, Chowpatty, and she takes me to her guru and says I can help her in her work at Central Props."

"When was she working there?" What was true and what was false here?

"Until she dies she works for Mr. Raven. They are not paying her so much, because she dresses as a hijra. She says, 'This is who I am.' Sami is very political. So she has to work outside normal hours for them, not in studio, and I am helping her. That is how we meet. She sees me making pictures. She says, like her father, my father was maybe an artist."

Sami's inheritance. "Or your mother," I said. A line from my mother's diary: *Rosalind is my book*. I looked up at the sky and saw its bronze fading to a sullen tint of lead. The air was opaque, saturated with vapour. "What about the men who beat me?" I said. "Those family snaps can't be the pictures they were after."

"Sami is knowing men high up in government. They come to see her in Great Palace Street, hijra prostitution area. And she is a very smart girl. She tells me that some customers ask hijra to lie on their backs and lift their legs so they can put their penis through into anus and pretend it is a woman. But people like Sami who do not like anus-fucking have a trick to put a hand behind." She clenched her fist and poked a finger into it in a graphically obscene gesture. "Man is thinking this is anus. So Sami makes more money."

"Why is that?" I opened my leafy fish parcel, but its fresh blast of the sea didn't revive my appetite.

"Men pay less money just for fucking through the thighs. Sami says Bombay is full of mills and factory workers. She says girls like her are *Chini Kharkana*. Means sugar factory. One day Sami tells me she can make even more money and stop people tearing down our homes. Because of some pictures a friend took."

"Pictures of these men with her? Blackmail, you mean? So these men were involved in property in some way."

"I never saw the pictures."

"Why come to me with this story, Sunila—what about the police?"

She shook her head. "Police are involved. And journalists have a passport."

"A press pass. It's different."

"And you are talking to Bina of Sami's pictures. People think you have them."

"You misinterpreted our conversation. I never had the pictures you mean."

"You said to one of the men about pictures, as well."

I stopped pushing the food around and stared at her. "How do you know that?"

Her eyes were lustrous with innocence. "Same men are threatening girls in Great Palace Street. Bada Johnny is telling me, one of the boys last night. He is friend of my friend Robi, the boy who spoke to you at Mistry's studio."

Bada Johnny: B, I thought. "Your boyfriend is a goonda—a gangster?"

Sunila shook her head and pressed her hands together in her lap. "Not a boyfriend and not a goonda, miss. Not such a bad person."

"On a cosmic level, maybe not. Personally, I hope his next ten reincarnations are as cockroaches. This Bada Johnny—does Robi know him well?"

"Once he was political, with Shiv Sena. That is how Robi knows him. Now he is just small-time crook. And he ran away from the killing of Sami."

A tinny cover version of Michael Jackson's "Thriller" wafted through the walls to us from some other astral plane. "How was Sami killed?"

Sunila started to cry, absolutely silently, holding her head back the way professional models are trained to do to prevent smudging their mascara. But it didn't work. Kohl gathered around her eyes until she had the dark sockets of an Oedipus mask. "Robi's friend is there, miss," she said, when she could speak again. "He saw big boss cutting her. She is dying slowly. Finally they are drowning her, he thinks."

"Not in the sea."

"No, miss. In a bathtub."

Cycles within cycles, I thought, never quite repeating. Drowned in a foot of water. The legs slip up, the head slips down, you pass out; it's as easy as washing a baby. Except that Sami was poisoned. "There was cyanide."

"They are splashing it on her, stuffing rags of it in her mouth."

"Why?"

"They say that will teach her for—"

"For what?"

"She stole something from them." Sunila stopped, changed direction. "Now Bada Johnny told Robi I must be very careful, because big boss and other man, Chota Johnny, are looking for me."

B and C. "And the big boss—he's not Indian, is he?"

"Acres."

"Acres, you call him?" That name rang a bell, but not loud enough to pick out any tune. Something I'd read in the newspaper.

"Coming and going in Bombay for many years. He wants Sami to tell where the photos are, miss, and at first she says nothing. But . . ." Sunila was weaving back and forth in the chair like a solitary mourner at Sami's funeral. My brain recorded the movement, doubting its sincerity. This is not genuine, I thought. She has seen this in a film, this image borrowed from a classical tragedy. "Sami is in the bath and very pale, so pale. The bath is full of blood. Finally she says, 'With Sunila's pictures. My father's pictures.' And then something like Gol or Gul. Not knowing anymore what she is saying. All I know about Sami's pictures is she told me once they are with a friend who knows how to keep a secret. She says, 'His lips are sealed.' Why isn't she telling those men the truth?"

"Because she knew if she told them they would have no reason not to kill her."

"But they are killing her anyway. Cutting and cutting her—"

"Sami said her photos were 'with Sunila's pictures.' " I had to stop the words. "And 'my father's pictures'—what did that mean?"

"I don't know. Sami made many drawings of me. Maybe she had those with the photos of her father, of Mr. Prosper. But I am not knowing where they are now."

I pushed my food away for good. "She thought *Prosper* was her father? That's crazy! Why would Prosper give her away? He's dying to have a son."

"But she is not a real son, she is hijra." Sunila wiped her face with her sari. "Later, she says, even her mother is killing herself because of this."

Maya. When she realized there would be no more sons.

"She is using these pictures of Mr. Sharma to meet him." Sunila traced the outline of the leaf plate with her finger. "Then she starts badly to want the operation. So she begins blackmail. If she cannot be real son, maybe real daughter is better. Also, she is in love with a man. This makes her real woman for him."

Sunila hung her head and explained that she herself was too frightened for the operation. The fear had started when she assisted the midwife at a castration ceremony at Bina's. The midwife had a line to Mata, the Mother Goddess, and as such could afford to set restrictions: isolation before the operation, no sex or spicy food, no mirrors. On the tenth day of isolation, at three in the morning, Bina's girl was taken from her room and ritually bathed. Naked, she sat on a stool and began chanting *Mata Mata Mata* to put herself into a trance. She took a plait of her hair in her mouth.

"To bite down on. For the pain," said Sunila, "and I held her arms tightly."

The midwife separated the penis and scrotum with a fine string. She made two diagonal cuts and sliced off the offending genitals. A piece of bamboo was forced up the uretha to keep it open and blood was allowed to flow out, to wash away germs as well as the last trace of masculinity. The first menstrual flow.

"Bombay doctors are only for transsexuals," said Sunila. "They try to stop the blood too soon for us. Operation makes us *Nirvan Sultan*, meaning like a king."

The ancient Greeks also liked their painted boys, I thought. Is India a reflection of how life was? Or of how it is going to be? All the boundaries blurred.

"Tell me about the pictures," I said. "You knew Sami—where could they be?"

"There is Zarina, who was Sami's flatmate. I have the address, but it is too dangerous for me to go there."

I had another thought. "Do you know Sami's real name?"

She shook her head, then smiled shyly. "But sometimes I am calling her Surya, like the sun-god."

Of course. Every Bombay film has to have a few gods thrown in. Searching for a classical image, I had been offered one, straight from Prosper's notes: Apollo's half brother, the mercurial Hermes—god of gateways, crossroads, boundaries—who appears to mortals in the form of a messenger, representing mutation and transition, from whose name came Hermaphroditus and the Hermetic art, the science of alchemy. And how could a gilder's daughter not recognize Hermes? I switched off the tape and stood up. "This may be more than I can handle, Sunila. But I'll think about it. How can I get in touch?"

"Robi always knows how to find me." She leaned forward. "You *will* help hijra? I loved Sami, miss. She was my sister and my mother."

"And where's a girl without her mother, right?"

AN AIR MASS LIKE THE MONSOON WIND, STRIKING A VERTICAL OBSTACLE LIKE A mountain range, is forced to ascend. Often it does not have sufficient energy to surmount that obstacle, so it tends to go round the barrier rather than over it.

"How can we identify the approaching air mass which has sufficient energy to climb over an obstacle in its path?" my father used to ask.

I need to remember the answer.

Driving to my hotel I could see that the roads had been scoured by dust to a glassy finish that bounced back any available light and then fractured it into a kaleidoscope of colours. The earth was still waiting for its seasonal booze-up. But no one except a meteorologist would claim that the monsoon had not yet started.

5

THE NEXT MORNING, BOMBAY'S METEOROLOGIST-IN-CHARGE forecast that the rains would arrive in thirty-six hours. If I lived that long.

The television news said that for thirty years the earth had been suffering a deficient phase of the sun. The sun's diameter was smaller than average, accounting for three decades of low rainfall. Better monsoon times were ahead, the meteorologists promised, which meant that flooding in Bombay would get worse, because all the streets and compounds had been tarred or cemented over. The rains could no longer seep back naturally into the earth.

I bought a stack of newspapers in the hotel bookshop and started chasing the names of property developers, my own personal land reclamation project. *Ever see what acid does to a face?* I tried to block out Caleb's words and concentrate on the job in hand. *Middle of a crowded street, no one sees a thing.*

I discovered that Bombay was a boom town, property prices rising at 40 to 50 percent a year. You could buy a small flat with just enough room to swing a mother-in-law for about a million American. If you wanted to escape her, you could get an option on a twenty-five-thousand-dollar two-bedroom, Swiss-style chalet built around a famous guru's ashram in the country. An Indian answer to the holiday time-share: enlighten your soul while lightening your wallet.

Our prophets used to come out of the East, but the modern communications industry had reversed the trade winds of revelation. The new evangelists were Americans preaching *The Art of Public Speaking and Salesmanship*. Or *How to Succeed in Advertising*. Bombay bookshops and small ads were full of the religion of self-improvement.

Every secretary who answered the phone was a convert. Clutching the
bible which told them, "You are who you think you are!" they claimed
to be vice presidents and managing directors, just as in Italy they
would have been *dottores* or *professores*. Getting to the brains behind
the drones was like shaking hands with an octopus: I kept winding up
with the suckers.

By midmorning, when Ashok rang to invite me to lunch, the only
thing I was sure of was that Misters A, B, and C weren't the kind of
people who advertised in the yellow pages. I told Ash I had a few
things to finish but they would be done by about one. "I'll get a taxi.
Thomas is busy doing some research for me."

"I will collect you from the hotel."

"By the way, Ash, you don't happen to know Anthony Unmann,
do you?"

"I believe one of my uncles taught him at Oxford. Why?"

"I'll tell you later. Is your uncle still there?" He was. At Balliol.

With lunch at Ashok's favourite Goan restaurant to look forward
to, I set off for the microfilm library Ram had recommended. He'd
given Sunila's story about Prosper a credibility rating of minus five,
with an outside chance that Sami's father had worked as a technician
or extra with Sharma. His advice was to stick to the property angle.

It was important to find out whether Sami had been talking about
squatter camps or chawls. The chawl blocks—tenements of four or
five storeys that had been built to accommodate factory workers—had
identities, actual addresses, usually linked to the nearest textile mills.
The squatter camps were entirely different: random drifts of the dispossessed, amorphous as coral reefs.

"The people there are like polyps," Ram said, "but instead of
separating lime from the seawater the way a coral polyp builds its reef,
you have these lost people dividing Bombay's usable debris from its
tidal wave of waste to build the skeleton of a camp. God help you if it's
anything to do with those. Indiranagar, the squatter colony in front of
Santa Cruz airport, has about thirty thousand people. And Dharavi is
the largest slum in Asia, three-quarters of a million people squeezed
into half a mile of shacks. The slum equivalent of the Great Barrier
Reef."

Each encampment had its own elaborate structure consisting of
communities from the same part of the country who had brought their
customs and trades to Bombay. "The camps have a higher proportion
of Bombay's workers than any other city group," Ram said. "A third
of all our unskilled labour live there."

Not even the most cynical politician would claim that they could ever afford to house these people properly. They had to be marginalized to be affordable, pushed to the outskirts, where they wouldn't upset the tourists as much. They were part of a long tradition of cartography where marginalized people belonged, quite literally, to the margins of maps, the borderlines, beyond which lived the edge monsters—centaurs, harpies, mermaids, hybrids of promiscuous unions between different species.

I see myself this way, and Sami. Two hybrids, out on the edge of the map.

IN THE LIBRARY, I STARTED WITH THE ADDRESS SUNILA HAD GIVEN FOR Zarina, to check who held the property deeds. But I couldn't find the address listed on any map. When I asked the library clerk, he said he had a feeling that it was near Great Palace Street, perhaps part of a block backing onto the old Goliath cinema complex. He brought down a map of the city and put his finger on a road.

"There's no street name," I said. "Why do you think that's the one?"

He shifted uneasily, as if his skin had shrunk to a less comfortable size. "It is just a gully, madam, a space between the roads. Building name is what counts: Goliath Palace. See how it is connected all round to this other street almost like palace walls? On this western side is Goliath Cinema."

"But how did you know that?"

"Famous building."

"So famous it's not listed in the address book or the map?" Why was I surprised? As Herman Melville said, No true places appear on maps. Maps are pieces of theatre, poetic abstractions designed to conceal more than they reveal, especially in Bombay, where, like the itinerant traders and opportunists who settled it, the substance of the city is essentially nomadic; it's always moving on. A place whose tourist maps include pictograms of as-yet-unbuilt hotels but not squatter camps that have existed for thirty years is best mapped by a series of ideas rather than by thoroughfares and public highways.

The clerk seemed to be trying to pull the skin of his arms down over his hands. They were very small and delicate, like a girl's. He checked to see no one was listening. "All this area around Goliath Cinema is famous for boys . . ."

"Hijra?"

"Some hijra, more zenana: boys pretending to be hijra to make more money. Cinema is all boarded up. Still, you might be trying to check its owners. They may be same as owner of chawl." He warned me it might be an old deed, whose name had not been updated to reflect present ownership.

But trying to find a listing for Goliath in the Bombay address book—or in any book—proved impossible. In Bombay phone books, names may be listed under their employer's name or under the name of the person who first installed the telephone, or under whoever paid the most for an entry. Categories were constantly shifting, and as mobile phones and fax machines arrived and street names were updated to reflect current political beliefs, the dialling code for a fishing community today became by tomorrow a code for the inner city.

Squinting at the rows of white-on-black lettering on the flickering screen I reflected, not for the first time, on how in a computer era we are all in the hands of the cataloguers, the people who choose which box to put us in. Not a century that respects Renaissance men, those transgressors of the single index entry.

This system had the usual peculiar juxtapositions and missing links—cinemas under *Houses, Movie* (impossible to access without correct placement of the comma); stories of Indian film directors listed not under *Film* or *Indian Film* but under *Movie Journalism, Indian*. After an hour, I gave up on Goliath and started on Prosper, on the off chance that Sunila's story had some basis in fact.

Thanks to his spectacular history, my sister's husband was relatively easy to trace. His public face, at least. Prosper Sharma had been born into the kind of family the media loves. It had everything: money, talent, connections, looks. He had married into the same background, perhaps a few rungs up in terms of wealth, and although Maya's downwards slip from classical music into the movies had initially been frowned upon by her own family, it was given a certain credence by Prosper's early artistic success.

A golden, glittering pair who had it all to start with and added a shiny skin of fame to what they had been given. A dynasty waiting to happen. All they lacked were the children: no mention anywhere of the misfit son.

I kept fast-forwarding the early days. Pictures of a young Caleb, so darkly beautiful that at first I didn't recognize him as the prototype of the bullish man I knew. Like Bombay, he had put on weight and his skin had lightened and yellowed with age. But here he stood proudly between the older Maya and Prosper, grinning like a Roman urchin into the camera.

Click. The year Prosper won the Oscar for Best Foreign Film.

Click. The year Prosper was nominated for Best Director at Cannes.

Click. The year Prosper opened a film festival in Hong Kong.

They made an unlikely trio, a fact which the screen magazines were not slow to pick up on. BOMBAY BOY'S METEORIC RISE! FROM CHOWPATTY TO CHOW MEIN! A NEW COMET IN THE SHARMA FIRMAMENT! THE PRINCE AND THE PAUPER: *Former scene-shifter and draughtsman at Island Studios, plucked from his pauper's life by Guru Sharma.*

Caleb smiled less each year.

Still no offspring. I tried the birth announcements over a period of two years, sure that any child born to such an illustrious pair would have been splashed across the headlines. Nothing in any of the papers.

I spent thirty minutes reading up on the malaise that had afflicted India's film industry in 1986–87, the year before Maya died. Thanks to the *Guide to Indian Periodical Literature* published by Gurgaon's Documentation Service, there was a letter Prosper had written to the Film Development Corporation in January 1987, complaining of the corporation's withdrawal of funds from his current project. Long before Maya's death it had been a bad year for him. To get financing for a film, it seemed, even producers of Prosper's calibre would have to go hat in hand for a loan to the big financiers—construction magnates, diamond dealers, whoever had the money this year. Interest rates could be charged at up to 60 percent, depending on the fame of stars signed up. But that was only the beginning. After that, another loan had to be found to pay off the first financier. And so forth.

As I was about to close Volume 23, Jan–Mar 1987, and get some lunch, I glanced down the page from *Economics, Cinema (Indian)* to *Evidence, Criminal.* A familiar name caught my eye: A. Tagore. Scanning idly through the list to see what this Tagore had written, I found that he or she was listed as the author of a six-page article, "Psychological Techniques in Investigation, from Mogul Times to the Present," in the August issue of something called the *CBI Bull.* It's just barely feasible, I thought; he's a historian, after all. It's not really his period, but maybe he's moved on a few millennia. I checked the guide's front index. It cross-referenced a detailed list of publications, and under *CBI Bull* was its full name: *Central Bureau of Investigation Bulletin,* New Delhi.

I started to mine older and then more recent editions of the guide. In one, six months after Rajiv Gandhi's death, I struck gold for the second time. Under *Crimes, Political,* a long essay in the *Indian Police Journal*: "Political Assassination and VIP Security—Why We Fail": A. Tagore. Then again, three months later, in the *Police Research and Development Bulletin*: "Standards of Investigation, Improvement, and Innovation": A. Tagore.

There must be other Tagores with the initial A, I thought. But when I got to the Oct–Dec 1987 issue of the *Indian Journal of Criminology*, published just six months after Maya's death, it became clear that ancient buildings and lost causes were not Ashok's only passions. The article would have seemed dry to anyone but a fluent criminologist. Or to me. It was called "The Effect of Water Immersion on the Detectability of Certain Antigens in Dried Bloodstains: A lecture given at the Police Research and Development Bureau, Ministry of Home Affairs, Bombay, by Professor Ashok Tagore, D. Phil. (Oxon.)."

The transmutation of blood and water into a body of evidence. Bloodstreams from a body of water. Maya, with her poor smashed face in a puddle of monsoon rain. Me with my head in the sand.

The greatest number of listings under A. Tagore were credited to the *CBI Bull*. I chased up a book called *The Police Dilemma* by R. Singh to find out a little about the Central Bureau of Investigation. Mr. Singh said that the CBI was created in 1963 to collect criminal intelligence and investigate cases of corruption. It had interstate jurisdiction and international ramifications.

> Although the Research and Analysis Wing (commonly known as RAW) is more politicized, and was once regarded as Mrs. Gandhi's personal secret police, the CBI's own political fallibility has always been exposed when it has in any way threatened the interests of powerful political personalities holding important portfolios in Central Government.

To some extent, Mr. Singh concluded, the CBI could be considered the FBI of India, with all that institution's strengths and weaknesses. Exactly the people the government's top brass would call in should they have a sex scandal threatening one of their senior staff. And Ashok had pretended to be vague about criminal procedure.

I closed the book and rubbed my eyes. I know what iss *your* nem, Ashok: you're a fucking spook. Those articles in the police bulletins proved it. I felt as if another door on my past had slammed shut. At the very least, Ashok was sitting on the government fence, and until I knew more about Sami's clients, I didn't want any government reps tagging my movements.

From a pay phone near the library I rang Ashok to cancel lunch. His servant told me that he had already left to collect me.

6

Bunny had dropped off the photos of Maya, confirming what the photocopies had suggested: something or someone had marked Maya before she fell. And six years later, similar marks had turned up on the corpse of a hijra called Sami.

"A fresh corpse?" Satish Isaacs said on the phone.

"Not that fresh," I said, "but it was when the photos were taken. Do you think you could tell from police photos whether these wounds were made by the same weapon that made the ones on the hijra? Or hazard a guess?"

"No guessing necessary," he said. "If your corpse is scarred as mine is, then almost certainly the weapon used was a double-headed scalpel on a swivel neck."

"How could you be sure?"

Satish was indignant. "I reproduced this hijra's wounds to scale. And we use such scalpels here, so I had perfect opportunity to make copy cuts of the wounds."

"What do you use the scalpels for?"

"Their swivel heads make them useful for delicate cutting of parallel circles—in gold leaf, for example."

Ashok was waiting for me in the hotel lobby. He did not look like a spy, but I guess that was the point.

"Ah, Rosalind," he said, and smiled.

"I'm very sorry, Ashok, but it turns out I won't have time for lunch after all. Something has come up. Prosper wants to see me."

"I'll drive you. We can eat later."

"I couldn't possibly impose on you. I'll get a taxi."

"We'll go in my uncle's car." He was quite determined. All I could hope was that the car journey would give me time to sort out his motives.

The uncle's ancient Ambassador started with a sound like an electric blender. "Now," Ashok said, "tell me how your research goes."

I stalled for a while, but he was good at asking uncomfortable questions that were difficult to avoid without revealing my suspicions of him. Eventually, withholding only the details of Sunila's identity, I told him Sami's story, figuring that if he were CBI, he would certainly know about it already.

"Where did you get this?" he said.

"One of Sami's hijra friends."

"And did this hijra name the property owners who were being blackmailed?"

"She wasn't specific—government officials, politicians involved in demolition of the chawls."

"What nonsense!" Ashok's words were expelled as if he had bitten into a piece of rotten fruit. "Enforced slum demolition is another myth perpetuated by the commercial cinema. It hasn't been policy with the government since Sanjay Gandhi's time. These days it is a direct route to political defeat. The chawls and squatters' camps are seen as enormous vote banks, and the way to cash in your cheque is by supporting squatters' rights, thus ensuring big donations from the gangsters who are the slums' real landlords. It is these gang lords who are the profiteers, subletting public space, squeezing rent money out of every inch of pavement. And why should men like these be worried about such photos damaging their reputations? More likely your friendly hijra is planning to use those photos—if they exist at all—for a much less altruistic motive. So unless you have found some concrete evidence that supports her story . . . Have you, Rosalind?"

Yesterday that extra probing question would have meant nothing. Today it triggered a warning wave of static. "Nothing special," I said, staring out the window at Chowpatty Beach. We were passing the end where the city's gay community gather. "But there seem to be lots of people in this city who are not quite what they appear to be."

Silence hanging between us like dirty laundry. Then: "Whom did you have in mind, Rosalind?"

I gave it a heartbeat before answering. "Prosper, for instance." Watching his hands release their tension on the wheel. "Basil Chopra said that Prosper's *Tempest* is partly based on Ovid's *Metamorphoses*. Not exactly my field of expertise. Do you know anything about Ovid?"

Ashok raised one black eyebrow. "The *Metamorphoses* is a lengthy work. Have you any particular section where you would like me to begin?"

I shrugged. "With a metamorphosis."

"It is full of them. A chaotic universe subdued into harmonious order, men and women turned to trees, stones, stars. But let me see . . . there is the girl Caenis, who rejects marriage only to be raped by Neptune, the sea god. Her compensation is to be turned into a man, Caeneus, no longer vulnerable to martial or sexual wounds. Is that what you had in mind?"

On the horizon, a half-inch stripe of dark navy-blue cloud was cracked into segments by the occasional flash of lightning. The storm was moving closer. "Why would Prosper pick that aspect of *The Tempest* to explore?" I said.

"Considering how the generations of men have passed from the age of gold to that of iron," Ashok recited, *"how often the fortunes of places have been reversed, I should believe that nothing lasts under the same form. I have seen what once was solid earth changed into sea, and lands created out of what once was ocean."*

This was cryptic, even for him. "I have no idea what you're talking about, Ash."

"Ovid. Book 15. The 1955 Innes translation. Applicable to the transformation of Bombay from islands into peninsula." His dark eyes flicked from the road to me. "Or perhaps Prosper supports W. H. Auden's view that Caliban represents the sensuality Prospero has unwisely neglected in favour of his art."

"What's your view?"

"Oh, mine is not so imaginative or enlightened. Just the typical civil servant's sympathy for any attempt to impose order on the world, however vain."

We climbed into the wedding-cake Gothic of Malabar Hill, where the British left their legacy of colonial architecture to Parsi industrialists, Gujarati diamond merchants, and Goanese construction magnates, not to mention movie moguls. Moguls of all sorts, the artist on the beach had said. Sami's visitors.

"Do the people in these houses realize that half the population of this city lives in slums?" I spoke without thinking, forgetting that Ashok lived on this hill.

He took the comment as a personal affront. "Are people in the West aware that half the world lives below the poverty line? This city is simply the world on a smaller scale, except that here we have to confront our failures in person, not just in newsprint. And there is a living and an education to be found in Bombay, which has made it a magnet for the dispossessed."

I pointed to a barefoot shoeshine boy. About the age Sami was when her mother gave her away. "You call that a living? For the price of a tank of petrol you could give him a real life."

"I don't presume to play God."

"When I was young, I thought you *were* God, the way Dad described you. The man who walked over the Hindu Kush with nothing but two bearers and a trunkful of books. The man who filmed the white tigers. The man who spoke seventeen languages including Sanskrit."

"Only seven, I regret. And Sanskrit is not a spoken language."

"Exactly."

We pulled up to Prosper's apartment block, left the car, and walked up to the doorman. "Rosalind Benegal and Ashok Tagore to see Prosper Sharma," I said.

The man frowned. "Actually Mr. Sharma is at his studio, madam."

I smiled and said there must have been some mistake.

Ashok was silent until we were back in the car. "I can see now that lunch was indeed out of the question. But for some other reason than the one you gave me."

"Don't make a big deal of it, Ash. Prosper and I just got our wires crossed, that's all." I checked the rearview mirror for inspiration, pretending to adjust my nonexistent makeup. That's what girls always do in the movies. It seems to work for them. Moving my face a bit closer, in case it was more convincing with less distance between me and the mirror, I saw a car slide into the driveway of Prosper's block, a white Mercedes. Two men in the front seat, one with Ray-Bans and a cheesy complexion. Something about the driver's face.

I opened the door and ran towards the Merc. It started to reverse very fast. There was a pile of bricks and broken masonry next to me. I picked up the remains of a carved acanthus leaf and threw it at the Mercedes as it copped a U-turn in the road. The stone leaf cracked the driver's window and he put up his arm to ward off a cascade of shattered glass that never came. The back end of the

Merc slewed out and the big car wallowed into the traffic. There was the grinding of metal on metal and then someone screaming. It might have been the man who had fallen off the roof of an overloaded bus.

The Mercedes drove around the wreckage and disappeared.

Ashok appeared beside me. "Wait in the car, please," he said, and went to see what he could do to sort out my mess.

It was twenty minutes before he came back. "What we call here a 'denting' situation," he said. "No one killed and no one seriously hurt. I have given them some money to pay for the damage."

"Shouldn't we take them to the hospital?"

"They preferred the money."

"I'll pay you back."

"You've done enough. I'll take you to the hotel so you can get on with whatever it was I interrupted so inconveniently." A marble profile, cold to the touch. He started the car and drove for several minutes in silence. "Rosalind, why are you determined on this course?"

"Why change the habit of a lifetime?"

"You are following a pattern, then," he said. "That is reassuring. I was worried that you were turning to anarchy as a solution."

"You told me to find an Indian solution: what's wrong with anarchy? Plenty of precedent here. Isn't that what the monsoon is?"

"In the monsoon one finds a deeper logic than that of pure science."

"Yeah, right." Here we go with the Hindu mumbo jumbo, I thought.

"Each of our monsoon festivals symbolizes radical disorder followed by drastic reordering. A cycle." We passed the shoeshine boy again, or perhaps a different one. "I am more concerned with this obsessive cycle *you* are involved in."

"What do you mean?"

"Over the last few years you have lost so many of those close to you, Rosalind, and I can see that this makes you feel very isolated. One response might be to further isolate yourself"—he was choosing his words carefully—"and to seek out those who are equally isolated. To ally yourself with them and deliberately place yourself outside the family. I wonder if, perhaps, you were hoping for more from your sister than she is now able to give?"

"You mean, am I jealous of my sister? Look, those men in the car beat me up. I'm sure one of them murdered Sami. And my sister may be married to the man who ordered them to do it. You want me to sit here and chant Om?"

"Has your sister asked you to get involved to this extent, Rosalind?"

I hunched my shoulders. "She's frightened of Prosper, I think. Anyway, it's what I do."

"If you have any concrete evidence of Sami's murder, you should give it to the police. Do you have such evidence, Rosalind?"

"The police here are a joke," I said. "A friend tells me that Asia's largest market for smuggled goods is run under the noses of Bombay police headquarters, not far from the Customs House. One smuggler actually built himself thirty-eight stalls and let them out on payment of a ten-thousand-rupee kickback."

Ashok's eyes narrowed. "So India has a corner on corruption, has it? Well, if you wish to apportion blame, look to Britain, from whom India inherited the genes of its civil service. Or to Lord Macaulay, who bequeathed us the roots of our criminal court. One of the reasons that so many stories are spread about our police is that they are seen as the legacy of an alien power. First the Moguls imposed their institutions and customs on our Hindu society, then those were absorbed into the British system. Now our constable is distrusted by the law, disliked by the people, and classed as a scavenger in respect of his poorly paid position. Yet the greater part of the police are basically honest, despite having to live in worse conditions than all but the poorest criminal. And this greater part of the police believe in the system which the British bequeathed them."

"The police in Britain aren't that well paid either, but they seem to do all right."

An expression of disdain slid over his face like the glass partition closing in a taxi, effectively cutting off any further dialogue. He made no other attempt to draw me into his camp until we reached the hotel. And then I could see in his face what it cost him. "I'm giving that lecture tonight—" he said.

"What, another one?"

He persevered. "It's at the Film Academy at eight. There will be Indians there who are neither villains nor victims." He put his hand out to stop me leaving. "*I see the right path to follow, yet take the wrong one.* That too is Ovid."

I widened my eyes as if I'd seen a revelation. "What could I possibly add to that pearl? How about: 'You take the high road and I'll take the low.' No, wait, I have it: 'I used to live in a sewer. Now I live in a swamp. I've come up in the world.' "

He shook his head. "I'm sorry. I do not understand what you are trying to say."

"Ida Lupino," I said. "*No Way Out*, circa 1950. Or maybe Linda Darnell. One of the bad girls, anyway. They get all the best lines."

7

Aт TWO O'CLOCK I DIALLED ASHOK'S UNCLE IN OXFORD.

"Thirty years, Miss Benegal! But let me see . . . Anthony Un-mann . . . yes, it's coming back—odd chap, but clever . . . rather gothic tastes, I seem to remember."

"And his friend Prosper Sharma?"

"Prosper?" His old man's voice was quavery. "But of course! The cricketer!" His voice fading, drowning in monsoon interference.

"What did you say?"

The old voice reappeared. "Sent down for something or other . . . or perhaps it was that chap Unmann." He cast around through his memory file for a few facts. But no, there was nothing more.

"Could you see if anyone else remembers, Professor Tagore? It would be enormously helpful. You can ring me anytime. Professor? Are you there?" The line was dead.

From the small screen next to me a talking head read the weather report. Static edited the voice into a series of surreal highlights:

"Tandoori murderer blames monsoon stress—"

". . . on the Bombay nuns' case. A posse of detectives inspected the room where two nuns were burned to death, still used as a school-room for street children—"

". . . in Delhi, during record-breaking night temperatures of 120 degrees—"

"We dream with our eyes open—"

". . . desperately awaiting the monsoon, in Calcutta, where local elections were disrupted by unruly Marxist workers, who killed the labourers engaged in whitewashing over the graffiti of Karl Marx. The corporation responsible has agreed to have the graffiti repainted as—"

". . . evidence. The woman's breasts had been burned away. Po-
lice were alerted when neighbours complained that the man had been
roasting pork . . ."

A horizontal streak of lightning cut across and the screen went
black. Reception produced the usual excuse. "Yes, madam. Monsoon is
very close."

SATISH ISAACS WAS ON HIS WAY OUT, HE SAID WHEN I RANG, BUT I COULD MEET
him at Mohammed's, a chicken merchant in Crawford Market. He told
me I would feel right at home there, because the stone flooring came
from Scotland and the exterior reliefs had been designed by Rudyard
Kipling's father. In fact, the carvings of what could have been subti-
tled "Noble Peasants Inspired by Labour" were reminiscent of something commissioned by Stalin and his cronies.

From Badshah Cold Drinks Depot I bought a sherbet of mango
juice so fresh that the tannin from the fruit's skin puckered my mouth
like strong Glasgow tea. The vendor directed me to a great cathedral
of meat. It was late in the day to be shopping, so most of the huge
meathooks that descended from the ceiling were empty of their fleshy
chandeliers, but the noise of the fat, iridescent flies was overwhelming, adding a buzz of tension to the shouts of the butchers, who waved
their cleavers like conductor's batons, desperate to get rid of the
remaining goods. The sticky smell of blood reminded me of the
morgue.

I found Satish holding a wiry chicken upside down while he
squeezed first one of its thighs and then the other. He waved the
chicken in the air by its legs. "A very good *murgi*—no, Miss Benegal?"

"I'm not much of a bird fancier." I produced Bunny's photos in
their brown envelope. "Don't put these in the pot by mistake."

"Oh, she won't go in the pot yet. First a few days of corn and rice
under a basket in my yard, then the slaughter, then—Bob's your uncle—*murgi korma*." He nodded to the butcher, who tied the struggling
bird's legs together with twine, taped its beak shut, and stuffed it
headfirst into Satish's tartan plastic shopping bag, printed with the
words *Souvenir of the Silver Jubilee*. Satish opened the envelope and
examined the pictures with some interest. "Very likely the same
weapon," he said. "But I will get some blow-ups done to be sure."

"One more thing, Satish. A book was stolen from me the other
day—*Fine Arts of India and Pakistan*, originally from your reference
library. Why do you think anyone would want to steal it?"

"No idea, Miss Benegal, although it is an expensive book, now out of print."

I passed him the sheet of Sami's sketches. "You've got a much wider knowledge of Indian art than I have—do you recognize this figure of Shiva?"

Satish put his glasses on. "Very fine," he said, "but not of Shiva. I believe this is a drawing of Skanda, one of Shiva and Parvati's children."

"Never heard of him."

"See here, the peacocks drawn at the bottom of the paper?" Satish pointed to a series of thumbnail sketches. "Skanda is the young god of war and his mount is the peacock. The artist has also given the god his spear. And then he has added the triple ash stripes, the mark of Shiva, on the figure's forehead."

"Hindu gods have always given me problems," I said. Krishna I can deal with. He's got the flute, and that great reputation in the sack—six thousand milkmaids to date. Not to mention the blue skin. Any god slips into my bedroom late at night with a glint in his eye and a pelt of cerulean, a celestial hide, a blue hue to his epidermis, I know what to expect. It's the 330,000 other gods that throw me, and all those incarnations of Shiva and Vishnu. "So that's it? The peacock and the spear equals Skanda instead of Shiva?"

Satish smiled. "Not quite, no. This artist has amused himself with stories of Skanda, Miss Benegal. You see these six motherlike figures? And the stars drawn next to them? Possibly these are the six mothers of Skanda, the Krittakas."

Raw meat and too many gods. "I thought you said Parvati was Skanda's mother."

"That is so. Yet some birth myths are saying Skanda is the son of Shiva but not of Parvati, for Parvati was not able to hold Shiva's divine seed."

"So Skanda was Shiva's bastard son?"

He smiled. "In a way—but bastard son of a great god! Skanda was given to his surrogate mothers to raise: the Krittakas—your constellation, the Pleiades, isn't it? Pleiades, from word meaning to sail, so called by ancient Greeks because they are considering navigation to be safe from rise of that constellation to its setting."

I had a good idea why Sami would be interested in an illegitimate, motherless son. But where had she seen the statue? "Where is this image from, Satish?"

He shook his head. "Perhaps this was drawn from the sandstone carvings by Kushan sculptors around Mathura, which would explain why the artist used red chalk. We have more than one copy of this book you mentioned and it is having a very fine section on Skanda. You are welcome to look through it when you come to collect your photos tomorrow."

8

THAT NIGHT I WENT TO HEAR ASHOK GIVE HIS LECTURE, TO meet the other India.

No doubt about it, the man had set himself a quixotic task. Unlike Britain, which has become an encyclopaedia culture, a museum culture, dedicated to ambering each phase of its progress before trundling on, India is not so bound to the physical relics of its own past. This has always been a nation of storytellers who believe in improvisation around a central structure, and storytellers are renowned for leaving out the boring bits, which is how many Indians view their old buildings. Unless they have the postcard concession out front.

"The film you are about to see is a catalogue of the architectural leprosy caused by India's disregard for industrial pollution," Ashok said at the end of his brief talk. "You may be more interested in building India's future in computers or electronics than in preserving its past. You may feel that we should put money into saving our people before we try to save our architecture." The spotlight softened his lean features and gave them the courtly expression of an Elizabethan miniature by Hilliard. All he lacked was a ruff collar. "But we need to do both."

"Arrogant bastard, isn't he?" a voice behind me whispered, so close that I felt warm breath stir the hairs on my left shoulder. It was Caleb Mistry.

I turned back to the screen and tried to ignore him.

THE BIG PICTURE: *A leprous head, its skin further pockmarked and worn away by pollution*. Super 8, I guessed, blown up to 35 to fit the screen, the grain in the film mimicking the cratered skin. The head belongs to a smoke-ravaged stone goddess on a temple in Ahmadabad.

Shot in low light, the fast film stock deliberately pushed far beyond its optimum speed.

The leg of an amputee dissolves into: a pillar on the tomb at Agra, given movement by the lag typical of old Vidicon tubes under decreased light conditions, where the image smears as it moves across the camera. Ashok could not avoid the storyteller's syndrome, turning documentary into drama. What a newsroom would consider unusable, Ashok had employed to drive home a feeling of loss and mortality with the skill of a young David Lean. The film stock's technical flaws encouraged a blurring of vision, the metamorphosis of stone into skin.

That whisper stirred my neck hairs again. "Cheap tricks."

A gush of rusty liquid from the water tap that had been drilled into a painted Rajasthani dancer's chest on a wall in the desert city of Jaisalmer.

"A bleeding heart," Caleb said, oblivious of his neighbours' scowls. "How appropriate for this gathering of Nehru's babies."

And so it went, Ashok's plea for a reversal of the death sentence on his past. The first film of his I'd seen. Punctuated by Caleb.

At the end, we moved out into the courtyard, and the anonymous men who serve in India drifted through with trays of whisky and fruit punch. There was the rumour of food later, which in Bombay terms meant midnight at the earliest.

I looked over Ashok's audience. All the men had wives and children, all the women were dressed in vivid saris that made them look like a flock of gorgeous parakeets. It wasn't just that my plumage was wrong; in my grey Gap T-shirt and black linen trousers I felt like another species.

"Well done, Ashok," said one earnest gentleman. He turned to a portly old man on his left. "Did you see? Even Caleb Mistry turned up to get some tips!"

His friend checked to see that Caleb was far enough away. "Myself, I don't rate Mistry's work at all. All those romances between middle-class girls and shady though likeable characters with jail records. Pure tosh!"

"I think you are being overly harsh. I've always seen those films as his attempt to evolve a new idiom, don't you see, a kind of neorealism within the constraints of commercial Hindi film."

I moved away at this point and Ashok came over to my side. "Let me introduce you to the choreographer . . ." somebody or other, he said. I looked at the woman's flesh pressed against her silk blouse and saw Sami's crosshatched shoulder.

"And this is one of our best young writers on . . ." I think Ashok said politics, but it may as well have been joss sticks. A smooth face convinced of its right to reproduce. A political joss stick who knew where he was going and where he'd come from and why he was here. He just wasn't too sure about the rest of us.

That familiar, harsh voice behind me again. "Nothing raw, everything cooked."

Ashok turned around. "Ah, Mistry, I am flattered by your attendance. I didn't realize you were interested in architectural preservation."

"I'm not," Caleb said, smiling at me. "But without a villain the spice of Hindi movies is lost."

Turning my back on Caleb, I said, "It was a good film, Ashok, but I need some sleep. Or something." Waiting for Ashok to change the direction I was headed.

"I'm not sure what more I can offer," Ashok said.

I heard Caleb move away, imagined what he would have offered. "Sorry, Ash, I just don't fit in with the Happy Families crowd. They're the same faces you see at events like this all over the world. Only the colours have been changed."

"Perhaps your father was right when he compared you to the monsoon," Ash said, his voice unusually bitter. "Or some other overwhelming entropic force."

"An overwhelming *what*?"

"If you'll allow me a euphemism, I would call entropic forces the reluctance of nature to have order imposed upon it."

"As it happens, despite my general lack of a classical education, I do know what entropy is. Disorder," I said. "Second Law of Thermodynamics: things fall apart. The law that defines the arrow of time, as they say. If entropy decreased, time would start running backwards."

There was a gold Mercedes parked in front of the theatre. The passenger door swung open and I got in. Caleb sat in the driver's seat. As I reached to close the door, Ashok was watching me from the theatre steps, his worst suspicions confirmed.

I know how a cyclone is conceived, but how does it chart its course? Like a born-again Christian with the Bible I could quote Piddington's meteorological poetry and read into it whatever message confirmed the course I had chosen already. Not the safe route, the profitable one, sailing around the edge of the storm. My compass is set straight into the eye. A collision course.

9

Tours of the city, one, two, three.

"I want to show you my Bombay," Caleb said.

The city as a conveyor belt to chaos. He drove too fast, and I tried not to see the crash that was always just seconds away, staring instead at his profile, searching its fleshy contours for a hint of the finely drawn youth in his old photos.

"Where did you first meet Prosper?" I asked.

His jaw tightened. Something there, hidden. "I used to take him on walking tours," he said. "I took him to cafés where you could eat fresh mussels for a couple of paise, places where they can make a meal out of a handful of dried roots and some rice with its husk still on. You know all that gritty reality in his films the critics go wild for? I showed it to him."

He hurled the Merc into a narrow road of wooden buildings that were decaying with age, girls leaning against open doors, girls framed in upper windows overlooking the streets. The noise from cheap videos, transistors, and street vendors was incredible. We were driving so slowly, caught in an eddy of sexual window shoppers, I could hear a soup of languages from all over the subcontinent. *Choleee kay peachayayay . . . Choleee kay peachayayay . . . Choleee kay peachayayay*: that song bouncing off the walls.

"This is Falkland Road," Caleb said. "Two and a half square miles of sex for sale. These are the cages." Barred compartments no bigger than train lavatories, a painted teenage girl in every compartment, like rabbits in a pet shop. The standard wooden booths found in every bazaar in Gujarat, for selling anything. "I was born here."

He turned the car down a lane and parked it, giving a boy nearby a handful of rupees to look after it. "Come on." Caleb grabbed my arm. I tried to yank it back, but he pulled me along by the wrist. "You're so interested in the preservation of our heritage, I want you to see mine."

There were Shiv Sena symbols scrawled on every available wall. An old man walked by with a brass incense burner on the end of a pole which he swung into the open girl cages as he passed. "To get rid of the stink," Caleb said. I saw a fat man standing in the doorway of one of the cages talking to an older woman. Behind the couple was a very young girl. The woman pulled up the girl's skirt and pointed at the hairless genitals. The man nodded, gave the woman some money, and she drew a curtain across the door and left him with the girl.

"I don't want to do this," I said.

"We used to walk here, me and your brother-in-law. I knew everyone then."

My arm was red where Caleb held it. There would be bruising tomorrow. Tears before bedtime, Gran would have said. "Any of the old gang left?"

He shook his head. "Girls don't live long in the cages, despite their protein-rich diet of spunk and junk."

"I don't believe you," I said. "It's a story, another bit of poetic licence to sell movies. I've heard a new one every day since I got here. Once upon a time in India . . ." Thinking: I'm not ready for this. Wanting to put my hands to my ears, as I had done before, when my mother told me the things her father used to do.

He turned off the street abruptly, hauling me through a doorway and up four flights of narrow, stinking stairs. At the top sat a fat woman chewing paan. Her hair had been hennaed the colour of brick dust, but not for several months; there was a broad stripe of grey down the central part. She and Caleb haggled for a few minutes in a language I didn't understand. "Are you speaking Hindi?" I asked. To fix my identity, a person who questions.

"Marathi," he said. He pushed me down the corridor and opened a turquoise door. The woman was barely out of sight. He pulled my top over my head and unfastened my bra. He undid my trousers and pulled them down. Then he shoved me up against the door, unzipped his jeans, pressed his hand on my throat so hard I could barely breathe, and pushed himself inside me. All I felt was the doorknob pressing into my backbone. *This is how the dead live.*

When he had finished, I walked a little way into the room, making a neat list of details in my head. Compass points, the map of Caleb: a mattress on the floor, a faded poster of Shiva taped to the wall, a chair next to a window that overlooked an unlit inner courtyard. In one corner of the yard a girl of about ten or eleven was squatting to pee. A man watched her, rubbing his crotch.

"It smells of fish in here," I said.

Caleb smiled. "No. It smells of women who can't afford to wash enough. Or who simply are not giving a shit anymore." His language had started to slip gears, shift down. "Wait there." He went down the hall for a few minutes and I could hear him arguing with the old woman. My skin felt clammy, fluey. You are a receiver, I thought. So receive. I switched on the tape machine in my bag. "Sound effects, Falkland Road." Trying to put some distance between this man and myself, even if it was only the thickness of a microphone. A demarcation line between who I was and what the landscape was turning me into.

Caleb came back with a couple of joints. He lit one and offered it to me. I shook my head, but was grateful for the spicy smell of the dope. He inhaled deeply. "Home sweet home. The house I am living in as a kid. Prosper was teasing me that I would never get my skin free of that ancient, fishy smell of women—or of Ma. She was born in the Koli fishing village at the end of Colaba."

"Who taught you English?"

"I had lots of teachers. When I first started with Prosper he encouraged me to watch old Hollywood movies whenever I wasn't working. Sitting in the dark, practising Sinatra: 'Show me a guy who has feelings and I'll show you a sucker,' or Glenn Ford in *Gilda*: 'Statistics show there are more women in the world than anything else—except insects.' But my favourite was Hitchcock: 'Some people are better off dead. Like your wife and my father, for instance.' *Strangers on a Train*. Prosper told me to watch it. Called it 'a seminal work.' Seminal—the kind of word you use when you get your education from books. When he first said it I got all excited. Thought it was something to do with sex."

"So that's how you learned—from the movies?" I was standing next to the mattress. Caleb pressed on my shoulders until I sat down.

"My dad used to amuse himself teaching me and Ma. He left to go back to Britain when I was ten. Ma went into the cages after that. I lost my virginity to one of the hookers downstairs when I was twelve." He inhaled deeply again from the joint, then rested it on the edge of the chair. "Shall I show you what she did?"

"No." I sat perfectly still, refusing to play the game.

Caleb took one of my hands and put it on my crotch. "Rub yourself," he said.

"That's not how I do it."

"It doesn't matter. Go through the motions." When he'd got himself worked up with his hands, he said, "This time I'll wear a rubber. I didn't learn to use them until I was fucking society girls like you who didn't want to get pregnant. Most of the girls here were so junked out and hungry they hadn't had periods in years."

It was over in a few minutes. Sexually, it didn't do a lot for me. But it passed the time. It cleared out the tubes. It shut the voices up.

Caleb peeled off the condom and threw it in the corner of the room. "That's called a 'shot' in local parlance. Or 'short time.' Two fucks equals two shots." He picked up the joint again. "That's what I remember," he said. "Strictly business. Once she got me going she lay back and thought about her dinner or her next fix, or whatever hookers think about. I might as well have been fucking a corpse." Caleb looked down at me. "Like you."

"I thought you were."

"Would you prefer me to knock you around a little next time?"

"Why are you treating me like this, Caleb? Do you hate all women? Or just the ones you sleep with?"

He stared at the glowing end of the joint, watching while the head of ash slowly curved down with its own weight. "I treated you the way you've been asking to be treated since you got to Bombay. Anyway, all products of the British public school system like a bit of rough, isn't that what they say?"

"That's what they say. But I never went to public school. I'm a working-class kid. Made good, just like you. My grandfather was a butcher, son of a clerk." *Big red hands. Like raw meat, my mother said. But he always kept his nails clean.* "My grandmother was a peasant like your mother." Both of us damaged, Caleb. "Sorry to disappoint you."

"Not like mine," he said. "My mother wasn't a peasant, she was a whore knocked up by some Englishman who promised to look after her and then buggered off back to his wifee in Britain. My friends were other whores' kids. A real ethnic mix. The gangs who supplied the cages specialized in tribal girls from Nepal, Assam, Kashmir. Difficult virgins were handed over to a rape artist."

"*Salaam Bombay.*" Trying to hold on. "It was a movie, Caleb. I saw the movie."

He stood up and walked away from me, turning with his back to the window so his body was silhouetted, his face invisible. "You people, you think you know us. You've seen all the Hindi films about the slum dwellers whose blood runs with the milk of human goodness. Or the poor villagers who are downtrodden, yet remain upright and honest. The prince and the pauper separated at birth but both growing up with their nobility still evident."

"You're the expert. You made those movies."

The calendar pages flipping over, Bombay film style: 1988, Hema Malini plays both the weak subdued girl and her boisterous sister; 1990, Dilip Komar plays the cowardly brother and simultaneously his clever and courageous twin.

"That's all crap," he said. "I watched my first murder when I was eight. It was nothing special. Badly cast by Hindi standards: the heroine wasn't pretty, the hero wasn't sympathetic. When I was ten, Ma's pimp sliced off the nipple on her left tit with a knife and then poured acid on it. I nursed her. But she went back to him. What you call an enlightening experience. That's what forms you. And once you get out of the swamp, you do what's necessary never to slide back. *Never.*"

"What about the Shiv Sena movement? What about that poet from the chawls who writes in Marathi?" I am saying it to both of us: there is good in where you came from, in what you were, not only in what you have become.

"Namdeo. Let me guess." His voice was contemptuous. "You read about him in a book and then you signed up twenty pounds a year for Action Aid: *On the day I was born I was an orphan. The one who bore me went to God. I was tired of this ghost, Haunting me on the footpath . . . So I ate shit and grew. Give me five paise . . . Give me five paise . . . and take five curses in return.* The first poem of my own people I ever learned. The first one not taught to me by Prosper. Not Shakespeare. Not fucking T. S. Eliot."

"Why did you come to Ashok's film?"

"To see you."

"For this?"

"To find out if you'd taken everyone's advice and given up the private-detective shit. I wouldn't like anything to happen to that face of yours." He took one last toke on the joint and flicked it out the window. "Although I prefer your sister's."

"Too bad she's happily married."

"Is she?"

"She'd never leave Prosper."

"She told you?" He gave me a grim little version of a smile. "If you love your sister, you better hope she does."

"What do you mean?"

"Your sister has money, hasn't she?"

"Some. Nothing major unless she sells off her family's estate in the south."

He raised his hands. "Well, Prosper hasn't exactly got a great reputation with women, has he?"

10

AT THE RITZY I WENT STRAIGHT TO MY ROOM AND RAN A BATH. While the tub filled, I looked up "entropy" in my pocket dictionary. "Energy existing but lost for the purpose of doing work," it read; "a measure of the degradation of the universe; strictly bound to temperature. Energy flows from a hotter object to a cooler; in the process, the systems become more disordered." And here I was moving from Britain to India, trying to reverse the process.

The hotel bathroom was painted an unfortunate shade of aquamarine that gave my skin the pallor of a day-old corpse. Trust me, I know that colour. The mask of my face submerged under the shimmer of the badly foxed mirror. I supered onto it the drowned features of Sami. I held up my hands and saw the exposed sinew around her wrists. This was not the portrait I had come back to India to find, not the family snap I wanted to stick in my album. Of the old India that flickered through my personal home movies there seemed not much left.

I washed three paracetemol down with cold beer and lay on my bed watching geckos catching insects on the ceiling. One of the more successful geckos got so fat and heavy with bugs he fell from the ceiling onto the bed and bounced. He looked a bit stunned. I knew how he felt.

Lying wide-awake with closed eyes, staring at the inside of my eyelids, I finally gave up on sleep and started to read the book I'd bought about Shiva, a mercurial deity who is morally ambivalent and delights in flouting human rules. Vishnu is the god of accepted behaviour, representing all the orthodox Hindu qualities—devotion to caste and home, support of the family unit over the individual. They say he satisfies the large group of us who are looking for security, certain knowledge, and the strength of community. He is the god of the mid-game. The boring bits. Dangerous, beautiful, phallic Shiva stands on his retinue of badly behaved and irreverent dwarfs and nature spirits, the *ganas* and the *yakshas* whom he has tamed and keeps in service. He is Lord of the beginning and of the end.

While I was comparing two illustrations of Shiva—spot the difference, grasp the subtleties—I noticed the photo caption next to them of a building frescoed with dancing girls: *By an unknown Rajasthani artist*. It reminded me of Sami, another unknown Rajasthani artist, whose only mistake had been to try to stick her head above the wall of invisibility. One of the images in Ashok's film came back to me: a modern wall stippled with the broken remnants of old temple carvings. I had seen that wall before—in the town of Sonavla, on the railway line from Bombay to Poona. When had Ashok been there?

"Surely in meteorology, as in astrology, the thing to hunt down is a cycle," wrote S. A. Hill, in his Indian Meteorological Department memoirs. "And if that is not to be found in the temperate zone, then go to the frigid zones or the torrid zones and look for it, and if found, then above all things, and in whatever manner, lay hold of it, study it, record it and see what it means."

I was stuck on a circular track, a cycle that never quite repeated. But I had no idea what it meant. Closing my eyes, I dreamed of a Michelangelo's *David* whose head sprouted geckos' tails and snakes like Medusa's.

THE SNAKES WERE TIGHTENING AROUND MY HEAD UNTIL IT STARTED TO RING. Ashok's uncle in Oxford. He had remembered about that Sharma fellow.

"Sent down, he was."

"So you said." I looked at the clock. Three in the morning.

"Yes, yes, but there's more, you see. He never got his degree."

"That's it?" I said. "That's what you rang to say?" Prosper Sharma did not get the degree he claimed for himself on his letterhead. More solid evidence for his murder trial. Along with my cocktail-napkin monsoon chart and the remarkable similarities between Sami and Skanda, god of war.

"No, no. Also it was widely believed he was covering for the other chap."

"What other chap? Blame for what?" It was too early or too late for this.

"Didn't I say?" He sounded surprised. "That chap Unmann. He and Sharma smuggled a tart into their rooms. Got reported. Terrible shame. Sharma was a magical batter. Now that I think of it, the tart might have been a man." He stopped to squeeze his spongy memory. "That's it. A man dressed up as a tart."

"A *transvestite*? You're sure?"

"Or some such gothic creature . . ."

We were both shouting to be heard over the static. The man in the room next to mine pounded on the wall to shut me up. Once again, the line went dead.

11

Big face is singing to me. As my saffron-skinned lover moves closer, disembodied, I can see horizontal video lines, fractured colours. Then, in the kind of twist where one part of your unconscious self speaks to another, I hear myself say, "But this is a dream—and so badly shot." And Basil Chopra's reply: "Of course, dream sequences are obligatory in Bollywood, along with family melodrama and a comic figure passing through."

I woke up with a numb right ear caused by having passed out with my head resting heavily on a copy of *Gods, Demons and Others* by R. K. Narayan. It was an Indian edition, cheaply printed on what looked and felt like toilet paper. I must have sweated into it in the night, because the smudged words "outlines melting or emerging" could just be read on my right cheek.

Outside, yesterday's black stripe on the horizon had swelled to enclose half the city in a wall the colour of mussel shells. There was a petrified silence everywhere. How had the Scots, that shade-loving species, ever survived this climate? *"Once upon a time,"* my mother said, *"when white people first came to this coast, two monsoons were the age of an Englishman, not more. And we have lived so much longer, Rosalind. Too long."*

The old voices getting louder. I splashed my face with cold water to get rid of them and put on my thinnest white Marks & Spencer's knickers, part of me that will be forever British, one half of my cultural inheritance. Over them I slipped a long muslin dress in terracotta, the colour of the earth I wanted to get down to.

Then I rang Shoma Kumar, exchanged a little preliminary chit-chat, and asked her if she had ever heard of Prosper or Maya having had a son—maybe an illegitimate one. She seemed genuinely astonished by the idea, her antennae out for a story. "I'll tell you what, Shoma—you give me an idea about Prosper's prowess as a lover and you can have first bid on any juicy titbits I uncover."

"As a lover?"

"You said Caleb was hung like a Coke can. I figure you could tell me what Prosper liked in bed."

She went uncharacteristically coy, said she couldn't go into details. The most she would say was that he was a director through and through. "You mean he likes to watch?" I said, trying not to think of my sister. But she wouldn't add any more details.

I called Satish Isaacs after that to make sure the photos were ready, then Ram to see if he'd had any luck tracing the Goliath Cinema's owners.

"I've tried to access the info," he said. "But whoever owns that building has covered their tracks pretty well. I'll keep trying."

As soon as I put down the phone, it rang again. The hotel operator said that a Mr. Ashok Tagore had left a message. "If he rings back, tell him I'll call later."

AT THE CENTRAL PROPS UNIT, SATISH HAD MADE BLOW-UPS OF THE PHOTOS OF Sami and Maya. If not identical, the wounds were close enough to make a very strong link.

"And here is that book you were interested in," Isaacs said. "There is a large section on the images of Skanda." He pointed at one photo of a sandstone figure standing in profile. "This one I think is very similar to your drawings."

The figure bore a remarkable resemblance to the one in a sketch of Sami's, even to the chip out of the figure's left ear, although Sami had drawn hers from a different viewpoint. "Is there one of this taken full face, like the drawing?"

He shook his head. "It is an old photo. Artist most likely drew from the actual piece. But I will check the collection, in case we are having perhaps photos in another source." He got out a pair of thick glasses to read fine print and flipped through the index. "Ah no, there won't be any better pictures, I'm afraid. This picture is of one of your brother-in-law's pieces. Last time a complete photographic study of the Sharma collection was done was sometime in the early sixties, which explains the poor quality of the reproduction." He took off his glasses and smiled happily at me. "But why are you worrying, Miss Benegal? You are having an advantage over all of us in that you can view the original any time you wish! Only to be paying a family visit to the Sharma residence."

But when had Sami paid her visit?

"Borrow this book for a couple of days if it interests you, Miss Benegal."

12

Thomas was back with me, looking smug after the tips he'd been paid to escort a Saudi oil sheik and his wives from one diamond merchant to another. But he was worried about my future. He told me that the old Goliath Cinema, a complex the clerk at the microfilm library had said might be Sami's last address, was not a place for a nice girl to go. I thanked him for his concern and asked him to come back for me in two hours.

On the road where Thomas dropped me there was a billboard for Caleb's current film: NEVER BEFORE! A LOVE STORY PLUS SEVEN MURDERS! THE MEAN STREETS OF AAMCHI BOMBAY BY NIGHT, MIDDLE-CLASS SHIVAJI PARK BY DAY: LET SLEEPING UNDERDOGS LIE! As usual, I didn't recognize good advice even when the underdog came up and bit me in the leg.

The address Sunila had written down matched a five-storey building far enough outside the main hijra prostitution roads to be quiet, but still close enough for action. It took up a full city block backing onto the Goliath Cinema. The complex must once have been very beautiful, a nineteenth-century mansion, or maybe even an old mill, built at a time when mills were designed like palaces.

The bottom two floors were devoted to cheap enterprises of a kind to suit the local clientele: all-night bars; shops selling vibrators, batteries, and henna; quacks with dubious medical qualifications pushing herbal remedies for sexually transmitted diseases. CURE VD: DRINK AH-MED'S TEA! said one sign. To get to the residential floors, I had to walk into the central courtyard under a carved stone archway probably built to allow carriages to pass. There were eight apartments to a floor and a common latrine and leaking tap in the yard. Zarina's address was up five flights of stained concrete steps, past doors left open to allow what little breeze there was into these people's claustrophobic lives. I could see men stretched out on the floors in the late-afternoon heat, arms flung across their faces against the light.

Someone had made an effort with Sami's last home. A simple whitewashed pattern of woven flowers and leaves had been painted around the door, and two flowering plants stood in pots on either side, recently watered. But there was no answer when I knocked. As I was about to leave, a tall, bare-chested man in white pyjama bottoms came out of the flat a few doors away.

"If you are seeking Zarina," he said, "she has not been here for a couple of days." He saw me looking at the watering can he was carrying. "I water them for her when she's working."

"You must be a good friend," I said. Or a pimp.

"It's not what you think. I'm a scriptwriter."

I clocked the run-down state of the apartment block.

He shrugged. "It's a buyers' market. When I *was* a scriptwriter, I used to work late, just like Zarina. She's a good cook, coming from same neck of the world as me. I'm Hindu from Bengal and she is Muslim from Bangladesh. So speaking different languages. But Zarina and I forged a kind of culinary friendship over mustard-fry fish and steamed banana blossoms. We share common nostalgia for *ilish*, a fish Bengalis are comparing to their women—very tempting on the outside, but get too close and you choke on the bones. Do you know it?"

I shook my head. "Did you know Zarina's flatmate as well—Sami?"

The watering can slipped in his hand. "Sami's dead. I don't know about that." He started to retreat back into his own flat.

"Don't worry. I'm not with the police." I flashed my BBC pass. "My name is Roz Bengal. I'm trying to find some photos of Sami's for a friend of hers."

"What friend?"

"Sunila, another hijra. She said that Sami took these photos to stop some clients pulling down her friends' homes."

"I am knowing nothing about photos, but I know Sami was trying to protect this." He waved his arms in the direction of the courtyard. "Although the developers are not exactly pulling it down. It is being recycled."

"*This* is the building Sami was trying to save?"

"Not much, is it, for anyone from the West?" His expression was ironic. "But well over a thousand people are living and working in this block, up to fifteen in some apartments. Recently it was sold for rede-velopment as luxury hotel complex with multiscreen cinema and spa facilities. Using up fifty times present resources, of course, because our foreign guests are taking very unkindly to power cuts and water shortages that we, as a backward nation, are taking for granted."

"Who are the developers?"

"They style themselves Goliath Corp.—you can see breadth of their vision in a poster on the cinema—but this is only a blanket to cover a multitude of sinners."

What had the beach painter told me? "Any idea where I might find Zarina?" I said. "In case she knows about the photos?"

"She's freelance." He stopped, reluctant to give me details. I waited.

"Sometimes she is working one of the bars near Great Palace Street," he added grudgingly. "Bar None, it is called. Most places round here are for zenana, but there is hijra mother who is running rooms above this bar. You might try there."

"Do you remember whether Sami ever mentioned someone called Gol or Gul?"

"Name is ringing a bell . . . I think Sami is having a friend named Gul. Long time ago. I remember him only because he is cripple of some kind. Sami is always adopting cripples."

He returned to watering. End of interview, I thought. But before I reached the stairs he called out in the wistful voice of an exile asking for letters from home: "Please, if you see Zarina, remind her that it is nearly monsoon: time for making resolutions—and *khichuri*. No need to shop, I have onions and ginger and eggs to deep-fry, and even special *atap* rice. She will be knowing what I mean."

"*Khichuri?* Oh, you mean kedgeree."

He shook his head. "That is bastardized British version. Ours is a more refined dish, the layers of flavours being infinitely more subtle."

I left him pinching the dead flowers off Zarina's plants.

THE BAR NONE WAS A GRIM PLACE, WITH THAT PARTICULARLY ASIAN DISRE-gard for artificial lighting which makes rooms always either too dark or too bright. Every stain and fleshy wrinkle was deepened by the hard, bluish-white glow of overhead strip fluorescents. The walls were painted a glossy hospital green that had bubbled and discoloured with terrible seepages. The bar was a wood-grain Formica table with a collection of half-empty bottles and stainless-steel cups on it to drink from. The furnishings were armchairs covered in an array of unnatural fabrics that made you sweat or itch or both.

Girls were washed up around the edges of the room in conjugations which seemed arbitrary, nothing to do with inclination, like the magnetic cohesion of shells, seaweed, and driftwood on a beach, in whose casual groupings and separations patterns can be discerned that lack either logic or durability. There were fine, dark Malayali and Bengali faces; pale, green-eyed Muslims from Kashmir; snub-nosed Gujaratis; and tiny Nepalese with the matte skin of Chinese porcelain dolls. A few sarcastic cracks at my female presence rippled the waves of indifference as I entered, but the interest sank quickly. The life of Bina's family of hijra in the country had appeared to have some dignity and grace, but these girls were beached here in the neon life, washed out as well as washed up. I sat flicking through the screaming headlines of back issues of Shoma Kumar's magazine, *Screenbites*, that lay on the sofa: "GOOD BOY BAD BUSINESS: Nohsin Khan Unmasked!" "A STUD OF THE LUSTIEST KIND: The New New Strain of Love!" "OUR NEW ANEETA SETS PULSES RACING WITH HER WOW FIGURE AND PEARLY SMILE!" The articles were just as educational:

WHY VILLAINS SMILE EACH TIME THEY ARE SLAPPED

Every slap means money! Today the villain is omnipotent on Hindi film screens. Like the hero used to be, he is swashbuckling, debonair, and able to make females swoon with his suave and snakeish charm.

A few furtive customers came and went, and through the tinny Hindi film music playing from a small transistor the sound of creaking floorboards could be heard above. This bar had all the sexual appeal of a small-town hairdressing salon, except that here, the final result would be even tackier. After an hour of sweating into my knickers, I figured I'd established enough credibility to ask the dark Malayali next to me if she knew a girl named Zarina.

"Zarina is most popular here, when she is deigning us with her presence. But this is not very often, because she is not one of the hoi polloi. She used to have a very rich steady boyfriend, but I have not seen her for many days."

I described Zarina's neighbour. "No, that is actually the nice man who is living next to her," she said, "photographer."

"He said he was a scriptwriter."

"Yes?" She lifted her heavily plucked eyebrows. "Maybe in another life. Now he takes pictures." She giggled. "Dirty pictures. Such a sweet boy, but not interested in Zarina for sexual purposes. Her boyfriend was tall, like this neighbour, but more well built and dressed in Western clothes and shoes of the very best sort."

She wouldn't go any further. "Was her boyfriend married?" I asked. "Did he wear a ring?" Prosper wore a ring.

She shrugged. "Married, unmarried, fathers of many, all kinds come to us."

"What about a cripple named Gul—a friend of Sunila? Do you know him?"

One question too many. I was starting to sound like a cop. The other girls had gradually stopped even the pretence of chatting. I heard the stairs protesting and a stout, ageing Richard Nixon in drag appeared at the doorway. "Oh no, this is Auntie," whispered one of the girls. "Here comes trouble."

"You there," said Nixon, pointing at me. "You tourist! What are you doing here, scaring off my business? Pissing or get off the pot!" She clapped her cupped hands in a peculiar way the hijra have and then held one hand out and rubbed her fingers together. "Just because we are not having that tool which makes you happy at night, you cannot come here for nothing."

"I'm sorry," I said. "I'm looking for Zarina, for a friend."

"Your friend wants Zarina, he pays much money."

"Not for that, just to talk."

"Not for *that*!" She spat the words at me. "No fuckee-fuckee, just talking? But talking too costs money."

"I'm sorry, this was a mistake. I'll leave."

Halfway down the street, I heard someone call out "Miss! You have forgotten this!" One of the Kashmiri hijras, waving a copy of Shoma's magazine. I started to tell her that it was not mine, but she pushed the magazine into my bag anyway.

"You are lady who is trying to stop these goondas who are hurting the hijras?" The hijra looked me over. "Why are you doing this? You are not hijra."

"Everybody has to have a hobby."

"People are saying BBC will make a difference. But you must be careful in this neck of the woods. Zarina is being badly beaten. Maybe I think her boyfriend is doing this. Or his friends. She got away. But last night goondas are back, asking after this Sunila girl, and some stupid person is telling them that Sunila has a good friend called Robi who is working for Caleb Mistry."

"Do you know the boyfriend's name?"

"I must go." She tapped my bag. "Very good article about Hollywood makeup."

I turned to the article on Hollywood makeup, not expecting much. Scribbled in the margin next to "Before and After Pictures of Madonna" were the words *Gul the leper Little Flour Scool of English Goliath 4–6.*

Even the dingy concrete skin of Zarina's block was white now against the dense, steely mass of monsoon clouds. There was still no answer at her door, but I noticed a piece of paper poked under her mat. It was written in English.

Zarina—The burst of the monsoon is the day on which vows should be taken on how long to fast and when to observe <u>silence.</u> Remember monsoon poem:

> *By thunder and lightning frightened*
> *Every woman hugs her husband close,*
> *Though well his <u>guilt</u> she knows . . .*

I put the paper in my pocket, wondering idly what the neighbour's handwriting was like.

13

THERE WERE FIVE HOURS TO KILL UNTIL THE MEETING WITH Gul, so I had Thomas drop me back at the microfilm library Ram had recommended. This time I switched directions and started at the end, with Maya's death. It was listed separately from Prosper's file, under *Suicides*. I was still looking for a property link, working backwards through the old gossip about Prosper's affairs, the hints of his flings with Nonie and Shoma Kumar, the recent twilight years living off the glow of previous hits, without either commercial or critical success. Headlines: SHARMA: RISING EXPECTATIONS, REDUCING RETURNS! SHARMA: MAJOR HYPE, MODEST HITS! SHARMA'S ISLAND: SINKING FAST?

A film in fastback: I could see the errors of judgement Prosper made before he made them. The split with Caleb telegraphed long before it finally happened. First the fall, then the decline of the Sharma empire. I read the clippings on Maya's plunge, hoping to find some trick of the light that put Prosper at the scene, or a glimpse of Acres or Unmann in the crowd scenes.

Tired of the fruitless chase, I reverted to my old library habit of relieving boredom by idly flipping through any interesting stories that caught my fancy. Or confirmed my prejudices, I could hear Ashok say. Outcries over police brutality and incompetence. A writer called P. V. Nath pleading in 1983 for autopsy facilities to be made available at each police station, with officers posted who had adequate knowledge. "There are items like post-mortem examinations of corpses," he wrote, "for which the current setup is extremely inept."

I read letters to the editor about a gang that had been used by top politicians to kidnap student leaders from Delhi University in 1980, and of the senior police officer who had tried in vain to smash the gang. He was quoted in *The Times*: "We are powerless to stop the growth of this mafia when it has politicians' backing. If we arrest them, they will simply be bailed out."

I read of other suicides, bride burnings, dowry deaths, young wives who had killed themselves after failing to cope with the pressure of maltreatment meted out by their in-laws. My eyes skipped restlessly, missing headlines, losing dates, losing track of time. Scrolling quickly past yet another story of a woman's fall, I stopped suddenly and felt the tunnel vision of *déjà vu*. A small headline: *Wife's Monsoon Despair Pushes Her over the Edge.* I flipped through the opening lines again to the date: 20 June 1973. Almost fifteen years before Maya's death.

Police have rejected hints of foul play in the death of a woman found yesterday after falling from the balcony of her seventh-storey apartment in Bombay. Neighbours say she had been depressed for months and sounds of weeping had been heard on many occasions. "I blame it on the monsoon, and on the fact that her husband is so often away for his work," said one woman. "Everyone knows no joy is greater than union of lovers during monsoon, no sorrow deeper than separation at this time. Most common theme of Indian love songs is longing of lovers for each other when rains are in full force." The dead woman, Sephali Mistry, twenty-two, is survived by husband, Caleb, and daughter, Nonie. Weather permitting, Mr. Mistry returns today from Delhi, where he is on location with movie moghul, Prosper Sharma, shooting a version of Shakespeare's *The Tempest.*

This is the colour of the atmosphere before the cyclone strikes. A lurid red, I thought. *Bright crimson.* The colours of melodrama. How many more of these circles on the ground? I wondered, ideas sparking in my head like loose wires. I blinked away the computer blur and read the lines more carefully this time; then trawled the files again for any mention of Caleb's early years, to find out more about how the street kid had managed to climb out of the dung heap. It took a long time. My eyes were blurring with screen fatigue. But I found the connection.

It used to be a more common crime among the lower echelons of Bombay's gangsters. For anyone farther up the criminal ladder it wasn't profitable enough. A film becomes popular, on the scale of *Jurassic Park*, say. Everyone wants to see it. So someone with capital buys up all the seats, and has his touts sell the tickets on the black market at triple or quadruple the price.

The year is 1967. A judge recommends severity in sentencing a ticket tout arrested outside Bombay's biggest cinema. The sentence reflects the boy's link with more serious crimes. In particular, with his practice of stealing gold which has been melted down into "biscuits."

They never catch the ringleader. The eighteen-year-old ticket tout is released after serving a short sentence, largely because the esteemed director Prosper Sharma steps forward and promises to give the accused a respectable job to keep him out of mischief. It is considered to be very generous of Mr. Sharma, who, after all, was the injured party: Goliath Cinema, where the boy is arrested, is one of a chain inherited from the family of Mr. Sharma's wife.

The young criminal, Caleb Mistry, proves worthy of his patron's trust.

In 1973, Caleb has been working for Island Studios for six years. In 1974, following his first wife's suicide, he remarries—a beautiful socialite—and is rumoured to be making an experimental film of his own, *The Cyclone*; 1974 was a golden year for Caleb Mistry.

But 1973 was the year he stopped smiling into the camera.

That explained *The Cyclone*. The replay of Caleb's wife's death, not of Maya's. Two more wires connected. I felt as if the tight band around my head had loosened suddenly, the way we used to feel at the burst of the monsoon, when southwest winds over north and south India would meet and increase in strength, coinciding with the disappearance of a belt of high pressure.

I shut off the microfiche and got the librarian to make me a few copies of the relevant newspaper files.

"BUT THE FACT THAT SHARMA OWNS SAMI'S BUILDING DOESN'T PROVE HE HAD anything to do with her death," Ram said, when I rang him from the library, "or even remembered that he owned the place. Guys like Sharma have so much, they—"

"Suddenly you're the voice of reason. What about this biscuit business? Have you ever heard of it?"

"As in McVities?" His voice was mischievous.

"Ram."

"Sure. If you're smart, and you've got cash coming in that you don't want going straight out into the taxman's pocket, you melt down your undeclared gold into portable gold biscuits, sort of oversized coins, a common way for respectable Bombay people to store black money. Trouble is, if you get it nicked, you're out of luck, because you can't complain to the authorities. Good news for the crooks."

"But how would the crooks know who has these gold biscuits?"

"You can figure that anyone in a business with no fixed price, where a lot of cash changes hands quickly . . ."

"Movies, drugs, prostitution . . ." I said.

"Property, video piracy . . ."

"And who better to tell me about video piracy, right?" The day before, Ram had confirmed the source of his newfound wealth.

"I've heard you can get good info on who's got the biscuits from the police. For a price. They get a kickback from the goondas."

"MADAM, YOU ARE BACK HOME AT LAST," THE HOTEL RECEPTIONIST SAID.

"So it appears."

He told me that Ashok had rung several times, and there was a message as well from Basil Chopra. "I have written it down this time clearly," he said, "because last time you were complaining so much about my writing, and Mr. Basil Chopra is saying you will understand."

"Fine, get on with it."

"This is it, now I am quoting: 'Tell Miss Roz Bengal that the monsoon finally reminded me. The tempest. It happened while we were filming, years ago. Caleb had begun directing. It was to have been his first picture. Then the tragedy with his wife happened. *Thou didst prevent me; I had peopled else / This isle with Calibans.* Tell her she has the face of Caleb's first wife. The one who died. The dead one.' And he has found the manuscript you wanted. He did *say* you would understand."

"Yes, yes, I see. Thank you."

Partner recognition is not highly refined amongst amphibians. A bullfrog's mating song can be heard up to a kilometre away, but for him a female is anything which is soft, has the appropriate width, and moves. A male of one species has been known to find a female of another species buried deep down in the mud, pull her out by her hind legs, clasp her back to his breast, and copulate with her until she dies from the incompatible poison in his diversely coloured skin. He may continue his mating for hours after his partner's death, stimulated by the movement given to the corpse by his own passionate thrusting. He may even continue copulation with the mud.

Sometimes I think we haven't moved far up the evolutionary scale.

I went to the bar and drank something that aged me prematurely. To keep up my strength I ate several bowlfuls of peanuts, the most widely travelled food in the world. And half a bowl of pickled onions. "Onions are high in vitamin C," I said to the bartender, in case he was worried about my health, "good for hangovers." These were more widely travelled than was absolutely desirable.

1 4

We SAT IN BASIL CHOPRA'S CONSERVATORY DRINKING FRESH lime soda with crushed mint. "I didn't really know her," he said. "No one did. She was rarely in the public eye."

"You must've known her face enough to link it with mine after twenty years."

"It was a memorable face," he said simply. "Although not a memorable mind to go with it; that I do remember. A simple girl, barely a word of English, completely devoted to Caleb, always looking up at him with adoring eyes. She was small, rather undernourished. A reflection, perhaps, of their earlier, more difficult time together. I think it was her smallness and daintiness that stopped me from putting your faces together immediately."

"I'm hardly petite."

"All girls today are taller than their mothers and grandmothers. I think it's the food. Almond sweets, my dear?"

"I'm fine, thanks."

"You don't mind if I do? They're from a most delicious little shop not far from Crawford Market. My driver brings them to me."

"You say you didn't know her very well—why? You must've met her on the set."

"One would think so, but you know, I don't remember her coming to any of the parties. Of course, there were a lot of them then, and a lot of people wanting to meet one." Basil cast his lashes down modestly.

"What about photos—there are newspaper pictures of Prosper and Maya and Caleb together. Where was Sephali?"

"At home with the children, I suppose. How can I put it? Moviemaking is like a closed family unit, at least for the duration of the filming, a mafia that is hard for outsiders to break into. Prosper and Caleb were rather a special instance. Caleb was just finding his feet, working very hard to learn the business and then studying whenever he had time off, trying to improve himself. Prosper was remarkably patient with him, terribly close—almost like a father. Caleb was invited places very early on that he would never have got into without that push from Prosper. Perhaps that's why he didn't bring—what was her name again?—Sephali. A tree. White flowers opening at night and shed by morning. The irony is that the tree is meant to have been a princess who fell in love with the sun. When he deserted her, she was burned. The tree grew out of her ashes."

"What grew out of Sephali's ashes—Caleb's career?"

"You could put it like that. There was the faintest hint of a suggestion from Maya and Prosper that perhaps Sephali's presence did not do much to assist Caleb's social standing. She was basically"—he cast around for a polite word—"unsophisticated, the first Mrs. Mistry, and terribly young, although it was easy to forget that under all her paint and cheap finery. That was the other reason I didn't equate your face with hers at first. She looked more like you after . . ."

"After what?"

"No, really, this is too morbid."

"Go on."

"After the fall."

"You saw her after she'd killed herself?"

"I saw the photos Caleb had. Like the death masks they used to take in plaster. He kept the pictures with him for months, poor chap. I think it was the guilt."

"So what you're saying is that Caleb was embarrassed by her and quite glad to see the back of her. Which explains why he married again so quickly."

"Embarrassed by her—yes—but certainly not glad to see her go. No, dear girl, not at all. The boy was quite broken up by her death. Couldn't work for months. And then became very odd indeed."

"Odd? Was there any question of its not being suicide?"

"Absolutely none. The little girl—Nonie—saw it all. She made a very reliable, very sad witness. The neighbours found her curled up in the bathroom. I say—are you all right, dear girl?"

"I'm fine." She was in the bath when I found her, I had told my father.

"It was to give Nonie a mother that Caleb married again so soon. Certainly the second marriage was nowhere near the love match the first had been."

"Although more suitable for his position."

"Of course." Basil stopped. "I am only telling what is true, not what is fair. One can't help wondering if Caleb's rise would have been quite so meteoric with—"

"With Sephali? The second wife was a more graceful flowering bush, then?"

He looked amused. "What a taste you have for metaphor, dear girl." He glanced at his watch. "Now, I don't want to press you, but you did say . . ."

I stood up. "Yes. Sorry to have kept you. Thank you, you've been most helpful."

He smiled rather vaguely. "Have I? I'm so pleased." As he shook my hand at the door, he looked searchingly into my eyes. "You seem a bit peaky. I don't think this monsoon weather agrees with you."

15

At FIRST I COULDN'T FIND ANY SIGN OF A LITTLE FLOWER IN the crowded strip of commercial enterprises that supported the old Goliath Cinema.

It was easily missed, a shop not much wider than its doorway, no windows, the sign advertising its existence slightly more upmarket than the rest by virtue of the flower painted on it. Not the usual charming but rough folk art, this was an elegant, long-stemmed rose of decidedly European heritage. I pushed past tall filing cabinets to the desk and rang the bell on it, my skin already soaked from the inadequate ventilation. A man as narrow and cramped as the shop appeared.

"I'm looking for Gul," I said. "I'm a friend of Sami's."

The narrow man grunted and disappeared.

"He speaks almost no English." A disembodied voice from behind the desk. A shadow moved, resolving itself into a leper on a skateboard.

"I am his voice and his dictionary," the leper said. He had a pronounced American accent. "And you are the lady from the BBC."

"You must be Gul." I looked more closely at him. "You seem familiar."

"My name is Gulab, like the syrupy sweet. But Sami called me Gul: the rose. I have seen you at the Taj Mahal Hotel, where I sometimes go to beg. And at Chowpatty Beach. On the morning you talked to the police I was putting flowers on the place where Sami was found. And later. Beach painter is a friend of mine. Sami too was a friend. More than a friend. We met many years ago when she gave me scraps from the Taj kitchen, where she worked once. And she was also my teacher. I loved her." It was said very simply. "She gave us all hope."

"Gulab." A face flickering at the edge of my memory.

"A rose by any other name would smell as sweet. I learned that from Sami. My parents named me before this . . ." He gestured at his body.

"Your English is very good. But you sound American."

"I am getting my accent from the hippies in the sixties. How old do you think I am?" His face was folded like a topographical map of hilly country. Fortunately, he didn't wait for an embarrassing reply. "I have fifty-seven years. And in all those years only Sami is treating me as a man."

"What do you know about Sami's photos?" I said.

His leonine face folded itself further into grief. "I know they are sexual pictures and they are getting her killed. That is all. For several years now Sami is having a life I am no longer involved in."

Followed by eunuchs and lepers, my sister had said. "So it wasn't you who was with Sami when she was harassing my sister, Miranda Sharma?"

Gulab lowered his eyes. "Yes. For this I am ashamed. But only once am I going with Sami. And I am sorry."

"It may have been your name Sami spoke as she was dying. I thought you might know where the photos were."

"If I was knowing, I would long ago have given up these pictures to the men who want them. People here can find other homes, as I have done. It is not worth the deaths. But Sami is giving them misguided belief that they can have some power." He disappeared into a dark recess of the shop and came back with a flowered card folder. "Only pictures I have are ones she is drawing for me."

Inside were sheets of drawings by the same hand who had sketched my Skanda. These were on graph paper, each figure measured, as if the artist were planning to scale the work up. "Did Sami ever draw you?" I said, trying to place that elusive connection, wondering if his face had been one of the sketches in the margins of the stolen book.

"Does it surprise you?" He smiled, the corrugated roof of his face creasing horizontally as well as vertically, turning him from a lion into a Pekinese. "We were once very good friends, you know. But these other drawings I keep at my home. However, if you wish to see, I am most pleased to be showing them."

"Is it near here, your home?"

"Jehangir Baug, one of the squatters' colonies on the outskirts of Bombay."

"Then I don't think I'll be going there tonight. How about tomorrow? Where can I get in touch?"

"Go to STD telephone office near giant billboard on Cadell Road in the morning. I will meet you there."

"How will I find it?"

Gul laughed. "No problem. I am living quite near giant billboard. And all taxi-wallahs are knowing this road because it is on edge of Jehangir Baug, where the finest illicit hooch in Bombay is made. You will be able to smell it when you get there. So delicious it is and so profitable that all our hutments are electrified. Some people are even having to work only nine months a year brewing and then return to villages to buy land. Not like my parents, who are somewhat in the grips of ruthless hooch baron."

"What time?"

He looked surprised. "When you arrive in the morning, I will find you."

SATYAJIT RAY SAID THAT CINEMA AS A MEDIUM IS CLOSER TO WESTERN MUSIC than to Indian, because in India the tradition of inflexible time does not exist. Music here is improvised; the same piece can last two hours or fifteen minutes. "It is nothing which resembles a sonata or symphony with a beginning and an end, irrespective of who the conductor is," Ray said. The duration of an Indian song depends on the musician's mood, the temperature, the time of day. Only jazz comes close.

But cinema is a composition bound by time. I thought about the movie being made by Prosper, and wondered how advanced his production was, and where its director had been when two men were torturing Sami to death. *Every woman hugs her husband close, though well his guilt she knows.* I was haunted by the thought that Miranda knew what her husband had done. Or half-knew, my half sister. Perhaps she only admitted it to herself on those nights when futility weighs you down like a heavy blanket in hot weather.

IN THE RITZY BAR, I SAT NURSING A WARM KINGFISHER BEER AND reading the screenplay Basil had given me at his house. Caleb had turned *The Tempest* into a story about the colonizers' contempt for the people they colonize. Judging by Prosper's handwritten alterations, the erosion of Caleb's vision had been gradual but not gentle. The result was a script that justified instead of condemning each succeeding ruler's right to rule.

But it was Prosper's notes in the spaces between the scenes and at the end of the manuscript that gripped me. Like the script, they too charted an evolution from condemnation to justification, another kind of erosion of identity. Here was a magical sentence: *My purpose is to tell of bodies which have been transformed into shapes of a different kind.* Prosper had marked it "Metamorphoses," adding, between the lines: "Ariel as a hijra? Sprites and demons recruited from Bombay circus dwarfs or . . . ?" I stared at his tiny, crabbed handwriting— "Sami and her troupe of malformed friends?"—until the meaning of the phrase dropped into place and I realized where I had seen Gulab before. One whole section of the jigsaw was in place, but the facts were still as slippery as jellied eels.

The receptionist at Caleb's studio told me over the phone that Robi was just completing a scene. Sunila's friend came on the line a few minutes later, out of breath.

"Robi? It's Rosalind Benegal. I want to get hold of Sunila."

He coughed. "I can pass a message if you are wishing it, miss."

Then it occurred to me that he could be of more use than Sunila at this point. "I need to get into the Central Props Unit after hours. Do you know how I can do that?"

"That is depending on which part of unit, miss. Some parts are having less security than others."

"What you call the Museum of Wounds. There are some things belonging to Sunila which may be there."

"Where are they? I could look for them tomorrow when I go to work."

I didn't like the eagerness in the boy's voice. He didn't exactly inspire trust. But I needed his help. "It would be too difficult to explain. Could you get me into the museum bit tonight? Do you have a key?"

He laughed. "Better than that, miss. I have Sunila. Man on gate is liking Sunila very much. I will bring her along." He finished work at eleven and would meet me outside the Props Unit between eleven-thirty and midnight. I just had to hope it wasn't one of Raven's nights for extracurricular work.

Thomas answered his mobile phone on the second ring. He did not think it was a good idea to go out so late on a night when the monsoon was sure to strike. "But nevertheless I am collecting you as requested, madam."

SCATTERED RAINDROPS THE SIZE OF TEN-PENNY PIECES WERE BOUNCING OFF the pavement as I got into Thomas's taxi. The big nimbus clouds that had been massing on the horizon all day had swelled up miles high, flattened and chiselled by the wind into a giant version of the marble quarries I had seen once at Carrara, in Italy. While these enormous, polished slabs rapidly blocked out what was left of the moon and darkened the road to a slippery black snake, scaly with cars' head-lights, the temperature started to drop very fast.

"Monsoon coming," Thomas said, winding up his window.

Lightning flashed above us, and there was an immediate crack of thunder, a hesitation no longer than a quick intake of breath, and then the rains burst through, wave after wave of white, rippling sheets of water. The car instantly lost traction and surfed towards the wrong side of the road. Another vertical wave of water pushed us back out of danger. Sealed inside, it was like watching a movie of the storm with the sound turned up too loud: real time telescoped; what should have taken hours took minutes. In a kind of cinematic slow motion, streets turned into torrents and then into waterfalls, floating lesser cars than the Ambassadors away, capsizing rickshaws. The battery-powered Madonna on the dashboard suddenly lit up, and the plastic

Shiva ornament behind me swung wildly as we swerved to avoid collisions.

"Traffic is not disciplined," said Thomas. "You don't know actually who is going to take a left turn and who a right."

People appeared out of every doorway and stood in the streets with their arms spread wide. I saw a woman close her eyes and turn her face upwards as if in prayer. If she had opened her mouth, she might have drowned. As it was, the rain pouring down smeared her lipstick and made the kohl under her eyes run. Her features were washing away, leaving a smooth slate on which to paint a new face. No one could mistake this rain for any other. It was not rain at all. It was as if the world had turned upside down and the oceans were pouring onto the land in one last great tidal wave. As if the sky had fallen and liquid had become solid.

"We should go back, Miss Benegal," said Thomas.

"Keep driving. It's not much farther."

But there was no sign of Robi under the entrance to the Props Unit. We sat in the car opposite the building waiting for him to turn up, while all around us the weather roared. At midnight, Thomas said that perhaps the young actor had been delayed at the studio because of the weather. Or perhaps he had gone home. Fifteen minutes later he said that perhaps we should be going home as well.

"Perhaps this storm is sent with healing breath, / From neighbouring shores to scourge disease and death," I recited. Thomas gave me an odd look. "You should like that, Thomas. An introductory poem from the fifth edition of Henry Piddington's *Hornbook*."

My mother used to do this in her manic periods—pass on scraps of my father's favourite poetry, always out of context. Just lines, not whole verses, links in a chain to a firmer reality than her own. She called it my inheritance, which wasn't far from the truth. I would find notepaper covered with scraps of obscure quotations stuck to the fridge with a set of magnets shaped like vegetables. The magnets had once belonged to my grandmother, plastic carrots and turnips and potatoes that were as close as my mother got to roots.

The rain gradually let up enough so that individual drops were visible again. When those stopped, the noise faded to a soft, dripping silence. A sealskin night. I remembered this from my past. The violence of monsoon rain seldom lasts more than an hour or two. A serenely clear sky supervenes. There is a feeling of anticipation. I watched as a huge rent appeared above us, tearing a swirling, yellowish cavity in the sculptured edges of the massed clouds.

"No one is here, miss. Only that one car down the street and us. Your friend is not coming."

I glanced over my shoulder. A white Merc. A starburst of shattered glass on the driver's side. My brain took too long to make the obvious connection. I was thinking of Piddington, who warned mariners of cyclones that are contemporaneous, sometimes so near to each other that they travel along parallel tracks, or move forward on tracks which form such angles that the two storms must meet. At the meeting of these two storms the violence and chaos contained within the circumference of each is not doubled but multiplied exponentially. It breeds like frogs.

I climbed out of the car and ran across the street, slipping on the slick road. There was no need to beat down the door to the Props Unit; it was already open. Slumped at his desk in a deep sleep, the guard was oblivious to my entrance. I shook his shoulder roughly and his head slipped off his arms, a dark red contusion on one side of his face. I hesitated, torn between common sense and my need to protect that figure whose corrugated wax features held the clue to my one tangible piece of evidence. Ran back across the road.

"Thomas, call the police."

"Please to be waiting here if there is trouble, miss. Police phones may be out."

"There's no time. Sunila and Robi might be inside already."

"I am coming with you." A gentle brown man six inches shorter than I, with a head full of poetry and movies.

"No, Thomas. If I don't come out in the next ten minutes and the police don't show, you'll have to drive to the station and get them. I don't know the way."

"You have no reason to go in there. These people are not your family."

I pulled myself away and crossed that road for the third time.

17

As I opened the doors from reception into the prop unit's offices, the rain started up again and the lights went out. My pocket torch sent a thread of light ahead of me to where blue emergency lights burned here and there, giving the inner landscape a lunar hue like that of a hand-tinted black-and-white film. My own footsteps were inaudible, drowned by the rain outside. I felt someone watching me from the shadows, flicked my torch beam over the watcher: a framed photograph of Nehru, father of modern India, stared down at my passing, his lean, patrician features disapproving in the dim light. Next to him was a bad painting of his only child, Indira Gandhi, that made her look suspiciously like Golda Meir. And then Indira's sons, Sanjay and Rajiv. Gandhi after Gandhi, the Congress Party disappearing down the corridors of power into the distant future.

I stopped and listened again, hearing a noise that was wrong for this place. The mew a young kitten makes. From one of the workbenches near me I grabbed a gilt Shiva the size and weight of a bowling pin. The sound came again, louder this time. I stuffed the torch in my pocket.

The door to the Museum of Wounds was slightly ajar, a white light inside as well as the dim blue emergency lights. Keeping my back flat against the wall, I edged along far enough to see through the gap. The museum room was L-shaped, its longest leg bending away to my right. The door was in one corner of the short leg, angled so that I couldn't see the rest of the room to my left. I gambled that the noises were coming from the other side of the L. If I crouched down and stayed on the side of the room where Satish kept his standing figures, I would be protected from view.

I have never been good at gambling.

Slipping through the door, I was about as invisible as an old lag in a police lineup. My fellow players' blue shadows stretched all the way to my feet, elongated by two big torches set low on the floor, an out-take from one of those German Expressionist films of the thirties. A tall man in a white suit with his back to me. A boy in a chair. A short man sitting in another chair between a pale latex man with his face caved in and another whose neck had been severed nearly to the spinal cord. The short man was smoking a bidi and looking bored. My first thought was that Vikram Raven was working late and the tall man was one of the studio hairdressers employed to make wigs for Satish's models. There were big clumps of dark hair lying around the boy in the chair and little remained on his scalp. A victim's haircut. The two men turned towards me in surprise. The boy didn't move. It was Robi. The kittenish noises were coming from the bloody hole where his mouth had been.

"Why, Miss Rosalind," said the man in white, "I guess my guard wasn't doing his job."

"Acres."

"How nice of you to drop in on our little party," he said, and smiled pleasantly. Then a heavy weight dropped on my head and no one said anything more.

When I came to, I was in a chair next to Robi. His wrists and ankles were taped and he appeared to be unconscious. Considering the shape he was in, it was better he stayed that way. Acres had pulled up a stool and was sitting in front of us swinging one of his legs back and forth and humming. He was wearing a black T-shirt emblazoned in gold glitter with the words *Jurassic Park Is Coming!* and he held my Shiva in one hand. B or C was next to me, the man without the limp. His machete was resting on my upper thigh. Both men looked very relaxed. Acres was holding a straight razor in one hand and wiping blood off it with his handkerchief.

"It seems my guard wanted to see what you were up to before interfering," Acres said. He held up the Shiva. "Is this what you were going to use as a weapon?" B or C laughed. Acres's arm shot out and he hit Robi on the side of the head with the gilt figure. Its curved elbow sank in just behind the boy's ear. Acres dropped the statue. "Not bad," he said. "The thing is," he went on, as if I had just interrupted an ongoing conversation, "we're having trouble getting any info out of your friend here. You might be able to help."

I shook my head to get rid of the dizziness. How long had it been since Thomas rang the police? If I told Acres where the pictures were, would he kill us anyway? Could I stall him long enough for the police to arrive?

Acres took my movement for a negative. "I was hoping you'd listen to reason when you'd heard my proposition. I'm a reasonable man. See—we haven't even tied you up. So this is it: for every question you don't answer, we do a little more persuasion on your friend. How does that sound?"

Before I could speak, he stepped over to Robi and very casually, not pressing hard, ran the razor down the side of the boy's face. Acres's expression of concentration was that of an artist enjoying his work. As if he were painting with a triple-zero brush dipped in red, a fine line of blood appeared behind his razor, slowly thickened, and started to run. Acres stopped just before he got to Robi's throat, then stepped back to admire his handiwork, looking at me for approval.

"Stop," I said, feeling tears running down my cheeks. "My driver has gone for the police."

Acres laughed. "You trusted a Bombay taxi driver?"

He cut Robi again.

"Stop it!" I said. "Tell me what you want to know."

"Still pretending innocence." He shook his head, made a click of annoyance with his teeth. "This thing is useless. I used to have a draughtsman's scalpel that left perfect parallel cuts just like train tracks, but I lost it."

"Sami. You used it on Sami."

He nodded thoughtfully. "You know, I think you may be right. But where did I leave it?" His hand darted out and slashed Robi's face deeper this time, leaving a bloody cross on his cheekbone. "X marks the spot," he said.

"You're insane."

"Just a little fun—any port in a storm, right, C? Or is that any hole in a port?"

The man called C laughed.

"You see, we know the pictures are here somewhere," said Acres, "because we followed the pretty boy and found the room like this." I noticed the carnage around me for the first time, Satish's best works smashed. "And him here in the middle of it all." Acres gestured with his razor in Robi's direction. The blade caught the boy almost accidentally in the shoulder, slicing through his shirt.

"I know where the pictures are," I said. It wasn't going to be possible to stretch the time out until the police came.

"Is this bothering you?" said Acres. "But I thought you liked to play rough. And you must know, a lover of traditional Indian culture like you, this is *Ambubachi*, the three days which mark the start of monsoon. My mother was very religious, a real god-licker. She taught me that even if the rains start and then stop, the monsoon isn't certain until the skies open enough 'so that the red earth flows like blood.' That's what she used to say. Good, isn't it? The earth bleeding so you know it's ripe."

He smiled and stabbed the razor into Robi's leg. Blood spurted up onto Acres's suit. "Fuck," he said. "Would you look at that—and this is Armani."

"Stop it! I've said I know!"

"I'm just teaching pretty boy here a few lessons, aren't I, sweet?" Acres lifted his jacket up to look more closely at the blood on it. "This job is going to cost me a fortune in dry cleaning. Maybe I should switch to cigarettes." His eyes came back to me, the expression blank. "Now where did you say those pictures were?"

"Inside the leper."

"The leper?" He pressed the lit cigarette in his hand against Robi's cheek.

I thought I was going to be sick.

"Maybe you need some time to cool your brain," Acres said. "Don't you think Miss Rosalind could do with some cooling breezes, C?"

C said something that made Acres laugh again. "C has another suggestion, but personally I'm not that fond of white meat. I like my chicken cooked longer."

"I'm serious," I said, the words coming out rough. "They're inside the leper over there at the back of the room." Gulab, preserved in wax, his lips sealed.

Acres walked over to Sami's masterpiece. He smashed the skull with his fist. Nothing. He pulled off the arms and legs. Still nothing. He began to slash the clothes on the figure's twisted torso methodically, back and forth, back and forth, tic-tac-toe, until a large brown envelope slipped out of the leper's brocade waistcoat, its top two layers cut to pieces. Acres opened it, pulled out some ten by eights, and grunted with satisfaction.

C moved a little away from me to see the results of his boss's work.

I kicked over the torches and started running, bouncing off a soft body. Living or latex, I couldn't tell.

I ran through the next room, knocking over figures and chairs, aiming for the stairway up. But when I was halfway across, the lights went out again and I overshot the mark. Put my hands out for the stairs and felt books instead. The library. I pulled tables of books over behind me, feeling old pages cling and tear as I kicked them aside.

I came to a room with big photographic lights around the edges and a velvet-covered table in the centre. Voices several rooms back. Banged my fist against a switch marked Strobe Timer and slipped through into an antechamber with windows high up and open. I slammed and locked a flimsy door that one good kick would break. Pushed a table against the wall and climbed up. Footsteps entered the photographic studio. Under the door I saw the flare of a strobe. A voice cried out. The strobe went off again. I looked out the window and realized why no one had bothered about closing it. The oily black surface below was not tarmac, it was water. No beach, just pilings of rubber tyres emerging from the sea.

The strobe stopped flashing. I heard Acres's voice talking to one of the other men. Kicked off my shoes. The only way out was to swim along the shore until I hit one of the old East India docks. A grainy newspaper image floated into my head, of the Bombay Port Trust steamer *Zephir* lifted by a monsoon sea and smashed against the sea wall at Ballard Pier.

The voices were outside the door to my room now. A small man put his shoulder to the door. I shone my torch out again down the side of the building and caught the shine of wet boards. There was a dock directly below. With one last look into the face of a smiling Ganesh, I pulled myself through the window, hung for an instant by my hands, and dropped down.

act 4

AQUA REGIA

Gold, insoluble in all single acids, can be dissolved in a mixture of nitric acid and hydrochloric known as aqua regia—royal water—*because it dissolves the noble metals, or in a solution of alkaline cyanides in the presence of air or an electric current.*

1

I DID NOT HIT THE DOCK, I HIT THE WATER, BADLY, AND IMMEDI-ately felt the pull of the waves dragging me under, throwing me against the pilings and rubbing one side of my body raw on the barnacles.

Ways of dying: drowning. First the panic. A cocktail of water, air, and mucus produces a froth that clots the lungs. The conscious struggle ceases as the final convulsions take over.

Ways of dying: poison. A victim of strychnine poisoning experiences a claustrophobic feeling of restlessness and impending suffocation, followed by a series of contractions more violent than childbirth, and like that great expulsion, the muscle seizures are interspersed with periods of rest. You suffer a terrible thirst. *I would not die such a dry death, my mother said, with the strychnine berries still in her hand.*

In my dreams of her I am always swimming.

Join the drowners, a voice says, very close.

How do you escape the interior pursuit? I sucked up the last inch of air, my eyes burning from the salt. Grabbed something firm on the surface of the waves. Drifting on my back, one hand flapping like an inadequate fin, the other arm wrapped around that precarious floating island, I am a sea creature, caught halfway in the transition from water to land. Pictures inside: scrabbling at buttons to save herself; the autopsy, her lungs pale and distended as carnival balloons, washerwoman's hands. The washing of ten tides will never clean. Criminals in the old days, hanged on the shore at low tide and left for three high tides to pass over them. A fine white foam on her mouth. Bathwater dragging liquid out of her blood. Water for water. Blood chlorinated as a public pool.

To suffer a sea change, into something rich and strange.
I'm caught in nets like caul round a foetus.
The swell of the sea. The knell of the sea.
"You're dreaming," someone says.
Dreaming of fireflies as I drown. Let the punishment fit the crime.
"You're dreaming, Miss Benegal."

THE KOLI FISHERMEN WHO PICKED ME UP IN THEIR NETS MUST HAVE MIS-
judged the monsoon, or perhaps they were so desperate for money
they couldn't afford to miss the chance of a day's fishing, whatever the
risk. Usually they haul their boats up onto the beach well before the
first storm breaks, transforming the hulls into temporary shelters by
the simple expedient of turning them upside down and hanging rough
thatched roofs over the top.

They were alerted by Thomas, who had returned from his unsuc-
cessful visit to the police and patrolled Prosper's building looking for a
back entrance. He saw me fall and waved down the fishermen coming
into shore. They'd used their nets to catch me, pulling me in still
attached to my floating island, which turned out to be the Styrofoam
packaging from a crate of Coca-Cola once destined for Saudi.

I had mistaken the fishermen's lanterns for the fireflies of Kerala
that strung our trees like Christmas lights after the violent monsoon
rains had stopped. It was the Christmas just after I turned four that
my mother gave me my first taste of strychnine. "Once upon a time,"
she said, "when white people came to this coast, two monsoons were
the age of an Englishman and not one in twenty English children born
on the islands lived beyond their infancy. You have lived much longer,
Rosalind. Take this," she said, "to keep the snakes away."

It was the right dose for killing, but the seeds are very tough and
difficult to powder, even in a mortar. They hurt my teeth. I tasted
enough to feel the first claustrophobic strickening, but not enough to
die. And our gardener was watching her. "The monsoon is not good
for English ladies," he said later to my father, after they had taken the
seeds from my mouth and given Mum a sedative. The gardener never
could be convinced of my mother's Indian connections. "Too pale for
India," he said. Not pure enough gold.

The next time she tried the seeds on me I was more suspicious.
Mild doses of poison build up the immune system.

Between the intermittent downpours in the monsoon there would
be nights just like this one, lit by stars and fireflies, splattered with the

blood-red skins of cochineal beetles and filled with a raucous chorus of frogs. *The rain was like a chess player,* said the poet Subandhu, in another monsoon, fourteen hundred years ago, *while yellow and green frogs were like chessmen jumping in the irrigated fields.*

We might as well have been frogs and fireflies, those fishermen and I, for all the understanding we had of each other. When they brought me into shore I tried to tell Thomas about Robi, but he must have thought I was delirious, shouting about wax corpses and lepers and watery cells, my arms tight around that Coca-Cola float. He took me to a hospital, where the nursing sisters gave me a shot of something to make me sleep so deeply that no dreams rose to the surface. Everything went dark, a climactic feature associated with the monsoon: one cannot tell day from night; the clouds block out the sun.

2

I WOKE TO THE SOFT FLUID SOUNDS OF HOME, THE MELTING vowels of a Malayali nursing sister singing to herself, probably a St. Thomas Christian, as most of them are, so-called because a watery Malayali legend has it that Thomas the Apostle landed north of Cochin in A.D. 52 and converted the locals in Kerala from their Dravidian version of Hinduism to his newer superstitions.

"Later he was stoned to death on a hill outside Madras."

The pretty nurse looked startled at my voice.

"Oh, you are awake," she said, reverting to English.

"My name is Rosalind Benegal." The mystery of who I am solved in two words. Half sister of Miranda Sharma, I thought; the butterfly pinned to the green baize with five more. But are we even half sisters? Sometimes I think my life to the age of seven was all a dream. It has that unreal movie flicker to the edges, the 1950s heightened Technicolor that yellows the greens and turns every sea turquoise. Sometimes I think I wove that past out of odd threads trailing from my relatives' clothes, and ever since I've been unpicking the stitches.

"Sister-in-law of Prosper Sharma," I muttered. Six for the glass case.

It wasn't until I woke several hours later to hear the monsoon rain roaring against the hospital windows that I remembered. Miranda was leaning over me. "The hijra, like Shiva, have the power to bring rain," I told her, which seemed a logical thing to say. "Robi was with Acres, but where was Sunila?"

"It's me, Roz. I've had you moved to a private room. You're going to be fine." She pulled up a chair and sat down by the bed.

"Did they find her? And Robi? Is he here too?"

She held my hand. "Relax and sleep, Roz. You're a little bruised and scraped, but it's a miracle you didn't drown. You can thank Coca-Cola. The nurses said they had to sedate you before they could pry your fingers off that crate."

"How long?"

"You can probably come home tomorrow."

"The men in the boat and Thomas. Robi's with the other corpses. I told them."

Miranda looked puzzled. "They were wonderful, Roz, and your driver brought you right here, then got in touch with me. Thomas, is it? He kicked up such a fuss in the police station that they finally had to go and investigate. Too late, of course; but the guard corroborated Thomas's story, and so did the wreckage inside the Props Unit."

"What time is it?"

"Two o'clock in the afternoon. You've been sleeping for hours. Prosper and I were very worried. He was here earlier."

"I feel so guilty," I said.

"About what, Rosalind?" Miranda's voice was as gentle as the nursing sister's.

"That I left. That I couldn't stop what happened." I was talking about Robi, but it could as easily have been about my mother. The guilt I wear like a second skin.

Miranda took the comment to refer to my mother. "You did what you could, Roz. Dad told me. And at some point you have to save yourself."

"Their great guilt," I said, "like poison given to work a long time after, now begins to bite their spirits." My father's words to me after the funeral. When we could not meet each other's eyes. Had I said it or dreamed it?

"What was that, Roz?" This time her watch said two-thirty. I had lost another thirty minutes. "You keep drifting in and out of consciousness," Miranda told me.

"Nothing. Something Dad said a long time ago." I cleared my throat. "He said guilt was a slow poison."

She shook her head. "He never said that kind of thing to me."

"He didn't need to. You were legitimate."

Miranda's fingers clenched on mine. "No, Rosalind. He didn't say it to me because he was closer to you."

"Sorry," I said. Apologizing for what?

"It's all right."

She was doing her best to throw me a rope from the lifeboat. All I had to do was to swim through a few dead bodies. But the effort was too much. I was trapped by the need to assess my sister's complicity. How much did she know? There were degrees of guilt—what was hers? I turned my face away to make the next words easier. "Last night," I said, speaking slowly and clearly, "Prosper's business partner, Acres, made me watch while he tortured a boy to get some photos implicating government officials in corruption. Officials involved in a property deal with your husband. They'll have killed Robi by now, and possibly Sunila, a friend of your Sami's. Sami, Prosper's daughter, son. The one Prosper gave away when the boy was only nine."

Miranda let go of my hand. "What are you saying?" Her back was pressed flat against the back of the chair. "Prosper doesn't have a son," she said. Then: "Why are you doing this, Roz?"

Why was I? I had come back to India to reclaim part of my history and put the rest on trial, only to discover that my past, like the islands of Bombay, no longer existed in its original form. I wanted to hold up that old abortive prescription and ask Miranda if she recognized her mother's handwriting, or her father's. Our father's. And what it made her think of loving families.

"Why would I lie, Miranda?"

She didn't have to say it. Because you're mad. Like your mother. She stood up, turned away. "Nurse! Miss Benegal needs more sedation."

"It all adds up," I went on, doggedly trying to win her over. "At the time Maya died, Sami was always hanging around Prosper's studio, hoping to catch sight of him—or maybe she just wanted work, I don't know. Either way, she saw something that day that she was too frightened to report. But she remembered."

"Prosper wasn't there." She was shaking her head.

"Somebody Sami recognized, somebody she knew was connected to Prosper."

"No," Miranda said, her back still to me, "other people would've noticed."

"No one was in the building. I checked: even the guard on the door was outside watching a parade. Anybody could have gone in without being seen. No one even saw Maya enter. Sami must have used the story to blackmail Prosper."

Miranda turned back towards me. "Sami never blackmailed Prosper."

"How do you know?" I was amazed by the conviction in her voice, although I don't know why. I've seen wives of multiple rapists just like this.

"I know because my husband told me. And I believe him." She spoke her lines in a stale, weary voice, like an actor reading from a script for the tenth time. "After that creature had been trailing me around Bombay for a few weeks, I went to Prosper. He told me he'd given money to Sami years ago because he felt sorry for her. Then she got fixated on him, and when he married me she was jealous."

"And Acres?"

She hesitated. The script had a few missing pages. "Prosper regrets that connection. It's only that he can't bear to lose his studio. And he blames himself for Maya's death, and for the fact that Sami involved me."

I was sure she was ad-libbing now. I could hear the nurse's footsteps coming. "I don't understand the kind of ties binding you to Prosper, but I know that the ties binding Prosper to Maya got so tight they snapped. He was responsible for her murder as surely as though he pushed her off that balcony himself." In my head I asked, How's your love life, sis? Anything unusual to report? Is your husband into flagellation, buggery, coprophilia, or any other of those great public-school traditions? Is that why you twitch every time he pulls the strings?

In the end, tact wasn't necessary. Miranda had left.

I WOKE LATER TO FIND TWO SMALL UNIFORMED MEN SITTING PATIENTLY BESIDE my bed.

"So, madam, you are awake," said the one with the kind of moustache usually attached to a plastic nose and spectacle set.

"You are perhaps now ready to answer some questions," said the second, who had a face as smooth and shiny as a hard-boiled egg.

"Did you try to find Robi, the boy from Caleb Mistry's studio?" I asked. "Or Sunila, the hijra who was supposed to have met me at the Props Unit last night?"

They exchanged looks with one another. "Ah yes," said the moustache, "this tale of master criminals and mysterious photos your sister has been relating. But we are thinking that perhaps now you might like to alter this and tell us for example what you were doing at the Props Unit after hours on a stormy night?"

"There were three men," I said patiently. "One was called Acres, a

European or American who has been living here off and on for many years. He was wearing a T-shirt advertising the movie *Jurassic Park*." I could hear how crazy it sounded, and tried to speak clearly through the fog of drugs. "Black. With gold lettering. He is something to do with property. The other one is called Chota Johnny, and a third man—probably a guy called Bada Johnny—might've been around too, because someone knocked me out."

The two men looked at each other and smiled, then made some notes.

"A man called Acres involved in property wearing a *Jurassic Park* movie T-shirt—most amusing," said the egg. "But *Jurassic Park* the movie has not yet even come to Bombay, actually. And your sister is informing us that you have been most depressed lately. Added to this is your beating and . . . humiliation at the hands of villains several nights previously."

"Who wouldn't be?" I said.

"Sorry, madam?"

"I *said*: who the *fuck* wouldn't be depressed!"

The egg scowled. His scowl lines made him look like Humpty-Dumpty after the fall. "No need to use bad language, madam. Perhaps such things are occurring because you have been straying into areas which are not actually concerning you. Your hotel confirmed you have been drinking most heavily, last night in particular. And on several occasions you have been abusive for no reason, the receptionist said."

"This is unbelievable. Am I on fucking trial for unladylike behaviour?"

They made more notes, my words not even denting their bureaucratic shells. Men in suits would be the death of me yet. At that point the nurse returned and told the two cops they would have to come back later.

I lay in bed for a while wondering whether Gul had waited for me. It was long past morning. Would he still find me if I went to the STD telephone office on Cadell Road? At least I had a telephone in the room, and for once, despite the monsoon, it worked.

But Ram's voice on the other end was surprisingly hesitant. It seemed they had gotten into his studio, stolen any computers they could carry, smashed screens on the others, peed on loose papers, and ground software into the floor. All our notes were gone, including the forensic stuff from Ram's cousin. The message was clear. And Ram had decided to take the hint. For the two weeks or more it would take the builders to put his place back together, he was shifting his surviving Mac to the Fort Aguada Beach Hotel in Goa.

"I'm sorry, Ram. But at least I still have all the original material."

"Then let's hope for your sake that the bad guys know less about the editing process than they do about our movements over the past week. Listen, Roz, why don't you come with me? Chill on the beach, drink a lot of ice-cold coconut toddy?"

"I can't. I'm sorry, Ram."

Ram said he wasn't sure I should be leaving the hospital so soon, but agreed reluctantly to pick me up and drop me at the Ritzy.

3

As soon as we pulled away into the traffic, I started in on my catalogue of Prosper's guilt, twenty minutes without stopping, aware only of the steely taste of the air in my mouth.

"You sound pretty wired, Roz." Ram spoke very softly, the way you do with a nervous animal. "It's not that I don't believe you. I do. If anyone needed evidence to prove we've got too close to something big, they only have to look at my studio." He paused to allow his words to sink in. "But a lot of your proof is pretty off the wall—all this business of Sami drawing motherless gods or whatever because she was Prosper's illegitimate son, and Prosper selling off forged gold coins—not that you have any except genuine ones. It may be true, but it's nothing the police could act on."

"Look, Ram: who has access to the Central Props? Who has contacts inside and outside to sell the goods? Who has been losing money hand over fist—"

"Most of this isn't even illegal," Ram interrupted. "Prosper has a right to sell his cinemas, no matter how many poor bastards he dumps on. And this link you're making between him and John Dee and the hijra—that's *really* wild."

"But you've seen his script notes—"

He shook his head. "I've been talking to a friend of mine in the effects business and he says there's a perfectly legitimate reason for Sharma's interest in Dee. This effects guy told me about the computerized animation techniques Sharma's been using for sequences in *The Tempest*: men turning into women and then into snakes and fish, storms brewing in mirrors, Jacobean magic sequences that turn into computer magic. Not the usual Bollywood effects that look like they come from a Christmas cracker. This is cutting-edge stuff. And Pros-per is planning to computerize some of Dee's navigational drawings about the search for the Northwest Passage to the Far East—he thinks they may have inspired Shakespeare. There was this guy—Orelio?—whose atlases were called 'theatres' before they were called atlases."

"Ortelius. He published the *Theatrum Orbis Terrarum* in 1570."

Ram nodded. "Ortelius—that's the guy. It seems your brother-in-law has got hooked on the idea of the Elizabethan stage as a kind of map of the world, with the early map books as miniature theatres. And he's using that as a visual concept for part of the set."

There didn't seem to be any point in arguing with Ram. I was too tired, maybe from my swim in the sea, maybe from lots of things. "So you think I should just forget about it?"

He was trying to let me down gently. "Walk away. People do it all the time."

I stared out the window at the oily waves that were pounding Chowpatty Beach with a sound like mortar fire. "I take it you won't help me anymore."

"I didn't say that. But on one point at least I think you're wrong. If Acres has the photos, the hijras are no longer in any danger."

"He's won, you mean."

"It happens, Roz. Not just in India. Why not talk to Ashok? If he really does have the kind of government connections you suspect, you could hand everything to him."

Even to Ram I didn't want to admit that I suspected Ashok of being involved, if not directly, then at least in the cover-up of some seedy but influential government official who had been snapped in bed with Sami.

THOMAS ARRIVED AT THE RITZY NOT LONG AFTER RAM HAD LEFT. HE AC-cepted my profuse thanks with a modest shrug. I warned him what had been done to Ram's studio. This met with a similar gesture of dismissal. "All in line of duty, madam." But when I asked him to take me to the STD phone booth near the giant billboard on Cadell Road he turned around in the taxi and stared. "I am sure you are not meaning Cadell Road, madam—perhaps some other road that sounds like it? Cadell is no place for Western ladies."

"Then I should fit right in. And, Thomas, can you make sure no one follows?"

"As in the movies, madam?" His eyes sparkled and he started the car with a rev like a 747 taking off. "*Dirty Harry* is having a very good chase, I think, and Nicholas Ray's masterpiece of the film noir, *They Live by Night*, and then there is *The Driver*, of course, which I am thinking is a classic of the genre—"

"Just lose them, Thomas. If they exist."

He copped a fast left down the first narrow alley we came to, a shortcut through a hotel parking lot at a speed that lifted the old Ambassador airbound on the first bump, and then crossed a main road in the teeth of oncoming traffic, leaving a barrage of horns honking behind us.

"Of course," Thomas said calmly, "very best chase sequence of all times is taking place with Steve McQueen in *Bullitt*."

4

As we approached Cadell Road, litter began to sprout like grass, lawns of debris grazed by cattle, dogs, goats, and pigs. The smell of decay mingling with the stench of bad distilleries and sewers overflowing from the monsoon was only slightly relieved by whiffs of ozone from the sea. Shelters built out of every conceivable waste product of the market system were supplemented with wooden packing cases stamped with their port of destination: Singapore, Bangkok, Calcutta, the closest these people would ever get to a package tour.

Thomas pointed to men walking along the road carrying sodden hessian sacks labelled *Indian Potash* or *Polchem* under their arms. "These sacks are for rain, madam. Test of good monsoon in Maharashtra is when gunny sack that peasants drape over their heads and shoulders stays damp enough to breed insects. All is quiet now until the rain starts again. Finally this place will become green and bright with flowers. Also, of course, rain will wash less than substantial shelters down the hillsides and floods will bring cholera and malaria."

"You were right, Thomas. It looks like every beggar in Bombay lives here."

"No one to beg from, madam. No, these people are self-employed, supplying city with a vast pond of cheap labour."

"A pool; we say a pool of labour." I watched a mink-brown naked boy washing himself from a big can labelled *White Emulsion*. "Why on earth would any farmer want to leave his land and come to this godforsaken place?"

Thomas said that the huts were only masquerading as urban slums; in reality, they were imports from the poorest Indian countryside, and the people in them clung to their old life as much as they could. He pointed out that some of the huts were still roofed in coconut matting, as they would be in coastal villages, and waved his hand towards a line of shelters. "Look, madam, the farmers come because when their crops fail they have nowhere else to turn, but there is always work here—see how many significant enterprises are operating along this road."

Without Thomas as a guide, the significance of these enterprises, each one enclosed in a shelter the size of two phone booths, might have eluded me. There were tea shops selling chemical soft drinks that left you thirstier after drinking them, recyclers of waste, tyre retreaders for the legion of cyclists, typing booths where men transcribed job applications to computer firms on archaic metal typewriters, astrologers to recommend auspicious wedding dates for young futures traders, fortune-tellers who would forecast a rosy future for hopeful stockbrokers, vendors of chocolate bars so high in wax that they never melted, even in the summer heat: stick a wick through them and you could use them for candles. To me, these people's hold on Bombay life was tenuous at best. But in fact they were like the birds who live on the back of an elephant, feeding on its ticks. When the larger beast began to die, they could fly away.

"You see, these are going concerns, madam. This is not such godforsaken place. Look at that sign there." He pointed to a freehand sketch of Ganesha that had been painted over a hoarding advertising suntan lotion, almost obscuring it.

"What does it say?"

"*Sunder Mumbai, Marathi Mumbai.* Means '*Beautiful Bombay, Marathi-speaking Bombay.*' In such places, you see, they have new god, god of politics, Shiv Sena. And Ganesha, Bombay's favourite elephant god, is joined with this."

"If we meet no gods, it is because we harbour none," I said.

"Sorry, madam?"

"Someone said that to me a long time ago. You can take it to mean that teacher's reprimand has been duly acknowledged by his humble student."

We stopped in front of an STD phone office whose side was painted with another fat Ganesha. "Please take care," Thomas said. "People here are not always filled with milk of human kindness, especially towards white tourists."

I was about to declare my birthright once again, then gave up.

Maybe his vision looking backward in the mirror was clearer than mine looking forward.

Inside the STD shop the man behind the desk shrugged and wobbled his head when I asked for Gul. His male customers made comments that I didn't need Marathi to understand.

I strolled around the few feet of shop, reading the ads on the walls. When this literary diversion palled, I stood in the sun outside. After thirty minutes, I dodged through the traffic to Thomas. "Are you sure this is the right place?"

"Most certain, madam. Look—you are standing in the shadow of giant board." He pointed to the silhouette of a snarling giant straddling a row of corrugated-iron huts, a message blazing in flaming unrecognizable letters across his chest.

I went back into the shop and asked again for Gul, this time miming a skateboard, an act of theatre which kept the new set of customers sniggering until I slipped outside again and sat down in the dust to wait for my conscience to be satisfied. I felt I owed it to Sunila, to Gulab—even to my sister, in some obscure way. After an hour of this, Thomas got out of the car and came towards me.

"It will be dark soon, madam. I think it is time for us to go." He looked around for a handy quote to cheer me up. "See that sign? In India, poetry is everywhere!"

I glanced up wearily at the handpainted sign he was pointing to, a cartoon doctor in a turban holding his stethoscope to the engine of a lime-green car.

> *Recipe for monsoon chills:*
> *Gripping tyres*
> *Wiping blades*
> *Steady Hands upon the wheels.*
> BY ORDER: TRAFFIC POLICE

"Hardly poetry, Thomas. The rhyme only works if you pronounce wheels as 'wills,' the way Indians do."

"Yes, madam? Like so many of Mr. Shakespeare's rhymes, isn't it?"

At that moment I felt my bag move. A small boy ran off down the road away from us. Thomas shouted and chased after him, but the potential thief was too fast. I opened my bag to discover that my wallet and camera were still there. "It's all right, Thomas," I called out. "The little bugger wasn't quick enough." I noticed a folded sheet of paper tucked into my wallet. On the paper had been scribbled a rough map and an even rougher representation of a rose. Underneath was printed "Little Flower School of English: All grammatical needs personified." The thief hadn't been taking things out of my bag, he'd been putting things in.

FINDING GUL'S HOME IN THE SQUATTERS' COMMUNITY AT JEHANGIR BAUG would have been impossible without Thomas, despite the map. Like the maze in a dream, there seemed to be no exit and no way back to the beginning once you made the mistake of entering. We turned a succession of identical corners with identical screaming babies outside family hutments where identical women rolled out chapattis inches from the open sewage that curled in a sluggish stream on either side of the narrow path. The electrification that Gul had described so proudly did not help to disguise the squalor. Nor did it seem to illuminate the lives of these people. Long before we found Gul I would have turned back—or simply dissolved into the smell of shit and steaming rubbish. Everything was pressing too close, but at the same time falling away, as if my main computer were shutting down certain files to preserve the whole.

I wanted to get out my tape recorder, keep this place at the end of a mike. But Thomas stopped me. "Best not to," he said.

"This is what Hell will look like."

"Oh no, madam."

After his initial reluctance to lead me into the maze, Thomas was now determined to point out evidence of its dignity and enterprise: a girl having her hands hennaed; a woman with the predatory features of a Rajasthani tribal who sat embroidering a skirt in the burnt-earth colours of her desert birthplace; a garland of tuber rose framing the entrance to a concrete hut.

"Look!" said Thomas. "Thanks to Shiv Sena, people here are now having concrete drains."

Open drains. You stepped over shit to enter your home, you stepped over shit to leave. Progress: a life framed in shit. "What do you mean 'now,' Thomas: you mean it used to be worse here? That hardly seems possible."

He nodded. "Is possible."

"You seem to know a lot about this place. You're not by any chance a secret fan of the illicit hooch they produce?"

"No, madam." His voice was as subdued as I'd ever heard it. "I am knowing this place so well because I too am living here not so very long ago."

WE FOUND GUL AT LAST, SITTING ON HIS SKATEBOARD AND WATERING TWO tomato plants where they grew in rusted coffee tins outside the flap of his hut. He gave me a warm smile, which turned worried when he caught sight of Thomas.

"It's all right, Gul. He's a good friend," I said.

Reassured, Gul smiled again and waved me in. "Come in, come in, then, Miss Benegal. Almost I was giving up on your arrival."

On one wall inside hung a photoprint of Shivaji so shiny even the oily grime of the air here couldn't stick to it. Gul gestured for me to sit on an empty ghee can that passed for a stool. The floor was of concrete, like the drains outside. I tried not to think what would happen when the monsoon got worse and flooded this settlement. At least Gul lived on a hill.

On a cloth next to my makeshift stool was a small bottle of Limca. "Please, Miss Benegal. You must be thirsty."

"No, I couldn't possibly."

The furrows in his face deepened. "But it is for you."

"How kind." A vicar's wife in Jane Austen. I tried again. "I'd love it."

Formalities over, Gul got out a folder from behind a low table, the only other piece of furniture. On the table sat an old typewriter. "Sami gave me that," Gul said. "People round here are paying me to type letters and documents for them."

Inside the folder of sketches was a succession of images Goya would have died for. Gul laughing, in red chalk. Gul asleep on his skateboard in the sun. Gul with the pitiful face of the professional beggar caught perfectly in ten or twelve sure brushstrokes. Gul earnestly typing in the dim light of the hut, a pair of half-glasses perched on what was left of his nose.

"They're wonderful," I said.

He smiled happily. "Oh, she was a most talented person, Miss Benegal. How I wish you were knowing her. I am thinking you could have been friends."

"I am thinking so too."

Sami had drawn on everything from envelopes and grease-stained newspaper to paper from a place called the Hotel Rama, on whose surface she had done her first fantasy of Gul as a leper maharaja. And here were sketches of Sunila as well, done while the hijra was sculpting, her brow furrowed with concentration.

"The Hotel Rama—where's that, Gul?"

He looked away. "I think it is where she is working sometimes. But even more interesting are these last three drawings."

These must have been the final sketches for Sami's wax figure of Gul, painted in bright gouache like Indian miniatures, with gridlines drawn over the finished work to make scaling up easier. Perhaps it was the detail and colour that stopped me from noticing the headed paper on which the paintings had been done, but eventually its significance dawned. PROSPER SHARMA read the first line, in small, elegant type, and underneath was my brother-in-law's old address on Malabar Hill, the one he had lived in with Maya and, for one year, with my sister. Some of the more recent sketches had been drawn on Prosper's headed paper from his current address. One in particular interested me: a grotesque god in the foreground and a cartoon of Gul—his features heightened to make their similarity to the god's more apparent—peering out from behind.

Gul pointed to the god's face. "Sami told me that your brother-in-law had a statue in his home that looked just like me," he said proudly.

"So she'd been to Prosper's house?"

"Oh, I think so—many times. And to the house of a friend of his, a Mr. Unmann, I am thinking." Gul seemed surprised by the question.

"Is there a chance I might borrow a couple of these?" I said. "Not for long, just to get photocopies done?"

He took the folder back from me so suddenly that the drawings fell to the floor. By the time we had collected them, he was composed again. "It is important?"

"It could be, I think so. And I'll be very careful."

He handed the complete folder to me. "Remember, this is all I have left of her."

"One last thing, Gul—did you ever meet a friend of Sami's, a hijra called Sunila who worked as an artist on Chowpatty Beach?" I held up one of the drawings. "This is her portrait."

He shook his head.

"So Sami never mentioned a family photo, taken with Prosper, that she kept with these drawings of Sunila?"

Gul's face lit up. "Sami is giving me this few days before she is killed—oh, where has my head been! I forgot that she is telling me to give this picture back if anything is happening to her. But the name she used is not Sunila. 'Robi is taking care of it.' That is what she says. Robi, at Caleb Mistry's."

"A friend of Sunila's," I said.

Gul rolled his skateboard over to the table and reached into a drawer.

It was a family snap, one of the millions you skip past in albums. Overexposed, framed so that the feet are cropped off and there is too much sky above the heads. A small, worn photo, of a silver-haired young man with a sensitive face, a pretty woman in an expensive sari, a little girl standing somewhat apart from the two adults and holding the hand of a man whose body was out of the shot. The girl must have moved as the picture was being taken, for her face was out of focus. I stared at what I could see of it for quite a long time before realizing that she was actually a little boy wearing makeup and a *lungi*, the wrapped fabric pulled girlishly high under his arms.

Prosper, Maya, and Sami in uneasy celluloid alliance? Or just a starstruck little boy-girl in the presence of two famous people. The photo proved nothing. Sami—if it *was* Sami—was impossible to identify, and the anonymous crowd close behind the three figures indicated that the snap could have been taken anywhere. No firm roots on which to base a family tree.

"Did Sami ever talk about the day Maya died, Gul? I have a feeling Sami may know who killed her."

"Why are you thinking Sami knows such a thing?" Gul seemed puzzled.

"Because she was there when Maya fell. The photos—"

"I too was there, madam."

I tried to keep my voice steady. "What did you see, Gul?"

"A parade. Then a scream and a dead lady. I am pulling myself out of her way."

"Nobody came out of the building?"

"Watchman is leaving his post early on to watch parade. Shortly after first Mrs. Sharma is falling, man is leaving."

"Would you recognize him if you saw him again? I know it was years ago, but if you think carefully, your memory might bring him back."

"Nothing to do with bad or good memory, madam. This man is wearing a mask. Thus there is no possibility of remembering his face."

So that was that. I felt like crying.

We left Jehangir Baug by the path we had entered it, downhill through the smell of raw sewage, now cut with cooking aromas, and out between the legs of the giant billboard, Thomas stopping this time to get a fresh mango sherbet from the sherbet-wallah who had set up his stand under the painting of Ganesha.

Ganesha/Ganpati: remover of obstacles. Hearing the vendor rattle the ice in his sherbet tubs, I remembered my refusal to share the mango kulfi with Ram after our trip to the morgue. "Here's the money, Thomas, get one for me too."

We walked back to the car after our sherbets and I wondered how long it would take the ice to loosen my bowels. I needed something to wash everything out into the open.

"You know the trouble with this case, Thomas? No fucking facts."

He nodded. "But facts are like butterflies, madam. Most difficult to catch, and often lacking in beauty when finally pinned down."

His comment worried me. The Timeless Wisdom was starting to make some kind of sense.

5

THE RITUAL OPENING OF THE MONSOON IS A TERRIFYING TIME, they say, for a man's sins will find him out and spoil the crops for others as well as for himself.

From the train to Poona the next morning I could see that the dun-coloured dust was now mud with dun-coloured snakes of water turning fields into islands. Cattle stood up to their knees in water. Small rowing boats were tied to swamped banyan trees. Liquid seemed to have risen through the earth's skin, sweated out by the heat. Where rice had been planted, the water glowed fluorescent green, as if lit from beneath like an enormous swimming pool. Women waded through with their saris tied up between their legs, parting streams of floating litter.

I got a bus to Sonavla and stumped through the flooded landscape to Bina's bathhouse, where the tall hijra came to greet me. I had hoped Sunila might have gone into hiding here, but Bina's face, free of makeup and as rumpled and damp as old bedclothes, told me it wasn't likely. "You have news of Sunila?" At my expression, her wrestler's shoulders slumped. "She has disappeared, just as Sami did, leaving all her things but no message."

"There might be a clue in her room to where she's gone—may I look, Bina?"

She waved me up the stairs into a pale blue room, subaqueous in the monsoon light. But there was nothing to see—a folded quilt, a bad print of the Mother Goddess, candles, matches. I sat down on the bed.

She sat next to me. "You think Sunila is dead like Sami, don't you?"

"Maybe. We were supposed to meet the other night and she never showed." I pressed my fist against the bridge of my nose to release the pressure in my head. "I saw the boy who was supposed to bring her getting tortured."

Bina listened to what had happened, nodding several times.

"This is not your fault, miss. It was Sami, filling Sunila's head with stories. I knew this was getting bad when the other man came here the day after your visit. Looking for Sunila's pictures—for her, he said. A bad man. It was in his face."

I described Acres to her and she nodded once. "What about Robi, Bina—do you know where he lived?"

"You think maybe Sunila is hiding there?" she said, her face brightening. "But I don't know anyone called Robi. He must have been a Bombay friend."

I described Robi to her as carefully as I could, although both times I'd seen him he'd been covered in blood. The more details I added, the more her face closed up like a fist. When I ran out of description, she leaned far under the bed to pull out a small chest covered in hand-blocked paper. From the chatelaine of keys around her waist she selected one to fit the cheap lock. I was surprised she bothered. The chest would have been about as hard to break into as a package of breakfast cereal.

Inside was a drift of letters and postcards and a cardboard book on which the words *Family Album* had been carefully lettered. It was filled with pictures of Prosper clipped from movie magazines, with scrolls painted around each photo to simulate the carving on Victorian picture frames. Flipping quickly past these, Bina put her lacquered fingernail on one of the few genuine family snaps, of a young boy laughing. Not much more than a toddler, but with the beginnings of a feminine beauty already evident.

I'd been staring at the answer to part of my riddle for days. "Robi?" I said.

"I think you are knowing the truth, Miss Benegal. This is Sunila. Before she is hijra. My Sunila and your Robi are the same person. This is the album she kept with Sami. They were like sisters." She closed the book. "Now there is something else I must show you that I did not before. Because I was ashamed. Because it reminded me of Sami. Something I think she must have stolen."

It was Skanda. Unwrapped from the layers of flowered cotton in which Bina had hidden him, the little god, no more than six inches high, smiled up at me.

"I don't think she stole him, Bina. I think she made him."

THAT NIGHT I TRIED ON ONE OF SUNILA'S SKIRTS TO SEE HOW IT FELT: A woman dressed as a man dressed as a woman. I slept in Sami's bed and fell asleep with my headphones on, listening to the tapes of Sunila, her voice so clear it could have been coming from the next room. *Pictures in the sand. She says that my father must be an artist, as hers is. Sami is in love with a man. This would make her a real woman for him.*

In the morning, Bina gave me Sunila's few possessions, including the statue of Skanda. "They should be buried with her," she said, "but as we have no body . . ." As I was walking away, she called out, "Be careful, Miss Rosalind. Remember, this is the season of the serpent, the time of Vishnu's sleep, when he leaves the demons in charge and the night has lost its moon. It would be good to make *puja* at the feet of your spiritual guru."

"I'm not a Hindu."

"You are Christian, then?" she said. "Do they not make puja?"

"Some of them do, but I'm not a Christian either."

"So what are you? I know some people from the south are Jewish."

"Not Jewish. Not anything."

"But who are your gods to tell you what is right and what is wrong?"

"Meteorologists," I said. "The shipping forecast on the World Service."

"Very good, Miss Rosalind, I too listen to BBC weather, but in this season there is very bad reception, so communication with your god may be difficult. All gods are absent during Caturmasa. They hold themselves aloof from human affairs. I think maybe BBC is sleeping also, not only Vishnu."

6

Back in Bombay I had a shower and a lunch of cardboard toast spread with the curious red-and-orange jujube-flavoured paste that passes for jam in every hotel in India. Then I picked up the photocopy of one of the drawings Sami had done on the Hotel Rama paper and tucked it in a pocket of my bag.

The Hotel Rama address only half existed. All the buildings in the street were in advanced stages of terminal disease, some little more than leprous brick skeletons, others still held together by bandages of plaster. I assumed they had been abandoned after some historic monsoon storm of a previous decade. Until I saw the signs: BEAUTIFICATION OF BOMBAY.

"You are being ill advised in your choice of hotel," said a man to whom I showed my letter. He pointed to the end of the street, where I could see an alley between tower blocks of rubble. "This one is earning no three stars in Michelin."

I left him laughing at his little joke.

The alley was as hot and bright as the chimney of a furnace, twisting through destroyed courtyards and narrowing where shattered gateways had collapsed in waves of brick and mortar onto the path. I stepped over the head of a lion, the wing of a fallen angel, a single marble hand. The path ended at a tall building whose sign, HOTEL RAMA, had been laid across two rusted paint cans to form a bench. What remained of the hotel door had been used by someone as wood to build a fire under a saucepan made from a tin can.

I looked through the doorway of the hotel and called out, "Hello?" Only part of the roof was left, and it was so still inside that the faint breeze of my call made the water vapour in the air dance and glitter in the sun like gold flakes in a liquid suspension. Entering the hotel, one slow step at a time, I saw that the person who had been sleeping there recently had not worried about the building's stability: a stack of movie magazines lay open next to the sofa, and there was the impression of a body in the layer of crumbled plaster on the mock-leather fabric.

Turning out of the reception into what must once have been a corridor leading to the bedrooms, I called out again into the bright, hot emptiness: "Hello, is there anyone home?" The word "home" a curious choice in the circumstances.

No answer. I began to search the ruins, following footprints through the monsoon mud. In a previous incarnation the hotel must have been a beautiful house. There were fine bits of Edwardian plaster moulding clinging like tree fungus to the carved trunks of wooden columns, and a few of the rooms still had their original panelled mahogany doors: where the thick layers of glossy bright paint had chipped away, you could see the dark, fine-grained wood revealed beneath it like chocolate under a Smarties' sugar coating. In a room with no windows I found a Victorian bedstead that someone had broken up for firewood.

People had been using this hotel quite recently, even if they hadn't paid for the privilege. There were the sodden remains of small campfires in two of the rooms and someone had propped a broken fragment of mirror up against a wall, although vanity in such surroundings seemed sadly misplaced. I noticed that the mirror bore the traces of a gilded past. A dark maroon showed through where the gilt had worn, typical of old work using red clay as bole so that when the surface became distressed the colour revealed would be sympathetic to the gold.

I am a little shortsighted. Crouching to look more closely at the pattern of giltwork on the mirror, I discovered my mistake. No one had mixed graphite to get this shade of maroon. It was not red bole; it was dried blood. Far too much of it to be a shaving accident: a fine, lacy spray had spurted out of someone or something and hit the glass. I looked into the mirror, seeing the mask of my face with the spiderweb of blood splitting up its features into their individual parts like Mum's drawings for her shrink: my father's nose, my mother's eyes, my gran's forehead; then I stood up quickly and leaned against the wall.

There was a part of me in that moment that wanted to hop on a plane to a cold destination and leave my sister and all the others to their shared fate, whatever that fate was. The other 1 percent breathed deeply and reached into my bag, got out the happy-snap Minolta I always carry, shot a couple of pics of the mirror, broke off one of the more gory pieces, and stowed it in a plastic bag. It was only a small piece of mirror, but it weighed as heavily in my bag as an unpaid debt. Whoever had cleared out these rooms hadn't worried about doing a good job. I found a few disks of hard blue wax down the back of a sagging sofa and a couple of rags smelling strongly of chemicals in the corner of a cupboard, with several empty bottles of what I wouldn't be surprised to learn had contained potassium cyanide and silver nitrate. Had Sami set up her freelance forging business here on her own or had she been working with one of Vikram Raven's team?

I put the bottles, rags, and wax into my bag with the rest of the things in my backpack, then turned left out of the room and walked deeper into the Hotel Rama, alone in the sun with the blood and the sparkling dust.

I found the bathtub behind a door at the end of a narrow, caved-in corridor in a part of the hotel that still had most of its walls. The bath was reasonably intact, with all but one of its original ball-and-claw feet and six-inch stretches of white enamel that had not yet been chipped off. The Edwardian brass showerhead was green with verdigris, but someone had hung garlands of flowers over it and made a feeble attempt at cleaning the blood-splatter marks from the wall behind. They had not touched the tide mark of dark maroon about two inches from the top of the tub, where you usually find grease. I wondered briefly about the effect of water immersion on the detectability of certain antigens in these dried stains.

Operating automatically now, following procedures vaguely remembered from my years as a Peeping Tom into other people's lives, other people's deaths, I snapped the maroon stains on the walls and tub and scraped blood splatters from them into an envelope. I laid one of my Tampax containers for scale on the floor next to a clear footprint edged with blood in the plaster dust and snapped that too, searched around the rough edges of the bath to see if there were any filaments of textiles caught there, stuffing anything I found into another clean envelope. From time to time I walked out of the room and stared up at the sky before returning to the job in hand. I was nothing if not thorough. Before I left I took one last look around. Saw something gleaming silver in the dust under the bath. Thought of the buttons that drowning people often pull off their murderers' shirts. The ones you find later, clutched in their fists like strychnine seeds. Got down on my hands and knees and reached into the years of grime and dead flies and dirty lives.

The draughtsman's scalpel must have rolled under there or been kicked there by accident when they heaved Sami's body out to take her to the beach. I looked at its aluminium handle, etched with cross-hatching to make its grip firmer, and felt it lying cool against the heat of my hand, most of it washed and smeared with dark dried blood, just as the two parallel blades were.

Slowly, I let the knife roll down my hand and into an envelope, turning it from a weapon into evidence. As it rolled, the twin points of the blades lightly nicked my palm, leaving a curved line of bloody parallel commas in the flesh, as if a snake had struck again and again. Like the pricked red chalk patterns my mother used to make on flat water-gilded surfaces, where it was important to avoid denting the gold.

There seemed to be nothing more to do. I had no conviction that my evidence would change anything. One murderer more or less on the streets never stopped the next murder. Only the faces changed. But there were certain procedures to follow. There were certain beliefs that civilized people were expected to share. That all men are created equal. That the legal system equates with justice. That our sins will find us out in the end.

I walked back towards the Hotel Rama's entrance down a corridor I hadn't used yet. Long ago it had been painted lung pink, with kidney-red doorframes and wainscoting, an intestinal colour scheme that years of mould and mildew had turned rotten, something you would find in the viscera of a cancer victim.

As I passed the first room, I thought I heard a sound. Apart from the occasional scratching of rats and scuttling of cockroaches, there was now a buzzing in the air, as if an electric bulb were about to blow. There were several broken and missing floorboards in the room, so I held on to the doorframe, wary of my footing, and peered into the dark corners. All I could see was an empty room filled with rubble and debris, and another doorway opening onto what in more prosperous times must have been a dressing room. The buzzing came from there.

When I lifted my hand off the doorframe, it came away sticky and smeared with maroon. I thought it was the paint. I had a rhododen-dron that colour on the balcony of my flat in London. But nobody paints a condemned hotel. I stepped into the dark room, sliding around the edge towards the dressing room, talking into my mike to steady myself, trying to give an accurate picture, the words coming out unconnected to me, like the voice-over for a film:

"This is what the camera sees: sticky dark splashes on the floor, and two parallel slide marks mingled with footprints through the dust leading into the shadows, ending in the rubble of a partially collapsed roof. A rat sits on the rubble, worrying at something. It stands up and hisses as the tall, green-eyed woman approaches, then runs off. The buzzing gets louder. It is the flies."

Something sickly and sweet where the flies buzzed thickest over the rubble. I leaned forward and pulled some of the bricks away, and the feeding flies rose up in a cloud.

For a second I tasted undigested toast and jam in my mouth, turned away, and spat. Then I forced myself to look back at the mixture of bloody pulp and bone fragments and white gristle that had once been a man's face. Whoever had killed him had not bothered to hide the body very well. But they had chopped off his hands. Like the man in the ice house, I thought. And wondered, Did this one have gold in his pockets? The blood here much fresher than the blood on the bathtub. No one would be able to reconstruct dental records from the splinters of white enamel stuck to his bare chest. But then no one would want to.

I walked away from the mess, looking around for something to clean my hands. There was a dark crumpled rag lying in the shadow of the doorway. When I picked it up and wiped off what blood I could with it, I found that the rag was an old black T-shirt with gold glitter emblazoned across the chest, some of the letters obscured by blood: *J   ssic Pa k Is Coming!*

They tell you in India the stories of cobras who eat their own species, cannibals of the serpent world. In fact, this cannibalism occurs only when two cobras fix on the same prey and the larger of the two snakes devours the other in error while swallowing its dinner.

With Acres dead, who had the photos?

I got out my Minolta again and shot off half a roll of the body from different angles. A film camera would have given a better impression of the scene, but it would have been more difficult to find the point of focus in this low light. Focusing by eye is often impossible when you are using a wide-angle lens or when shooting against the sun or through fog or filter diffusers. And before focusing a lens visually, the cameraman has to ensure that his eyepiece is set to suit his own visual impairment. Her own visual impairment. Any slight astigmatism can pull a whole scene out of alignment. When I first started shooting videos of road accidents and murders, I was glad of the sense of removal a lens gave me, the way it made the violence unreal. I wanted a long lens now and the reassuring whirr of a camera ticking over. To drown out the flies.

I added the T-shirt to the bloody mirror in its bag and piled the bricks back up on that destroyed face and shoulders to provide at least some protection against the scavengers. When I heard a noise behind me that was not a rat, I waited for the blow. But there was just a soft voice asking, "He is dead?"

"Very," I said, turning slowly to face my questioner. Despite her flamingo-pink shalwar kamiz, I could recognize the telltale signs of a hijra. She was small for a man and very dark, with broad Bengali features.

"Who are you?" I said.

She dragged her eyes away from the rubble to my face.

I pointed at the bloody rubble. "Did you see who did this?"

"Goondas."

"Goondas?"

"*Dadas*, gangster men."

"Didn't they see you? How did you escape?"

"He catches me, but I get away."

"Who caught you? The man who did this?"

She shrugged and wouldn't look at me.

"Did you see who killed this person?" I said.

"Not killing. A man after is coming and pushing—that." She pointed her chin in the direction of the flies. "With his foot. I do not see his face." Stressing the word "face" oddly.

"What did you see of him? You must have seen something."

"His hand when he is putting it over my mouth."

"What did his hand look like?"

She shrugged again. "A hand."

"Big? Small? Brown? White? Any rings?"

"A ring—here." She pointed at the middle finger of her left hand. "Gold. Very nice. Big hand. Pale as dead ilish."

"Ilish?"

"Fish."

Ilish: the Bengali fish. Zarina. "What about his voice?"

"First he is saying 'Silence' in English. Then I bite his hand and he swears and tries to catch me, but I am faster."

"How long has the hotel been wrecked like this?"

"Long time. Since last monsoon maybe."

"What were you doing here if the hotel was wrecked? Did you come to put fresh flowers on the place where Sami died? Did you work with her here?"

She started to move away. "I am not answering all these questions."

"Zarina, you have to help—" At the use of her name, she ran. I tried one last time, calling out, "Did you like the khichuri, Zarina?"

It stopped her for a moment, and she turned and smiled. Then she was gone, running like a deer. I had about as much chance of catching her as I had of catching the next bus to Piccadilly Circus. So I packed up my things and headed back through the hotel to the street to find a taxi. If there were any more secrets to be turned up in the Hotel Rama, I didn't want to be the one to do it.

"What is to be your destination, madam?" the taxi driver asked me.

"My destination? Good question. Let's start someplace where they serve drinks with paper umbrellas in them," I said. "Take me to the Oberoi."

THE OBEROI ON NARIMAN POINT WAS INDIA REINCARNATED AS A DALLAS MALL. Enough pearly marble to drain a quarry, buffed up like the talons on a Soho tart, an eleven-storey atrium filled with plants from every tropical zone but this one, a high-level pool with a cascading waterfall to mime the monsoon downpour, and a string quartet of brown men playing white men's music—all those foot-tapping local tunes like "My Way" and "California Dreamin'," and "Chicago, Chicago (It's My Kind of Town)."

There had been a few eyebrows raised at my appearance when I asked for the day rate on a single room here at the Spaceship Oberoi, but—"Interviews," I said breezily. "I need a quiet room to do some casting for the BBC."

Usually I hate wasting good money on someone else's taste in ruched hotel curtains, but there's a time and a place for everything. I took advantage of the "environmental unit" in the health spa to computer-control a sauna, a steambath, and my own tropical rain storm. Just like Bombay in the monsoon season, but without the inconvenience. The cosmic dance of Hilton, Oberoi, and Hyatt: who needs gods or meteorologists when you have international hotels?

I put on a clean, if somewhat wrinkled, T-shirt from my backpack and went down to the bar with a glossy new image. Roz Bengal as consumer instead of consumed, that was the impression I wanted. But every mirror I passed reminded me of the stained one in my bag. Too many reflections. I badly needed a drink.

In the bar I ordered every cocktail named after a foreign location. "I'll have a Manhattan, a Singapore Sling, a Hawaiian Punch, a London Fog, a Tobago Teaser, a Moscow Cooler, and an Irish coffee," I said. "And then we'll wing it."

"You are wanting a table for your guests, madam?" asked the bartender.

"The bar's fine," I said. "Just line the drinks up and I'll knock them down. I'm not expecting company."

When I got to Hawaii, I asked the bartender if he had any snacks.

"Bombay Mix, madam, or finger foods?"

"Oh, finger foods, definitely. They would be just perfect." I had a snap vision of those missing stumps in the Hotel Rama and blinked the red away quickly. After Tobago, I found I didn't see them so clearly. And after Moscow, I felt ready to take on India again.

THOMAS ANSWERED HIS MOBILE ON THE FIRST RING. "I HAVE THIS INFORMA-tion you requested but have not yet copied it out neatly."

"Never mind. Give me the gist of it."

Thomas was most pleased to inform me that his mission to trace the *Ramayana* players had been accomplished satisfactorily, although he had to wade his way through several obscure Shakespearean quotations and references to little-known films before getting down to the facts:

Some members of the troupe who had played the *Ramayana* on the night of Sami's death had roles in Prosper Sharma's latest production of *The Tempest*, but they had disappeared. Some of the current troupe had also been junior artistes at the time of Maya's death, when Prosper was filming on Chowpatty. Every member of his company had worn masks that day, even production managers and assistant directors; an artistic device, Prosper said, to get the whole company in the mood of a revel (as if they had needed that, given Ganesha's festival erupting all around). They remembered the day clearly because it was so chaotic.

The same troupe were booked to perform an excerpt from Prosper's *Tempest* at Anthony Unmann's going-away party. "Today, in fact, madam."

"Today?" I had completely forgotten the date.

"Yes, madam. Today is thirteenth."

The day that Rupert Boothroyd, my expert from Christie's, was due to arrive. In a couple of hours. Time to lay my box of tricks on the table.

Let us examine the evidence, Your Honour: a piece of mirror, a scalpel, a bloody T-shirt, a couple of rolls of film, some tapes of a dead hijra, some drawings and a statue, a few newspaper clippings. What it came down to: no hard evidence tied Prosper or Unmann to the murders without the most fantastic leaps of imagination. I still needed a lure to get the snake out of his hole.

7

"AH, IT'S YOU, ROSALIND," ASHOK SAID, WHEN HIS HOUSE-keeper showed me into the library. "I wondered when I would hear from you again."

He was standing on a stepladder, holding a book in one hand and a portable hairdryer in the other. "The monsoon is terrible for mildew," he said. "During the rainy season I usually keep Christmas lights burning night and day along my bookshelves to stop the worst damp. But we have had so many power cuts recently I found my complete works of Shakespeare had turned the most melancholy shade of green. So I am having to dry the more precious volumes by hand." He held up the hairdryer and slowly got down off the steps.

"I have some things to tell you that might . . ." I stopped.

"That might?"

"Assist you in your investigations."

He frowned. "What investigations are you referring to, Rosalind?"

"I read some articles you wrote in the *CBI Bulletin.*"

His eyebrows rose slightly.

"The articles by Professor Ashok Tagore, D. Phil., Oxon." Come on, Ash.

"Yes?"

"And I looked up what the CBI is." His reticence was making me impatient.

"Ah yes. That would explain some of the comments you made a few days ago in the car. As it happens, a D. Phil. from Oxford University is not so unusual as you would think in the upper echelons of the Indian civil service."

"You can hardly call spies the civil service, Ashok."

He carried on. "And the name Ashok is a relatively common one. Even popular, I would say. A king of the Mauryan dynasty—circa 260 B.C., at a rough estimate—who was converted to non-violent Buddhism after a famously bloody battle. He forswore war as a means of conquest and exchanged many missives with the Hellenic world."

"So you're saying you're not a spy and didn't write those articles."

"Perhaps you should listen more carefully."

"Missives exchanged with the Greeks, with the enemies—what's that supposed to convey? Give me a break, Ash. We're on the same side."

"Are we? I am not entirely clear whose side you are cheering. It appeared to be Caleb Mistry's the last time I examined the evidence. Clearly, you have . . . ties with Mistry, a man who has in the past been involved in some enterprises that are—shall we call them questionable?"

"The biscuit business? I know all about that."

"You find it admirable?" His voice as cool and dry as bleached bones, picked clean of emotion.

"Not quite the same as murder, Ashok."

"No. However, it has come to the attention of the authorities that Caleb Mistry is not unfamiliar with the elusive Mr. Acres, a man you have accused of murder."

"Of course. Acres was one of the men who tied us up at Caleb's studio."

"There remains some doubt as to the verisimilitude of Mr. Caleb Mistry's story."

"What do you mean? He was tied up like me."

"Possibly. Prosper—"

"You believe Prosper's stories," I said angrily. "Why is it so important to you to blame Caleb?"

"You might ask yourself why it is so important for you to rewrite Caleb's history and to prove your brother-in-law guilty. Consider Caleb Mistry: the illegitimate son of a prostitute, a man who worked part-time as a pimp for several years, then in various positions in the underworld, with whose leaders he still maintains many connections, whatever he has told you. His first wife killed herself in mysterious circumstances. And incidentally, Mistry is not his real name. He adopted it from a Parsi—"

"And then there's Prosper," I said, unable to keep the bitterness out of my voice, "with his old school tie. A real saint. Well, let me tell you a few things about my dear brother-in-law."

Ashok listened with his usual distant expression to my theories about the connections between Sami, Prosper, Sunila, and Unmann, his attention only sharpening when I began to describe the scene at the Hotel Rama and how I thought it tied in to Sami's drawings. I didn't tell him about Gul or Skanda.

"You have kept all this material together?" Ashok asked, and when I nodded—"Then what you must do is to pass it over to the proper authorities. Although drawings are not proof of anything. Too much is artistic licence."

"That's it, Ash? You don't think I've earned any explanation?"

"Should the authorities inform me of further developments arising out of the material you have collected, be assured that I will pass on the information."

We might have been strangers discussing ancient history. "And just who are these proper authorities, Ash? What will they do?"

"What they can."

"What happens if the murders of a few hijra don't really count on the scale of the destruction of the career of some politician who likes buggering eunuchs?"

"There may be wider issues here than sexual preference, Rosalind."

"You'll have to do better than that." I stood up.

"Wait." Ashok pushed aside some of the books on his desk and sat down opposite me, indicating that I was to sit as well, as if I were a potential candidate he was interviewing for a job.

"How much do you know about the Shiv Sena movement?" he said.

"The basics."

"You know enough then to realize that it is—or was—a very sensitive political issue. Shiv Sena was begun by Bal Thackeray, the Maharashtrian cartoonist, with the aim of righting the wrongs done to the original people of this soil. Or so he claimed. Many Bombay people saw the Sena's cry of 'Maharashtra for the Maharashtrians' as a fascist one. It was disliked by south Indians, Jains, Parsis—outsiders in Bombay who were persecuted by the Sena when it first came to power. And the poor have always mistrusted politicians: in 1966, the year of its founding, the party had only eighteen supporters. But then the Sena vowed to protect *all* Maharashtrians from persecution—especially the poor and dispossessed—and backed up those claims by winning concessions from the government to install drainage and latrines in the worst chawls. So support for the Sena gradually built among the city's huge population of squatters and small stall holders, and as it acquired political power, the Sena became less narrowly Maharashtrian and more generally Hindu. Even Indira Gandhi supported them, at least while her father was prime minister."

"Why would she support a separatist movement?"

"To be seen to be on the side of the poor, I imagine. As I said to you a few days ago, the chawls are essentially huge vote banks."

"She wanted to cash in."

He shook his head at my flippancy. "Let us look at a few of the main characters in our story: Maya's father was a noted Parsi intellectual who contributed many satirical articles deriding Bal Thackeray, often mocking Thackeray's magazine, *Marmik*, which had a circulation of about forty thousand in the 1960s. The first weekly entirely in the Marathi language, and a political soapbox for Thackeray. Maya herself was no great supporter of the Sena, even less so after she married Prosper, a real outsider in Maharashtra. His family were wealthy Parsis from Lahore who moved to England before his mother returned here with Prosper in the late fifties, after his father died."

"At least Prosper's father gave him a name. Unlike Caleb's dad, who buggered off back to his wife in England."

"On the contrary: Mistry's father, a Mr. Falkland Williams, was a technical draughtsman and engineer employed in the reclamation of land in Bombay. He returned to England because he suffered from a rather common heart disease, of which he subsequently died."

Caleb, the engineer's son. "Why are you so well informed about Caleb's background, Ashok? Or interested, for that matter?"

Ashok unlocked a wooden filing cabinet, handing me what looked like a handwritten shopping list clipped to an English translation: a list of names and contributions to Shiv Sena dating back years. One name stood out: Caleb Mistry.

"For many years Mistry was a regular contributor to the Shiv Sena cause," Ashok said. "Over the past six years, as the Sena has been slowly replaced in popularity by other parties, Mistry has increased his donations, paying out what amounts to a hundred and twenty-five percent of all profits in his movies. And he has no other source of income."

"So? He supports the party of his mother's people and makes

more money than he declares. It's the black economy. The film industry gets paid largely in cash and it's full of people with suggestions of
how to hide the excess—property, gold mines, beer companies. What
has all this to do with the hijra murders?"

"There are extremists within the Sena, as there are in every political party—"

"You're saying Caleb's one of them?"

"It is more complex than that, Rosalind. Not everything is so cut-
and-dried. With the electoral victories the Sena has had in the last few
years, these extremists have seized the opportunity to stir up violent
agitation between the local Muslim population and those people who
think of themselves as pure Hindu Maharashtrian." Ashok's mouth
twisted into a pained smile. "It gets worse during Indo-Pakistan
cricket matches. And Mistry's associate, Mr. Acres—"

"You've got no proof of that association."

Ashok laid a yellowed piece of paper on the desk between us.
"From the Bombay police files, 1967," he said.

The document confirmed the arrest and subsequent sentencing for
traffic in gold "biscuits" of one Caleb Mistry and his cohort, Roberto
Acres.

"Acres managed to persuade an official to let him go. He disappeared from sight for many years. He is—*was*, if your hunch about the
body you found at Hotel Rama is correct—a gangster, a pimp, a
blackmailer."

"Acres never struck me as a candidate for knighthood." Caleb and
Acres. I found it hard to speak.

"He was also one of the Sena's extremist agitators. Not that I think
he had any political beliefs apart from those which lined his own
pocket."

"So he should make an excellent politician. But I don't understand—I thought Acres was American. How could he be involved with
the Sena?"

"His mother was Goan, in fact, but it is not so much Mr. Acres
who has been stirring the karahi—more his associates. He has also
been used on occasion by certain gentlemen in . . . in a party close to
the centre, shall we say."

"Playing both sides against the middle."

"A game at which our Mr. Acres was rather adept. Now I want you
to consider that Bombay is a movie city. Our film business is full of
north Indian Muslim male stars and south Indian Hindu female

stars—your brother-in-law's studio a case in point. Caleb Mistry's is pure Hindu, every man, woman, and child a Maharashtrian supporting the Sena, down to the humblest junior artiste."

"You think this Shiv Sena connection of Caleb's may have had something to do with Maya's murder?" I said. "But the other murders—of Sami and Sunila—were they political as well?"

"Let us say they might be made to *look* political. Mr. Acres has always kept that option open, as a possible wedge to drive between opposing parties. Can you see how a young woman with insufficient background information could do serious political damage in such a situation? Damage she had not necessarily intended?"

It was a good story. Another good story. "But what about the property and forgery angles I mentioned?" I said.

"So many angles. I am giving you their point of intersection."

I wondered what his motives were for revealing all this. "Tell me, Ash, which side of the political fence do you sit on? You really buy into the current government?"

"If you wish to reduce this discussion to simplistic terms, I am on the side of order. And without government there would be only anarchy." He was studying me carefully, judging his audience, how much of the plot to reveal. "What you want is a miraculous solution, Rosalind, but no such solutions exist. India is a country full of spurious miracles—the editor of *The Indian Sceptic* has exposed over fifteen hundred. My own ambition is to see just one real miracle before I die. In the meantime, we must make do with law and order."

"Shades of grey."

He frowned.

"Something Shoma Kumar once said about Prosper. Anyway, I'm not sure if there is much order, or no more than there is in the weather. Sometimes the monsoon comes and the rice grows. Sometimes it doesn't, and you die. There's not a damn thing you can do about it."

"Every man for himself, is that what you believe?" he said.

"And as many like-minded people as you can squeeze onto the raft. Mine's pretty small at the moment. It's being rebuilt a log at a time. I'm not sure if there's room for anything as big as a government on it just yet." I got up and walked around the room, picking my way gingerly through the leaning pillars of books. Next to the window was an impressive section on the Malabar Coast.

"Your father left me those," Ashok said. He had followed me across the room, and now reached from behind to get a book off the shelf, his arm grazing my shoulder as it passed. I could feel it through my thin shirt, and wondered if his proximity was deliberate or unconscious. "I keep them next to my favorite books of legends."

Turning my head, I looked into Ashok's dark eyes. "I find facts more interesting these days," I said. "Do you have any of Dad's books on snakes? There was a great one by a guy who filmed the spitting cobra. The trick was to get close enough so the snake spit its poison at your eyes, but not so close it bit. Too far away and the snake just makes a run for it. Apparently, the snake has to see your eyes staring right into his before it will spit. But this guy couldn't afford to get bitten again because he'd been bitten so often he was immune to the antivenin. One more bite, he's dead. So he uses his wife as bait instead. Of course, the wife always wears glasses—the saliva can't actually blind her."

I heard Ashok walk away, his steps heavy. "I am afraid I do not understand where all of this is leading."

Like hell you don't, I thought.

"But with Acres dead and the photos in the hands of an unknown party, there is little to be done, Rosalind, unless you agree to give the authorities what you have." Sitting behind his desk again like a judge.

"Did I say they got all the pictures, Ash? I'm sure I didn't." Watching his face tense up. A hit. "No, they missed one. There is one small piece of hard evidence."

"And who is this picture of?"

"Someone—how did you put it?—someone close to the centre."

I would have left then, without any formality. But Ashok was a follower of Hinduism, a religion which allows for an infinite number of second chances. At the door he put his hands on my shoulders and turned me to face him. "Consider this carefully, Rosalind. I think you are more loyal to India than you imagine. And remember what happens in India when the fuse is lit under religion and politics."

"Mother India—*Bharat Mata*—wasn't that the rallying cry when Indian patriots were trying to get independence from Old Mother Britain? Mom—she's always a potent symbol. But nationalism seems like a very unstable mother to me. One of those mothers whose own background gets in the way of the interests of their kids. And I'm not a nationalist: I've never cared for team sports."

8

Rain fell like a fist on Bombay, slamming all available oxygen into the earth, so hard that the taxi driver wasn't sure we would make it up the Malabar Hill.

"Unmann's party better be worth it," Rupert Boothroyd said, removing his wire-rimmed glasses to wipe off the steam for the fifth time since I had picked him up at the Taj. His cream linen suit, soaked through in the two-foot leap from hotel to car, now sported a high-tide mark at mid-calf. "And as I told you earlier, Miss Benegal, unless the forgers are very amateurish, which you assure me they are not, it's unlikely I will be able to tell if Mr. Unmann's collection is fake—a concept I find highly improbable, I must say, given his credentials."

Rupert Teddington Boothroyd was nice enough, for a man whose head was all brain and no chin, like a wedge being slowly driven into his back to force his shoulders up in a noncommittal shrug. Earlier in the afternoon he had spent a long time telling me that like most of the less informed press, I oversimplified methods of detecting forgery, ignoring aesthetic criteria and preferring splashy scientific revelations.

"Take paintings that have been overzealously restored," he said. "What emerges from technical examinations using infrared will still have to be cross-checked by an art historian. Journalists place too much value on signatures and their date of application. In fact, many artists don't put a name to their work until very late."

Until too late. My father had already taught me that lesson.

"And then, Miss Benegal, there is the difference in *purpose* between forger, copyist, and artist, where a historian may detect what a technical test cannot."

"What do you mean, a difference in purpose?"

"The artist is secure in his artistic identity and thus free to experiment with it, while a forger must cling desperately to an identity which is already established—someone else's, in fact. And as to copyists—in many instances, technical revelations simply reveal quite genuine restoration rather than deliberate counterfeiting. I have often been called in to examine Mogul miniatures, where there are many cases of eighteenth-century copies subsequently acquiring a decent patina of age without any intent to deceive, at least not by the artist."

"Does that apply to gold coins and medals as well? Were there lots of copies?"

"Very little of the coinage which flooded India survived, because most gold and silver coins were melted down for jewellery. Generally, the early coins we find are bronze. And bronze copies are easily made from existing coins, using the lost-wax method." Rupert was warming to his subject. "During the Renaissance, many artists who produced commemorative medals favoured lost wax. Later medals were struck like coins, heated metal disks forced between two engraved dies by the blows of a hammer. The process allowed large quantities to be reproduced, hammered out in a cold, crisp style like little soldiers."

"Nothing to identify the hand of the artist," I said.

He nodded. "It also led to a disillusion with mass production. Artists became more interested in the original wax models, and these, being rarer, acquired a value beyond their gold copies."

"Proof that an artist may supersede his material."

Rupert wasn't to be deflected from his course by questions of metaphysics. "In fact," he went on, "the Renaissance artists' interest in medals was linked to their love of classical coins. For proof, we need look no further than the numerous fake coins cast by medal artists like Dürer. And who, Miss Benegal, *who*"—peering over his glasses like a lesser horned owl—"could complain of a copy by Dürer!"

Boothroyd's natural forum was a perch in the lecture hall with a good supply of dead mice for company. I hoped he would be suitably pedantic with Prosper and Unmann. "What about faking sculpture, Rupert?"

"That depends on the material and the country. Hindu sculpture is difficult to classify, precisely because the personality of the artist is to an extent suppressed. The work is not intended to be a one-off masterpiece like the *Mona Lisa*. It is more akin to Michelangelo's *David*—"

"Why *David*?" An echo whose source I couldn't trace. The image of Sami came to mind.

"*David* was cast several times without loss of integrity. And in classical Roman and Greek work, as in Hindu, the same god is often repeated with subtle variations in iconography. Good forgers recycle—old canvas, worn stone—to reproduce the patina of age. Technical detection is easiest when there are a greater number of variables to test—paint ground, gesso, varnish. But with stone you have only the stone, so less can be done technically, apart from using ultraviolet, which will detect any recutting as a different fluorescence than the original—if someone had found a worn statue, say, and recarved the details to increase its value. Then again, different climates cause differing degrees of wear, like the 'priceless' Modigliani head dredged up from a Livorno canal that proved to be the fruit of four hours' work on an old paving stone by some students."

"So you'd expect an exterior stone statue in a monsoon climate to wear more quickly than the same statue kept in a London museum."

"Exactly. Bronze is more difficult to fake; its patina needs time to develop. Although the latest chemical bronzes, combined with exposure to salt air, can be terribly convincing." To lesser mortals, at least, he implied. "One must always remember the case of that 'quintessence of the ancient Greek spirit,' as it was called for so many years!" I hadn't the faintest idea what he was talking about. "The bronze horse purchased by the New York Met in 1923 and declared to be a fifty-year-old forgery in 1967," he said. "You must have heard of it!"

"What if a buyer suspected that a work had been acquired illegally," I pressed him, "but he'd already had its provenance authenticated by a respected art historian—such a buyer might not feel the need for a technical expert to check it, right?"

"Hypothetically. In fact, he almost certainly would not bother. If the historian were sufficiently grand and the price sufficiently low. Unless it was a question of insuring the work, that is. For an exhibition, say. Anthony Blunt pioneered the careful inspection of an artwork's documentation—"

"Anthony Blunt, the traitor?" I said.

He shrugged. "And distinguished art historian . . . Blunt's work means that provenance these days tends to be established by authenticating papers—anything from a letter to a diary entry." He smiled a bit ruefully. "And paper documentation is easier to forge than art."

"So you're saying that legitimate or illegitimate, it's just a question of a name," I said. "And in the end, all a name does is cover your ass." The key was here somewhere. All I had to do was find the right lock.

9

FOR UNMANN'S PARTY, MY GECKO-GREEN SHALWAR KAMIZ IN raw silk seemed appropriate. Fuck the earthy colours, I thought, let's go straight for the reptilian. I kohled my eyes, gelled my hair into a black helmet, and stood back to admire the effect. The corpse of Elvis in drag. It needed earrings, the ones my mother used to call "the chandeliers," a legacy from my great-grandmother—pure Chitrali tribal, like my mood. Beaten silver set with mirrors, they trembled and tinkled in heavy, cascading platforms almost to my shoulders. If I moved too quickly they'd put someone's eye out. I planned to swing my head with the zeal of a shampoo model.

Unimpressed by my glittering transformation from the crumpled hippie he had met this afternoon, Rupert Boothroyd stared grimly out of the taxi at the flooded streets, clearly regretting his decision to escort me to Unmann's. The car threw up a wake of water that sent pedestrians scurrying away under their huge, rusty-black umbrellas like enormous cockroaches avoiding a jet of detergent.

"I don't know what my friends were doing suggesting that I come here in this weather," Rupert said. "And Goa is not likely to be any better."

Our driver turned around and smiled. "Oh yes, sir. Goa is raining even more. All tourist posters are saying 'Come to Goa when it pours!' Here in Bombay will be arriving many Arab peoples just to see our monsoon falling out of the sky."

"I'm so pleased," Boothroyd said.

"You have the tape I gave you?" I cut in. "And you will be sure to give it to Ram Shantra at the Fort Aguada resort if and when your plane takes off tomorrow?"

Rupert hunched his shoulders miserably in acquiescence.

"Sir and madam are walking remaining distance," said our driver. "But not so far. Up there is your house, in what people are calling Street of Maharajas."

LEGIONS OF SMALL BROWN MEN WITH LARGE BLACK UMBRELLAS STOOD OUT-side Unmann's gates waiting to usher the guests through a dripping forest of tamarind, the trees swathed in mist like shrouded mummies. The house was large and turreted, and under its porte cochere were more servants holding basins of jasmine-scented water for us to rinse off the mud, with warm towels to dry our feet.

"It is rather splendid," Rupert whispered to me a few minutes later.

"In a House of Usher sort of way," I said, then glanced at the gnawed chicken bone he was holding. "Or maybe I'm thinking of Hansel and Gretel."

The marble entrance hall was flanked by twin mahogany stair-cases curving round to an open mezzanine lined with black granite urns. Overlooking the hall stood a welcoming committee of bronzes, a Bombay Mix of Indian deities and Victorian gods of industry. I had to give Unmann credit for style. To make a virtue of his leave-taking, he had wrapped all the furniture in yards of muslin and tied it like Christo sculptures, a frivolous gesture his ancestors clearly did not approve: walls of dead Unmanns stared down gloomily, their painted mouths fixed in perpetual grimaces of disdain, as if even the act of portraiture were a treacherous loss of sobriety.

We followed the other guests outside into a courtyard of Chinese glazed tiles, protected from any threat of rain by the embroidered canopy soaring over it, the size of a circus big top. Banks of bonsai trees, their trunks thick and contorted from years of tortured clipping, defined the edges of the garden.

"My great-grandfather had very Oriental tastes." Unmann's voice behind us.

"That makes sense," I said, "given that he made his fortune in opium."

My comment made Rupert uncomfortable. At each turn in the house I had seen his faith in my forgery story fade. Admiring a bronze dancing girl emerging like Botticelli's Venus from foaming waves of shredded newspaper in a half-packed crate, Rupert had announced loudly that she was certainly museum quality. "So kind of you to invite me, Mr. Unmann," he said now.

"This is Rupert Boothroyd." I smiled into Unmann's wary eyes. "From the Asian art department of Christie's. I'm taking him on the rounds of the great and good of Bombay. Tonight: you. Tomorrow: Prosper."

Unmann smiled back, but his eyes remained cool. "Delighted to have you here, Mr. Boothroyd. What a shame that most of my collection is already packed."

"Yes, we overheard a man saying you had sold up everything to some Kuwaiti oil barons," I said. "House and contents: 'lock, stock, and barrel.' "

"Not quite everything," Unmann corrected. "I have kept a few treasures."

In fact, we had passed rooms stacked with crates addressed to Unmann's galleries in San Francisco, Berlin, and London.

Leaving Rupert to chat up Unmann, I told them I was going to find my sister, intending to have a closer look at what Unmann was shipping out. "I'm afraid your sister wasn't feeling well, Rosalind," Unmann said. "But Prosper is here. Upstairs, I think, in the room beyond the musicians."

He pointed to a verandah that overhung the courtyard, where a band was playing a slow raga, a *des*, I thought, the late-night raga often combined with a *mallar*, or monsoon group. As I made my way through the crowd, the combined glitter of noble metals and precious stones bounced off the tiled floor in a laser show of rich and richer that made Gran's earrings quiver with class revolt. I swept a large whisky off a waiter's tray and added some ice with one of those claw-shaped silver tongs that are supposed to stop you from getting your germs mixed up with someone else's. "Ice is made from boiled water," the waiter told me.

"Good," I said. "I wouldn't want to catch anything I don't already have."

A fat pink man with a face like a well-sucked cough sweet— sticky, glistening, and round at the corners—winked at me from across the room. I stuck my tongue out at him and skated across the floor in the direction of those rooms of crates, knocking once on a big mahogany door that looked like a drawbridge before slipping inside.

A space the size of a ballroom, maroon velvet curtains fringed in gold, chandeliers caught up in muslin like girls in crinolined ball dresses.

The next room was empty except for some plaster casts of Victorian beauties peering out winsomely from under a torn billiard table. Beyond was another ballroom, a repeat of the first, but half the size.

Unmann had said he liked to gamble, and what bigger gamble could there be than to smuggle out a houseful of forgeries under the nose of a Christie's art expert and a generous slice of Bombay's ruling class? I checked off a list of the things Unmann was leaving behind for his Arab buyers: an empty packet of bidis that had been dropped into a chipped Chinese vase; a stuffed cobra coiled to strike, one eye missing; a bookcase full of such mildewed eulogies to British trade and industry as "The Personal Fortune and Memoirs of Sir Warren Unmann" in the *Economic History Review*, Vol. XVII, 1879. A sugar bowl lettered: *East India Sugar Not Made by Slaves*; a Copeland silver champagne ice pail, with painted swags of grapevines and five gilt baby satyrs supporting it; and the *pièce de résistance*: a tiered porcelain centrepiece in gold, turquoise, and flamingo pink, given by Queen Victoria to Sir Warren Unmann, with four life-size naked nymphs clutching vases of silvered glass striped in ruby with cut decoration, the kind of item that inspired Ruskin to proclaim, "All cut glass is barbarous." A sure conversation stopper at future Kuwaiti dinner parties.

If it stands still, swag it and gild it; if it moves, stuff it, could have summed up the Unmann family's approach to interior design.

I opened a few doors to see if there was anyone in the immediate vicinity. As the nearest sign of human life was a servant shooing peacocks out of the dining area below, I felt free to relax.

Using one of a set of silver fish knives as a lever, I prised off the top of a crate addressed to a Berlin antiques shop and found what looked like a 360-piece set of early Wedgwood china. Other crates held busts of various whiskered gentlemen.

What was I looking for? There is a theory in physics, my father taught me, that if two solutions are possible in an experiment, the one which is most aesthetically pleasing often turns out to be correct. "What is true is often what is most beautiful," he said. It would please me to discover that Prosper and Unmann, those genuine articles, were smuggling forged works of art. Therefore, I was determined to prove it true.

In the fourth crate the dark face of a bronze Vishnu smiled up at me through curls of pale newsprint. If it was a forgery, I couldn't tell.

"Madam!" A servant's alarmed voice came from the doorway behind me.

I turned around and said serenely, "Mr. Unmann has asked me for . . . for some more candlesticks to illuminate the function."

It was the word "function" that got him. He dipped his head and closed the door. After ten more cases all I had learned was that the bulk of the Indian artworks was destined for the three galleries called Goliath. I was puzzling over this when my brother-in-law's voice rang out: "Rosalind! What on earth are you doing?"

Prosper was supremely elegant in a raw silk kurta pyjama that matched the champagne in his hand. Behind him stood Unmann, smiling faintly, and Rupert.

"Ah, Miss Benegal," said Unmann. "So my servant was correct."

There was nothing to do but brazen it out. I tried a casual laugh on for size and felt it tighten uncomfortably round my throat. "Rupert, you should see—"

Boothroyd cut me off, his face filled with horror at the possibility of being linked with me. "Please believe me, Mr. Unmann, I had nothing to do with this."

Unmann smiled reassuringly at the dealer. "I'm sure of that, Rupert."

Boothroyd did a good impression of a spaniel fawning at his master's feet, keeping well back from the invisible boundary between my camp and theirs.

"I'll get her out of here, Tony," Prosper said.

"Nonsense. Dear Rosalind has just had a little too much to drink," Unmann said, his voice full of false bonhomie. "Come and have something to eat."

He seated Rupert and me at a long table wrapped in yards of muslin, Unmann between us like a referee. The condition of our fellow guests indicated that I was not the only one to have been drinking heavily.

"Tony told us he was saving that place for Caleb Mistry's latest . . . love," drawled a lean man with a camel's haughty stupid expression. "And of course we all know that the monsoon is a very erotic time." The girl next to him giggled. Her plump body and painted face reminded me of one of the plaster goddesses sold at Indian street markets on festival days.

Around the garden were ten more tables like ours, each seating about twenty people. Ashok was at one of them, watching me, his face impassive.

"I didn't know Ashok had been invited," I said to Unmann.

"Oh yes." He smiled. "Your friend Tagore is a prominent member of the Tilak Foundation, as are most of the guests here tonight. I thought you knew."

"Oh, look!" a woman said. Across one of the verandahs a large film screen had been stretched. On it, actors in Mogul court dress wandered through a downpour to a covered pavilion in an overgrown Persian garden. As the first dishes arrived on our tables, images on the film began to mirror our party. A collection of masked figures—dwarfs, acrobats, hijra dancers—carried elaborate plates of food to the courtiers in the monsoon pavilion, a scene shot through the arches of a Mogul palace so that it was framed by the stone as if in an Indian painting. Invisible musicians—whether live or on screen, it was impossible to tell—were playing the *Meghamalhar*, a raga that is meant to evoke distant echoes of thunder and the cry of peacocks.

"So clever!" said the woman next to Rupert. "Like old Indian palaces with their special balconies where nobility went to view the monsoon downpour."

I could hear Rupert: ". . . delighted to be included in this gathering of Mr. Unmann's friends."

"Yes, he will be so missed by our foundation."

"Foundation?" said Rupert.

"Our Tilak Foundation," said the woman. "A group of concerned people who are involved in preserving venerable buildings of historic interest to the nation."

At a lull in the party the woman's voice again carried across. "With squatters and so forth, the only thing to be done sometimes is complete gutting, preserving exterior only. But always we are trying to rebuild in original vernacular."

"Like the building attached to the Goliath Cinema complex in Bombay?" I said.

The woman was delighted. "Such a pity it was allowed to go to rack and ruin. A beautiful *haveli*, built in the Gothic style by one of our great nineteenth-century trading families, with lavish display of arcades and other such embellishments. But upon dispersal of family, house is falling into hands of lowlifes."

"Will you be able to save it?" asked Rupert.

"Thankfully, some foreign investors have agreed to preserve

building's exterior at least—in exchange for being allowed to convert it into a heritage hotel. But rooms will be furnished in old style so visitors may enjoy once more the glory that was India of yesteryear." Her eyes sparkled with enthusiasm.

"Thus making about a thousand people homeless," I said, "free to enjoy the glory that is Bombay this year."

"This is Prosper Sharma's sister-in-law, Your Highness," Rupert cut in.

Her Highness, whose face had dropped at my comment, revived at Prosper's name. "Dear Prosper! Such a strong supporter of the foundation. For this Goliath project he has volunteered the services of his team of highly skilled artisans to produce artwork in keeping with the period."

A man with a carnivore's mouth interrupted. "Miss Benegal, Tony has been telling us how Caleb Mistry and you were involved in a sticky situation at the ice house." He nudged the plump girl sitting between him and the camel and she giggled again. "Since then there have been repeated sightings of you two in even stickier situations."

Another man: "Under the Mistry spell . . . like her sister." The boiled sweet face.

"What do you mean—" I started.

The woman poked the man sharply in his ribs and he gave a small explosion of laughter. The rest of the table joined in. Feeding time at the zoo. On cue, Unmann passed a plate of rice stained the colour of a fake tan, garnished with squares of pure gold leaf. I pushed the food away.

"Oh dear, I hope he hasn't offended you," said a woman in nightshade purple.

Unmann patted my arm with his large pale hand. "Of course not," he said.

A schoolyard chant: *Pakistani, Pakistani, stuck his dick in Mummy's fanny!* The circle of little white faces closing in. Welcome home to Scotland, Rosalind. A hybrid consigned to the margins of the map with all the other edge monsters.

I stared at Unmann's hand on my arm, pale as a dead fish. *Ilish*: the word comes back. A broad gold ring on the middle finger. Before turbulence becomes fully developed, I thought, it must pass through several intermediate stages.

"You didn't get all the pictures, you know," I said to Unmann, smiling into his bleached eyes. "You left one behind." I patted my bag. "Would your guests like to see what you get up to in your spare time?"

A gamble. I leaned across to Rupert. "It's the Goliath galleries you should be checking out," I said.

Rupert was trying to fade into his Christo chair. "We must humour Rosalind," Unmann whispered to him. On the screen above us, Basil Chopra appeared, striding across the grass. The attention of the diners at my table was diverted.

"He's meant to be invisible, isn't that the form?" said the night-shade woman.

"Most difficult, given dear Basil's predilection for ghee."

All eyes except ours were glued to the film. The three of us bound up in this tight little web. Unmann's whisper softened still further. "You know about Rosalind's . . ." I couldn't catch the next words. Did he say breakdown? Tarring me with the brush of the unreliable narrator. It was such an old story, one I had heard so many times before. From my father. From the doctors, when Mum's symptoms were first diagnosed. "Her mother had Münchhausen syndrome by proxy . . ." Were these words being spoken? ". . . perpetrator typi-cally a woman . . . makes someone else ill, if necessary by force . . . Terrible thing . . . lasting psychological damage to the child, to Ros-alind—"

"Such an honour, a sneak preview of Sharma's *Tempest*," the camel man said.

A slim figure in the costume of Rama danced after Basil, and over the chatter of the dinner guests rose the voice track: *Now I will believe / That there are unicorns; that in Arabia / There is one tree, the phoenix throne; one phoenix / At this hour reigning there.* Perhaps if I had not spent days in the company of her photos, if Satish hadn't insisted on showing me every lifelike detail of his reconstruction, I might not have recognized her.

"Sami," I said. "Goliath. You see, Rupert? The same name as Prosper's—"

"Mothers poison their offspring," the whisper went on. "In princi-ple, they stop short of murder but—"

"It's the storyteller's disease," I said. "Münchhausen was a story-teller." I could feel the flow of events crossing that boundary from smooth to turbulent. *Once there was a time in India, my mother said, when all three of earth's methods of creation were combined. Incest, fire sacrifice—and dismemberment . . . A little cut, my mother said.* "You invent a story and then you make it come true."

"They make their children ill and then lie about it." Unmann saying that? "They often start with themselves. Not diagnosed . . . late seventies."

Boothroyd reached across Unmann to put his hand on my arm, and spoke in a voice that was meant to be kind. "Miss Benegal, you are not looking at all well."

"Patients often have a history of sexual abuse." Unmann or the doctor or my father or maybe I was saying as I shook off Boothroyd's arm and stood up so quickly my chair fell over, dragging the table-cloth with it. For several minutes after the glasses and plates smashed I could hear that storyteller's voice: *Once there was a time in India.*

When the echo stopped, Prosper was beside me. "I'll take her home, Tony." My brother-in-law, the murderer, put his arm around my shoulders.

"Enter Ariel, like a harpy. And Prospero, invisible," I said. "Aren't those the stage directions?" I snapped my fingers. "What a shame: you're still here."

The last thing I noticed as Prosper escorted me out of the garden was Ashok. That final, mysterious member of the Tilak Foundation. How he must have laughed when I came to him for advice.

"Straitened circumstances, Prosper?" I said, as he got into the driver's seat of an old Ambassador outside. "Everybody has a driver in India."

He started the car and pulled out into the road. "I blame myself for not believing your sister. She has worried herself sick over you. She told me of the accusations you made in the hospital and I rather unwisely put them down to your incident with those goondas. But the situation is clearly more serious." Mud splashed the windscreen, obscuring the view for several seconds. "I haven't got time tonight to take you to a doctor, which would be the best solution. I must return to Tony's." He glanced at me. "I'm taking you to our flat."

"Good. I'd like to see how my little sister is getting on."

We stopped in front of his apartment building. "Miranda will be sleeping by now," he said. "I don't want you waking her tonight. Perhaps tomorrow she will be able to talk some sense into you. Although I believe this has gone beyond what family can do. You need professional help." Unspoken: *like your mother*.

"Or I can talk some sense into her."

His mouth tightened. "This has to stop, Rosalind. I have tolerated the wild gossip you have been spreading around Bombay since you arrived. Because of your background and the state of mind it appears to have induced. But I am not prepared to listen to any more delusional and unsubstantiated accusations."

"Substantiation?" I could barely spit the word out. "Let me get this right. You want me to prove to you that you did it? Wrong country, Prosper: Kafka was an Austrian. But if you want substantiation, don't worry: I've got proof."

"Yes? Of what, precisely?"

"I dropped that photo of you and Sami and Maya next to Acres's mashed-in face in the Hotel Rama. And took a picture of it up close." Wanting to rattle him as he'd rattled me. "Which will shortly be mailed to newspapers and movie mags with all the rest of the stuff I have. It may not be proof that the police will buy, but I can't wait to see what the likes of Shoma Kumar make of it."

For a couple of minutes we sat and listened to each other breathe.

Then Prosper spoke, his voice as warm and full of promise as the barrel of a well-oiled gun: "No doubt you will do whatever you think will damage me, Rosalind. But I must warn you that the person who will be hurt most by your actions is your only sister, who has become increasingly worried about you in the last few days and who is at this moment confined to bed under strict doctor's orders for fear that she may lose her baby. A baby who will be your only nephew. As well as my *only* son."

After that we were both well behaved all the way to the penthouse. In the corridor of the flat I gave the picture frames a few light taps. But we both knew who was in control. "Just checking to see if the gilt has dried yet," I said.

"Please keep your voice down," he said.

He led me to the back of the flat into a large, airy room like a time capsule of India's past. The walls were lined with shelves full of statues and rare books, and between the statues were Mogul miniatures, framed collections of gold coins and medals, hundreds of desirable fragments in stone and bronze.

"Oh good," I said. "More books. I can catch up on my reading."

ASYLUM—THEY SHOULD NEVER HAVE GOT RID OF THE WORD: A PLACE WHERE people who do not fit in or can no longer pay their dues find sanctuary.

My mother had been released into the public domain for several months when I saw her last. Current government policy, another brilliant scheme to save taxpayers' money. They called it "an opportunity to interact with the public." As if that's just what was missing in the public's daily life, interaction with a few more schizophrenics and manic-depressives. All my mother wanted was attention. Suddenly there was no one to attend anymore, no one to listen to her stories. Instead, she got a selection of coloured tablets to collect every Friday morning at the clinic. Seven tablets per week for seven weeks, seven minutes per patient—that's what the consultant had it down to.

Callahan, P.? *Tick.*
Johnston, R.? *Tick.*
Paton, J.?
Paton, J.?

Jessica Irvine Paton—no trace of Indian roots in her name—never collected her seven tablets on that Friday in February 1986. The consultant was prepared to swear to it at the autopsy.

I watched the rain start up again and hammer on the window until the lights along Chowpatty Beach below vanished in the mist. Closed my eyes. Tried to remember something Ashok had said, years ago, about the West having music and instruments that end with a crescendo and a climax. "But we have the raga—a group of notes whose tune may alter with the wind. And our musicians play the sitar, an instrument that ends in a question."

Transcribing sitar music is like trying to map the sea, he told me. We make a black mark on a lined sheet and assume that by doing so we have control over it; it is in our power, a piece of firm ground fixed on the map. We can watch its erosion, chart its decline and fall. But the sound moves around underneath the mark, never quite the same, impossible to catch. A piece of sea, latitude 15, longitude 60, in the Indian Ocean, say, where a monsoon storm begins: does that particular bit of liquid have a fixed identity? Do the waves in it dissolve, or travel the world, or remain in one place, part of a larger, more orderly pattern? How does a wave change from smooth to turbulent?

When did my mother tip over from coping into not coping? Did India turn the tide of sanity? I know that my father became interested in chaos not long after he met her. Went on to collect the papers of Lorenz (*Irregularity: A Fundamental Property of the Atmosphere*), Swinney (*Onset of Turbulence in a Rotating Fluid*), Thompson (*The Borderline between Calm and Catastrophe*).

"You have all these instruments and computers," I said to Dad one day. "Why can't you tell exactly when the monsoon will arrive?"

He stared off into the distance, squinting slightly, as if the horizon held some complex equation he would be able to read if only he could see more clearly. "If we knew exactly the law of nature and the situation of the universe at the initial moment, we could predict exactly the situation at a succeeding moment." He traced his finger along a recent scar on my arm. "But it may happen that a small error in judging initial conditions will produce an enormous error in the final phenomena. When it comes to turbulence, prediction is difficult, I'm afraid."

I didn't know then that Dad was quoting the nineteenth-century mathematician Henri Poincaré, one of the first men to guess the implications of chaotic behaviour. We were discussing the monsoon's instability, but it could as easily have been my mother's. It taught me that perfect order is impossible in charting the irregular side of nature.

I walked over to a mahogany display case of gold coins and medals to see if any small miscalculations in the initial forgeries would be revealed as enormous errors when compared to the real thing. Before I got to the case, I saw the statue of Skanda on a shelf flanked by a row of books and a small bronze Shiva. Sami's bold draughtsmanship had given the figure a monumental quality that this Skanda lacked. Other than that, every detail matched the statue Bina had given me, right down to the arched curve of the god's left eyebrow, which gave the face such a quizzical expression. Her red chalk had imitated the mottled sandstone perfectly. Gulab had not been making it up; Sami had been here, standing where I stood now. This same bronze Shiva had been sketched in like Skanda's shadow in one of the preliminary drawings.

I moved one of the table lamps closer and took the Minolta from my bag to shoot off several photos at different angles, turning the Skanda figure in a full circle. When I'd finished, there was something about the god that still puzzled me, some discrepancy I couldn't put my finger on.

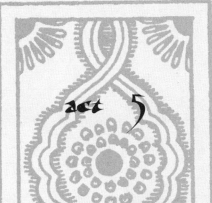

act 5

THE SEA AND THE MIRROR

By charms I raise and lay the winds, and burst the
viper's jaw.
Whole woods and forests I remove: I make the
Mountains shake,
And even the Earth itself to groan and fearfully to quake.
I call up dead men from their graves.

—Ovid, Metamorphoses *(Medea's speech)*

1

I AM DREAMING OF THE MEANING OF THUNDER. *HE WHO WAS
living now is dead . . . There is no water but only rock*. A wasteland.

Miranda's voice outside my door: "Nonsense, Tusker, I don't care
what Prosper said."

"Miranda?" I called out.

There were footsteps, the door rattled. "Have you locked yourself
in, Roz?"

I tried the door on my side. "It must be stuck."

Tusker: "Mr. Prosper's wish, madam. He said Miss Rosalind was
to be locked in until his return." His voice lowered to a whisper.

"I see," said my sister. "Well, you can let my sister out now,
Tusker. I will ensure that she does you no harm."

I was shocked by the change in Miranda. Her face was pinched;
her belly had swollen so much that her narrow back was bent under
the strain like overstretched strings on a bow. The joys of motherhood.
I wanted to help her, but I didn't know how to take the first step.
"Miranda, you look terrible. What's wrong?"

"What's wrong? My sister disappears from her hospital bed after
accusing my husband of murdering his eunuch son, and now the hijra
have put a chalk mark on our door."

"A chalk mark?" I asked, thinking that Miranda sounded like a
different person. Gone was the sweetness, to be replaced by someone
fiercer and less reasonable.

"It's what the hijra do when a male child has been born in their
territory." She turned away and rested her hand heavily on a table.
"They mark on your door with chalk, and then they come back on his

naming day and they do horrible, lewd performances, and they look at his genitals and threaten you if you don't give them money."

"They wouldn't do that, Miranda. What could they threaten you with? And how would they know where you live?"

"They know these things." Her voice had begun to rise. "Every hijra guru has control over a neighbourhood. Her *chelas*—her disciples—comb houses and maternity hospitals ceaselessly to find out where male children are born. They may want my son, to replace theirs."

"You can't really believe that, Miranda."

But Miranda was past common sense, uncommon in expectant mothers at the best of times. Putting my arms around her awkwardly, I made comforting sounds while she cried, watching from a distance to see if this was how sisters behaved.

"I'm hungry," Miranda said, after the tears had stopped. "I'm always hungry. I feel as if my body has been taken over by an alien organism."

Tusker took this as a message to disappear into the kitchen, reappearing a little while later with a tray on which there was a basket of hard-boiled eggs, a banana sliced into some yoghurt, a bowl full of butter-yellow mangoes, an Edwardian silver teapot, and a jug of orangey-pink pulp with a long silver spoon in it.

"Freshly squeezed mangoes," he said proudly . . . "You slurp them up with spoon."

The teapot was engraved with the initial *C*. "What's the *C* for, Tusker?"

He glanced at Miranda. "Initial of first Mrs. Sharma's family," he said.

Miranda gestured around. "Most of these things are . . . were her family's." She smiled. "I tell Prosper that if worse comes to worst with his studio, we can always flog this stuff. It would be nice not to have to compete with such a glorious past all the time."

"Maya's past wasn't all that glorious," I said. My sister's face froze. "Oh God, I didn't mean that how it sounded," I said. We sipped tea for a few minutes. Then I came to a decision: "Listen, Miranda, I want you to know that this . . . obsession I've had—it's over." Her expression was hopeful but not quite believing. *He who was living now is dead*. "Whatever happened or didn't happen to Sami," I said, "I'm going to let someone else deal with it."

Her smile was my reward. Perhaps in a while it would relieve the guilt.

"I wish Prosper was here." Miranda looked over at Tusker. "What time did he leave?"

"Mr. Prosper drove out very early to Island. Last day on set, he is saying, and he is winding everything up, returning very late tonight for a much needed rest."

Miranda insisted that I borrow a shalwar kamiz of hers, its fine cotton the colour of freshly brewed Earl Grey. After a shower, with the smudged kohl washed from my eyes, I almost looked like her—a nice middle-class Indian woman. When I reappeared in the living room, Miranda stopped what she had been saying to Tusker to admire my newfound respectability. "That's my favourite outfit. It suits you." Tusker started to speak again and she cut him off with a shake of her head. "No, Tusker. I am absolutely not returning to the hospital, whatever Prosper told you. I was there all night. I'll go again later, when he's back." She laid her head against a pillow, exhausted from her brief display of spirit. "About those photos you wanted, Roz."

"Forget it," I said, thinking, The hospital? But Prosper said she was here last night.

"Prosper found them for me."

"Prosper?"

She nodded. "You see? You were wrong. I must have slipped them into one of Dad's old books, with some early pictures of Mum." She pointed to a book on the coffee table. "Then I forgot all about them."

I picked up the book, a biography of Benvenuto Cellini, the brilliant sixteenth-century Florentine who showed no compunction about killing anyone who got in his way, until he was thrown into prison for the murder of a rival goldsmith. The photos of Maya's death were in good company.

"I don't know why I put them there," Miranda said, "but you can keep the book. I think it's one of your mother's that Dad brought back from Scotland after . . ."

"Yes." There was an inscription on the flyleaf. "To Jess—the book you wanted, although I think the *Libro dell'Arte* would have been more suitable, whose author learned from Giotto that nature is the artist's best master." Trust Dad to turn a gift into a sermon.

"You'll want to keep these," I said, passing over some pictures of my father with Miranda's mother. On the back was written: *Taken in 1959.* Before Mum arrived. "They look happy."

Miranda nodded slowly. "Daddy told me they were. He said he loved my mother in a different way than—"

"That's all right, Miranda. We can talk about this when we are both less tired. You should rest now." And I didn't want to be here when Prosper got back. I kissed her goodbye before she could say anything further. On the way out, the doorman sketched a bow and called respectfully, "Good day, Madame Sharma." I didn't bother to correct him. In my sister's clothes I had acquired a new identity: mother of a rich man's son. A seal of approval stamped on me like a bar code.

AT THE RITZY I SCANNED MIRANDA'S PICTURES QUICKLY, BUT THERE WAS NO sign of Acres or anyone else I recognized.

The phone rang: "Madam, it is about your bill. British Broadcasting Corporation have cancelled their Amex card."

"*What?* Why would they do that?"

"There is a fax here from London office which perhaps explains the situation."

"Read it to me."

"It is a private transmission, madam. And quite lengthy."

"Read the gist of the bloody fax to me."

"No need to take that tone, madam. Gist of it is that head of BBC Features Department is saying you are no longer working for him, everything you do is entirely your own responsibility, Amex cancelled."

"Does he say why?"

"They have received information of behaviour practised by you in public place which is considered unbecoming to a person of your position. Also misuse of BBC name. Your bill comes to six hundred and seventy-two pounds sterling—"

"Do you accept travellers' cheques?"

"—and twenty-four pence, given current rate of exchange. BBC has also blocked your usage of travellers' cheques bearing their numbers."

Shit. "No problem. I'll pay you later. In cash." I hung up and checked my wallet. There was about enough cash for a couple of beers and one taxi ride. Who had been pulling strings at the BBC? Did Prosper have that kind of influence? I rang my sister to see if she could tide me over until I sorted the finance, but the line was engaged. So was Ashok's. "Great," I said, in the general direction of the print of Alpine meadows and romping Heidis that hung over my bed.

The pictures of the woman who had started this chain of events lay all around me on the bed, with the coins I had stolen from Prosper's collection before leaving his little gallery this morning. From living to dead in two rolls of twenty-four. I looked again. Added them up like playing cards. Seven hands of six, one of five. The last pile was one short. Forty-seven pictures. Lots of times a picture or two doesn't come out in a roll of film, I thought, staring at the blurred figure of Sami in mid-frame. And then suddenly out. My sister was using a motorized camera. There should have been a continuous stream of snaps of Sami walking out of frame, not this sudden jump. I emptied the negatives out, switched on my bedside lamp, and held each strip up to the light one at a time, reading the numbers. One strip missing: the wide shots of Prosper's studio.

The phone rang: "Madam, there is long-distance call for you from New York, United States of America. A Mrs. Nonie Irving."

For a second I had no idea whom he was talking about. Then the name clicked: Caleb's married daughter. "Put her through."

From Nonie's voice, no one would have guessed she was Indian. If anything, her accent was American. These Mistrys were quick studies. "Hello? Miss Benegal? Sorry to ring so late—late our time, anyway— but you left an urgent message on my answering machine two days ago. I've been away."

"It's about your mother."

"My mother's dead, Miss Benegal. She died when I was a child."

"Yes, I know. But I wondered . . . how?"

"She killed herself. And it's hardly urgent: that was twenty years ago."

I explained why it was urgent, playing up the possible connection between her mother's death and the recent murders that had been taking place in Bombay.

"There was no question of murder in my mother's case," Nonie said.

"How can you be sure? They said that about Maya Sharma's death and she had the same cut marks on her arms as your mother's."

"Maya Sharma's case is another matter, in no way related to my mother."

"But how can you be sure?"

"Because she had done it before."

"Who?"

"My mother. Her cuts were self-inflicted." Her voice monotone, all emotion squeezed out.

I drew in my breath. "What did she use? A knife?"

"If you must know, Miss Benegal, she used a double-headed scalpel. And if you want any more of the gory details, get them from my father. It was his knife."

She put the phone down.

I felt the room sink in on me, thought of that first night with Caleb in the ice house: *"Did you know that in murders of extreme passion, a killer always betrays his pathology?"* A small error in judging the initial conditions, as my father had said. Not wanting to believe it. I laid my right hand on Blanford's *Indian Meteorological Vade-Mecum* of 1877, as men used to do with their Bibles before going into a battle from which they were uncertain to return. Blanford's starting point was to determine the centre of the monsoon circulation. Detailed knowledge of conditions in that centre, he said, offered him hope for predicting a monsoon's development. I put on a dark shirt and fixed my mikes to the inside of the collar, where their foam heads were virtually invisible, then called a taxi.

2

THE DRIVER HAD TO DIVERT DOWN A BACK STREET ALMOST IM-
mediately. "Cobra nest," he said, by way of explanation. "Police are
closing street."

Streets and paths in India are often closed off by the police if a
nest is discovered. Young snakes are venomous from the moment of
their birth, the cobra venom so potent that even elephants are often
killed by bites, if they are bitten on tender parts of their bodies—the
soft places between their toes, the tip of their trunks swinging down to
pick up a bunch of logs. They die in three to four hours unless the bite
is noticed early enough and treated with antivenin. A human can die
within fifteen minutes. The symptoms are typical: otherwise quiet people become abnormally agitated and suffer vision disabilities and severe dizziness. Their body reflexes slow down. Respiration is difficult.
Since arriving in Bombay, my symptoms had started to accelerate.

When I was frightened by the snakes in Kerala my father coun-
tered fear with a poem by Vidyapati from the fourteenth century:

> *Oh gentle girl, the rain*
> *Pours on your path*
> *And roaming spirits straddle the wet night.*

"The winged water cobra inhabits standing and slightly flowing water," my father said. "A king cobra's head can grow to the size of a
man's hand, its body to over fifteen feet long. It leads a secretive life
that few men see. Remember that very often he will not bite if you
show him that he need not fear you. He does it to protect himself.
When he spreads his hood it is like the peasant who holds a burlap bag

over his head to keep out the monsoon." Balancing fear with poetry. Counting serpent tales out on my toes like the story of the little piggy who went to market.

One: The proportion of his body raised indicates his degree of agitation. Up to one-third in extreme cases. "How tall is that?" I ask. His hand above my head. "Five feet on a fifteen-foot snake." The height of a child tall for her age.

Two: A cobra is charmed by the swaying body of a musician, not by the flute.

Three: Spreading the hood while keeping the body flat on the ground is indicative of fear and readiness to flee.

Four: An upright position without the spread hood indicates mating interest.

Five: Ordinary cobras strike in a forward, downward direction.

Six: A king is the only cobra which can move forward while in an upright threat posture.

Seven: It is much less aggressive than many smaller serpents.

Eight: It feeds almost exclusively on other snakes—even deadly ones like the krait and the Indian cobra, naja naja.

Nine: It is the only cobra which does not need to attack from above.

"We are arriving at Caleb Mistry's studio, madam," the driver said.

Ten, what the fuck was ten?

Ten: Often the king cobra will first execute a feint with his mouth closed before attacking.

I was taught at my father's knee to see venomous snakes as roaming spirits in search of the high ground. No wonder my sense of morals is so warped.

CALEB WAS IN HIS DIRECTOR'S CHAIR WHEN I WALKED INTO THE STUDIO, laughing up at one of the actors. His laugh froze into that unreadable Rajput curl when he saw me, a smile like a moustache, a disguise. A real ladykiller's smile.

"You might be interested to know," I said conversationally, when I was close enough so that only Caleb's immediate associates could hear, "I've been talking with your daughter about her mother's death."

He stood up and took a few quick steps towards me, the slapping sound of his flip-flops exaggerated by the wet floor. "Perhaps we should continue this in private," he said. I followed him into his office and he told me to wait there while he sorted the studio out.

Edited highlights of Caleb's comments floated in from outside, enough to let me know that what was left of my reputation was being destroyed. I wandered around the office, searching for evidence in his favour. The room looked as if he had just moved in or was about to move out. On the desk were the cardboard models I had been told Caleb still produced for every set, the scalpels and spare blades he used to cut the board strewn across them. *A double scalpel,* I thought. Old letters, reviews, and newspaper clippings were piled onto film books—Ray, Truffaut, Brian De Palma, Hitchcock. Paperbacks of poetry in a language I guessed was Marathi. Photos everywhere—hundreds of them, a historical labyrinth of photographs: his daughter; himself as a young man on some early film sets; the miniature of a young woman with a boy; a formal photographer's portrait of a dark, coarse-looking older woman, perhaps his mother.

In one drawer I found a stack of gold coins, some as crisp as the day they were minted, some slick with use, like old soap, the images on them no longer decipherable. Running my fingers over the patterns, I thought of how an expert gilder must plan his work around the drying time of the gold size he is using. Yet in every career there comes a time when the gilder misjudges what he can gild in one time, or is called away during a session to find, on his return, that the size has become too dry. Caleb has left me too long on my own. He has miscalculated.

I put the coins in my pocket.

By the time Caleb had finished with the cast, I was on the sofa again with my backpack clutched against my chest. Armour-plated. He came into the room, closed the door, and walked over to me. "So you've been talking to my daughter. And something she said brought you here."

I smiled at him, my lips stretched like a jester's. "A high proportion of men who kill women first pick out partners who seem stronger, or who have attributes they envy, maybe a higher position in society," I said. Like Maya, I thought. "Have you heard of Ted Bundy, the American serial murderer? He said that if he'd been raised in a different background he would've taken to stealing Porsches instead of murdering college girls." I pushed the mike farther under my collar. "Later, they don't care who they kill, of course."

"Meaning what?"

I picked up one of his scalpels. "Maya and Sami were cut with a knife like this one, with double blades. Your wife used the same kind of knife on herself."

His hand came up in a fist. I thought he was going to hit me, but all he did was pull a tool box towards him, find what he wanted inside, and hand it to me. A double-headed scalpel, the twin of the one I'd found in the Hotel Rama. "They're not uncommon, Roz. You think you're the only person to have noticed I use these? Or that my . . . wife used one as well?"

"So it wasn't you who forced Maya off the balcony?"

"Nobody forced her."

"I saw the cuts on her, Caleb. They matched Sami's."

"Read the autopsy. Maya wasn't killed with a knife; she died from the fall. Someone showed her Prosper's next three-picture deal and the fine print specified no Maya. Prosper had signed it. Maya was written out. Her life was over. She jumped. Poetic justice." He laid the scalpel back on his desk. "You of all people should know why people commit suicide. Because they have no more hope. Or no escape." His voice was bitter. "Or because there are too many demands they can't fulfil. Maya had lots of enemies. She was a liability. The backers wanted a younger face."

"Your daughter's."

"Prosper gave Nonie the lead without any push from me. And then he honoured her by inviting her into his bed. He didn't marry her, of course. She didn't have the breeding."

"Is that why you hate Prosper so much? Even after all the help he gave you?"

"That's right. Prosper was my mentor. My guru. He taught me the tricks of my trade, gave me books to read, told me how to behave in public. What would help my career and what would hurt it. Remade me in his own image."

"Like a father."

The noise Caleb made only vaguely resembled a laugh. "Oh, much closer than that. More like a mother. For a long time I would've done anything for him." He stopped. "Almost anything."

"Even get rid of his wife."

Caleb sat down beside me, pulled my shirt up, and ran his finger down my backbone. As long as he concentrates on my back, I thought, he won't see the mike leads. "Is that what you want to hear, Roz? Yes, I suppose I got rid of Maya for him. In a way." He paused at the bruise where the doorknob had dug into me at the hennaed woman's house. "Do you know that the Mother Goddess often appears as the castrator of her mortal consort? One of the sources of her anger is his rejection of her." He pressed the bruise. "I thought you could be like that the first time I met you. A ballbreaker. Like Maya. Of course, she was no mother. She was a harpy. Like you. You're no mother, are you, Roz?"

"What do you mean?"

"Miranda told me a lot about you. Like what your mother did after she heard you'd killed the kid."

My father must have told her. "I had an abortion. Not that big a thing. Not *murder*. In case you can't tell the difference anymore." My parents used to do this. Tear at each other. Poison each other by opening old wounds. "Why would Miranda tell *you*?"

"That's what lovers do," he said, and watched my eyes carefully, to see his words sink home. "Offer confessions as tokens of trust."

So that's what they'd meant at Unmann's. "How long has it been going on, with Miranda?" Words like teeth being pulled from my mouth without anaesthetic.

"It was over months ago, once the novelty of fucking Prosper's wife wore off."

"So you never slept with Maya."

"What makes you say that?"

"The novelty: you said the 'novelty' of fucking Prosper's wife."

He stood up again, restless, turned, put his hand around my throat from the front, a strangler's hold. Released it. Sat down. I let out my breath. He still hadn't noticed the mikes. "I had a go," he said, "in my barefoot way. She wasn't interested. Maya hated me. She always blamed me for getting Prosper interested in rough trade. But Prosper had that inclination long before he met me. She was going to bring everything crashing down around his head."

"Harpies were always associated with whirlwinds and storms."

"What?"

"Prosper taught you about film and in return you tried to seduce his wife."

"It was his idea. To ease her into retirement—his words, not mine. But I wasn't good enough for her."

"Tell me about her."

"She couldn't have children, that was her problem. Childbearing gentles a woman. I think it's the pain." He pressed the bruise on my back again, so hard this time it made me feel sick.

"What about Sami?" I said, hoping to surprise him into truth. "Wasn't Sami Maya's child?"

He shook his head. "I think not."

I felt let down. "Whose, then?"

He put his hand up and ran it down the side of my face, cupping my chin in his palm before letting go. "I don't know—some other unfortunate bitch who got messed around by Prosper. Not a legitimate birth."

He had his hand between my legs. It felt good. What had Unmann said about erotic preferences? They don't always come up to our moral standards? I put my hand over Caleb's, ran my fingers over the fleshy part. Then dug my nail in.

"How did you get rid of Maya?" I said.

At the medical clinic near our home in Kerala I used to watch cobras being milked of their venom. The thing about a cobra is that it uses up a fifth of its poison with each bite. Except in artificial milking situations, when about half the total stored in its glands is released. You milk the poison by getting the snake to bite again and again. After several bites there is only enough venom left to produce a feeling of ecstasy in the victim. Or coma.

He pulled his hand away and put the blood to his mouth. "I didn't. I told you that already. Anyway, if you're going down the drainhole, what difference does it make who pulls the plug?"

"It bothers me. What I keep wondering, what I keep going over in my head is: whose idea was it to get rid of her, Prosper's or yours?"

"You know the story. I was a humble assistant at the time. Who do you think pulled the strings?" He stood up and walked around the room, stopping to pick up the miniature of the young woman. "If you really want to know who was responsible, you should have a look at Prosper's book of shooting scripts.

"All through the spring of 1986, Prosper had been complaining about Maya. He never said he wanted her dead, not in so many words. But the implication was there. A suggestion, a laughing aside during a screening, an allusion to Caleb's criminal past, some probing questions about how far old friends would go for a few thousand rupees. One day he said to Caleb, 'I need a script for Maya.'

'What kind of a script?' Caleb asked him.

"Prosper said he was thinking of a scene where there was a fall from a balcony. An open door frames a shadowed figure—two of them; one; we can't quite see. One shadow pushes the other backwards into the sunlight. Maya stumbles, turns towards us, screams. Falls. We see cuts on her body that might have been done by a killer, but then again might be self-mutilations, a cry for help. No one is ever sure.

Like my wife, I said to him." Caleb stared at the miniature. "The bastard just nodded and remarked casually that yes, such a death would have dramatic effect. 'This will be Maya's last starring role,' Prosper said. 'Make it a good one and I'll ensure you get a picture to direct.' "

"What did you do?" I said.

Caleb turned back to me. "I had to be sure of his meaning. So I went away and wrote a script. Not a good one—it wasn't necessary. But precise about details. When and where and how. Brought it back the next day and gave it to him."

"Maybe he didn't realize the implications."

"He knew. In my script, the fading star survives. In a wheelchair, true, but she lives on. As a famous playback singer, in the best tradition of Bollywood. He changed it. Little red ticks all the way through. And then a red cross."

"A red cross?"

Every change in Prosper's shooting scripts had to be initialled by him in red. He would go through them, leaving red checks and initials on the changes he approved, crosses where he did not.

"And then?" I said.

Then he got to the fall and said no. That wasn't what he had in mind. A red cross. One line: "Rewrite as previously discussed."

"What was your decision, Caleb?"

Caleb held up his hands and used them as a viewfinder to frame my face. "Let me tell you a movie," he said. "This is how it starts. This is the beginning. You have to picture it, an opening scene something like Hitchcock's *Strangers on a Train*, with a series of symbolic following shots on feet going first one way and then the other. The right way. The wrong way."

The bastardized version, I thought, the Bombay version. *Strangers on a Train*: two men discussing their capacity to commit murder. One of them backing out of the deal. But which one?

"I handed the script back to Prosper and he stapled it into his book, the one his crew call *Atharva-Veda*. Told him it wasn't really my kind of movie. He asked did I have anyone else in mind. So I gave him Acres's number."

"Acres worked for you?"

"We used to have an arrangement. These days Acres is an independent. That's why he used the scalpel on Maya—to keep me in line. If I ever decided to rat on him, Acres could always drop a hint about my first wife's death. Let the police make connections. Or maybe the knives were Prosper's idea. Prosper and Acres have forged a partnership based on mutual suspicion. Did you know Prosper's in hock up to his sensitive eyebrows? To build that great independent studio of his he sold his family estate—or Maya's, should I say: he married her for her money. And unless this current venture is a hit, his studio goes to the developers. Prosper made a big mistake when he let Acres get the upper hand."

Caleb walked across the room, opened a locked drawer, and tossed some photos at me. They were not what you'd call art shots. The focus wasn't good. I couldn't have picked my brother-in-law's bare ass out of a police line-up. But his profile and his silver hair were instantly recognizable. And there was no denying the face lying there on the pillow under him. The face on Chowpatty Beach.

"Sami's pictures?" I said.

"Some of them. The ones I'm interested in."

"At least my sister won't have to worry about whether he used a condom."

"No?"

"Apparently Sami had a neat trick with her fist." I looked up at Caleb. "Where did you get these?"

"The photos? From Zarina's neighbour, a photographer and part-time scriptwriter I've used from time to time. He kept a few negs. It was a trade-off. I offered him the writing job on my next picture."

"I found Acres's body, Caleb. Someone had chopped off his hands. Like the man you found here in the ice house."

"You think everyone in the film world doesn't know about the man I found here? Like they know about my double-headed scalpels? Gossip is the Bollywood telegraph. In any one of Shoma Kumar's rags you can read all about my daily life, my work methods, even how often I am taking a shit. You think I'm so stupid as not to know that?"

I wanted to believe him. But something still wasn't quite right. "Why did you say Maya's death was *poetic*, Caleb?" He shook his head. I went on. "Because you abandoned your first wife, as Prosper abandoned Maya, drove her to suicide when she didn't fit your new image, the image Maya and Prosper created for you? And then she killed herself while you were away making notes on how to behave when winning the Oscar? Is that what you blamed them for? Your own guilt?"

His face turned a dull red.

"I have a portrait of her here, if you want to see," he said. "One of those pathetic ones they paint over photos to try and make them look as if they've been in the family a long time. She saved up to have it done, to give herself a respectable past." He went to the chest of drawers and got down the miniature he'd picked up earlier. "I met her when she was working in the cages. We were never married."

I looked more carefully this time. Buried in the stylization of the painting I could just see the resemblance to me that Basil had mentioned. "Basil said I was like her," I said, and thought, Lots of women are killed because they look like Mom or stepmom or little sis. I remember reading that somewhere.

"Basil has always had a good eye for a woman."

"But she looks so young. Even with all the makeup. I thought it was a picture of your sister and you."

He touched the image. "She *was* very young. Fifteen. The boy was two."

"Who is he—her brother?"

"Ah, Rosalind." Caleb walked across to the chest of drawers and placed the picture back in position, tracing the outline of the boy's face with his fingertip. "Not her brother. *This thing of darkness I acknowledge mine*. My son. He . . . died. When he was very young."

"Sami was very young too when Prosper got rid of him. Did Prosper send Acres to kill Sami? To kill his own son? How could anyone do that? Send a man to murder your son and your wife and then go on working with him?"

"There are different kinds of murder."

"And some are more painful than others. Like the ones where you use a knife."

Caleb flexed his hands on his thighs. "I'm not trying to excuse him. I'd be the last to do that. But maybe Prosper didn't realize Sami was his son. There is no real proof. There was the blackmail, as well. For a son to blackmail a father. Or perhaps, in the end, everyone is expendable. I think . . . for Prosper, it's to do with the fear of falling."

The phone rang and Caleb answered it. "Yes. Yes," he said. Then: "I got them. But what are you doing with the others?"

Watching his profile, with its slightly elongated Indian ear, so typical of the carved gods Prosper displayed in his home, I realized what had been missing in the statue I photographed the night before. Or what should have been missing. In Sami's drawing and in the photos in Satish's fine arts book, there had been a chip out of Skanda's left ear, as there was in the statue Bina had given me. But not in Prosper's Skanda.

"So where do I find Prosper's great work, if that's what I have to see to get proof?" I said to Caleb when he hung up the phone.

"What? Oh, the book. He keeps it locked up in his office at Island. But that should be no trouble for an ingenious girl like you."

I thought about the state of my finances. "It shouldn't, but my regular driver has another job today and I'm temporarily out of pocket: no cash for a cab fare. Plus I heard on the radio coming here that trains have been cancelled because of flooding on the track."

"Money problems?" Caleb was focusing on the conversation again. He reached into his pocket for some paan and chewed it for a second, his next words coming on a breath of cloves. "You want to do this badly enough?"

"What—nail Prosper? Absolutely," I said, trying to forget the promise made to my sister.

He put his fingers under my chin and turned my face away from him to face the light. Putting ticks and crosses at high and low points, I thought, where the resemblance to his dead wife did and did not align. "Amazing. To look so like someone and be so different." He spat some paan juice on the floor. "You won't stop until there is some kind of a confrontation, will you? You might wreck your sister's life and bring down a lot of people with it. But that won't stop you."

"Things have gone too far."

He changed the conversation abruptly, started talking about juggernauts. Had I ever seen the festival in Orissa devoted to the god Jagganath? Did I know that this god and his chariot were the origin of the word "juggernaut"?

"I'm tired of stories, Caleb."

But he was determined to tell me one more. About the juggernaut chariots that carried the god's image, so huge that they swayed through the streets like ships under sail. Dragged by thousands of fanatical pilgrims, who, in their enthusiasm to speed the god faster and faster, often fell and were crushed to death by a chariot which had been built too high, too top-heavy.

"The belief that they throw themselves under the wheels deliberately is largely exaggerated," Caleb said. "A distortion of foreign journalists. Usually it is by accident. They fall, and the momentum of the chariot is such that it cannot stop."

"The only juggernauts I know about are the articulated lorries that rumble past my flat in London and keep me awake," I said.

Caleb nodded, as if he hadn't really expected me to be interested. "I'll get my driver to take you to Prosper's," he said, "and I'll make sure he carries a tarpaulin in case you run into any heavy going on the road."

3

THE MERCEDES WAS A BEATEN-UP WHITE SEVENTIES MODEL whose front passenger window had a spiderweb fracture held together with tape.

"Seems you had a bit of an accident," I said to the driver. His eyes flicked across to the cracked window.

"Yes, madam." Paused. Checked my eyes. "Car was stolen and then found."

"Did you catch the thieves?"

"No, madam. Car thieves are very tricky in this country."

After forty-five minutes, the sky started to get dark, although it was still hours until dusk. Half the sky was the blackish maroon of a bad bruise, closing rapidly on the blue. "Wall clouds," the driver said, pointing at the horizon. "Where thunder and rain is. Cyclone coming." He switched on the radio, hitting it with his fist to make it crackle into life. "This is the BBC World Service . . ."

"I am trying to improve my English," he said, turning the dial until he got a local station.

"*We interrupt our regular programme to broadcast an added cyclone warning from the Bombay Meteorological Service. The worst phase of the cyclone which has been skirting the Maharashtrian coast and approaching the city at 300 to 500 kilometres per day is expected to hit at between midnight and three o'clock this morning with winds of up to one hundred and twenty kilometres per hour spiralling around the centre . . .*"

"Are you Marathi?" I asked. The driver's dark eyes met mine in the mirror.

"Of course, madam. All people working for Mr. Caleb are pure Marathi. He is only hiring Marathis."

"Purity isn't always such a good thing, you know." Thinking about the photos Caleb had got from Zarina's friend. The *Bengali* scriptwriter. Not Marathi. "The strength of pure gold is increased by alloying it with other metals." A sermonizer, like Dad.

"I know this, madam. My grandfather was a goldbeater." From the mirror, his eyes smiled mockingly.

"How did you meet Caleb?"

"I picked his pocket." He grinned. "Like my grandfather, I too have always been interested in gold."

We drove on through a ferroconcrete vision of the future, suburbs built in a housing style reminiscent of public swimming pools and mid-American gas stations, all painted glossy Toytown colours, the architectural vernacular of the mafia in Italy, Zanzibar, Sicily, and everywhere else.

When we reached the last of Bombay, the drowned land poured away on either side of us. The road was a river, widening where the tarmac had flooded. Often we had to drive up onto the banks on either side to avoid floating in potholes that had become small seas. A mirror on the world, everything upside down: where the water was highest I saw people sitting on the roofs of their houses making lunch over fires lit on the corrugated iron, with their goats and chickens around them in a circle. Smoke from the fires rose lazily to disappear into the low cloud of saturated vapour that hung in the air.

"*Pralaya*: the Cosmic Deluge," said my driver. "When peacocks and elephants are dancing, we say. An inauspicious time for travelling. A time when the borders between living and dead vanish."

We passed the tomb of a royal minister, the turnoff to a battle-scarred former citadel of the warrior Shivaji, the road to Ahmad-nagar, where the Mogul emperor Aurangzeb died. We detoured onto a muddy track around a lake that might once have been a valley, driving at the same speed as a swimming cobra whose body was longer than the car.

"Nagas also are looking for high ground, madam."

Nagas, the snake deities propitiated by barren women in the time of the monsoon. The gods who bring sons as well as rice. I felt as if I were in the grip of a tide washing me back and forth like the jetsam thrown overboard in time of danger, goods jettisoned from a wreck that remain underwater, abandoned, until they are discovered by a deep-sea diver and pinned like gold coins to the felt of a museum. Or left below the water, a risk to other ships.

The weather was getting worse. You could feel it pushing against the heavy Mercedes, resenting every mile we gained. It took us more than two hours to travel the ninety-odd kilometres. Finally, we turned down the side road that led to Prosper's studios near Sonavla. The sign that once had read ISLAND had already been partially dismantled. In its place was the beginning of a cutout figure, still only half-painted. I recognized the figure's five o'clock shadow. It was the one I had stared at all over Bombay, my screen lover of the kipper complexion, my larger-than-life hero.

"What does that lettering say?" I asked.

The driver glanced quickly at the giant figure as we drove past, and then his gaze flicked over at me. "It says 'Another Exciting New Development of Goliath Enterprises.' " He pointed to a temple inside the compound, like a half-built spaceship from an old *Eagle* comic. "You see—ashram and temple will be in the centre when building is complete. People on holidays will be coming here to meditate with gurus. Latest concept in vacations."

"Gul, Gol . . . iath," I said. "Of course." That's what Sami was saying when she died. Where Gul the leper lived. Not the giant billboard: the Giant billboard. And Unmann was building a temple, "his last good work"—or was it an ashram?

The storm clouds were right overhead now. It was so dark that the driver had to switch on his headlights. Through the studio front gate I could see a few lamps lit in the distance, but the heavy steel gate itself was shut firmly, its top rimmed with barbed wire. For some reason there was no sign of the watchman—or of anyone else, come to think of it. I rang the bell and pressed the intercom underneath, announcing, "Rosalind Benegal, come for a surprise visit." Nothing happened. I rang again, listened to static.

Then a click from the door's lock and it began to swing open. I got back into the car, singing, *"Choli ke peecheeeee,"* my voice rusty with tension. The driver glanced back at me. "What's beneath my blouse?" I said lamely. "That's what it means." As if he didn't know.

We drove through a deserted world, all that remained of Island, most of the streets under water. "A little Indian empire, perfect in every detail," I said.

A quarter of a mile down a long, curving street I saw a hut with lights in the windows. We stopped a hundred yards from it, and the driver turned off the car ignition. "Wait," I said. "There's something wrong." The door to the hut opened. A figure appeared, black against the light. Two figures. I opened the door, jumped out, and started walking towards them.

"Now this *is* a surprise." The dry, cultivated tones of Anthony Unmann stopped me halfway to the hut. "If it isn't Miss Benegal, come to visit two lonely old men in exile. Everyone else has gone to celebrate in the big city. Unfortunately, I am leaving as well. Things to wind up, a plane to catch, that sort of thing."

He walked slowly down the steps away from the door. As he came closer, the features of the man behind him were illuminated by the beams of the Merc. Acres, my brother-in-law's business partner. A miraculous reincarnation.

"Well, well," Acres said. "We can't seem to scare you into shutting up, or drown you, or blow you up—what's next?"

"Acres," I said. "But the Hotel Rama . . ." My usual perceptive commentary.

"Ah, good, you thought that gentleman was our Mr. Acres." The amusement in Unmann's voice was clear. "But no. Just a seedy purveyor of lewd and badly focused photographs. Not at all creative, that fellow, except in his demands. Mr. Acres took care of him. Now I'll have to leave you, and trust Bob to make sure you get whatever you need." He nodded as he walked past me to Caleb's car and got in. I heard the car's ignition turn. It started to reverse away to the right. The gears changed with an unhealthy grinding sound. As if in slow motion, the Merc picked up speed and accelerated back the way it had come. At the first curve, its rear lights vanished, leaving me with instant replay, a flashback of misread signs, the final links in the coil of half-truths and lies.

The photos from Zarina's neighbour, a photographer and part-time scriptwriter I've used from time to time.

You aren't going to stop until there is some kind of a confrontation.

I remembered then who Caleb's wife reminded me of. Not just my face—Sami's: *This thing of darkness I acknowledge mine.*

Perhaps, in the end, everyone is expendable.

"Looks like it's just you and me, Miss Benegal. Now, what can we find to amuse ourselves? Shall we finish that chase scene we started the other night?"

I didn't wait to hear more, but turned and ran towards the centre of town, keeping to the mud, where my sneakers would have more purchase than Acres's Italian loafers. After a minute I could hear him slipping and swearing behind me. There were two options. If I could get to the canteen, if it wasn't locked, there would be knives, something to defend myself with. Maybe I could barricade myself in. *Until when?* The second option I didn't want to contemplate yet. Acres was gaining fast. I had to remember my guided tour. I turned left past some bathhouses, then right again up a street full of suburban bungalows. Right at the life-size statue of Shiva. Left, then right, I thought. Acres was close now. No canteen. One more turn. Catching my hand on the corner as I felt myself slipping down in the mud, with his harsh breathing behind me. Pushing myself as hard as I could. The mud deeper, a thick soup around my ankles, slowing me. Up the steps and into the dark kitchen. I grabbed the first thing to hand, an iron pan, still filled with oil. Holding it with both hands, I threw it at Acres's face as he came through the door after me. There was the wet sound meat makes when you hit it with a hammer. His head slammed back against the doorframe. I heard him cough "Bitch." He was holding his face, slower as he pushed himself upright and came after me, sliding on the oil. Not slow enough. In his other hand a razor. A farcical scene from a bad film, sweeping everything behind me to trip him, never quite far enough ahead.

There wasn't time for the element of surprise that would have given me my chance. I dodged out the back door of the canteen, feeling rain and wind slam into me as I came around the corner into open ground. I heard Acres fall on the wet kitchen steps behind me. The rain was coming down so hard I couldn't tell the difference between solid and liquid. Ran blindly, pointlessly, colliding with pomegranate trees, shrines, fake tombs; no longer hearing Acres.

And then I was safe, among friends. An audience of hundreds under a well-lit shelter. Some watching gravely, some dancing, playing, eating, as if they didn't care. *Why didn't you stop this?* I said, and saw that the crowd was absolutely still. Stone still. Wiping my eyes of rain I put out a hand and touched cold marble that a trick of watery light had caused to dance and move. Weathered marble Vishnus, their faces impassive as Ashok's. Parvatis, coquettish, with sandstone breasts like melons. Faces like my own and Miranda's in a hundred incarnations. Prosper's graveyard of props. I stood behind a tall unknown warrior, resting my head against his cool shoulder, trying to catch my breath.

"I know you're there, Roz," Acres said, his voice coming to me through the rain, far away. "Who are you talking to? There's no one here but you and me."

The second option. But I had lost my bearings, couldn't calm myself enough to bring back the walk with Salim. I saw Acres's shadow before he saw me and pushed forward with all my strength, rocking the warrior until he started to fall.

"No!" Acres said, and stepped aside. The warrior caught him a glancing blow as the heavy stone brought down a figure in front, and then another, another, tenpin bowling. I ran like a rabbit out of the shelter, Acres behind me, around one too many corners. A dead end. A white marble wall. A door at the top of the steps that didn't open. Down the steps again, I turned and saw the figure behind me slow to a walk as he realized what I'd done.

"Time to play," he said.

I saw a passage in the earth, a tunnel to forestall the inevitable, and fell to my stomach to half-crawl, half-swim into the mud under the steps like some not quite amphibious creature attempting evolutionary reversal. Acres laughed, leaped forward, and grabbed an ankle so coated in mud that my sneaker slipped off and my bare foot slid through his hands like a wet bar of soap. I pulled my legs up behind me to the side of the cave, the crawlspace under the steps.

And there we sat for a few minutes catching our breath, the rabbit and the snake. Except the snake was too well fed to fit through the hole.

"Can't you hear the rain coming down, Miss Rosalind?" he said, when the rattle of his breathing had calmed to a rasp. "Your hole's going to be filling up soon."

We both knew I had run out of options.

Acres shone the light of a pencil torch into the space where I was pressed about four feet away from him. Or maybe an arm's length, with the razor extension. His hand came in and made a tentative sweep in front of me. The next time the sweep of the blade was closer. It just caught the side of my foot, so sharp I barely felt it. I buried my legs in the mud as a frog will do when threatened, feeling something hard against them, a bottle. I wondered if I could break it and use it to slash Acres's arm. If I had the energy. He must have clipped the torch to the knife somehow, because when he swung the blade back and forth viciously the pencil light traced a figure eight in the dark.

"Have to make this knife a little bit longer, Miss Rosalind," Acres said. "But not much." His voice was friendly. "Might have to test it out first. You ready?"

He pushed his head into the space and shone the torch on it, so I could see he was grinning. Talking in a low, monotonous voice. A stream of obscenities. Telephone sex: I'll do this to you and this and you'll cry, you'll beg for more, you'll never get enough. I know you want it. That's what you like.

Where do they get it from?

His arm came in slowly, waggling, a spoof. Knowing he could cut me whenever he wanted, he started stropping the knife on the ground, getting ready to shave my legs. "Fee-fi-fo-fum!" he said.

Off to my left, there was a low sound like air escaping from a bicycle tire and I thought I saw movement, a slight stirring.

In my panic I had found a way to a second option after all.

I shouted at Acres, "Come on, you asshole, you fat cocksucking psycho!"

He lunged wildly. I could have told him it wasn't a good idea to do that. The shadow that was not a shadow on my left grazed Acres on the side of his hand, missing him in the strobe effect of his torch.

"Shit," said Acres, dropping the razor and shaking his hand and then his head hard, a man stung by a bee, trying to clear his vision. "What the fuck was—" The shadow struck again. More efficiently this time. It went for his head.

Acres cried out just once; then his arm fell, his body sagged and flattened out, becoming part of the mud. The shadow retreated back to the high ground. We stayed like that, quiet, peaceful, and absolutely still.

The rain got heavier until even the high dry ground started to dissolve into mud. After a while, a long coil of dark rope slipped out around the island of Acres's unconscious body and swam off in search of less crowded quarters. I crawled over to the dark mass that was Acres and felt around it, pushing my hand into the slime to find the torch and razor. I switched the light on and then quickly off. The two puncture marks were quite clear on his cheek. The flesh around them was already starting to swell and discolour. Switching on the light again, I ripped a strip off my shirt to wrap the razor in and put it in my pocket. Then I tried to push the heavy, limp body out from under the steps. The first few heaves made no impression on it at all. I couldn't get a grip in the mud. Every shove at Acres's head made my feet slip and his arm flop over, and I wound up with my ear filled with mud, the dead weight of Acres's warm hand pressing my face down into the slurry. A warm embrace. Soon that voice would start up again with its shopping list of obscenities. I wedged one leg against the steps and heaved on his shoulder. His hand rose up as if to call a taxi, and there was a sticky, reluctant noise like the sound of old vegetable parings being sucked down a drain. I heaved again, pushing against the side of his face as well, my hand sliding off his cheek, getting a grip on his ear. A definite shifting, a sort of belch. A drain unblocked. The rain helped. I waited a few minutes and eased him out an inch at a time. Finally there was enough room to slither out from under the steps myself. My legs were so shaky from adrenaline and cramp that I had to hold on to the wall to steady them. I stood there and let the rain wash over my face. When I shone the torch onto my watch it was still not quite midnight.

My other sneaker was nowhere in sight. It annoyed me, that missing sneaker. I wasted several minutes looking for it, finally squatting down to feel underneath the bloated mass at my feet. No luck. But I felt the bulge of his wallet in one pocket and pulled it out. The sight of the cash inside and Acres's gold Amex cleared my head. I realized it was more important to get inside than to find my shoe. Even if the full force of the cyclone didn't get this far, it would be bad enough. I gave Acres one last look before wading off through the rain and wind.

It took me about twenty minutes of false turns to find Acres's hut, on a slight rise, dryer than the rest of the studio lot. My backpack lay where it had dropped when I ran. The door to the hut was still open, the interior small but dry, with a cot bed in one corner, a desk piled with books and files in another, and a fan overhead, still whirring round. A pack of cigarettes lay next to an ashtray full of butts. As if Acres had just stepped out for a few minutes to take the air.

I looked in the mirror over the cot and saw strands of seaweed hair trailing over a grim white skull. The only things alive in that face were the eyes, yellow-green as a cat's. "Next year, I promise, it's the beach vacation," said the skull.

I would have liked a warm shower. I would have liked a Bloody Mary, made with lots of Tabasco and Worcestershire sauce and a curl of lemon rind, the way they made them at my favourite bar in London. And a slice of hot buttered toast with salty Marmite. The hut didn't run to that. There was a mobile telephone, however, which I presumed was dysfunctional. A prop, like everything else here.

But encouraging crackling came from the receiver when I picked it up, if not much else. Acres must have believed in this phone: he had written a couple of telephone numbers next to it on a pad from the Hotel Rama. One of them struck a tune in the discord of my brain: Caleb's studio.

On the bookshelf above the desk I spotted the *Fine Arts of India and Pakistan*. Inside the book was the familiar warning:

Reading through the book more carefully this time, studying it as one would a text set for a particularly difficult exam, I got an inkling of why the thieves had taken it from me. The margins were full of Sami's beautiful thumbnail sketches, and not only in the section devoted to Prosper's collection. This was her last will and testament, my inheritance. Every couple of pages she had copied the figures, drawing them from different angles, enlarging details not seen in the photos. Where had she found the reference for that cobra headdress, the dancer's foot, the fold of an ear? Next to the photos she had scribbled dates. I had no idea what the dates meant, but I recognized the faces she had copied. My silent stone audience had their twins in these photos.

In a locked filing cabinet which I forced open with a knife and a few swift kicks to the lock, I found Prosper's black book: an old ring binder about four inches thick. It was a treasure trove of shooting scripts, storyboards, photographs of film locations in Kashmir, Cochin, Pondicherry, snapshots of famous Indian stars of the last thirty years, scraps of Mysore gold silk for a dancer's costume, the painting of a mask for a remake of the *Ramayana*, stills from his own and other directors' films, quotes from poems and plays and works of meteorology recording historic storms that related to his own personal *Tempest*. Is this how the mystery of a man's life is pieced together? I wondered. A scrapbook of odd memories, mirrors within mirrors, like Van Eyck's Arnolfini portrait.

Prosper's book charted the history of more than one tempest. Here was the script Caleb had told me of. Just as he'd claimed, the crucial scene matching Maya's death step for step with Caleb's complete set of storyboards, drawn with a skill that matched Sami's, each scene given Prosper's red tick of approval. And like all Prosper's scripts, this one was typed on a standard form with a date at the bottom that proved it had been written a few days before Maya's death. Whether this constituted evidence any court would accept I had no idea. But it convinced me.

Prosper had added his own notes to Caleb's few brief pages of dialogue and stage directions. There was a comment taken from Hitchcock's shooting script for *Strangers on a Train*—"Bruno decides to compromise the hero, Guy, by placing Guy's lighter at the scene of the crime"—and from Truffaut's interview about the same film with Hitchcock, Prosper had cut out a scrap of dialogue:

T. This picture is systematically built around the figure "two." Both characters might very well have had the same name, given that both villain and hero are obviously a single personality split in two.

H. Correct. Bruno has killed Guy's wife, but for Guy, it's as if he had committed the murder himself.

Not so much a diary as a confession. It explained why this book was locked up.

In another section he had extracted an excerpt from Hitchcock and Truffaut talking about *Vertigo*, the film in which Jimmy Stewart watches his lover throw herself off a building:

T. What was it about the book on which you based *Vertigo* that appealed to you?

H. The hero's attempts to re-create the image of a dead woman through another living woman.

The last half of Prosper's book was a diary devoted entirely to *The Tempest*. For years he had played with its themes and characters, distorting Shakespeare's intentions, manipulating the story to fit his own desires, reading into it an acquiescence that wasn't there.

The storyboards were masterpieces of detail: projections of chaotic wave patterns, diagrams of Shakespeare's original outdoor stage lighting, retouched Polaroids. The final computer-generated twist was incomprehensible to me, although I thought Ram would understand it perfectly. It was to take place inside the caves on Elephanta Island, where the cameras would record screens broadcasting different versions of *The Tempest* while a magical studio storm raged outside. It looked like the kind of thing that could all go terribly wrong.

On the date of my arrival in India I found this quotation in Prosper's book: *Bengal light: black sulphide used as a shipwreck signal, or to illuminate the night*. For each day of my visit, Prosper had a different quotation in his black diary. As if I were part of his film and not my own.

In the filing cabinet with Prosper's book was a brown envelope containing the rest of Sami's pictures. Solid evidence at last. I recognized many of the faces, although there were no blazing stars on the political stage. Then I thought, Evidence of what? Of this particular act. But not of murder.

Lying down to rest on the narrow bed, I sank into a cloud. My eyes closed. Outside, a giant vacuum cleaner was trying to suck the hut up into the sky, the oddly reassuring sound of someone else's hand playing with the Fast Forward button for a while.

4

WHEN I OPENED MY EYES, THE WIND AND RAIN HAD SUBSIDED and there was a bright moon outside. I shone the torch on my watch: 4:15. If the cyclone had hit as predicted, this would be the eye of the storm, marked by clear skies and no rain or wind. I had about three to four hours before the eye passed and the storm-force winds picked up again. If I started walking now, I was bound to find someone on the road foolhardy enough to be driving into Bombay.

I put Prosper's book into my backpack with Sami's photos and stepped into the moonlight. Even in this manufactured world you could hear the sound of growth in the air, a moist squelching from the ground, and outside the studio compound I could smell that the dead dun earth was coming to life again.

At school in Scotland I had read a story of the Deluge that paralleled the Hindu one of my youth. It was the Greek legend in which Deucalion and his wife, Pyrrha, land in their ark on Mount Parnassus after the flood. They pray to Zeus to ease their loneliness. "You must cast behind you the bones of your mother," he tells them, and they take this to mean the stones of Mother Earth, and when they cast these behind them, men grow out of the stones cast by Deucalion and women from those cast by Pyrrha.

I put my hand into the side pocket of my bag to take out the little package I had been carrying with me ever since my mother's death, letting the old dried strychnine berries trickle through my fingers like breadcrumbs as I walked.

Seven years ago I had told my father a story. It went like this:

I came back and found my mother half dead in the bath. She had taken strychnine, something she'd tried before in Kerala, but in smaller doses, always in such low concentrations that they acted as no more than a stimulant to her system. And to Dad's conscience. She had tried halfheartedly with aspirin and sleeping tablets in Scotland when Gran died. She had told me so many times that she wanted to kill herself that it had become part of the wallpaper of our relationship. I told Dad that Mum was already suffering violent strychnine contractions when I found her this time, which was true, and that when I tried to touch her she went into convulsions and slipped underneath the water and drowned. Very quickly. Too quickly to save her.

Which could have been true. It would be typical of strychnine poisoning.

I said that I did not ring the police or the ambulance immediately but sat and waited for hour after hour. Until the water was cold. My father came to Scotland from Kerala to testify on my behalf. He said that Jessica had attempted suicide on several previous occasions. She had access to the berries because the two of them had recently been on a visit to Kerala, where she had met an old gardener who kept a supply of the berries for himself.

The visit had not been successful?

It had not been successful. They had agreed that the visit, the "second honeymoon," as the local papers called it (not realizing that there had never been a first), was not a success. Jessica was unstable anyway, he explained, and her own mother had died quite recently, leaving her doubly bereft.

Dad was such a good witness it wasn't necessary for me to add what I had told Mum after the abortion. That I would rather be dead than risk repeating the pattern of our life. A shrink laid on by the local authority to ease me through the breakdown I suffered told me that I had not forgiven Mum for all the damage she had done to me.

Remember the game, she said. Put your arm around my neck. Help me, Rosalind. So I did. Put one hand around the back of her neck, cupping her head as you do when bathing a baby, and another under her knees. Slid her under the water, pressing down on her head until her nostrils were submerged and then her eyes. There was a lot of splashing. She put a wet hand out and grabbed my shirt. Or perhaps I imagined that particular detail. I can't really remember the sequence now. It is more likely that she became unconscious from shock immediately she felt the water rush up her nose. Such deaths have been documented many times.

I never told anyone that part. I carried it with me, wrapped up with the strychnine berries. But perhaps I imagined the whole thing. It's possible. The mind plays curious tricks on us.

This morning I was casting the weight of my guilt behind me like stones, berries like breadcrumbs along the road to Bombay. Just in case I had to walk this route again someday, in case the laws of Chaos are stronger than the Second Law of Thermodynamics; in case the Hindus got it right and we can turn back the clock and start again, with a slight alteration to the pattern.

I have always used walking to help me think. And sometimes not to think, to lose myself, as I do in the water. From my maternal grandmother, whose ancestors had footed it halfway across the ancient world and back, I learned these long, even strides. Out of one century, into another. Out of the past, into the future. At about six in the morning a lorry driver stopped to offer me a lift, and his family of five found room for me among the boxes of mangoes at the back.

On a street not far from Crawford Market, I leaped out, with the spicy scent of the fruit still on my skin. The driver spent a few minutes searching for his best mango, the kind where juice has oozed out of the stem end to harden on the orange skin like sticky crystal dew. He offered it to me shyly. "Gift of monsoon."

From Crawford Market I took a taxi to the hotel, slipping by the receptionist before he spotted me. It was eight o'clock. There was no sign of the winds strengthening, so it was possible that the cyclone had moved away from Bombay in the night, hijacked across the Arabian Sea to Oman.

The receptionist obviously had noticed me after all: the phone rang before I had a chance to run the bath. It was Ashok.

"I'm here in the hospital with Miranda," he said. "She has gone into labour prematurely. The doctors are sure she is going to recover. But it was a close call."

"What happened—was it the baby?"

"It *is* the baby. The baby is still in question. I think you should get here as soon as you can. Your sister keeps asking for you and"—he waited a few seconds before completing the sentence—"there was a bomb at her flat."

"Not Miranda." It felt as if he had kicked me in the stomach.

"A package addressed to you was delivered just before one o'clock yesterday. The doorman wasn't around, but one of the gardeners saw a man go up with it. Fortunately, the bomb was not a very effective one. Tusker must have answered the door—he took more of the bomb's force and has been in a coma ever since. But your sister wasn't making much sense."

One o'clock. At one I was on my way from Caleb's to Prosper's studio. "Why did the hospital ring *you*?"

"They tried Prosper first, but they weren't able to find him. They sent a man to the Sonavla studio and the watchman there said that the place was already locked up and Prosper had gone back to Bombay with some of the crew. Then they rang you, Rosalind. Miranda was able to tell them that much. When you weren't at the hotel, the receptionist gave them my number. Because I had rung you so often over the last few days. I have been ringing you every hour since I heard. Where have you been?"

"Making offerings to the Nagas," I said. "How is Prosper taking it? I presume he has heard by now."

"Not yet. We found out from his office here that he went straight to Elephanta Island yesterday to make arrangements for the last days of shooting that are to take place there. He must have got stranded by the storm."

Ashok gave me the name of the hospital and Miranda's ward. "Rosalind?"

"What?"

"Be careful. The doorman said he mistook you for your sister when you left her flat yesterday morning. He said you were wearing her clothes. And the doctors here say she wasn't supposed to have left the hospital anyway. It's possible that whoever sent the bomb thought you were still in the flat. They may try to rectify their mistake . . . I rang Mistry, you know, when I was trying to find you. He said he had no idea where you'd gone after you left his studio."

"He said that?"

"Yes. But you were seen driving away in one of his cars. A man recognized the car because it was a white Mercedes with a smashed window on the driver's side."

"I'm leaving now."

A package addressed to me. I knew of only one person who thought I would be safely locked in that flat. Prosper. Caleb knew where I was. And Acres had said, We can't seem to *blow you up*. At the time, my mind had been too busy to question his meaning.

The traffic was terrible. A tour of Hell. The drive magnified beggars, pollution, noise, stink. I kept repeating Ash's words: *The doorman mistook you for your sister*. Willing Miranda to recover.

5

Ashok was waiting for me outside the maternity wing, where Miranda lay in my place.

"Rosalind," he said, "your sister's had the baby. He's a bit small but seems to be doing well. Your sister is fine too, although very weak and drifting in and out of consciousness. She should rest now, but it might do her good to see you first."

Ashok left me in the private room where my sister lay, her face as pale as the linen sheet over her swollen belly. Miranda's eyes opened while I was looking down at her.

"Welcome back," I said, sitting down next to her. "You gave us quite a scare." Her mauve-veined eyelids barely fluttered. I took the hand that wasn't on a drip and stroked it gently. She had a sticking plaster over one eye and the bloom of a bruise on her jaw. Her lips moved and she moaned something I couldn't catch.

"I'm here, Miranda. It's me, Rosalind. I'm here."

Her lashes fluttered up, but her eyes didn't register. She mumbled again and I squeezed her hand. Slowly, her pupils slid round to meet mine. They still looked unfocused. She tried to say something. I put my hand on the unbruised side of her face, but it made her wince, so I took it away and held her hand again instead.

"I'm so sorry, Miranda." The chorus of my Bombay visit.

Her fingers moved in the palm of my hand, no more than the tickle you feel when a moth brushes against your bare skin. But I could feel the letters:

"Okay—yes, I'm okay, Miranda. Not hurt at all. And the baby's fine, we're all fine."

She smiled, squeezed my hand very softly, and closed her eyes, drifting off into her own country for a while. I waited for her to come back to me. "Do you know who did this, Miranda?" I felt her fingers flutter again. "I thought so." Ran my fingertip over her profile. My profile. "Sleep well," I said.

After an hour, a nurse appeared and said she thought Mrs. Sharma should rest now. In the waiting room, Ashok stood up from the bench where he'd been sitting. Over one arm he carried a neatly folded Burberry mac. The kind Robert Mitchum used to sport in noirish private-eye movies. A coat no Englishman would wear. "Did your sister give you any idea of who did this?" Ashok said.

"She didn't say anything." She didn't have to speak. We were two children underwater again.

"Are you sure? It could help us if she had."

"Us?" I stared at him until he dropped his eyes. "Prosper and chums are the only ones who believed I was in that flat, Ash."

He smoothed the Burberry, staring at the label for a minute. "Will you take a walk with me, Rosalind? We need to talk. In private."

We walked out into the hospital grounds side by side. Anyone watching would have thought we were new friends. But my first words were more of an ending. "It's over, Ashok. I finally put two and two together and came up with three: the Tilak Foundation. A group of like-minded people united to steal what's left of India and flog it to the highest bidder."

He turned to face me. "It's not what you think, Rosalind."

"Let me tell you what I think." Measuring my words out as carefully as medicine. "That you lied to me from the start about your motives, skillfully wove a new story to fit every new piece of evidence, played me like a marionette to entertain the audience while you picked their pockets, used my trust for your own ends—whatever they are. Until you got my sister blown up."

He ran his hand over his eyes. "I know you feel I'm to blame, Rosalind, but we were as much in the dark as you. Why do you think I joined the foundation? We had no firm proof; we didn't dare move too soon for fear of catching the little fish and letting the big ones get away once again."

"We? Who are you talking about here, Ash? Your chums in the civil service or your greedy fellow historians?"

"The Tilak Foundation is not a group of villains, as you seem to believe. Many of its members—of whom I am one—are entirely sincere in their aims to try to stop the destruction of India's heritage. They are

BOMBAY ICE / 357

responsible for installing such mundane things as modern drainage
systems in medieval towns, in providing irrigation systems to desert
regions where people would otherwise abandon their homes and join
the tide of homeless in cities like Bombay."

"What were you doing filming at Sonavla? It's too much of a
coincidence."

"No coincidence. One of the temples was being restored there by a
group of Mr. Unmann's artisans and it came to our attention that not
quite all the artworks were returned to their position in the temple. An
inquiry was set up. But by the time we arrived on site, the statues were
once more in place."

"Or so you thought."

"Or so we thought. Suspicion arose when an associate of mine in
Germany reported that artworks corresponding roughly to the ones
that had originally gone missing from the Sonavla temple site had
been sold in Berlin. We assumed the works being sold were forgeries
copied from the originals by master craftsmen."

"Of course." I let Ashok hear the sarcasm in my voice. "That
confused me for a while. I couldn't figure out why Prosper would need
Jigs at the Archaeological Survey if he was shipping forgeries. And
they had to be forgeries, because it is illegal to export artworks more
than a hundred years old from India without a letter from the
Archaeological Survey of India. As you were careful to point out to me
when you gave me Dad's barometer."

"Who is on trial here, Rosalind? Do you wish to convict the whole
of India? It's not a perfect system. Nothing is."

"So what did you do when you discovered there was massive fraud
going on?"

"There were wider implications that had to be considered."

"As I said before: there always are."

"If I had allowed you to bring down the entire Tilak Foundation,
as seemed to be your intent, it would have undermined everything for
which we had worked."

"So when you were stringing me that line of shite about Shiv Sena,
you knew all along the Sena had nothing to do with it."

"As usual, you are trying to make something cut-and-dried which
is more complex. Each detail is affecting another. To ignore one detail
for the sake of a convenient generalization would result in an enormous miscarriage of justice. To have singled out Mr. Unmann and
your brother-in-law would have reinforced the Sena's xenophobic

views. Certain eminent men in that party would have liked nothing better than to point the finger at foreigners. And India cannot exist in a vacuum."

"And now? What are you going to do about Unmann?"

"Mr. Unmann has already left the country. You refused to hand over what information you had. There was nothing we could do."

"And Prosper?"

"Justice under the law is not always what we hope for, it's simply the best we can do. I can only repeat what I said before, Rosalind. I would ask that you pass over to me what information and evidence you may have gathered in your unorthodox fashion and trust me to deal with the situation in the only way I know that does not lead to anarchy."

"Or what?"

His next sentence was spoken unwillingly. I could see he had hoped nothing further would be necessary. "Or I may have to take steps I do not wish to take."

Over the course of our conversation the tone of Ashok's voice, his whole attitude, had gradually altered. Now the ghost of an official walked between us.

"Give me some time, Ashok. I need to talk to my sister again."

"Your sister will sleep for several hours. There is nothing further for you to do here—unless you wish to see the baby?"

"No." Not with his bloodlines. "But I have some editing work I need to do on my tapes for the BBC."

"I thought the BBC—" He stopped abruptly.

"Had cancelled my contract? I wonder how you knew that. Was it the first of your reluctant steps, Ashok?" I turned back towards the hospital. "Tell me one thing: why trust me with all this information?"

"I am hoping that the broader implications I have outlined will influence you to make the correct decision."

"And if they don't?"

Ashok's was the voice of bureaucracy. "I can give you twenty-four hours in which to consider your options, Rosalind."

"And then what? The documents will self-destruct and me with it?" The System. It's the same all over the world. They try to convince you that you're doing what they want you to do for your family, your country, your religion. But in the end the same old people stay on top. "I'll tell you what I'll give you, Ashok, as a down payment on your trust. Hold out your hands." He held them out like a small boy waiting for a treat. From the bottom of my backpack I retrieved the stolen coins. In Ashok's left hand I put one of the ones lifted from Caleb's studio yesterday. In his right, one of Prosper's.

Ashok examined them carefully. "Where did you get these?"

"Do you know what they are?"

He held up his left hand. "This one is a genuine mohar of the mid-Mogul period," and, holding up Prosper's, "and this one is a fake. May I repeat the question: where did you obtain these?"

"From a couple of people who know a lot about impurity."

Twenty-four hours Ashok had given me. Enough. If Ram was back in Bombay, and if he was half the sound wizard I thought he was.

6

Ram was waiting for me at the studio of a friend who did the special effects for some of the biggest names in Bollywood films: flying monkeys, winged gods, multilimbed goddesses.

"Right," Ram said as I came in, his smile a little wary. "The tape you gave that Boothroyd bloke brought me back here, although he made you sound like even more of a nutter than usual. But before I get involved in this again, I want an update on the latest little sequence of events. You think Prosper sent the bomb. Why blow up Tusker and Miranda and half his own flat?"

I sat on one of the plastic café stools that served as furniture. "It was a mistake. Miranda had a doctor's appointment that Prosper made for her. She was supposed to be in the hospital overnight, not at home. Tusker was worried because he'd been told to leave me locked in the flat. Alone with the cook. The bomb was badly made. Clearly it was meant to destroy the whole flat." I forestalled Ram's disbelieving comment by passing him Sami's drawing of Skanda and the photos of the same figure in Satish's book. "See that notch out of the ear?" I pointed at the photos. "These are photos of Maya's family's collection, taken back in the late fifties, early sixties. Before this forgery scam started."

"You don't know that for a fact," Ram said, but I shrugged him off.

"Okay. Let's call it a logical assumption." I passed him the photos taken in Prosper's flat. The one-hour processing I had managed to find before getting here hadn't helped the quality. But it was still clear that Prosper's Skanda lacked the notched ear. And its face had been subtly changed. I laid the morgue photo of Sami next to it and her statue of Skanda. "For every forgery that couldn't be cast from a mould, Sami did lots of drawings from the original. She must have been in Prosper's flat to draw this Skanda, and when she came to make the copy, she altered the face slightly to give it features closer to her own. Then she stole the real Skanda—this one, with the notched ear, Prosper's original. See how it bears much less resemblance to Sami's photo? I think she and the other hijra artists who were killed had some plan to set up business on their own."

Ram shook his head. "I still don't get it."

"All along I was going on the assumption that Prosper's collection was genuine, that he and Unmann were simply selling copies they'd had made at the Central Props Unit under Raven's supervision. But they had a much grander scheme. Unmann knew that forgeries would not pass muster—to get the kind of money that mattered—with the collectors he had in mind. It was the originals they were selling, stuff they had access to through the Tilak Foundation. Authorized for export by Jigs, who probably gave them documents claiming the works were modern copies. I figure they started by ripping off temples in obscure towns where no one knew any better or was really interested as long as there was something to hang a garland on or to fill in the hole on the shelf. Smaller museums would lend them work, honoured to be given a mention in a foreign catalogue. Who would notice when the piece they got back was subtly different? If worse came to worst, Unmann or Raven could always say it was a genuine mistake, a mix-up at the factory—or at Island, where they stored the larger figures to give them the requisite patina of age.

"Then Prosper started to get needier. He had been eating into Maya's family collection for years. Finally, there was nothing left except an old insurance policy. That's why he wouldn't allow any exhibitions of his collection over the last few years: he couldn't afford to have the insurance experts in to value the work. And he certainly couldn't afford to have my friend Rupert Boothroyd poking his nose around. Rupert was a risk, even after I'd been thoroughly discredited at Unmann's."

"Who delivered the bomb?"

"A flunky of Acres's. I don't know. Miranda thinks it was Acres."

"She told you? I thought you said she wasn't speaking."

I nodded. "As good as told me. The first two letters anyway: AC. A game we used to play when she was a kid: tracing out words on each other's hands to see if we could read them like Braille. But I don't think he'd risk showing his face."

"Right," Ram said. "So where do we start?"

"You think you can do it?"

He nodded. "The first half, anyway. The rest, with a little help from my trusted friend here in FX and that shooting script you said you have."

Until Ram gave me his nod of acceptance, I hadn't realized how much I'd been counting on him.

WE SPENT HALF THE AFTERNOON IN THE SOUND ROOM.

"Look, Rosalind: the Protools system divides your strand of conversation into that wiggly pink graph line at the top of the screen," Ram had to explain computers to me in the language of the semiliterate, "and we'll make the person you're talking to blue and the background SFX lime green. See how that high peak of your voice just clipped his peak, his comment there—so we can't edit you out without losing his opening words. But here—this is better—you paused in real pro fashion and you can see the lime-green SFX line is almost straight—no peaks and troughs at all—so I can nip that out and no one will hear the difference. And if you want to give this comment of his even more drama, we could steal some of that earlier pause and slip it in between those two clauses of his. Then you'd really feel the strength of what is being said."

Ram looked over at me with eyebrows raised in a question. "I mean, if we're talking FTF situations here. It does slightly distort the original sense of what the guy's saying."

"Go for it." FTF: our old shorthand for "Fuck the Facts."

His eyes slid back happily to the screen. "I've saved the original edits on a separate master—in the unlikely event you want to tell the real truth someday." He was reeling through strands he'd already stored. "Okay, Roz—this is only a suggestion, but the beauty of these machines is that we can just slip this earlier clip in here and have a listen to see if it works and store it again if it doesn't without bothering with all that cutting and splicing of tape."

"Sounds good, Ram. Can you get rid of bumps in the edits like that one?"

He lined the stylus up between two points on the graph of my voice on screen and pressed the delete button.

"Easy as that," he said. "Anything else? I'll slip under it a bit of background street noise from the other recording and you won't notice a thing."

Ram assured me that the rest of our scheme was in hand. I left him one of the tapes we'd made, put the other into my bag, and took a taxi to the hospital.

ASHOK WAS LEAVING AS MY TAXI PULLED UP. WE CONFRONTED EACH OTHER ON the steps outside. "What are you doing here, Ash? Grilling my sister in her bed?"

He didn't have the grace to look embarrassed. "I was on my way to see you. Have you thought about what we discussed?"

"I have, and I think you're right. I'll turn the stuff over to you. But my twenty-four hours isn't up yet."

"Ah yes. Unfortunately, it seems there has been a general rethink, given the gravity of this situation."

"What does that mean in plain English?"

"It means that you have until 6 p.m. and then you must turn over everything to the authorities: the tapes, the photos. I mean *everything*, Rosalind."

MIRANDA WAS SITTING UP IN BED CRADLING HER BABY BOY. SHE LOOKED AT ME and beamed with the irritatingly endearing expression that all nursing mothers have.

"Isn't he lovely, Rosalind." No question mark in her voice. There never is.

"Yeah, he's wonderful." I've attended so many friends' births now I feel like a qualified midwife. I know all the patter. "If you like walnuts."

"Oh, Rosalind, all babies look like Winston Churchill when they're first born."

I was waiting for that. It usually comes before the one about how small his/her fingers/toes/ears are.

"Look at him, Rosalind—look how small his fingers are. Look— he's smiling at you!"

There's something about a baby's approval that is hard to beat. It's a shame they have to grow up.

"Don't you think he looks like Dad when he smiles?" Miranda said.

"He has a real ladykiller's smile, that's for sure." In fact, my sister's son bore no resemblance to anyone in particular. Still, I've known lots of babies who inherit no physical features from their parents, just a single gesture or mannerism. I looked more closely at my nephew's mouth, that smile so familiar, permanently curled up at the corners like a rajput's moustache. "Has Prosper arrived yet to admire the new addition?"

"He got back from Elephanta a few hours ago. He's over the moon."

"Miranda, I know this isn't the best time, but I have a kind of odd deadline and I need to ask you a couple of questions."

"Yes?"

"Do you have any idea who might have sent that bomb?"

"Ashok Tagore has already been asking me. I have no idea. Somebody crazy."

"So when you traced out those letters this morning . . ."

She looked down at her baby. "I don't really remember the last twenty-four hours very well. I think I was a bit delirious."

"Me too." We admired the little brown frog in her arms for a few more minutes. "What about your son's father—you still love him?"

Her chin came up and we stared at each other. "I always wanted a baby," Miranda said. "And it's funny how cocooned it makes me feel. As if nothing outside really matters." She reached out to me and I patted her hand.

"I'll be back later to play the proud auntie," I said, marvelling at how two people with so much in common could be so different.

In Ashok's lesson about ice, years ago, he had told me that the crystals in an ice tray generally have stable boundaries, because their solidification proceeds smoothly from the outside to the inside. Like a child sent away to school at an early age, I thought now. "In turbulent air, ice obeys subtler mathematical laws, growing outwards from an inner seed. With snowflakes, for instance, it is impossible to predict how fast the crystallization will proceed or how often it will branch. Boundaries are unstable. Choices made at any moment by the growing crystals depend on humidity, temperature, the presence of pollution in the air." He quoted the lines of a writer he admired: "The nature of turbulent air is such that each pair of snowflakes experiences very different paths. The final flakes are a record of the history of all the changing weather conditions they have experienced. The combinations may as well be infinite."

THOMAS'S EYES SPARKLED WITH ENTHUSIASM FOR HIS NEW ROLE. "MR. RAM'S friend has given me costume for you and instructions for tomorrow. And I have found some more information on subjects you requested."

I read the newspaper clippings in Thomas's car. They dated from several months after Maya's death. That's why I hadn't found them in any of my searches—and because, in inscrutable indexer's logic, the clippings had not been filed under Maya or Sharma. According to the pencilled name in the right-hand corner of each piece, they were listed under Goliath Productions.

GOLIATH GIVES STRUGGLING STUDIO NEW LEASE ON LIFE

Struggling movie mogul Prosper Sharma has had to watch sadly while his last five films have taken nosedives at the Bollywood box office. Six months ago he lost his beloved wife, Maya, star of stage and screen. But today he officially celebrated his ailing studio's new lease on life. "I owe it all to my old friend Anthony Unmann, and the backing he roped in from Goliath Enterprises," beamed the delighted studio boss. "Without their support, my Island would have been sunk!" he quipped. People in the know at Goliath (a dark horse in the city's booming property race) have said that the new agreement should benefit both partners.

"Great, Thomas," I said. "But have you managed to find me a bed for tonight?"

"Yes, madam, with my cousins."

I couldn't go back to the Ritzy, even though Acres's credit card and a little judicious signature forging had settled my bill. When I didn't hand over the right material to Ashok at six, the first place he and his colleagues would come looking for me was my hotel. Shortly after that, they'd hit Ram's studio.

"Bed is no problem," Thomas said. "Only I am hoping you do not mind quality of accommodation." He glanced over his shoulder. "You are sure you are not wanting a rest first before making this expedition to Mr. Caleb?"

"I'm sure."

Miranda hadn't answered my question directly, but it was as close as we were going to get to the truth. As children, playing the game of writing on each other's hands, we always had a problem recognizing when one word stopped and the next began. *The first two letters: not the murderer, the father. Not the father, the murderer.* A real ladykiller's smile.

7

Before we reached Caleb's studio i had ram's second tape in my little DAT and the volume cranked as high as it would go without distortion. This time I had made no effort to disguise the microphones. I felt very calm. A snake charmer, a metallurgist, a reader of meteorological signs. The little guard recognized me and waved me past with a smile. Caleb had probably given him time off the night that Acres followed me from Prosper's flat to here.

It was a break between scenes. One of the extras told me that Dadasahib was in his office at the back. I walked through the controlled chaos and opened the office door without bothering to knock. Caleb was stretched out on a sofa among all his plots, the floor around him papered with grainy ten-by-eight black-and-whites of a young woman who might almost have been sleeping, her face washed clean as bone. A dead face. Sami's face—and mine.

Caleb jumped up when he heard the door. For an instant Ram would have cherished, he didn't speak. Then—"Acres." One word, as I had, the night before.

"Mr. Acres should've stuck to safety razors."

"It's what you wanted, Roz," Caleb said quickly, "a confrontation." Like me, he could change his shape to fit the required role. Like me, I thought. He's like me. But I pushed the thought away.

"Last night I kept running the scene over and over," I said. "I could see how it all worked, up to a point."

"I was only involved up to a point," Caleb said.

"But the thing that kept bringing the reel up short," I went on,

trying not to listen to him, "was the question of why you would want
to hurt Miranda. What did you have to gain?"

"That was Acres. And Prosper. You have to believe me."

"They thought it was me in the flat. But you knew it wasn't,
because I was here. Still, you'd already had one son killed, I kept
saying to myself—Sami. Because his reincarnation wasn't quite what
you'd hoped for."

"No. I didn't know that . . . Prosper never told me, don't you
understand? And even if he had, I couldn't be sure Sami was mine. He
could've been in the same hijra family as my son and picked up the
story. It was a vague resemblance."

I pushed one of the photos on the floor with the toe of my shoe.
"He was a wonderful draughtsman, Sami. Like you. In other circumstances he might've made a good engineer." My voice was seductive as
a late-night DJ's. "Like his grandfather."

Caleb tried to interrupt me there, but I pressed on. "The equation
I couldn't figure is what you had to gain by killing your second son as
well. Miranda's."

"What do you . . . ?" he started, shaking his head.
"Who . . . ?" If I had wanted to then, I could have walked over and
pushed him to the ground. He hadn't known.

"She lied to me," he said. "She told me it was Prosper's." He
turned away so I couldn't watch him. "Get out of here. You've done
what you came to do."

I shook my head. "No. I haven't. Not yet."

"You've done enough," he said, and shouted to someone in the
studio.

Two big men appeared at the door. "Something wrong,
Dadasahib?"

Caleb waved his head at me. The two men moved forward obediently. I pushed past them into the open studio, where the crew had
gathered at the sound of our raised voices.

"You are not welcome here, Miss Benegal," said one of Caleb's
bouncers, coming towards me to take my arm.

I pressed the Play button. There was some distortion, because the
recording conditions had been less than perfect, but Ram had cleaned
it up enough so that you could hear quite clearly who was speaking. It
was Caleb, in this office, when I'd asked him why he hated Prosper so
much, and earlier, when he'd taken me to the brothel where he'd
grown up. But Ram had cut my question.

"Unless this current venture is a hit," said the tape, coming in clean on Caleb, *"his studio goes to the developers."*

The two men stopped walking towards me. Maybe they thought Caleb was throwing his voice.

"What about the Shiv Sena movement?" said the taped Rosalind.

"That's all crap," said Caleb on the tape. *"I am tired of this ghost haunting me on the footpath."*

The studio had gone silent except for the drip of the leaking roof and the hum of lights.

"Stop it." The real Caleb cut across the tape. You could hardly tell the difference between the two Calebs, real and taped. Modern technology is a bloody miracle. "I never said that."

"Didn't you?" I said. "It's your voice. I'm sure your crew would be interested in the rest of the tape. And they'd like to look at these photos of Sami." I threw one of the morgue pictures onto the studio floor, and the face rested on the surface of a puddle for only an instant before slipping under the water like an unfinished print in a developing bath of chemicals. "Knowing those old pictures of your first wife as so many of them do." I tossed another one towards Caleb and it spun out, a badly thrown Frisbee, and landed a few feet from the first. One of the crew picked it up and showed it to his friend. "I think you'll find Sami's resemblance to her is pretty striking. The story doesn't quite fit your image as a supporter of the downtrodden, does it?"

"Are these supposed to be evidence of some crime?" He had changed his tactics.

"No. But then there's my testimony. It might not convict you, but it would be enough to get a lot of people interested. Enough people."

The crew's muttering was much louder now. Caleb, used to a silent, admiring audience, must have been more aware of it than I was. He looked at our jury and then back at me, as if weighing what he knew on a set of scales. "Your testimony, yes. You'd have to stand up in court as an expert witness. In front of all those friends of mine who have watched you over the last couple of weeks. What would you say, Rosalind? What is there to say?"

Caleb waved to his two bouncers again, and when they hesitated, he started walking towards me himself, smiling, holding out his hand. "I don't think you'd expose yourself like that."

I listened to the wet slip slap of his plastic sandals on the floor.

"Try me," I said, and pressed the Play button again.

"Who is he? Was Sami her real name?" Ram had done a masterly

job of matching the interior and exterior of two different background atmos.

"*Ah, Rosalind,*" the taped Caleb absolutely unmistakable. "*This thing of darkness I acknowledge mine.*"

"*How could anyone do that?*" I asked him on the tape. "*Send a man to murder your son and your wife and then go on working with him?*"

There was movement in the shadows as people appeared from other parts of the studio. Everyone was listening. You could have weighed the tension in the air.

Caleb and I knew what came next. We understood the power of the spoken word in India, a country where a simple storyteller under a banyan tree can hold an entire village in thrall for hour after hour.

"*There are different kinds of murder,*" he said. "*I . . . didn't realize Sami was my son . . .*" The buzz of studio lights covered the editing almost completely. "*There was the blackmail, as well. For a son to blackmail a father . . .*"

I could see Caleb bracing himself for the climax of our little melodrama, glancing around at the cast and crew. He was a man who was used to manipulating his audience and could calculate to the minute how they would respond.

"*Perhaps, in the end, everyone is expendable,*" the taped Caleb said. "*It's to do with the fear of falling.*"

"How much of this is there?" he said, in real time.

"The whole story."

"All right, Rosalind, you can stop it now." He waved to our audience to clear away. When the extras had left us alone on the stage, illuminated like film stars by the arc lights, Caleb started to speak. You have to be careful, I thought, admiring his strange grey eyes and the curl of his mouth. He's going to be very convincing. "You asked me once why I hated Prosper. Now you see. He seduced both my children and cost me my son twice over. If he was my son." He looked at the pictures in the water. "Did you know that Maya told my wife she should send him away because he wouldn't do my career any good?" he said. "And my poor, ignorant bitch figured she was doing me a favour. She was so frightened when she saw how I felt about his disappearance that she clammed up for two days. Cut herself a few times to make up for it. And then found some of her old painkiller. Once a junkie, always a junkie. Didn't sober up enough to tell me until too late where she'd dumped him. By then he'd run away. Vanished."

I did not want to look at him now. Wanted to be reduced to a pair of ears, a recorder programmed to hear only the facts.

"Did Prosper ever tell you why he blocked the distribution of my first film?" His eyes searched mine.

"Tell me, Caleb."

It was his turn to look away. Something here that could not be said, even now. "Because I wouldn't give him what he needed. But my s . . . but Sami did."

"If you hated Prosper, why did you work with him on this Tilak scheme?"

He shook his head. "Not with him. I was working with Goliath, helping them to get control of Island. That was the deal I made with Unmann years ago: I'd line him up with the requisite people and he would help me bring down Island. I think it was Unmann who told Acres to use one of my scalpels, to make sure I was implicated, to keep me loyal." He stepped towards me. "Rosalind—"

"If you think this confession is enough," I said quickly, "it isn't." A voice in my head: What do you hope to prove—or disprove? This man will say anything.

"I'm not trying to . . ." He sighed. "Call it my epitaph. You know, there's an Indian poem I like, an old one. A man who's weary of the prolonged monsoon: *Arrows of water fall*, he says, *like the last blows that end the world*."

"*Who keeps so late a tryst?*" I finished the line for him. "My father taught me the poem when I was ten. It's by Vidyapati." I wanted to tell Caleb that villains don't recite poetry. It's not in character. Heroes of detective fiction are often literary. But not villains. Not even in Bombay movies.

Caleb smiled. "Clever Rosalind. Well, this is for you:

> *The earth is a pool of mud*
> *With dreaded snakes at large.*
> *Darkness is everywhere,*
> *Save where my feet*
> *Flash with lightning.*"

"*Your* feet," I corrected. "The lines are 'Save where *your* feet / Flash with lightning.' " I wouldn't let him have even that, the last line, the final monologue.

"Yes," he said. "Perhaps I should be singing this. My swan song." Looked down at his feet next to the photos I'd thrown. His bare feet and his paan-chewing, the only exterior evidence left of his years on the streets. Caleb, the man who consumed his own identity. He shook his head and shrugged. "Back in the swamp again," he said, and laughed. "This fucking country." He started to lean over to pick up one of Sami's pictures, and as he did, he slipped. I'm sure he slipped. That is how I remember it. The floor was very wet. He slipped. He reached out to stop himself from falling and grabbed the first thing to hand, a cable running into the wall, his fingers touching the six inches of bare live wires where they connected the 10,000-watt incandescent movie lights to a totally inadequate socket. There was a flash, a fishy, rubbery smell, and for an instant he seemed to clutch the wires tightly. But it was an accident. It's the electricity that causes that rigor, not the will. Everyone knows that.

There was a man in India who survived 4,000 volts and died from a tetanus infection of his injuries in the hospital afterwards. People have survived contacts with wires carrying 8,000 volts. Yet workers with long-standing heart disease may suffer death from relatively low electrical shocks. Caleb couldn't have received the electrical current for very long before one of his electricians moved to turn off the source. But Caleb was dead by then. His heart had been weak from birth, the papers reported later. It was genetic. It was in his blood.

For one instant when he gripped the wires, I had expected him to vanish in a puff of smoke and leave behind the smell of sulphur. Or to show some evidence of cyanidation, at least. I learned it at my mother's knee: the predominant process for extracting gold from its ores. "When an electric current is passed through a dilute cyanide solution," she told me, "gold can be deposited on other metals as an electroplate, a reaction that we often use for protecting and decorating base metals."

Perhaps it was *my* skin that should have shown traces of gold. It's a romantic image. Some director will use it one day. Caleb would've liked it, with his love of melodrama. But that is not what happens when you get wired up to thousands of volts of electricity. It fries the shit out of you. Still, there were some signs of electroplating on Caleb. The faintest tinge of gold on his hands and lower arms—flash marks that follow contact with high voltage, a classic reddish-yellow arborescent pattern. A tree struck by monsoon lightning. Sometimes there may be no abnormal marks at all on the exterior of an electrocuted body. But the central nervous system is itself electrically based, so an excess surge of current totally disrupts it. It simply overloads the circuit.

What had I hoped to achieve here? A confession, certainly. A tying of knots and closing of links in a long chain. I wanted to ask: Was it really Acres or was it you who pushed Maya? Were you guilty or innocent of Sami's death? And if guilty, how guilty? But the prisoner had left the stand before the prosecution rested its case. That's another thing they never do in the movies.

I walked back into Caleb's office and picked up the photos of the dead woman who might or might not have been Sami's mother. I opened the drawer of the desk to collect my own family snaps—of Prosper—and found as well an envelope with the word *Caleb* written on it, containing a strip of negatives and a photo of a crowd in front of a modern building. What distinguished this photo from any other bad tourist snap was the man leaving the building. He was wearing a mask of Rama. There was nothing else of note: dark hair, standard cotton kurta pyjamas, sandals, like every second Indian man on the street. I looked again—no, not sandals, flip-flops—and thought about Acres's passion for Armani and Gucci. The handwriting on the envelope was my sister's. I tore the envelope into small pieces and threw it away, put all the remaining photos and negs in my bag, and left the studio. No one stopped me. No one spoke to me. I was invisible, a shadow that passed through solid objects without disturbing them.

I GOT INTO THE FRONT SEAT OF THE TAXI NEXT TO THOMAS AND LET HIM TALK about movies, poetry, Shakespeare, anything he liked, as long as he didn't stop. "Have you heard of a film called *Prospero's Books* by a Mr. Peter Greenaway?" he asked, and carried on without waiting for an answer. "I am hoping someday it will come to a cinema near me so I may observe *The Tempest* given new lease of life with latest in computer technology. Wouldn't this be something, Miss Benegal?"

I agreed it would be something. Other than that, I didn't say much.

Thomas's cousins lived above an old costume-hire shop off Dr. Atmaram Road in the hawkers' paradise of Bhuleshwar. To reach their flat we had to pass through the shop, where the proprietor sat in front of a painted backdrop of Paris.

"His family is starting by supplying costumes for folk theatre," Thomas whispered, "but boom is coming with birth of mythological movies and TV series. Especially dream sequences, requisite of all Hindi movies, are good for business. Now he is stocking dazzling array from Snow White to Rani of Jhansi."

"This is the man who is helping us with our costumes for tomorrow?"

The cousins accepted my arrival as they appeared to accept most things, and after several cups of tea and a small plate of standard Malayali fish-curry rice, I felt sufficiently revived to ring Ram on Thomas's mobile.

"The heavy dudes have been round," he said. "Like you figured they would. Shouting about Caleb Mistry. They were no problem. But that friend of yours, Ashok Tagore? He could get blood from a stone. Lucky I didn't know where you were or he would've convinced me that it was in your best interests to tell him."

"Did you give him any inkling of what we have planned for Prosper?"

"Nope. When he pressed me, I gave him the photos you left and the tape we made, pretending it was only under duress that I would do such a thing. But he seemed more interested in some other photos he suspects you of having, that could damage a few of the government's nearest and dearest. That's what he thinks you're up to. Maybe you should ring him and relieve his mind so he doesn't let off any more of the heavy artillery before tomorrow."

"What about Prosper? Is he going ahead with the shooting at Elephanta?"

"So far as anyone knows. Barring a cyclone, he'll be there tomorrow with every last piece of space-age equipment in place. He's got exploding carriages, flying ships, an outdoor screen the size of Hyde Park, all linked up to computerized wind machines, cobweb spinners, fogmakers—the works, the whole cinematic bag of tricks, with a few from the Bronze Age thrown in."

"Then let's hope your friends don't fuck up."

"MAY ONE ENQUIRE WHERE YOU ARE RESIDING?" ASHOK ASKED WHEN I RANG. "As it seems that your last hotel bill was paid by a man whose lifeless body you reported having seen several days ago in the Hotel Rama."

"That was thoughtful of him, to settle my bill before corpsing it. By the way, how did you like my tape?"

"Most original," he said, "but I think there has been some mix-up in the information you left with your friend Ram. He seems to have given me only the photos of a woman long dead and a book on the arts of India. Then this tape . . ."

"You didn't like it?"

"It is most entertaining. Your young colleague is clearly a very talented editor. Unfortunately, the tape he gave us consists almost entirely of monsoon sound effects and commentary on the weather."

"It's what I'm here for, Ash. To chart the monsoon. Didn't the BBC tell you that when you rang them? And don't forget all that pertinent data I included about the Chaos theory. I seem to remember recording a long monologue on the formation of ice crystals at the top of a tropical storm cloud."

"Ah yes," he said. "I am quoting freely from your masterly editing job: 'Contrary to popular belief, Chaos serves not to destroy but to create. As a liquid crystallizes, it forms an exquisite pattern of growing tips not dissimilar to the aggregation of randomly moving particles . . . to the lightning path of an electrical discharge.' "

"There was nothing about electrical discharges on that tape," I said.

"Was there not? Perhaps then I have misinterpreted your concept of creativity."

8

Well before dawn, I felt Thomas tap my shoulder.

So now it begins, I thought. The last act. My Indian solution. I told myself that this was for my sister, and dressed as quietly as possible in my borrowed clothes.

"You have your script?" Thomas whispered as we left his cousins'. "Your work chitty? Your pass to the set?" I patted the beaded bag that had replaced my usual backpack and then checked again to be sure, as one checks endlessly for passport, tickets, wallet before leaving on a long trip.

"How do I look?" I said. One of the cousins had done my makeup the night previous, and I hoped that the few hours' sleep on it had only served to give me the requisite raddled appearance.

Thomas smiled and nodded. "All is perfection."

"What if the others don't get there in time, Thomas? What if the car Ram sent gets stuck in the mud?"

"What if, what if. Now you must be trusting in karma, like any good Indian girl," he said. "But if necessary, I too am donning such a costume."

"You're a Christian, Thomas. You shouldn't believe in karma."

"Whole of India is believing, madam, not only we poor Indians upon its stage."

"What an incorrigible poet you are."

We reached the docks from where the boats to Elephanta would leave. A crowd of extras had gathered already, yawning and stretching in the mist. Thomas drove down Ramchandani Marg and dropped me at the junction with Best Street, just past the Taj Mahal Hotel. Before I got out, we turned to face each other. "Go with God," he said. "I am awaiting you here this evening come hell or high water."

PROSPER HAD CHARTERED THREE OF THE SO-CALLED BIG BOATS TO CARRY HIS cast and crew the ten kilometres to Elephanta, where the lights, cameras, and props had been set up over the last two days. The crew and extras waiting for the boats were suspended in a pink cloud above the dock, as if Prosper's special effects had begun already. But it was only smoke from the bidis settling under the weight of monsoon air and shrouding the crew's feet. The spicy smell of the cigarettes was very strong. Essence of India.

It wasn't until Bina appeared with her small band of hijra and moved to where I stood on the dock that Ram's technical wizards separated themselves from the crowd, passing us with a grunted *Mumbai,* the password Ram and I had agreed on. Shortly after Bina's arrival, there was a shout from a beefy man near the boats and we started to board. I could see three other men of similar weight and height who were in charge of ensuring that no one without a pass got on. Fortunately, Bina and her strapping girls had received passes from Prosper's hijra dance troupe, who had been only too eager to trade theirs for the equivalent of three days' wages from Acres's wallet.

The humidity was building up again. Even halfway across the harbour the air was still as close as a bedsheet. Waves muddy with silt washed into the sea by last night's rains broke over the boat's gunwales, leaving a film of shiny mud on the deck like slip on a potter's wheel. "What are the crew talking about?" I whispered to Bina.

"There was a killing last night in a restaurant in Colaba where one of the crew was stabbed to death by a man at the next table. The man said the crew member had been staring daggers at him. Result of monsoon madness, everyone is saying. Other example of madness they are giving is Prosper Sharma filming during this season. Everyone is putting this down to lack of funds, which is worrying them because many have not been paid recently."

From what Ram had managed to glean through his network in the industry, Prosper had decided to abandon the realistic interpretation employed for the earlier acts of *The Tempest* and to film the last scenes as if they were being performed onstage. The action would become increasingly theatrical, until the film ended with the central actors static by the sea, reciting their lines straight to camera, like one of the *Ramayana* performances given on Chowpatty Beach.

"Prosper is deliberately using a technique from the early days of Indian cinema," Ram had said last night, "when filmmakers here drew heavily on the kind of theatrical framing you get in Victorian melodrama. But because of the cost of the actors and equipment he's using, and the fact that his access to Elephanta has been restricted to only short periods of time, he has to shoot a lot of it in one long take. Makes it better for us. But your little stunt at Caleb's has made security even tighter than usual." He had shaken his head at this point. "You know, there are no guarantees that I can pull this off, even with the talent I'm roping in for the day?"

"I have faith in you, Ram," I said. "And you are sure there will be the usual audience of VIPs on the set?"

"As sure as I can be. Everyone's fascinated by Prosper's new technology. They figure this is his last throw of the dice. He's even brought in some techno whiz kid from Spielberg's setup in the States."

GIVEN THE ROUGH SEAS, THE LAUNCH MANAGED TO MOOR WITH SOME GRACE at a pier of concrete blocks by the northwest end of Elephanta, where our passes were checked again. And there were other hazards. It was only a quarter-mile to the main caves 125 steps up a gentle incline, but those of us wearing bright jewellery had to fend off a continuous assault from acquisitive monkeys.

"We have monkeys like anything here in India," said one of the crew, aiming a dropkick at one of the creature's heads. Animal lovers do not survive long in India without a few monkey bites.

At the entrance to the caves, thick black cables from the movie lights snaked across the ground and two handpainted signs had been erected, large enough to accommodate three languages. The English version read: WAISTING TIME WAISTING FILM WAISTING RUPEES; the second sign ELECTRICITY IS DANGEROUS MORE THAN GUNS: TREATING EQUIPMENT WITH RISPEC.

Immediately to the left and right on entering the caves were two carved panels, one of Shiva as Lord of the Dance, the other of the god sitting on a lotus looking pretty pleased with himself, everything under control. We moved farther in, pressed by those behind us like sheep into a pen. Straight ahead through a forest of pillars was another huge Shiva, a good six metres high, this time as Trimurti, the three-headed Supreme Deity. He sat back in a deep recess, and at the base of his figure stood dwarfs with the leonine features of lepers.

Lighting was concentrated on this inner cavern, on Ardhanarisvara, in particular: "Lord who is both Male and Female," as my guidebook put it. Viewed from one angle, the figure's bisexual form was perfectly harmonious, its female face staring off serenely into a carved stone mirror that represented *maya*, or illusion. In front of this stone mirror another mirror had been constructed, apparently of polished obsidian, like John Dee's speculum in the British Museum. It was in fact a subtly disguised computer screen the size of a large television. When the lights were lit and the camera finally rolled, this double mirror would appear to be one, onto which a series of magical images could be projected.

I caught a glimpse of Basil Chopra's larger-than-life figure as he strutted to and fro in front of this false mirror, shedding makeup girls as a whale sheds blunt harpoons, while reciting his lines over and over to an unseen camera: "Welcome, sir, This Cell is *my* court . . . This Cell is my *courrtt* . . . This *Cell* is *my* court," struggling to tone down his stage projection for the sake of a subtler medium.

Between my crowd of extras and the figures of Shiva, six rows of fluted pillars with bulging pillowed capitals marched like massive pawns across a giant's game of chess, supporting a vast excavation some forty to fifty metres square. Under normal conditions this cathedral of stone would have given the impression of grandeur and space, but seething with people it was more claustrophobic. There was that breathless feeling of anticipation I have known only at royal weddings.

In the small western court somewhere off to our right was the control room where Prosper and his minions sat, a magician's cell devoted to cinematic mumbo jumbo. The gateway to the eastern porch was partially blocked off to prevent anyone from disturbing the mobile generators installed in the court beyond. They would provide the electricity needed for a spectacle of this scale. Each one was independently mounted on its own prime mover chassis to save the time—and the resulting loss of money—involved in having to disconnect all the lighting and reroute the cable whenever the filming shifted locations.

Every ten metres around the perimeter of this mass of activity stood one of Prosper's beefy stuntmen. Security was tighter than anyone had ever seen, the whispers said, because of the bomb and what had happened yesterday at Caleb Mistry's studio. No one knew quite what it was that had happened, only that it had involved "that crazy woman, Mr. Sharma's sister-in-law."

The surly villain standing guard over the eastern porch had his back to the narrow passage open behind him or he would have seen a small, masked figure appear in the gap and vanish again after briefly sliding his papier-mâché mask aside to reveal his face. It was Ram, mouthing a word at me, although he didn't stay long enough for me to read his lips. Behind its oblivious guard the eastern court should be humming, as planned, with its own brand of electricity—a negative charge.

I threaded my way through the crowd, nervously rerunning all the instructions Ram had given me yesterday and matching them to the realities of this set. What had seemed feasible while planning it on a simple diagram of these caves began to seem increasingly less so when faced with the grand scale of Prosper's last act.

Six rows of columns separated the extras crowded into the entrance at the north porch from the inner sanctum where Basil paced, Asia's answer to Orson Welles. To the right of the central rows, four colossal stone doorkeepers, the Dvarapalas, guarded a large Shiva shrine. They were still fierce, despite having had their lower bodies desexed by the Portuguese gunners who used these caves for target practice during a monsoon season a few hundred years ago.

I got no farther in my explorations than this shrine. Neither did anyone else who wasn't part of the inner circle. We were held back by the A-team of heavyweight bouncers. I would have to trust the facts gathered from Ram's informers. The Government of India Tourist Bureau had agreed to close Elephanta for Prosper only one day a month over the previous six months, and in that period he had shot most of the lesser scenes. His final extravaganza was to be filmed roughly in the order it appeared in Shakespeare's original fourth and fifth acts, with one exception. The traditional play within a play where Juno and Ceres (represented here by hijra in the guise of equivalent Indian goddesses) present their masque to the guests would be the last shot of the day. For this scene the whole cave had to be cleared to allow dancers, musicians, and effects people enough room to perform their miracles.

The original stage directions called for the goddesses and their attendants to vanish, but in Prosper's script they would continue to sing and perform outside the cave, filmed by a separate crew and directed by Prosper—who would appear on an exterior monitor, which the full daylight would reduce to a bleached but still potent figure. The vision of goddesses and dancers would be projected onto a screen behind Basil, gradually dissolving and fading away like all the other insubstantial pageants he had conjured up, in a dreamy cloud blown into the cave by the spinner, a special fan with a nozzle which dispensed a thin stream of glue used to construct artificial cobwebs.

"Move back, move back," a gruff assistant director shouted. One of his gofers rushed to distribute a final shooting script in the language of our choice, shouting to be heard over the waves of chatter. The collection of VIPs also received a copy of this document. I was staring down at this uneasy mixture of East and West when I heard Bina's voice behind me.

"Something is happening."

The cast and attendant VIPs fell silent as footsteps were heard climbing the steps up to the western porch. A tall silhouette sliced through the crowd, reflected light catching his shock of hair to give it the gleam of polished pewter. He was carrying a conductor's baton, which it was rumoured he used to conduct his orchestra of cast and crew. He raised it now for silence, and there was a flutter of applause.

"Ladies and gentlemen, the show is about to begin," my brother-in-law called out, for all the world like a ringmaster in the circus. "Those of you in the first scene, please take your positions. The rest of my colleagues and distinguished guests"—an elegant dip of the silver head in our direction—"pray be silent."

Without another word he turned on his heel and descended into the magician's control room. The clapperboard boy leaped to do his work. Prosper's disembodied voice cried over the loudspeakers:

"And . . . *action!*"

Abracadabra, I thought: *Enter Prospero, Ferdinand, and Miranda.*

A distant sitar plucked the first notes of the goddess theme. The gloom had long since dispersed, to be replaced by the unearthly light of big arcs by the time Basil's rich fruitcake of a voice rang out: *"If I have too austerely punish'd you . . ."*

Behind him, one layer after another of luminous gauze unrolled, each the size of Wimbledon centre court. Lit by an elaborate system of large angled lamps and sky pans, the translucent material did not so much conceal the cave walls as veil them in memories. They were at once stage clouds, deliberately mimicking those used in Jacobean masques and in the decorated frames of Renaissance maps, and dreams of Shah Jahan's youth, the high point of Mogul glory. Here was the mausoleum to his beloved wife, the Taj Mahal. Here, the shimmering, pearl-grey domes of the Moti Masjid at Agra, and the Red Fort of his City of the Ruler of the World with its golden letters on the ceiling proclaiming, "If there is a paradise on earth, it is this, it is this, it is this."

One final curtain came down behind the trio of actors—Shah Jahan's lost Peacock Throne. Basil reached out to touch it, and as he did, some trickery of the lighting made it vanish. There was an intake of breath from the audience.

In a break between scenes a few minutes later, I heard a man whispering softly to his companion, "Sharma was lucky to get Chopra and Shiraz out of retirement—not to mention the rest of the cast and crew. I'm surprised he has the money."

"That is why he is having to shoot so much in one day. Unheard-of, old boy. But he was forced into it by the conflicting shooting schedules of his galaxy of stars—and also by his mad determination to film that masque scene in one long shot running from this cave down to the sea."

Bina interrupted my eavesdropping. "When is Ram beginning?" She looked as nervous as I felt.

"I don't know, Bina. I haven't talked to him since yesterday. But I'm sure everything's under control." I hoped. "We have to wait for the agreed signals."

Despite the tight security, Ram had explained, several of Prosper's autocratic decisions would work in our favour. The first was that Prosper had insisted on his actors learning their lines and speaking them as if on a stage, a complete break from Indian movie tradition, where everything is dubbed. Prosper had also decided to direct the entire last two acts from within his control room. He would be able to watch the live actors performing on his monitor without seeing what was happening on the screens in the main cave itself. The images on the obsidian mirror and the large screen set into the wall in front of Trimurti's shrine were time-programmed to coordinate with Prosper's control panel. It wasn't the first time he had used this technique—he might be a gambler, but he was also a perfectionist: his team had fine-tuned the method on several commercial ventures over the past year.

Once again, the cathedral of stone rustled into silence.

"And . . . *action!*"

The real magic began.

Enter Prospero (in his magic robes) and Ariel . . . The shadowy, flickering words in beautiful sixteenth-century Islamic calligraphy were projected onto the walls of the cave while Basil strode through the forest of pillars intoning Prospero's opening lines to the final act: *"Now does my project gather to a head . . ."* and Ariel tumbled in behind the opalescent backdrop that represented Prospero's mirror.

As Ariel spoke: "Remember I have done thee worthy service . . ." from Act One, I knew that this was the moment Ram had been waiting for. Onto Ariel's backdrop was projected, not the image of Ferdinand, as it read in Prosper's shooting script, but one of Sami's morgue photos. There were a few whispers from the audience, swiftly silenced by a scowl from the assistant director, whose back was turned to the monitor. Clearly, Acres's hard currency spread liberally throughout the poorer technicians had bought us the required averted eyes and closed mouths that Ram had said we needed.

"Just as you left them: all prisoners, sir," said Ariel, oblivious to what was happening, and the first photo dissolved into a close-up of Sami's wounds. Ghosts of the hijra corpses appeared behind him and dissolved again, one after the other. Basil and Shiraz, old pros that they were, never once glanced at the screens behind, but I saw the stunt director shift uneasily from foot to foot.

Shiraz, famous for his comic roles in the 1960s, was playing both Caliban and Ariel. Now he held up the Shiva mask he used for Caliban and recited: *"This Island is mine by Sycorax my mother, which thou did take from me: when thou came first, thou stroked me and made much of me . . ."* The screen gave us first Sami's family snaps, then Maya.

The wave of murmuring from the crowd was louder. People on the floor suspected that something had gone wrong. But no one knew quite what: the process was too new to them and too professionally done. They glanced at their copies of the script and muttered, while Basil stared around, puzzled, an old bull at bay. I saw a figure leave the group of cameramen and move quickly towards Prosper's control room.

"As I told thee before, I am subject to a tyrant, a sorcerer," Ariel said, *"that by his cunning hath cheated me of this island."* On the obsidian screen of illusion, Maya's death mask and a grim black-and-white of Caleb's first wife. And that blurred, inconclusive photo of Prosper and Sami—if it *was* Sami.

Everyone realized then that there had been a terrible mistake. The cave erupted. A voice yelled "Cut!" over the loudspeaker. Basil finally turned to see what was projected on the screen behind him. The crowd of extras surged forward. A woman fainted. Accusations flew back and forth between the technicians responsible for setting up the screens. A small skirmish broke out over by the eastern porch, where the cobweb spinner and the biggest wind machine were located. It would have been worse if Prosper had not appeared in the doorway of the western porch at the moment when the first punches were thrown. By then, someone had managed to flip the switch on the computer and wipe the screen.

"I want every single pass checked," Prosper said. That was all. He disappeared again and left his best man in charge. Salim. That's what Ram had mouthed across the cave. I saw Bina watching me and I shook my head at her, pulling my veil well forward over my face.

My hijra makeup could not fool Salim for long; he knew me too well. He didn't say my name aloud, just tightened his lips and had two of the beefy villains march me down to the control room, where Prosper was waiting.

"Do you see the resemblance?" I said.

"To whom, Rosalind?"

"Sami."

His own mask slipped for a moment. "I presume the beard is your own?" He turned to Salim: "Was anything else out of order?"

Salim shook his head. "Only problem is we are having half the hijra expected."

"They're never very reliable," Prosper said. "That's the least of our problems. The most important thing is to get back on schedule so that we don't lose the light for this afternoon."

When Salim had left the room to Prosper and his two technicians, my brother-in-law turned his attention back to me. "Are you going to tell me how you did this?" He waved at the computer responsible for controlling the cave's screens.

"Impossible," I said. "I don't understand the first thing about computers."

Prosper nodded at the man seated next to him at the panel of multicoloured buttons and switches. "Well, this gentleman does, and he has successfully disposed of your disk and replaced it with our original. Did you really think it would be so easy to destroy months of work? Or that whatever little game you played with Mistry yesterday would work on me as well?"

I shrugged. "The way of justice is a tightrope, to quote your mate Auden's thesis on *The Tempest*. But it's the best we can do at short notice."

"Apparently you had even more delights in store for us." He waved the disk.

"I thought it might bring back some fond memories."

"It's a shame you have wasted such wit and ingenuity." He smiled, but it wasn't one of his Number 36 specials from the Chinese restaurant menu of charm. "You might have got somewhat further than producing cheap videos for late-night TV. Now we must get on with our work. I hope you enjoy the show."

There was a bank of monitors in front of us, each one representing a camera—half for inside the cavern, half for outside on the walk to the sea. Like Prosper, I could only watch the actors, not the screens behind them. But given the calm that pervaded the set, it appeared that nothing was out of place. The day unfolded on schedule, quietly and slowly, like any other day on any other movie set. Roll the cameras. Stop. Adjust the lights. Roll the cameras. Stop. Retake. Roll the cameras. Stop. Remove a hair from the shutter. Over the period of several hours while I watched my brother-in-law, it became clear that he was a real artist. A bit of an actor as well: he enjoyed having me as a captive audience.

At two-thirty Prosper nodded to his assistants. "Twenty minutes' lunch break," he said. "We're running late." When they glanced over at me, he added, "Leave a guard up there on the porch and also on the western exit. And bring us some tea when you come back."

He lit a gold Benson & Hedges and leaned back in his chair to enjoy it, closing his eyes with pleasure at the first drag of smoke into his lungs. He reminded me for a moment of Shoma Kumar, that day in the Taj Mahal Hotel. "Miranda keeps trying to get me to give these up," he said.

"Tell me, Prosper, what exactly is it that you did in bed with Maya and Shoma and Nonie and all those other girls?" And Miranda.

He opened his beautiful eyes. "What is it that you think you know, Rosalind?"

"Sami."

"I've never said I didn't know Sami. I liked her when I first met her, years ago. We were making a documentary in the Great Palace Street area. She fascinated me. Such a strange vehicle for that mixture of intelligence and—"

"Larceny? I know about the connection between you. The family snap."

"What is there to know?" His voice was so reasonable. "Sami approached me last year with that sad little photo she had. It seemed simple to solve the problem. She wanted so little. I just passed the information to Caleb and left him to deal with the situation."

"Caleb said you never told him that Sami might be his son."

"And you believed him?" Prosper's expression was amused. "Of course, you and he had some sort of . . . liaison."

"Why didn't you tell Sami that he was not your son?"

Prosper raised his eyebrows and thought back. "I don't know, really. At first I was amused by the suggestion that I could have fathered—"

I cut him off before he could come up with any more stories. "It was a way of seeing Sami again and still fooling yourself about the reason."

"You have mistaken my intentions. I genuinely liked Sami. She had extraordinary gifts. She was a talented painter and sculptor—"

"And forger."

"If she had been born in another century, she would have been one of the court favourites. There is a long and respected tradition of hijra romance in Mogul courts. I discovered that when I was researching the background for this film."

"I know about the long history. Even the *Kama Sutra* outlines the best ways to have sex with a eunuch. So you fucked Sami and discovered you liked it. And by letting her believe you were her father, you introduced her to the joys of incest as well. Then what happened?"

"You are always trying to turn one thing into another that it is not."

"I've seen the pictures, Prosper."

That slowed up the supply of charm for a while, but I could see he found the conversation fascinating, a harmless trip to the therapist, where you can leave all your dirty washing in someone else's laundry cupboard. Who would believe my word against his, after all?

"Miranda and I were not getting on . . ." he said. "The age difference, other things . . . Then she got pregnant. At first it didn't affect my relationship with Sami. Each time she asked for a bit more—but still so little. Until Sami saw some pictures in Shoma's magazine—of Miranda, pregnant."

"Classic situation. The mistress hadn't imagined hubby was still screwing wifee. But you weren't, were you? That's the irony."

"What makes you say that?" He smiled and shook his head at the suggestion. "The lovemaking had diminished, as it does in any long-term relationship. But not entirely disappeared. Then Sami started following Miranda. Just that, at first. Saying things to her. Later Sami moved on to threats . . . It seems she had those photos, and not only of me. She said she would show them to Miranda unless I gave her money for an operation." He was thinking back. "The operation itself would have cost twenty-seven saris, twenty petticoats, twenty-seven blouses, two dance dresses, nine nose rings, and two hundred rupees for the midwife. Plus Sami would have needed some extra support because she would have to take time off her . . . work, to live in isolation for a month, with a forty-day recovery period. Paltry, of course, to us. Although I did try to work out what the cost meant in her terms. But she had other demands, with political ramifications, that were not so easily satisfied. I could see things were getting out of hand."

"Your property deals involving the people in Sami's photos. So you had her killed. How did you think you would get away with it?"

"I'm a director, not a killer."

"You see something in your head and make it happen."

"This film may be my last chance, don't you see? Film is not a forgiving art form. It needs capital, distribution. And if I never get another chance, I have to go out on something good." He leaned forward, willing me to understand. "It was a very delicate position, negotiating capital for this film."

I started to laugh. "You mean the money you were ripping off from the Tilak Foundation. So Sami died for your art. I'm sure that was a comfort to her in her last hours. How did you arrange it?"

He shook his head and leaned back again, despairing at my inability to grasp the rules. "I arranged nothing. A friend took some comments of mine the wrong way. It turned out he had dealings with the kind of people who . . ."

"Encourage old wives to jump?"

Prosper smiled distractedly and looked at his watch. It was impossible to tell if he had regrets for what had happened—or felt nothing at all. I thought of Unmann, the first time we'd met at Breach Candy, that eely quality, too slippery to get a grip on. Two of a kind.

On cue, the small technician appeared. We proceeded without further hitch.

"We'll have a quick run-through of the masque," Prosper said over the loudspeaker. "And then roll."

The story so far: As Shah Jahan lies dying, "a metaphor for leaving the island," Prosper said over his shoulder to me, Shiva/Caliban dances in the mirror and reveals to his impotent master a vision of the future in the form of a play: the three goddesses and their troupe of demons, dwarfs, and hijra perform the ultimate defeat of the Marathi leader Shivaji/Ariel by Aurangzeb—but also the defeat of Aurangzeb and his Mogul empire in their turn, and the rise of British rule. The whole cave would be transformed into a series of living Renaissance maps—of battles won and lost, boundaries pushing forward and then retreating, the creatures on the margins of the maps—played by hijra and dwarfs as well—merging with the centre.

While Prospero/Shah Jahan recited his famous lines *"Our revels now are ended,"* the dancers would leave the cave—*"spirits melted into thin air"*—Prosper said, and join a huge throng carrying statues of Ganesh. They would march to the sea against a backdrop of monsoon effects projected onto a screen whose like I had never seen outside an American drive-in cinema. "Such an effect may have the added advantage of genuine weather effects," Prosper said, "if we are lucky enough for the monsoon rain to start up while we film—just as in Shakespeare's time, rain very often fell on the audience." Later, when the film came to be edited, both the parade and the monsoon effects would dissolve into the real monsoon storm that he had shot two days ago minus the actors.

"The baseless fabric of this vision—you see?" Prosper said. "And that march with the Ganpati images symbolizes India's rise as a Hindu state. We'll come back to that and fill the screen with it for Prospero's epilogue."

"Ganpati, remover of obstacles. Bit of a literal interpretation, isn't it?" I said. I couldn't believe the bastard actually wanted my approval.

Prosper dismissed my comment with a wave.

There were none of Ram's magic tricks to disrupt the dress rehearsal. It was a triumph, even without the computer screens in action or the special effects. And Prosper rewarded my tense silence with a smile of pure malice before turning back to the loudspeaker.

"Take a deep breath, everyone," he said to his audience in the cave, when the self-congratulations had died down. "This is what you've all been waiting for. Whatever happens—rain, storm, minor disasters—unless I expressly tell you to stop, I want you to keep the cameras rolling." He raised his baton to the technician on his left.

We all waited.

"And . . . *action!"*

The masque went perfectly. I was holding my breath as first one, then another of the images slid seamlessly onto screens: Mogul armies flickered across the pillars, the statue of Trimurti appeared to rise and greet Ariel, Caliban changed from a fish into a frog and back into Shiva. It was filmed theatre rather than cinema, but there was no denying the magic.

Once more, those old stage directions flickered across the cave's walls: *Prospero starts suddenly, and speaks; after which, to a strange, hollow, and confused noise, the Nymphs and goddesses heavily vanish.*

There was indeed a strange, hollow sound at this point. And for the first time, Prosper frowned. But Basil carried on, word perfect: *"These our actors, / As I foretold you, were all spirits, and / Are melted into air, into thin air . . ."*

As the goddesses and their attendants began their slow dance out of the cave, I heard the man at the control panel say, "What's that?"

"What?" Prosper said.

"There." The technician pointed at one corner of the screen, where up until now the cobweb machine had been spinning gossamer threads for Basil's "cloud-capp'd Towers." Something seemed to be going wrong. We watched, fascinated, as the web began to grow out of all proportion. More and more strands spun out into the studio. The big cooling fan—used between scenes to reduce the tremendous heat created by studio lights in that enclosed space—started up with a terrible rattle like giant eggbeaters. So did one of the wind machines. And another. Then everything happened at once. The gauzy back-drops painted with old maps of the diminishing Mogul empires, never meant to withstand anything more violent than one of Basil's substantial farts, were now flapping so violently they began to tear and fall in long strips around the huge actor. Slowly, his legs disappeared under a rapidly growing cumulous cloud of fabric. Still the old master carried on: *"The solemn temples, the great globe itself, / Yea, all which it inherit, shall dissolve . . ."* A small nymph, her legs tangled in skeins of gluey cobweb, fell against the biggest computer screen, on whose surface was a projected etching of the first Parsi theatre in Bombay. As the girl hit the screen, its surface shattered and sparks flew.

The technician was staring at Prosper, desperate for direction. Prosper said nothing. He sat rigidly, as if frozen to his chair. Then, as the nymph went down, he nodded his head. Seemed to be expecting it. When the fogmaker went crazy, he tapped his conductor's baton on the control panel in time to some beat that no one else could hear.

The fog machine started up. Small amounts of low-hanging mist were usually made by pouring hot water over troughs of dry ice and directing the resulting mist where it was needed with the help of a battery-operated fan. For larger fog and smoke effects, a special fog-making machine was filled with liquid and plugged into a power supply. This fog consisted of tiny drops of oil which could seriously damage equipment if not treated carefully. No one was treating them carefully at the moment: fog bubbled over the set like a speeded-up film of monsoon clouds, coating every surface in a treacherous slick and sending the less-sure-footed actors ass over heels.

By now, both technicians had stopped any pretence of work.

For the first time in ten minutes, Prosper spoke: "Keep rolling." Perhaps the tension was too much for him, I thought.

We had lost Basil in the fog, but his rich, invincible voice continued bravely: *"And, like this insubstantial pageant faded, / Leave not a rack behind."*

The golden balls which the props department had caused to remain in perpetual suspension on illuminated jets of water, a recreation of one of Salomon De Caus's magic tricks, began to spew out over the floor of the cave. Prosper's eyes were dragged inexorably to one of the outside monitors. I saw the musicians, who were too far back to guess what was happening, start up their eloquent refrain, the tabla player beating out a raga at a coke addict's pulse rate that was just about keeping up with my own. The massed wall of Ganesh pilgrims, watching the clouds of fog that the wind machine was blowing out into the daylight, assumed this was part of the master plan and raised their statues in preparation for their march to the sea.

"Keep rolling," Prosper said again, his voice very calm. He smiled.

Only then did I realize what was happening, and that he would win after all.

The entrance to the caves had been subtly reworked by the stage designer to resemble a slightly Indianized Jacobean playhouse, with the so-called heavens that covered and protected half the open stage given a Mogul cupola instead of an English dovecote. All the way through his film, Prosper had conformed to the Shakespearean "daylight convention," which permitted night scenes to be performed on a sunlit stage. Now, as the monitor recorded dancers, dwarfs, lepers, snake charmers staggering out of the cave, their hands held up to their eyes to shield them from such an abrupt transition into brilliant sunshine, the billowing artificial fog gave them the appearance of evacuees escaping from a terrible backstage fire. Framed on the mid-shot monitor, it was an image of overwhelming power.

My brother-in-law's film would be an artistic triumph. A masterpiece. *"We are such stuff as dreams are made on . . ."* said Basil. The camera slowly pulled back to reveal the full glory of Prosper Sharma's greatest spectacle.

At that moment, or perhaps a few seconds out of sync, the first hijra appeared: Bina, the veil she had been wearing discarded to reveal a second skin of latex, scarred like Sami's, the skin shredded and slashed into brocade, with wide bracelets of sinew wound round both her wrists. In fact, it *was* Sami's skin, in a manner of speaking, borrowed from Satish's model for the occasion.

Prosper started to shake his head. "No," he said, but too softly to be heard above the music.

A second hijra followed Bina, sporting a similar latex skin—Maya's this time. Soon a long parade of Samis and Mayas danced across the screen in front of us. And drowning out the live music was the sound of Maya's voice in that final playback song I remembered so well: *"Who is the winner, who is the loser, / and what is the price? / Father is the loser, father-in-law the winner, / and I, the bride, am the price."* A street vendor of pirate tapes had been happy to sell us a copy.

Still the camera pulled back. We could see that where the monsoon sea should have washed across that enormous screen above the cast, there was instead a moving tableau of Sami's stolen photos, copied last night and run sequentially so that they appeared to shudder in those jerky spasms typical of bad animation. Although you couldn't quite recognize Prosper, whose features were too distorted by the combination of screen clash and digitalization, other faces were more easily identifiable. Some of the faces had friends, business partners, political allies, or (worse) enemies among the watching VIPs. And as the film mixed from one familiar face and its less familiar naked ass to another in rapid succession, it was clear to everyone watching what was going on.

"Cut!" shouted Prosper, too late.

A series of explosions came from the biggest lights and they fused one by one.

"And print," I said.

epilogue
RETREAT OF THE MONSOON

In the last acts of Goethe's *Dr. Faustus*, the purified
Faust reclaims from the sea, with the help of
Mephistopheles, a stretch of submerged land.

—BASIL CHOPRA, Notes from Prosper Sharma's *Tempest*

So I AM LEFT WITH ALL THESE STORIES. AND WHO IS TO SAY which one is true?

In the bestselling biography of Prosper Sharma written by Basil Chopra years later, the old actor would claim that it was stress resulting from the epic scale of my brother-in-law's *Tempest* (effectively Basil's as well as Prosper's last film) that drove Prosper to the unforgivable acts which Bollywood gossip insinuated he had committed. If Prosper did indeed commit such acts. Basil was careful to point out that those ugly stories were only rumour, gossip, storytelling: the facts to back them up were few.

But rumour is a powerful weapon. It did for Prosper what the police could not, even after I had turned over the remainder of my evidence. Instead, Prosper was sentenced by a jury of his peers to a cell worse than any official prison, a cell completely lacking in magic: permanent removal from the spotlight. A future without fame, fortune, or influence, with no possibility of a reprieve. Bollywood, like its California counterpart, does not wish to be associated with losers.

THE WITHDRAWAL OF THE MONSOON IS A MORE DISCREET PROCESS THAN ITS arrival, although the country is still subject to an odd storm. A sixth-century Indian poet called this "the season of bright dawns, of fugitive clouds . . . when the lakes echo with the sound of herons, the frogs are silent, and the snakes shrivel up."

Towards the end of the monsoon, festivals are dedicated to drawing the gods back. At Diwali, the October festival that marks the official end of the monsoon, borders between the living and dead vanish and the dead are thought to be very close. But by October they still had not found Robi's body. And although I searched for Gulab many times outside the Taj Mahal Hotel, I never saw the leper again. The narrow man in Gulab's old school of English behind the Goliath Cinema explained to me that his former assistant had vanished one day and he had no idea where he might have gone. I thought of Ariel in Shakespeare's time, who probably wore some form of cloak labelled with the word "invisible" to denote invisibility. Poverty has the same effect.

Ashok went back to whatever mysterious work he did, and about a month after giving him my "evidence" I received a couple of newspaper clippings through the post. One reported that Goliath's foreign backers had pulled out of certain redevelopment plans (notably, the hotel complex behind the Goliath Cinema) because they considered Bombay's current political situation to be too unstable, a withdrawal that had been greeted with relief by the current residents of the Goliath complex, the paper said.

The other clipping concerned the recovery of a collection of gold mohars and stolen temple figurines. The Tilak Foundation was said to have put up the money for the investigation. No other names were mentioned.

I stayed on in Bombay until the monsoon turned into autumn, doing odd jobs with Ram to earn some cash, drinking beer, and watching my sister and her son grow fat and healthy. For Miranda never moved back in with Prosper; she moved in with me for a few months, instead. We treated each other with a careful tenderness that was still not quite certain, and we never spoke of Caleb and Prosper, even after the waves of scandal broke over her own head. People can recover from snakebite, I learned. Like alibis, orgasm, property prices, it's only a question of location and timing.

JUST BEFORE DIWALI, I HAD AN INVITATION TO A BONFIRE NIGHT PARTY FROM an old friend at the British Embassy in Bombay. The time seemed right to reclaim my British identity, what was left of it. To go home— or back, at least.

Thomas had to leave as well. His friendly Saudi oil millionaire had booked him for a tour of the subcontinent. Before he left, I gave my friend the statue of Skanda and a small bag containing the gold coins stolen from my leading men. "For all your kindness, Thomas. I'm sure you will find a good buyer somewhere in your thieves' market."

"But I have been most amply rewarded already."

"Please. I insist. Or I stay in the car. *Let your indulgence set me free*."

"Epilogue, Prospero," he said and, smiling, pushed my gifts into his bag.

I asked him what he would do with the money. "Go home to Kerala and live the good life? Buy your own fleet of cars?"

"Oh no, madam." His eyes were bright. "I think I will go to Paris—or to Cannes, for the festival of films. And see Mr. Louis Malle, who was always telling me to look him up if ever I am having such luck as to be in France."

I burst out laughing. "Life isn't like the movies, Thomas."

"That is a most depressing idea." He shook his head. "Who is saying that?"

"Woody Allen, I think, and he should know. But I'll tell you what, Thomas—you get to Cannes, and if Louis doesn't show, *I'll* meet you there. On the boardwalk in Cannes. Next year's festival. It's a date."

THE BONFIRE NIGHT PARTY TOOK PLACE ON THE FIFTH OF NOVEMBER IN THE compound of the British High Commission. We had warm English beer and cold greasy sausages on sticks and jacket potatoes burned in the fire. Everyone stood around stiffly in true British fashion until they got drunk enough to bitch about absent colleagues and discuss when the next shipment of Rose's lime marmalade was due. The houses inside the compound wouldn't have looked out of place in Surrey. The lawns were snooker tables. The flowers were hybrids from a London suburb. All Bombay's smell and ambivalence had been excluded. The only Indian thing was the branch of a huge tropical tree reaching over the wall.

After the children went to bed, there was dancing and more drinking and it almost felt like London. Suddenly, although there was no breeze, a leaf the size of a flag fell out of the tropical tree to impale that smooth green lawn like a sword. One of my friend's Nepalese servants crossed the lawn and removed it. No one seemed to notice. But raising my eyes from the spot where the leaf had been, I looked across the diplomatic jungle to see Ashok Tagore, very handsome in a pale linen suit. He tipped his glass in salute and made his way over.

"Our hostess tells me you intend to stay up all night and catch the early-morning plane back to London. Would you consider having breakfast with me before you go? I know a place that starts serving *jalebis* and fresh curd about 3 a.m. And I have a certain proposition of work that might interest you."

"Did you see the leaf, Ashok?"

He nodded. "I know its Indian name, although, sadly, I cannot give you the Latin."

I wasn't really listening. "That was a real fuck-you leaf, wasn't it?" I said.

Ashok's eyes lit up; then the corner of his mouth twitched and his whole face broke into a grin. "Indeed," he said, "sometimes the Anglo-Saxon has a certain precision that is absent in the Latin."

ONE THING THAT FOLLOWED THE SCRIPT: MY SISTER AND I HAVE REMAINED close, despite the distance between us, just as Basil had outlined to me so long ago, the good and the bad siblings together after a long separation and much gratuitous violence. The map of my family reassembled.

TWO YEARS AFTER THE MONSOON THAT TOOK PLACE IN MY THIRTY-THIRD year, a London newspaper ran a small headline on page 17: BOMBAY VOTES TO CHANGE CITY NAME TO MUMBAI. I tried to remember the poem Ashok had quoted on that last night in Bombay. How did it go?

> *I flick through some foreign verses,*
> *But find in them no traces*
> *Of the shade of this monsoon rain,*
> *something something something . . .*

Then the bit Ashok said was like sitar music:

> *No story quite resolved*
> *Not ending at the end,*
> *But leaving the heart uneasy.*

And I looked at the pictures my sister had sent me of her son and wondered if Miranda ever worried about the genes he carries, or about who he will take after, as I worry that within me I carry the genes of that old Scottish guilt.

ABOUT THE AUTHOR

LESLIE FORBES was born in Vancouver, Canada. For the last twenty years she has worked in England as an artist, travel writer, and broadcaster. *Bombay Ice* is her first novel.